KT-485-083

HENRY LAWSON

UQP AUSTRALIAN AUTHORS

This is a series of carefully edited selections which represent the full range of an individual author's achievement or which present special themes in anthology form.

General Editor: L.T. Hergenhan,
Reader in Australian Literature,
University of Queensland

Also in this series:

Barbara Baynton edited by Sally Krimmer and Alan Lawson
Rolf Boldrewood edited by Alan Brissenden
Christopher Brennan edited by Terry Sturm
Marcus Clarke edited by Michael Wilding
Robert D. FitzGerald edited by Julian Croft
Joseph Furphy edited by John Barnes
Henry Kingsley edited by J.S.D. Mellick
James McAuley edited by Leonie Kramer
David Malouf edited by James Tulip
John Shaw Neilson edited by Cliff Hanna
Nettie Palmer edited by Vivian Smith
Hal Porter edited by Mary Lord
Kenneth Slessor edited by Dennis Haskell
Catherine Helen Spence edited by Helen Thomson
Randolph Stow edited by Anthony J. Hassall

The Jindyworobaks edited by Brian Elliott
Writing of the Eighteen Nineties edited by Leon Cantrell
The Australian Short Story edited by Laurie Hergenhan
Eight Voices of the Eighties edited by Gillian Whitlock
Australian Science Fiction edited by Van Ikin
Colonial Voices edited by Elizabeth Webby
New Guinea Images in Australian Literature edited by Nigel Krauth
Five Plays for Stage, Radio and Television edited by Alrene Sykes

In preparation:

Xavier Herbert edited by Frances de Groen and Peter Pierce
Henry Kendall edited by Michael Ackland
Barnard Eldershaw edited by Maryanne Dever
Banjo Paterson edited by Clement Semmler
Christina Stead edited by R.G. Geering and Anita Segerberg
Eleanor Dark edited by Barbara Brooks and Judith Clark

HENRY LAWSON
Stories, poems, sketches and autobiography

*Selected and edited with an
Introduction and Bibliography by*

BRIAN KIERNAN

University of Queensland Press

First published 1976 by University of Queensland Press
Box 42, St Lucia, Queensland 4067 Australia
Reprinted 1980, 1982, 1985, 1987, 1988, 1991

Introduction and notes © Brian Kiernan 1976

This book is copyright. Apart from any fair dealing
for the purposes of private study, research, criticism
or review, as permitted under the Copyright Act, no
part may be reproduced by any process without written
permission. Enquiries should be made to the publisher.

Typeset by University of Queensland Press
Printed in Australia by The Book Printer, Victoria

Distributed in the USA and Canada by
International Specialized Book Services, Inc.,
5602 N.E. Hassalo Street, Portland, Oregon 97213-3640

Cataloguing in Publication Data
National Library of Australia

Lawson, Henry, 1867-1922.
  Henry Lawson.

  (UQP Australian Authors).
  Bibliography

  I. Kiernan, Brian, ed. II. Title. (Series).

828.2

Library of Congress
Lawson, Henry, 1867-1922.
  Henry Lawson / selected and edited with an introduction
and bibliography by Brian Kiernan.

  (UQP Australian Authors)
  Bibliography: p.

  I. Australia — Literary collections. I. Kiernan, Brian.
II. Title. III. Series.

PR9619.2.L3A6   1985   823   84-28047

ISBN 0 7022 1231 8

Contents

Acknowledgments   ix

Introduction   xi

Note on the Text   xxv

SECTION 1   Retrospect (c. 1903–8)

Editor's Note   2
A Fragment of Autobiography   3

SECTION 2   1887–92

Editor's Note   68
A Song of the Republic   69
Faces in the Street   69
The Watch on the Kerb   72
Andy's Gone with Cattle   72
A Neglected History   74
The Roaring Days   77
The Teams   79
The New Religion   80
Middleton's Rouseabout   84
Freedom on the Wallaby   84
A Day on a Selection   86
Two Boys at Grinder Bros.'   92
The Drover's Wife   96
The Bush Undertaker   104
The City Bushman   112

SECTION 3   1892–94

Editor's Note   118
Letter to Aunt Emma (Mrs. Brooks)   119
Hungerford   121
That There Dog O'Mine   125
Some Popular Australian Mistakes   128
The Union Buries Its Dead   131
"Rats"   136
In a Wet Season   139
"Dossing Out" and "Camping"   143
Australian Bards and Bush Reviewers   147
Stiffner and Jim (Thirdly, Bill)   148
Preface to *Short Stories in Prose and Verse*   155

SECTION 4   1894–99

Editor's Note   158
Remailed   159
Going Blind   163
The Geological Spieler   168
An Oversight of Steelman's   176
Letters to George Robertson   181
Reedy River   185
But What's the Use   186
The Star of Australasia   187
Mr. Smellingscheck   192
The Uncultured Rhymer to His Cultured Critics   195
They Wait on the Wharf in Black   196
"Pursuing Literature" in Australia   202
Crime in the Bush   211
The Iron-Bark Chip   217
Past Carin'   222
Second Class Wait Here   223
Letter to Earl Beauchamp   225

SECTION 5   1899–1901

Editor's Note   230
The Loaded Dog   231
Telling Mrs. Baker   238
Joe Wilson's Courtship   251
Brighten's Sister-in-law   278

"Water Them Geraniums"   298
A Double Buggy at Lahey's Creek   324

SECTION 6 1901–2

Editor's Note   345
The Sydney *Bulletin* (extract)   346
Send Round the Hat   358
The Shearers   374
A Sketch of Mateship   375
Drifting Apart   377
A Child in the Dark, and a Foreign Father   385

Select Bibliography   392

Acknowledgments

Acknowledgment is made to Angus & Robertson for permission to use letters from *Henry Lawson: Letters* edited by Colin Roderick (1970), and extracts from "The Sydney *Bulletin*" and "A Fragment of Autobiography" from *Henry Lawson: Autobiographical and Other Writings* edited by Colin Roderick (1972).

Introduction

This selection is intended to introduce Henry Lawson the writer. While, like any editor, I have wanted to represent the best of Lawson's work, to include only the best would fail to convey the way in which he found his identity, pursued his preoccupations, and related himself to the world around him through the act of writing. Lawson the familiar artist is found within the very much larger body of work by Lawson the writer, who was a professional deriving his income from newspapers, magazines, and book publishers (though he was never to exist solely and adequately on his writing). Between the best of the sketches, short stories, and verses and the inferior, and between his "imaginative" work generally and his "non-imaginative" writing, there are many links. In his journalism, his autobiographical writings, and his letters can also be found the dominant themes of his fiction and verse. These reveal a continuity of concerns, illuminate his personality and his artistry, and show his critical involvement with the changing society he lived in.

The complex unity of Lawson's work and personality (at least until the early years of this century) is observable from "A Fragment of Autobiography", here placed first. This is Lawson's portrait of the artist as a young man, more valuable as an imaginative record, and record of the imagination, than as a factual biography. It shows us the growth of the artist's mind: significantly it starts not with objective facts such as the date of his birth (1867), but with his earliest memories which recur throughout his writing. Memories of the abandoned goldfields and the late rush to Grenfell, of the era when the railways were replacing Cobb and Co. coaches, of the bullock drivers like "Jimmy Nowlett" and the drovers like "Dave Regan" who used to camp down on the flat, of his childhood chores on his father's selection, provided the historical setting and experience for much of his work. Sometimes there is a personal note that seems to relate suggestively to his fiction, as when he remarks that like Joe Wilson's son he was "an old fashioned child". "My father and myself (with intervals of many years) were also Joe Wilson's of strenuous moments. The incident of the child having convulsions was taken from the cases of my younger brother Peter and my own son Jim", Lawson wrote in 1916 (see Colin Roderick, ed., *Henry Lawson: Letters*, p. 248). And the painful recollection of how he was called "Barmy" by his schoolfriends and later his young workmates, reminds us of the early "Arvie Aspinall" sequence of stories, here represented by "Two Boys at Grinder Bros.".

At the centre of the autobiography's account of grinding labour and continual shifts to "make a go" at something else, or somewhere else, are the figures of his parents, the kindly, gentle foreign father and (as she is most often) "the mother". The story of Louise Lawson's escape from the routine poverty of country life to the metropolitan publishing world is at least as remarkable as Henry's own (which she occasioned), although he gives it scant mention in his autobiographical writings. Clearly, it had been easier for him to relate to his father and to remember him generously. She is "Mother" when remembered reading *Robinson Crusoe*, Edgar Allan Poe, or Adam Lindsay Gordon to her children; "the mother" when her literary ambitions are recalled, although Lawson can acknowledge sympathetically the special lack of opportunities for women in the bush. Interestingly, Lawson refers to himself as having been a "good" school pupil in the sense that he was a model student, "a self-torturer and a nuisance to my playmates". This ironic sense of "good" has been applied by psychologists to family situations like Lawson's own, and in its terms Louise was a "good" mother to her eldest child — imbuing him with her own frustrated literary aspirations and encouraging his, inducing that dissatisfaction that drove him, despite acute self-consciousness, to long for "something better — something higher — something different, anyhow", and which was to take him "from Mudgee Hills to London town". But by then he had come a long way from the experiences he had turned into art (as we see him doing also in the autobiography) and could only occasionally recapture them tellingly, as he does in "A Child in the Dark, and a Foreign Father", placed at the end of this selection.

The references Lawson makes to Louisa reading to her children from the *Australian Journal* and English and American classics remind us not only of the literary influences upon him (Dickens, Bret Harte, Mark Twain, and others he mentions in the autobiography) but also of the local literary-historical background to his work. In his younger years, the best known Australian writers were those he mentions in his autobiography:

Henry Kingsley, Marcus Clarke, Adam Lindsay Gordon, Henry Kendall, and Rolf Boldrewood. The first three were Englishmen for whom Australia was a strange land; rightly or wrongly, the response of these colonial writers towards the bush has been summed up for later generations in Marcus Clarke's phrase "weird melancholy" (a phrase which Lawson echoes in his autobiography — and this is also the "dominant note" of his descriptions of the bush, compare "In a Wet Season"). By the time of Lawson's death, in 1922, Christopher Brennan's major poems had appeared; Kenneth Slessor, the first important "modern" Australian poet, had begun publishing; the first volume of Henry Handel Richardson's *The Fortunes of Richard Mahony* (and also her first two novels) had been published in England; Katharine Susannah Prichard had also published three novels; Vance Palmer verse and stories; and Louis Esson a number of plays. In Lawson's lifetime a transformation had occurred in Australian culture generally and he was at the centre of its literary developments.

For generations of readers, Lawson has been the most "representative" of Australian writers. His own generation saw him (from quite early in his career) as amongst the first to delineate the life of the nation and to express its characteristics. For subsequent generations, Lawson formed the images and expressed the ethos of those formative decades in the development of the nation from the end of the gold rushes to Federation. For many writers and critics Lawson's techniques and attitudes provided models, a distinctive national traditional, to be observed in literature and life. In what sense Lawson was "representative" is an issue critics have discussed since Lawson's own day, at least since his verse "debate" with "Banjo" Paterson and others in the *Bulletin*. One sense in which he is "representative" can be seen in his concern to establish the human "types" of the society in which life presented itself to him: in his writing generally there is a whole gallery of types, mostly down on their luck, representing (from the start of his career) both country and city — the selector, the itinerant worker, the larrikin, the confidence man, the ragged-trousered philanthropist and philosopher, and the women and children who were the real victims of a raw society and an inhospitable landscape or cityscape. Lawson wrote from within their experiences, and they formed part of his immediate audience.

In arranging this selection I have tried to illustrate Lawson's emergence as a writer, as he outlines this in his autobiographical writings. Some of the early verse and prose, including some impressively brash editorializing from the *Republican* (which his mother bought), are presented in chronological order of composition — broadly, the order observed throughout the selection, as well as it can be determined. These early compositions express very well the ferment of radical social and political attitudes in the eighties and nineties. Although the "Fragment of Autobiography" ends before Lawson's trip to Bourke and the tramp to Hungerford which, with his childhood and later marriage, was one of the central experiences affecting his art, it is clear from the work that he wrote on his return — some of it amongst his finest — that his imagination and sympathies were stirred by discovery for himself the reality of the "Out Back", which had so often been idealized, and falsified, by previous writers.

It is apparent from a chronological arrangement of his work that Lawson established himself first of all as a poet, that there was no precise distinction between "stories" and "sketches" in his fiction concerned with the presentation of "typical" scenes from Australian life, and that simultaneously with the apparently direct notation of what he observed he tried his hand at more "literary" fictional structures. Spasmodic attempts at writing well-made (to a formula) magazine stories relying on strong plotting and very often resulting in melodramatic contrivance, factitious pathos, and "ironic" reversal continued throughout Lawson's career. Economic necessity probably motivated some of these efforts, but Lawson's unjustified pride in "The Hero of Redclay" (not included here) reminds us of the tired conventions that were to hand, as closely as in the columns of the *Bulletin;* he resisted them in the best of his prose. The conventional short stories are not well represented here, only at their best in such humorous examples as "The Loaded Dog" or "The Iron Bark Chip" which, though relying on a strong "story line", do have the virtues of the realistic sketch in their introduction of "typical" characters and a way of life, and some leave disturbing reverberations after their climaxes — such as we find in the macabre sense of humour that ends "The Loaded Dog", or the insight into an alternative code of ethics at the end of "An Oversight of Steelman's".

Although Lawson established his reputation as a poet, was thought of first of all as "the poet Lawson" throughout his lifetime, and as such received flattering praise ("I think you are the greatest poet Australia has produced" George Robertson, his publisher, once wrote in a letter), the comparison of the prose with his more "literary" (because formal and rhetorical) verse shows revealingly where his art can be located. In the "Fragment of Autobiography" he refers a number of times to the "faces of the street" (as he does elsewhere in his autobiographical writing) — the urban poor he would see around Paddy's Market. One of his early poems given here has this title and expresses his humanitarian concern, and also towards its end his youthful revolutionary fervour. In this poem, the experiences Lawson relives in his autobiographical writings are generalized, the emphasis is thrown on the writer's attitude rather than on what he observes through the window onto the street, and the jauntily swaggering rhythms ("deadly-in-earnest ring" and "thunderous reiteration" of refrain, as Lawson recalled it in "From Mudgee Hills to London Town", an autobiographical piece unpublished in his lifetime) are at odds with the human experience that ostensibly inspired the verse. In the autobiography, and in an earlier *Bulletin* piece "If I Could Paint", the particular memories of the harassed mother hectoring her children are relived and dramatically presented. Here is another of these memories of individual human faces, the one with which this section in the autobiography concludes, as it originally appeared as a *Bulletin* "par" on 6 July 1895:

His Mother's Mate

The haggard woman sat on a step under the electric light, by the main entrance of the theatre. She had a child on one arm, two more beside her, a pile of papers on her knee, and a cigar box, full of matches, boot-laces and bone studs, on the pavement by her foot.

A gentleman stepped out of the "marble bar" opposite, stood for a moment on the kerb, glanced at his watch and then across at the theatre. He crossed over, and put his hand in his pocket as he reached the pavement.

"Paper, sir?" cried the newsboy. "Here, Y'are, mister — *News, Star.*"

But "mister" had noticed the woman and walked towards her.

"Paper, sir! *Star!*" cried the boy, dodging in front; then, with a quick glance from "mister's" face to the newswoman.

"It's all right, mister! It's all the same — she's my mother . . . Thanks."

The contrast between this paragraph and the verse of "Faces in the Street" is telling. The prose presentation is sharp, particular, and dramatic. The author is "written out" and the objectively narrated facts, ruthlessly selected and arranged for maximum effects, speak for themselves. The gain from shifting the focus from the author himself and his response (as in the verses, the other prose versions) to what affects him — and comes directly through the sketch to affect us — is immense. The comparison of other "short stories in verse" with their prose versions — for example, both versions of "Brighten's Sister-in-law", or "The Fire at Ross's Farm" with "The Bush Fire", or "Past Carin' " with Mrs. Spicer's account of her marriage in " 'Water Them Geraniums' " (both included here) — is similarly in favour of the prose, in terms of convincing rhythms and enlivening details.

The basis of Lawson's best prose fiction lies in the sketch or the anecdote represented by this *Bulletin* "par". Any general and theoretical distinction between the "story" and the "sketch" (of character types, or of aspects of town or country life such as is found in "Hungerford") or the anecdote (an incident, such as "His Mother's Mate", which again reveals the typical) is difficult to draw. Lawson himself seems to speak of "sketches" more often than "stories", and his fully plotted stories, more often than not, show him going to literature, to established conventions, rather than to life for his inspiration. An early example of his attempts at conventional magazine entertainment is "The Third Murder" (not included here), about sleeping in a haunted house. The narrator thinks that he must have imagined voices and noises but later discovers that an actual murder had been committed in the house that night. At the same time as he was trying his hand at such stale fare, Lawson was extending the sketch, or brief vignette of characteristically Australian life that formed a staple contribution to the *Bulletin* and other papers, into an individual, story-length form. Thus, "A Day on a Selection" gives humorous particularity to general experience that must have been familiar to thousands of readers who, like the author, had grown up in the country. "The Drover's Wife" combines the sketch, of a typical bush woman, with the anecdote of the snake, which is again a typical experience. Although it is rather obvious that this story has been structured to present general experience through a particular instance, the form emerges from the experience embodied in the story (the train of events leading to the killing of the snake) rather than being imposed by the use of an extraneous plot. "The Drover's Wife" appeared in Lawson's first collection of stories, *Short Stories in Prose and Verse* published by his mother in 1894. This slender, badly printed volume contained some other of the best and most familiar of the stories, " 'Rats' ", "Macquarie's Mate", "The Bush Undertaker", and "The Union Buries Its Dead", suggesting how quickly Lawson developed his true talent for fiction after his trip to Bourke.

The last-mentioned of these stories, "The Union Buries Its Dead", is an arresting example of the rapidity with which Lawson reached artistic maturity, developed his technique of the "involved" narrator speaking in the vernacular, and presented his vision, a vision to which irony is essential. So authentic is the speaking voice here that we might be uncertain whether Lawson is "writing up" an actual incident he had observed back of Bourke or imaginatively inventing this funeral to capture the essentials of life as he saw it. To what extent this might be a sketch from life is, however, beside the point. What is important is the authenticity of the narrator's voice as he presents details which are both disturbing and comic. This sense of fidelity to facts, to life, is heightened by the narrator's insisting that he has omitted the stock properties of Australian fiction. This intrusion, as it might seem, heightens the effect of realism: the conventions of the facititious "story" are rejected in favour of the direct observations of the realistic "sketch", and the identification of the anonymous narrator with the author at this late stage reinforces our sense of this story's truth to life. In this passage Lawson comes close to his contemporary Joseph Furphy who through his narrator Tom Collins in *Such is Life* similarly rejects the romantic literary conventions which prevented writers from seeing Australian life realistically.

The apparently casual style of "The Union Buries Its Dead" is lean, spare, pared away to essentials so that every detail contributes to the narrator's complex attitude towards life. Through him we see men living on the margin of life, so much so that their values and existence are definable only in contrast with the absolute of death. Yet the universal ritual of burial calls forth what is residually and minimally human in these hard cases. There is no sentimental idealizing of "the Bushmen": the horseman, "who looked like a drover just returned from a big trip", knows what he ought to do and joins in the procession (as Clancy of the Overflow would have done); however, he is easily induced to fall out and go to the hotel instead. The anti-heroism of the story is summed up in its title, which ironically calls to mind the valour and pageantry of the American Civil War (as illustrated in the papers pasted over the hut walls that Lawson in " 'Water Them Geraniums' ", remembers seeing as a boy).

In "A Fragment of Autobiography" Lawson writes "My diggers are idealized, or drawn from a few better class diggers, as my Bushmen are sketched from better class Bushmen", and we have to allow that by "idealize" he meant something closer to "romanticize". But in his letters, articles, sketches, stories, and verses he did not consistently idealize in this sense at all. From his letter from Hungerford we can see how shocked he was by the discrepancy between conventional notions of bush life and the reality he discovered. "Some Popular Australian Mistakes" (written at about the same time as "The Union Buries Its Dead") and other articles reject the literary conventions in which bush life was usually described, even by those who lived there. The stories and sketches derived from his trip to Bourke and beyond, and his verse "debate" with Paterson, reject these conventions and insist realistically on other images. But Lawson at this time did "idealize" in another sense, in the sense of abstracting "ideal types" from the society he encountered outback and remembered from his earlier years in the country. The unnamed Drover's Wife is an early example of a stereotype that embodies the characteristics of a general class; later, in Mrs. Spicer, Lawson was to dramatize her more memorably as an individual. It is usual however to find the same name recurring in clusters of writings and sometimes recalled many years later.

Jimmy Nowlett and John Bullock (old school-friends in the autobiography, who appear in a number of stories), Dave Regan, Jack Moonlight, Barcoo-Rot, One-Eyed Regan, The Oracle, Johnny Mears, Peter M'Laughlan the bush missionary, Mitchell the swagman, Steelman the sharper, and Joe Wilson are all social types who recur in many stories, sometimes at the centre, at other times on the periphery. Steelman and Mitchell in their series of stories often become devices to disguise the fact that Lawson has nothing much to say and to allow him to pretend that it is really someone else who is spinning this yarn or indulging in facetious "philosophizing". (Such a device Lawson adopted in his declining years in the persona of John Lawrence to provide his rambling journalistic copy with the semblance of fiction.) For these reasons, only a very small proportion of the Mitchell and Steelman stories, those that can stand with the best of Lawson's fiction, have been included here.

Lawson's habit of pursuing these types through series of stories inevitably led to the question being asked, in his own day by A.G. Stephens and by other critics later, whether these ought not to have been organized into a unified sequence. Hovering behind this question is the speculation whether Lawson could have written a novel. From the letters to Robertson printed here, we can see that Lawson interpreted Stephen's preference for a "single plotted, climaxed story", one that would enable Lawson to develop "characteristics" as being a preference for the novel, or at least "something connected". The implicit assumption of this speculation, that the novel is a superior form to the short story or story sequence, is false — the quality of a work of art is not inherent in the form adopted but in what the artist creates within that form. But if we were to speculate on the sort of novel which Lawson would have written, to realize his critics' expectations of his novelistic potential and to contain his imaginative world, it

would have to be Tolstoyan. It would have to cover the period
from the end of the gold rushes, though perhaps going back to
Eureka, to the years of radical nationalistic fervour and social
unrest before Federation, at the least (while, like *Anna Karenina*,
remaining open to further historical developments). It would
have to embrace the life of the city, the countryside, and the
straggling margins of settlement in the bush beyond. Its
characters would be predominantly working class, chiefly
itinerant seasonal workers; its hero, like Joe Wilson, a socially
representative figure, incorporating (like Tolstoy's Levin) much
of the author's private experience; its heroine one of those women
whose life is severely restricted but whose desire for something better, if only for her children, gives her a tenacious grip on what she
must endure.

To bring all of Lawson's world from the stories, sketches, and
verse — and his direct concern with social issues in his other
writings — into a single work of fiction would necessitate a very
large novel indeed, and one crammed with minor, comic figures.
It would have to be at least as ample as Henry Handel Richardson's *The Fortunes of Richard Mahony*, which "covers" Lawson's
period of the post gold rush decades in both city and country
(Australian and English, another relevant possibility for Lawson's
"novel") for its study of a man and his wife with contrasting
temperaments. To compare Lawson's sequence of four Joe Wilson
stories with Richardson's Tolstoyan novel is to appreciate how
imaginatively Lawson discovered that extended form he was
searching for without imposing an artificial "literary" pattern on
life as he saw it. The great strength of Richardson's novel is its
powerful sense of the "fortunes" of life, the possibilities cir-
cumscribed by the exigencies of love, birth, and death. Similarly
through Joe Wilson we are made aware of the course of life for the
individual — courtship, parenthood, death, and the effects of
time on youthful hopes and human relations. The emotional
power Lawson generates through his more economical means
compares very well with Richardson's. Both we feel have seen life
whole and honestly, yet Lawson's art is the opposite to Richardson's. Instead of attempting to show all of man's estate, Lawson
selects those significant moments that can suggest more than they
show, that can stand for the essential experiences of life for many
other Joes and Marys.

The technique has something of impressionism about it, a seiz-
ing of the dramatic moment that although itself fleeting can suggest much more experience behind it. Lawson in his autobiography expresses his interest in the graphic arts, and "If I
Could Paint", a *Bulletin* article — written ten years after the

famous "9 x 5" Exhibition — includes subjects similar to those Roberts, Streeton, and McCubbin chose to represent Australian life, subjects that Lawson had already employed in his stories and sketches. He also mentions subjects, such as Eureka, which would lead to grandiose, crowded canvases of Academic proportions (comparable perhaps to his more rhetorically inflated verse); but his expressed ambition, which relates to his writing and to the Impressionists' interest in capturing the fleeting moment that is both individual and typical, is "to paint Australia as it is, and as it changes".

Lawson's interest in graphic expression, in the literary "sketch" and in "drawing from life" suggests aspects of his realism. Applied to any particular artist this term demands explanation and qualification. With Lawson it means his drawing on what he had experienced or observed himself for his best work rather than on literary conventions, even Australian ones, which he felt distorted the truth. The sketch, often impressionistically brisk, but implying the general and typical, is the basis of his fictional art. In " 'Water Them Geraniums' ", the central story in the "Joe Wilson" sequence and the greatest of Lawson's stories, the sketch of Spicer's farm has its source in Lawson's childhood memories; it is both an exact historical record (which is why it appears quite appropriately in Manning Clark's *Select Documents in Australian History*) and an evocation of the typical selector's domestic way of life. Mrs. Spicer's son in the story is an unindividualized version of "Jack Cornstalk", a composite figure Lawson created for a series of journalistic sketches of the typical country lad. Here is the sketch of "Jack Cornstalk in His Teens" as it appeared in the *Australian Star* in 1899:

> A boy in his early teens; a boy of casual appearance and offhand manner; a frank (painfully so, sometimes), sociable, 'open' freckle-faced boy; a man of the world in his speech, and a bushman in his knowledge of sheep, cattle, and bush work. He swears early and easily as a rule, has 'the slang of the bush on his lips', and promptly adopts improvements in the Australian language as they drift in from the out back. He knows more about certain subjects — upon which it is an undecided question whether a boy should remain in ignorance or not — than does the average city boy five years older. He appears, as often as any other way, seated astride a three-bushel bag thrown across the ridge of the old selection house, and wearing a dilapidated straw or soft felt hat, any manner of coat or jacket that is old, worn, and comfortable, a cotton shirt, and a pair of moleskin trousers, too large for him, or

home-made, and of a cut that would look as well back to front
— gathered under a saddle-strap or greenhide belt, and rolled
up above the knees of his sun-blotched shanks for some reason
of his own (to save them from the dust and sweat of the horse,
maybe, or with the vague idea of giving the impression of leggings). He says 'Good-day mister!' or hails you as, 'Hi, mister!'
(or missus). He says it's hot — or 'blanky' hot — or asks you if it
isn't. He is affable, and ready to discuss the probability of our
ever going to get a little rain, or any other bush subject. He is
sympathetic, philosophical, and fatherly with regard to your
trouble (if you have any), and without reference to your age.
He wants to know if you 'seen' any horses (or cattle), or,
maybe, 'a cove on horseback', along the track; if he is on a
strange track he wants to know how 'fur' it is to the next place.
He often mildly surprises a property-holder by asking him if he
wants a 'man' to knock round.

As a surplus boy on a selection he becomes possessed of a
horse, saddle, and bridle 'of his own' — the saddle the most
precious possession, because it is usually the hardest to get —
and starts out to work his way to Queensland and the Great
North-West. In an extreme case — say he is the son of a wretched, poverty-stricken, and hopeless selector — the old
broken-winded horse is given him, in a burst of fatherly
generosity; the flaps, stirrups, etc., of a dilapidated and long-
disused saddle, are fastened together with wire, whipcord, and
greenhide; a bridle, 'faked' of odd bits and saddle-straps; he is
made a present of a new pair of blucher boots (which were too
small for his father), an extra pair of white cotton socks, and
an old coat; and, maybe, at the last moment — a softened moment — of a small fortune, in the shape of five, or even ten
'bob'. He 'sheds no tears on leaving home' — if he can help it;
but perhaps, something comes over father suddenly as he goes
through the novel ceremony of shaking hands with his boy —
he turns away abruptly, and, in short, 'acts queer'; and
mother's drawn, sunburnt face pales a shade, and her haggard
eyes fill involuntarily — for the first time in years, perhaps.
These things move young Jack to hammer more vigorously
with a stick on the gable end of the old horse, and to fling his
heels wildly against the sides in his hurry to get a start in the
rusty machinery inside. Maybe his instinct tells him that what's
out of sight is, happily, out of the minds of both parties (to a
great extent) in the bush.

To compare this with the scene in the story when the Spicer boy
arrives, on the same horse, with the shout of 'Hi, missus!' is to ap-

preciate not only how important the exact details are to Lawson's imagination (especially the five shillings and the extra pair of white cotton socks) but also the dramatic refinement that has taken place in the fully fictional version — which tells us as much about Mary as it does about the boy himself.

Another aspect of Lawson's realism is his adoption of the vernacular, its rhythms and diction, for his narrative voice rather than a more elevated (and distanced) "literary" style, and his observation of how people really speak, as compared with how characters in fiction were usually shown as speaking. As with Mark Twain, whom he read and admired, Lawson's adoption of colloquial rhythms and "low" diction is a conscious rejection of romantic attitudes towards the life he wants to present realistically. (Early works like "Some Popular Australian Mistakes" and "The Union Buries Its Dead", referred to previously, make this clear.) An emphasis on Lawson's realism does not — as is sometimes implied when this term is employed — deny his imaginative organization of the details he has drawn from life. The selection and organization in the "Joe Wilson" sequence is subtle and imaginative — those geraniums, for example, which are pathetically real yet can also suggest a longing for "something better — something higher" that Lawson himself knew so well. The realist's eye for detail, such as the finger poked through the hole in the handkerchief, or pieces of string inked to look like shoe laces, is also the imaginative artist's perception of the significant image to express complex emotions.

The best of Lawson's writing combines the immediacy and particularity of the sketch (qualities so often disablingly lacking in the verse) with an imaginative communication of the sympathy he feels for the implied "general case". The figure of the mother at Paddy's Market that haunts his prose as it so obviously haunted his memory is a recurring example of imaginative sympathy and detached dramatic presentation working together. The balance between sympathy and control is delicate, sometimes precariously so (as when Lawson comments on the children of the poor in " 'Water Them Geraniums' "). The tendencies it contains artistically can be seen out of control elsewhere in his work: the tendency to sentimentalize, to melodramatize, to moralize. At one extreme there is a tendency to simply document; at the other a tendency to "fictionalize", to turn a neat plot. All these tendencies in the body of Lawson's work can still be seen in the "Joe Wilson" sequence, but here they are pulled tautly into tension with each other.

The "Joe Wilson" sequence is the crown of Lawson's artistic achievement. Completed in England, published first in

Blackwood's Magazine and the same year in *Joe Wilson and His Mates* (London-Edinburgh, 1901), it also marks the peak of his literary career. Lawson had another collection of stories published in England that year, *The Country I Came From*, and a further one, *Children of the Bush*, the following year. He was flatteringly, and perceptively, received by Edward Garnett, and other prominent English reviewers. It was a great personal triumph for the boy from Mudgee hills, with only a few years formal schooling, who had been afflicted with deafness at a most vulnerable stage in his insecure life: now he seemed to have the truly metropolitan literary world before him. Yet in 1902 he returned to Australia, separated from his family, seems to have attempted suicide, and the following year began the series of admissions to hospitals for alcoholism, and later, imprisonment for arrears of alimony that persisted for a decade. Lawson the writer continued to turn out stories, sketches, articles, and verse, especially verse, but Lawson the artist was only dimly and fitfully to be perceived in this large body of work. Why his talent disappeared and how representative his later work is are questions which have led to speculation and enquiry. Clearly, however, he was a sick and disturbed man after his return from London, and what social representativeness his work has is often at the crudest and most vulgar level of jingoism and racial prejudice. The young republican humanitarian, who had "dreamed of dying on the barricades to the roar of the 'Marseillaise' — for the Young Australian Republic", became in middle age a loyal imperialist bristling with military metaphors, as excited by the Allies' cause in the Great War as he had been by unionism as a young man.

The impossibility of selecting a representative amount from his writings after his decline which would maintain any balance with the quality of those he produced earlier has lead me to present a cross section of Lawson's work from his formative and artistically mature periods and leave it at that. Those who consult the later prose (in the collections edited by Leonard Cronin and Colin Roderick) will find some characteristics of the earlier writer. He still pursues characters and themes through series of stories: the "Elder Man's Lane" group, those dealing with Benno the bottle-o and Previous Convictions, an old lag. The "Elder Man's Lane" stories particularly impress the reader as being drawn — too directly — from life; lacking imaginative drive they are a rambling, facetious, maudlin (as the embarrassing title suggests) writing up of experiences. Behind these, and most of the later water, is a nostalgia for the past, for the days of horse-drawn traffic and a lost communality, that is inconsistent with Lawson's earlier presentations of life in just those days. In a sense, he could

be seen as retracing his steps in his later work. As the war kindled
enthusiasm for a cause, enthusiasm with a quite contrary
ideological basis from that of his youth (not that Lawson was ever
consistently committed to any ideology), the passing of the way of
life he had known as a young man in Sydney led him to romanticize the past, as he had as a younger writer idealized the "golden
days" which he had never known himself. The difference was
that, sadly, he had now lost the ability to "paint Australia as it is,
and as it changes".

Note on the Text

Lawson revised many of his best known works, some a number of times. Some of his changes simply corrected printing errors, others altered the substance of what he had written previously. In addition, editors "improved" his copy without always securing his agreement, and newspaper editors often cut it. New editions of his work appeared during his lifetime, which he could comment on even if he could not control them completely, and many more have appeared since he died. Whenever new type is set there is the possibility of further errors appearing, and also the opportunity for editorial "interpretation" of possible accidental or substantive errors in earlier settings.

The fullest account of textual problems can be found in the introductions to Colin Roderick's editions of the *Collected Verse* and *Henry Lawson: Commentaries on His Prose Writings*. Dennis Douglas's article "The Text of Lawson's Prose" in *Australian Literary Studies*, December 1967, reveals how unsatisfactory "standard" editions of Lawson were until Professor Roderick's appeared.

The text of this selection has been based on editions published in Lawson's lifetime and approved by him (at least tacitly). Unless otherwise indicated, his last revised version of those pieces which appeared in a number of editions has been chosen. Although the last revised version has generally been preferred, the arrangement after "A Fragment of Autobiography" is broadly chronological to illustrate Lawson's "development" as a writer. The date of first publication, which determines the order in which most pieces appear here, is not always a reliable guide to the date of composition (Lawson complained particularly of the *Bulletin* keeping a back log of his contributions) and has been departed from when there is a marked discrepancy between it and the known date of composition. It is however, a broadly chronological arrangement: no point would be served, for example, by printing "Brighten's Sister-in-law" out of its normal order simply because it was the first written of the Joe Wilson stories. The sources for the versions printed here are given in the editor's notes to each section. Manuscripts and typescripts have been consulted for the few pieces unpublished in Lawson's lifetime.

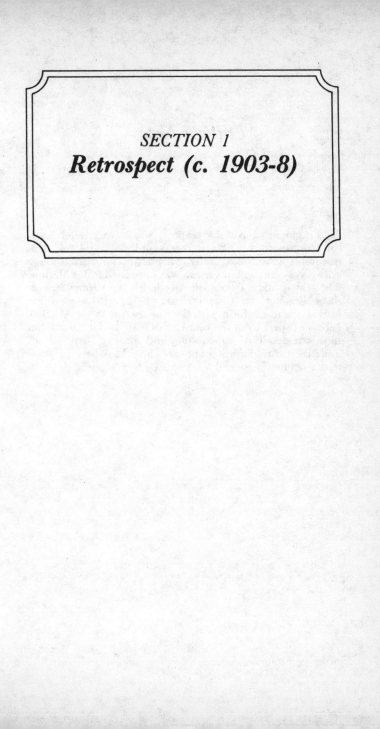

SECTION 1
Retrospect (c. 1903-8)

Editor's Note

A "Fragment of Autobiography" was written after Lawson's return from England, between 1903 and 1906. This uncompleted autobiography is his last major work, though only a very condensed version was published in his lifetime. The text is taken from Colin Roderick (ed.) *Henry Lawson: Autobiographical and Other Writings* (1972) with some slight alterations to conform with the manuscript in the Mitchell Library (apart from the usual modifications for consistency in minor details of punctuation and spelling, such as "ise" and "ize"). An alteration appears on p. 12, where an alternative reading suggested by Dennis Douglas is inserted.

A Fragment of Autobiography

I.   *The Tent and the Tree*

I had a dreamy recollection of the place as a hut; some of my people said it was a tent, on a good frame — for Father was a carpenter, but Mother tells me that he built a little bark room in front, lined with "scrim" papered with newspapers, with a white-washed floor with mats, a fireplace in front, by the side of the door, and a glass door! — relic of the rush, I suppose. The tent was the same that I was born in, on the Grenfell goldfield, some three years before, and had been brought back to Pipeclay. There was a tree in front of the tent — or hut — a blue-gum I think, and I know it had a forked trunk; and on the ground between the tree and the hut had stood a big bark publichouse, one of seven in the gully in the palmy days of Pipeclay. Some of the post holes were there yet, and I used to fall into them, until Father filled them up. Pipeclay had petered out before my people went with the rush to Grenfell. Pipeclay was a stony barren ridge, two little gullies full of digger holes caving in, a little brown flat, a few tumble-down haunted huts, an old farm or two on the outskirts, blue-grey scrub, Scotch thistles, prickly pears, Bathurst burrs, rank weeds, goats, and utter dreariness and desolation. But the hills were still blue in the distance. I took screaming fits, they said, and would lie down and roll out of the tent, through the room and across the flat till I was tired; then I'd sleep. But this was before I became conscious of the World.

That tree haunted my early childhood. I had a childish dread that it would fall on the tent, I felt sure it would fall some day. Perhaps I looked up, and the white clouds flying over made the top of the tree seem to move. The tent and the tree are the first things I remember. They stood there back at the beginning of the World, and it was long before I could conceive of either having been removed.

There was Father and Mother and a baby brother, but I *seemed* to come into the world alone — they came into my life later on. Father said that I suggested throwing the baby down a digger's hole, or drowning him, like a surplus kitten. They say I got a tin of jam one day and obstinately denied it, though my mouth, hands, and pinny were covered with jam: which was strange, for I was painfully and unhappily conscientious and truthful for many long years.

When I was about three, or three and a half, I read the paper, they tell me — or at least I thought I did. I'd get it and stare at it hard, and rustle it as I'd heard it rustle when Father turned it. About this time I was butted by a billy-goat — and I carry the scar, and several others, on my head to this day — but I don't remember the goat. It belonged to Granny. Grandfather had bullock teams and a sawpit. Granny lived in an old weatherboard place, that had been a publichouse, about a hundred yards further along in the World. I used to go to Granny's and get coffee. I liked coffee. One day she told me that the blacks had come and drank up all the coffee and I didn't like the blacks after that. I don't remember that the old lady had any special points about her, except her nose and chin, but I was extremely fond of her until the day she died. When I was about four and my brother two we had a song about Aunty — Aunty to come. Sometimes Mother would tell us that if we sang that song Aunty would come, and we'd sing it, and sure enough she'd come while we were singing it, and rush in and kiss us. We thought it very wonderful.

Then a tremendous thing happened. Father built a two-roomed slab and bark hut over on the flat on the other side of the gully — and on the other side of the World as it was then; and Grandfather came with a load of stringy-bark slabs, and stringy-bark poles for a kitchen. And Granny and the rest were going to Mudgee (about five miles away) or to some other place away out of the World. The dining-room had a good pine floor, and there were two dogs, and a church with a double tower, and a sentry on the mantel-shelf, and the sofa tick had a holland cover — I remember this because we weren't allowed to get onto it. About this time I was put into knickerbockers, and "come a man", and began to take an interest in lady visitors. I had two pair of pants, one of tweed and the other of holland I think, and one morning I tore the dark pair on a stump. Then a young lady came — a jolly, stylish girl whom I greatly admired. I was called but didn't show up for some time. I'd washed my face and damped my hair and combed it, but it was too wet and all in furrows. I'd dragged the holland pants on over the tweed ones. I shook hands with the young lady and hoped she'd excuse me for keeping her waiting, but the fact of the matter was, I said, that my trousers were broke in a rather awkward place. I told Mother later in confidence that I didn't think she was very ladylike or she wouldn't have laughed so. I was very hurt about it.

But we didn't seem to live in the new house any time before a more tremendous thing happened. We were in a cart with bedding and a goat and a cat in a basket and fowls in a box, and there were great trees all along, and teams with loads of bark and rafters, and tables upside down with bedding and things between the legs, and buckets and pots hanging round, and gold cradles, gold dishes, windlass boles and picks and shovels; and there were more drays and carts and children and women and goats — some tied behind the carts; and men on horses and men walking. All the world was shifting as fast as ever it could.

Gulgong, the last of the great alluvial or "poor man's" rushes, had broken out. And it seemed no time, but it must have been months, and may have been a year or so, before a still greater thing than ever happened. Father's party had bottomed on payable gold, and we went with Mother and some aunts on a trip to Sydney. We saw Grandfather at Mudgee — he was up with one of his teams, I suppose: it was in a publichouse and Grandfather was singing songs; and we saw Granny at Wallerawang, where the railway was, and where she'd gone to live. I remember little of the coach journey down, except that I felt smothered and squeezed once or twice, and it was jolly. I must have slept a lot.   We want to sleep on chairs in the waiting room at the railway station, and when I woke up somebody said it was Sydney, and there was a lot of smoke, and it was raining.

I remember little of Sydney, except that we stayed at a place in Castlereagh Street and the woman's name was Mrs. Kelly. We must have picnicked at Manly Beach or somewhere, for we had a picture at home of a Newfoundland dog with the sea behind him, and that picture meant Sydney to me for a long time afterwards. Mrs. Kelly had a swing in her back yard, and one day I was swinging high and told Mrs. Kelly's little girl that I was going right up to Heaven, and she said I was a very wicked little boy to say such a thing. I couldn't understand why. Mrs. Kelly's little boy taught us to say: "Ally-looyer! I hardly knew yer!"

I must have seen and remembered Pinchgut, or else Mrs. Kelly's little boy told me about it, for when I returned to Gulgong I informed a lady that I'd found out where babies came from — I was quite sure they came from Pinchgut. I had a new suit of velveteen knickerbockers, but I don't remember what Charlie had. One day we got out in the street and the door shut behind us, and we got frightened, and lost, and knocked and hammered at the wrong door, and it opened and we went into the wrong house. It was awful, but they didn't hurt us. The girls took us up in their arms and kissed us and gave us cake, and one of them took us home. I remember that Mrs. Kelly was very angry about it, because, she said, it was a bad house; but we couldn't see anything bad about it — they might have kept us there, or killed us, or given us to a policeman; we thought it was a good house.

But a more terrible thing happened. There was a hole in the fence, where some palings had fallen out, at the bottom of Mrs. Kelly's yard, and through there there was a coach-builder's or wheelwright's shop — I worked there afterwards — with a big heap of chips and shavings at the bottom of their yard, against our fence. One day Charlie and I got through the hole and started to put shavings and chips back through into Mrs Kelly's yard for her to light her fire with. We thought it would be a pleasant surprise, I suppose. But all of a sudden a man came running down the yard with a saw in his hand, while another man shouted to him from the shop: "Cut their heads off, Bill! Cut both their heads off!" I don't know whether I got through the hole first, or Charlie, but there wasn't much time between us. When they soothed us and got us a little calmer we were both determined that we wanted to go straight back home to Gulgong at once.

I remembered even less of the journey home than I did of the journey down. There was an inn where we stayed for a night, so we must have taken the coach journey by van and not by Cobb and Co's. The landlady knocked at the door and asked if we'd take in another little boy to sleep there for the night, so the place must have been full. There was trouble in the morning about a bottle of smelling salts I broke and something I split on my knickerbockers.

Then the hut on Gulgong, and Father had killed a pig. Mother asked us if we knew him again, and I said to him, "Ally-looyer — I — hardly-knew-yer, Father!" And Father seemed surprised.

He was always working, or going somewhere with an axe

or a pick and shovel on his shoulder, and coming home late. I remember watching for the glint of his white moles in the dusk, and sometimes following him out again after tea, when it was moonlight, and he went a little way with the axe on his shoulder to split firewood from a log. He worked in a claim in the Happy Valley, and again on the Canadian Lead. I had childish fancies of Happy Valley, because of the name, but I saw it in after years, and a more dismal hole of a gully I'd seldom set eyes on.

Sometimes we'd go for a drive round the fields in a cart with Mother and one or two other diggers' wives and stop at a claim where one of their husbands worked. And if it was his shift below his mate would sing out, "Below there! Peter! (or Tom!) Here's someone wants to see you!" and he'd be drawn up all covered with yellow mullock. I have an idea that those diggers didn't want to be bothered by their families while they were digging for gold.

Strange to say, there were periods during my childhood when I seemed to live alone: when Mother and brothers, but not so often Father, seemed to go completely out of my life. Maybe I dreamed a lot, or perhaps they were away on visits. But I remember a cubby house and a boy they wouldn't let us play with afterwards because they said he was a bad boy. As I grew the feeling of loneliness and the desire to be alone increased. I had a fondness for dolls, especially wooden Judy dolls, and later on developed a weakness for cats — which last has clung to me to this day. My Aunts always said I should have been a girl.

Aunt Phoebe was living at Gulgong and she had a sewing machine and a parrot; and there were honeysuckles in front of her house (we called huts houses — or "places" when they had more than one room). I believed the parrot understood people and I used to talk to him a good deal. I used to be there often, and when I was about six I fell in love with an elderly married lady who kept a lolly shop next door to Aunt Phoebe's. Her husband was away and she seemed lonely. She was forty or fifty and she had moles and a moustache. I remember I went into her shop one day, to buy lollies; she was busy sewing, and she was worried, and she said "Oh bother!" and it hurt me so much that I cried. I'd come in the back way and so I went into the kitchen and dried my eyes on a tea towel. She seemed greatly affected and comforted me, and gave me a lot of lollies — and she wouldn't take the penny. I didn't go in to Aunt Phoebe's until I felt quite sure my eyes were all right. I kept big things like that locked up tight in my heart, but the lady told Aunt. I was a very sensitive child.

And there were the diggers, grand fellows — Harry Brentnal and Jack Ratcliffe and the rest of them, and we had money boxes. And there were circuses — and one day we were walking with Aunt and she said, "Look quick! There's Maggie Oliver." And I looked and saw the most beautiful woman I had ever seen. She was fixing up a vine round a verandah. And one night, in a place they called a theatre, I heard another most beautiful woman sing:

> "Out in the wide world, out in the street,
>   Asking a penny from each one I meet.
>   Cheerless I wander about all the day,
>   Casting my young life in sorrow away!"

That infernal song haunted me for years, especially the last line. There was a pretty woman, living in a hut near us, who used to sing "Love Amongst the Roses" and have a black eye. I said I wanted to go and fight her husband — but perhaps she loved him. About this time I used to tell people that I was going on for seven. I seemed to stay going on for seven for a long time, but I began to feel old.

They said that Gulgong was done, and one day Mother and Father packed up all the things. Next morning we were waked early; there was a dray at the door and we heard a great scraping overhead. Suddenly we saw the sky and next moment were nearly blinded by a shower of pungent stringy-bark dust. Father was taking off the roof of the hut — for we carried the house with us in those days.

We were back at Pipeclay again. There was someone living in the new house on the flat, so we camped for a night or so with the Spencers. They had also shifted onto the flat and built a slab house. They used to live in a hut near the tent by the tree, but I didn't remember them then. I wanted to go across the gully with some of the Spencers' children and see the tent we used to live in, but they told me it was gone. Anyway I wanted to see for myself, or see the place, and whether the tree was still standing, but it was getting dusk, and the gully was full of dangerous digger holes, so we weren't let go. We'd brought the lining of the Gulgong hut with us — "scrim" or bagging with the newspapers still pasted on it, and our table stood outside, where the dray had dumped it with the rest of the load; so we children pulled a big piece of the lining over the table, and let it hang down all round, to make a cubby house, and we all got under —

Spencer had a big family and it was a tight squeeze. And we compared notes and got chummy and told stories. They were the first playmates we had, and we theirs, and we were chums until we were scattered.

The tent and the tree were gone, and Spencer was making a garden there. But the tent and the tree still stand, in a sort of strange, unearthly half light — sadder than any twilight I know of — ever so far away back there at the other end of the past.

II. The Old Bark School

Notwithstanding our old trip to Sydney, which we had almost forgotten — and it's strange how boys forget things of their childhood which come back to them as men — notwithstanding our trip to Sydney, the World was encircled by the Mudgee Hills, with Pipeclay as a centre. Mudgee, the town, five miles away was inside the World: Sydney was somewhere on the edge of the World, or just behind. I used to describe Sydney as a place 170 miles from Pipeclay.

The World could not be flat because of the hills — we children settled that amongst ourselves. Later on we decided that it couldn't be round, for the same reason. But we took it for granted, what we saw of it. The sky was part of the World, of course, and a dome, just as we saw it, and it ended all round where it touched the hills or flats. The sun — this was my idea — went down behind the ridge across the Cudgegong River, and then all round, behind the Mudgee Mountains, and behind old Mount Buckaroo in the west, and then rose again. It took him all night to go round. These conclusions of ours gave our first schoolmaster a lot of trouble later on. Heaven was up above, where the stars were; God was everywhere; and Satan and the other place were "down there". It was wicked to point at the moon or swear, or tell lies; it was also wicked to say "devil".

There was the ghost of old Robertson in his deserted slab hut: young Fred Spencer saw him one night through the cracks in the slabs. And there was the ghost of old Joe Swallow in an old stone hut at the foot of Sapling Gully; and the Chinaman's ghost at the Chinaman's grave in Golden Gully; and the Hairy Man in Long Gully. We wouldn't go through any of those gullies after dark. We children used to go out on the flat in the moonlight and sit in a circle, and talk about these spooks till we frightened each other, then one would start to run home and the rest would follow screaming.

Father worked at building and carpentering, round about the district and in the farming town: Spencer at fencing, clearing, etc. on surrounding runs, and, sometimes for wages in a claim. I have described such homes as ours many times in other books some were better and some were worse. There was a period of tin plates and pint pots and brown ration-sugar, bread-and-treacle and bread and dripping. Cows, pigs, and fowls came later, and there was milk, butter, eggs and bacon. There were times when the Spencers lived on bread and tea and "punkin pie". Perhaps I couldn't realize the sordid hardship and poverty of it now. We couldn't then because we knew nothing better, and so we didn't feel it.

I hope, in another book, to go deeper into the lives of Bush people — there is no room here. There was hardship and poverty, squalor and misery, hatred and un-charitableness, and ignorance; there were many mistakes, but no one was to blame: it was fate — it was fate. The misery and unhappiness that had to be and couldn't be helped. There were lonely foreign fathers, speaking broken English and strangers to their wives and families till the day of their death. A friend, who knows me, writes. "Treated ruthlessly, Rousseaulike, without regard to your own or others' feelings, what a notable book yours would be!" Yes. But what good purpose would it serve, even if I could find a publisher? Looking back, from these, the dark days of my life, to my boyhood and childhood, I can find many things that were bright and happy and good and kind and beautiful and heroic — and sad and beautiful too.

I don't want to write a bitter line, if I can help it, except it be against my later self. I want to gather all the best things I can remember and put them in this book; and it will be none the less true. Perhaps it will be the truest I ever wrote. The dead of our family have rested for many long years, the living will rest in good time — and I have grown old in three years.

Shortly after we returned to Pipeclay my brother Peter was born. I spoke of my money box on Gulgong — I had two pounds ten and I was given to understand that it went to buy Peter. He was bought from a Chinaman — not the vegetable variety, but the sort that used to come round with boxes of drapery and fancy goods slung on their poles. I still stuck to the Pinchgut idea, but a Chinese hawker did call at

the house on the morning of the day on which the new baby
was sprung on us, and that settled it as far as we children
were concerned. I didn't think that Peter was worth two
pounds ten as a baby, and couldn't see why I should be
called upon to pay for him. I thought it very unjust and
brooded over it a bit. My sense of injustice was always very
keen. The Spencer children had been found in wombat
holes and they said that that was better than being bought
off Chinamen, anyway. But we retorted to the effect that
they hadn't been paid for.

There was an old camp for bullock teams on the flat.
"Jimmy Nowlett" and "Billy Grimshaw" and others of my
earlier characters used to camp there, for quite a spell
sometimes in bad weather, or to spell their bullocks, which
they'd put it a paddock or back in the ridges. And they'd
patch up their waggons and make new yokes, etc. I've seen
the great wool teams, with bales packed high, rolling along
the rough road like ships in a gale; or bogged to the axle
trees with two or three teams of bullocks yoked to one load
and trying in vain to shift. It was cruel for the bullocks. I've
seen them go down on their knees and bellow under the
blows from the heavy handles of the bullock whips. When
Jimmy or his mates were in trouble with their teams we'd be
called in and shut up out of hearing. Great flocks of sheep
went by in sections, and mobs of bullocks: "Wild cow! Wild
cow! Keep yer bloody dogs inside!" "Dave Regan" and others
of my drovers used to call with their dusty pack horses. I
remember Jimmy Nowlett ground up some charcoal and
mixed it with axle grease and rubbed it on my brother,
Charlie's, face: he rubbed it well into his chin and cheeks
with an extra layer under his nose and assured him that it
was the very best whisker seed — the only genuine article,
and told him to be careful not to rub it off till the whiskers
sprouted. Charlie was a sight, but he screamed and kicked
and wouldn't be washed, and had to be put to bed with the
whisker-seed still on.

Log Paddock had broken out, opposite the old Pipeclay-
rush, on the old, level, creek and river frontage land grant
that had shoved the selections back into the barren stony
ridges. I remember the claims being bid for. Down at the far
corner of the other end of Log Paddock the old farmers had
built a little slab and bark chapel. See "Shall We Gather at
the River?": *Children of the Bush*. They got a school teacher
to camp there and paid him 6d or a 1/- a head for the
children. We went there first, in charge of some elder

children. I told him that my name was Henery Lawson, and they say he spelled it that way. His was Hanks. I remember little or nothing of that school, except great spitting and hard rubbing on slates.

Hanks, they say, used to talk about "improving our moral minds". There was a hedge or roses — a most uncommon thing — round a lucerne paddock on the bank of the creek, on a farm near the school, and, one day, in lunch hour, some of us went to the farm and asked permission to pick some roses and were told to take as many as we liked. We came late back to school, each child with a big bunch of the flowers. Hanks was waiting for us, and, as we came up, he took the roses, bunch by bunch, tore them to pieces, and scattered them on the ground, then he marshalled us in: "Mary Cooper, Elizabeth Cooper, Bertha Lambert, Henery Lawson, William Harvey, etc. etc. Stand up! You are guilty of the crime of stealing — stealing flowers from a neighbour." Then it occurred to little Bertha Lambert to say, in a meek voice, "Please, Sir, Mrs. Southwick said we could take them." "Serve out slates," said Hanks, and he turned to the blackboard and started to set [the lesson? Or "sob" for "set"?]

About this time there was an incident which left a very painful impression on my mind for years. We had a quince tree at our place and were strictly forbidden to touch the fruit, which was not ripe at the time. One day my brother Charlie pulled a quince, and persuaded me to have a bite. I was always very fond of quinces. I believe that he gave me the bite out of pure good nature, but the theft was detected — there were few quinces on that tree — and Charlie blurted out in terror that I had taken a bite anyhow. I was stung by a sense of injustice and my indignation was roused, for I reckoned that he had only persuaded me to have a bite for fear I might tell on him — or that he wanted me to share the punishment in case of detection. Bursting with indignation, and a perverted sense of injustice, I denied that I had touched the quince at all. Charlie stuck to it, I was believed because I had always been truthful, and he was severely thrashed. He begged me to confess and save him ("Henry, you know you did it! You know you did it!"), but — I don't know what devil possessed me, save that I was horrified as a liar — but I stuck to the lie and he to the truth and he got a second dose and was sent supperless to bed. It was a miserable night and a miserable week for me. I don't think a boy was ever so conscience stricken or a little soul so self tortured. He forgave me next morning, after breakfast, and might have forgotten all about it in a day or two, had I let him. I tried every way to "make it up to him" — he told me not to bother; I said I'd confess — he told me I'd be a fool if I did, and tried his best to persuade me out of it. But, months after I confessed. They didn't thrash me; better if they had and had done with it.

About this time — or I may have been a little younger — I began to be haunted by the dread of "growing up to be a man". Also I had an idea that I had lived before, and had grown up to be a man and grown old and died. I confided in Father and these ideas seemed to trouble him a lot. I slept in a cot beside the bed and I used to hold his horny hand until I went to sleep. And often I'd say to him: "Father! It'll be a long time before I grow up to be a man, won't it?"; and he'd say "Yes, Sonny. Now try and go to sleep." But I grew up to be a man in spite of lying awake worrying about it.

Father and a few others petitioned for a "provisional school" at Pipeclay — it was Eurunderee now, the black name had been restored. Father built the school. It was of bark. I remembered the dimensions for a long time, but have forgotten them now; anyway it was a mere hut. It was furnished with odds and ends thrown out of the public school in Mudgee, when the public school got new desks, stools, and things. Father made blackboards and easels and mended the rickety furniture. The books, slates, and things were all second-hand and old.

I believe the population of Pipeclay to have been obstinately, mulishly honest, whatever else they might have been; but Pipeclay, in common with many worse and some better places, disliked mounted troopers. The men and women were uneasy when one was round, the children were frightened and they hid, and every dog on Pipeclay hated a mounted trooper and would bark himself into convulsions when one appeared on the scene. Perhaps the people disliked the sight of the trooper and were embarrassed by his presence because they *were* honest and poor. Bush children are generally shy of strangers, but I can't account for the dogs — unless it was the uniform. Young Fred Spencer once told my brother and me, in strict confidence, that when he was about ten years old he caught a trooper, tied him to a tree, cut stringy-bark saplings and thrashed him. And when he was tired his father thrashed him. And when his father was tired his uncle thrashed him. And then they let him go. I doubted Fred but Charlie believed every word. Fred's ambition was to become a jockey: he is now one of the best riders in the west and has ridden many races. Charlie was undecided as to whether he'd join the bushrangers or the mounted troopers — a state of indecision not uncommon amongst boys before our time, for both troopers and bushrangers came from the same class.

A selector, an Irishman, named John Tierney, was selected as schoolmaster. He had served in some capacity in the Army in Africa, a paymaster or something. His strong points were penmanship, arithmetic, geography and the brogue; his weak ones were spelling, English grammar and singing. He was six feet something and very gaunt. He spent some months "training" in the public school in Mudgee, and had a skillion built onto the school, where he camped. I don't know whether he made his own bed, but his sister-in-law used to send his meals up to the school — one or other of us children used to carry them. I remember carrying a dinner of curried stew and rice, in a cloth between two plates, and a lot of the gravy leaked out. I suppose the dignity of Pipeclay wouldn't have stood his cooking for himself.

The Spencers went a couple of miles over the ridges at the back of Pipeclay to a slab and shingle public school on Old Pipeclay. Maybe their father thought they would get a better education. We went there later on — on account of a difference, I suppose, between our people and Tierney. There were a good many Germans round; the majority of the farmers were Germans — all the successful ones were. There were a good many Irish and the yellow and green had not faded yet. So there was fierce sectarian and international bitterness on top of the usual narrow-minded, senseless and purposeless little local feuds and quarrels; but there is no room for these things in this book.

The first day, one day in the first week at the Bark School, was a great day in my life, for I was given a copy book and pen and ink for the first time. The master believed in children leaving slate and pencil and commencing with pen and paper as early as possible. While setting me my first copy he told me not to go back and try to "paint" the letters. I am following that rule in this book, with reference to sentences. Better to strike out than paint. We had learned our A.B.C. — and about a Cat, a Bat, and a Fat Rat — somewhere in the dim past.

It was Robinson Crusoe, by the way, who taught us to read. Mother got a *Robinson Crusoe* and used to read to us of evenings, and when she'd get tired and leave off at a thrilling place, we'd get the book and try to spell our way ahead. By the time *Robinson Crusoe* was finished we could go back and read the book through from beginning to end. I wonder if Defoe had any influence on my style? Speaking of books, I was presented, at school break up, with a copy of a book called *Self-taught Men*, for "general proficiency". My people, for some reason, considered it a very appropriate present. But I wasn't a self-taught man: the world taught me — I wish it had taught me common sense and the business side of my trade.

Then the bother commenced. The master explained the hemispheres to us on the map, and doubled it back as far as he could to show us how they were intended to come together. We hadn't a globe. I thought the hemispheres should come round the other way; my idea was that the dome of the sky was part of the world and the whole world was shaped like half an orange with the base for the earth, but I couldn't account for the other half. The master explained that the world was round. I thought it must have something to rest on, but I was willing to let that stand over for a while, and wanted the hill question cleared up. The master got an india-rubber ball and stuck a pin in it up to the head and told us that the highest mountain in the world would not have the ten thousandth (or somethingth) effect on the roundness of the earth that the head of that pin would on the roundness of the ball. That seemed satisfactory. He it was, I think, who tied a string to the neck of a stone ink bottle, and swung it round, to illustrate the power of gravitation and the course of the earth round the sun. And the string broke and the bottle went through a window pane. But there was no string from the earth to the sun that we could see. Later on I got some vague ideas of astronomy, but could never realize boundless space or infinity. I can't now. That's the main thing that makes me believe in a supreme being. But infinity goes further than the supreme.

A favourite fad of the master's was that the school, being built of old material and standing on an exposed siding, might be blown down at any moment, and he trained the children to dive under the desks at a given signal so that they might have a chance of escaping the falling beams and rafters when the crash came. Most of us, I believe, were privately resolved to dive for the door at the first crack. These things pleased Father when he heard them, for he didn't build things to come down. When the new school was built, the old bark school was used by the master as a stable and may be standing still for all I know.

Our school books were published for use in the National Schools of Ireland, and the reading books dealt with Athlone and surrounding places, and little pauper boys and the lady at the great house. The geography said, "The inhabitants of New Holland are amongst the lowest and most degraded to be found on the surface of the earth." Also: "When you go out to play at 1 o'clock the sun will be in the south part of the sky." The master explained this and we had to take his word for it — but then it was in the book. The geography also stated that in bad seasons the "inhabitants" of Norway made flour from the inner bark of a kind of tree — which used to make Father wild, for he was a Norwegian. Our name, of course, is Larsen by rights.

There was a M'liss in the school, and a reckless tomboy — a she-devil who chaffed the master and made his life a misery to him; and a bright boy, and a galoot — a hopeless dunce, a joker, and a sneak, and a sweet, gentle, affectionate girl, a couple of show scholars — model pupils the master called 'em — and one who was always in trouble and mischief and always late, and one who always wanted to fight, and the rest of them in between. The children of the Germans were Australians — and children are children all over the world. There was Cornelius Lyons who rolled his r's like a cock dove and had a brogue which made the master smile. And there was the obstinate boy, Johnny B———, who seemed insensible to physical pain. The master called him out one day. "John B——— stand out!" Johnny stood out. "Hold out your hand!" Johnny held out his hand, the master struck it, Johnny placed it behind his back and held out the other, the master struck that and Johnny put that hand behind and held out the first; the master set his teeth, so did Jack — and so on for half a dozen strokes. Then suddenly the master threw down the cane, laid his hand on the boy's shoulder and spoke gently to him — and Jack broke down. Looking back, I don't think it was fair — Jack could have claimed a foul.

And there was Jim Bullock whose "eddication was finished" at the Old Bark School. "Oh, yes," he said to me, years later, while giving me a lift in his dray, "John Tierney finished me nicely."

Amongst the scholars was a black gohanna. He lived in a dead hollow tree near the school and was under the master's immediate protection. On summer days he'd lay along a beam over the girls' seats, and improve his mind a little, and doze a lot. The drone of the school seemed good for his nerves. They say a black gohanna haunted the tent I was born in, and I remember one in the house on the flat — I used to see the impression of his toes on the calico ceiling when he slithered along overhead. It may have been the same gohanna and he might have been looking after me, but I had always a horror of reptiles.

Sometimes, when the master's back was turned for a minute or so, one of the boys would cry suddenly: "Girls, the gohanna's fallin'." And then you'd hear the girls squawk. One form of alleged punishment in the Old Bark School was to make a bad boy go and sit with the girls. I was sent there once, by mistake. I felt the punishment, or the injustice of it, keenly; but I don't remember that I minded the girls. I grew extremely and most painfully shy of girls later on, but I've quite grown out of that now. In fact, I rather like sitting with them.

I was slow at arithmetic — it was Father who had the mathematical head — but I stuck to it. I was, I think, going into compound fractions when I left school. In '97 when I went to teach a native school in Maoriland, I could scarcely add a column of figures. I had to practise nights and fake up sums with answers on the back of the board and bluff for all I was worth; for there was a Maori girl there, about 20, as big as I am and further advanced in arithmetic, and she'd watch me like a cat watches a mouse until she caught me in a mistake. I was required to give the average attendance to two points of decimals, and I had to study, and study hard, before I could do it.

My handwriting was always wretched, stiff and cramped and slow and painful, and it used to worry me a lot. I changed it many times, and it was only after I went to England, about three years ago, that I struck a sort of running round hand which enabled me to keep within a dozen paragraphs or so of my rate of composition.

The master used to spell anxiety with a "c": i.e. anxciety — and many other words to match. I spelled Friday with a "y" for many years, was always in doubt as to whether the "i" or the "e" came first in words like recieve[*sic*] or believe; I spelled separate with two "e's" and blare "blair" — and so on, and so on. Mr. Archibald said I used to be a whale at spelling, and some of my early copy should be interesting reading. A comp. who used to set my work up on the *Boomerang* used to complain that my spelling was demoralizing him. It worried me a great deal, I was very sensitive about it; I'm not now — not a little bit — I leave it to the comps. Strange to say, my punctuation was good — that must have "come natural". It's a good plan to get rid of as many stops as you can.

I was fond of grammar at the Old Bark School, and made rapid progress in "parsing" or analysis. I don't bother much about grammar now — it used to worry and cramp me and keep me back too much when I started to write. My composition was always good.

Until I was seventeen and went for a few months to a night school in Sydney, I knew of no monarch of England other than Queen Victoria — except for a very vague idea of a King William the Fourth.

I shared the average healthy boy's aversion to school; in fact it developed into a positive dread, and before I left I had almost a horror of going to school. Yet I was a "show scholar" or "model pupil", as the master put it. There were two of us, and I can't decide now whether we were the makings of noble men or simply little involuntary and unconscious sneaks, but am rather inclined to the latter opinion. It seems hard to reconcile the fact that I hated, or rather dreaded, school with the fact that I was a model scholar. Perhaps the last fact accounted for the first. I dreaded school because I was sensitive, conscientious, and a model scholar, and I had never yet been punished, and it was a strain to keep up the reputation. I was always restless, fond of walking, and I hated confinement. Perhaps that is why, when I started to write, I used to do most of my work after midnight.

The boys went kangarooing and possum hunting and had their games and superstitions and a contempt for girls, as boys have all over the world. Some played the wag and stole fruit, and told lies and went swimming. I was too conscientious to play truant, and I had a horror of lying or stealing. I might have been happier had it been otherwise. But I couldn't resist the swimming. The water-holes in the creek were full of snags and treacherous, and we were strictly forbidden to bathe there unless one of the elders was with us. After a swim we used to rub our faces, necks and hands with dust lest unwonted cleanliness should betray us.

I was extremely, painfully sensitive, and almost, if not quite, developed religious mania at one time (when I was about fourteen). The mother was very highly strung and had religious spells. (We went to the other extreme later on in

Sydney, during the free-thought craze of the eighties, and became free-thinkers — or thought we did.) Father always professed to be a free-thinker, and he studied the Bible. He was one of the hardest working, kindest hearted men I ever knew. I have known him, after a hard day's work, to sit up all night watching a neighbour's dying child.

I was painfully, unhappily "good", a self-torturer and a nuisance to my playmates. I remember, one day, the master, with woeful want of tact, gave me a note to take home, informing my people that my brother had played truant from school that day. Charlie was waiting for me outside the school paddock and begged me not to take the note home — to save him and tell the master a fib. He pleaded very hard, but I had to deliver the note. I suffered a great deal more than he did.

I was strong, as proved in school games, and no coward, as was also proved, but I wouldn't fight under any provocation, because I thought it was wrong. Charlie would, on the slightest excuse, and he often wanted to fight for me and gave me a great deal of anxiety on that account. Years after, when we were grown to men, Charlie, who had learned to use his hands, backed me in a fight (girl the indirect cause, of course) and I lost, after spraining my ankle. He was very proud of me on account of my pluck, but he bitterly cursed my lack of science.

I began to be a lonely, unhappy boy, and to be considered a little mad, or at least idiotic, by some — my relatives included. My aunts said it was a pity I hadn't been born a girl.

Father built a new sawn-timber hardwood house on the flat, with a galvanized iron roof and a brick chimney, which last was the envy of neighbours who had only slab and clay chimneys.

The mother went to Mudgee for a while, and when she came back she brought a little stranger and foreigner into the family. We were tall and dark on Mother's side and generally supposed to have descended from gipsies. We were hot-headed, impulsive, blindly generous, and open-hearted and suspicious by turns. Father was short, nuggety, very fair, with blue eyes; he was domestic, methodical and practical. The little stranger, one of twins, was the first and last creamy-skinned blue-eyed baby in our family. She only stayed a little while — long enough for us to call her "Nettie", short for Henrietta (Granny's name). When the baby fell ill Mother took her to Mudgee and she died in the room she was born in. (I was born in a tent, Charlie in a bark hut, Peter in a slab house, and "Nettie" and her sister in a brick one.) When Nettie was dying they sent Mother out of the room, and she sat on a log in the yard — sat very still, they said, staring up at the stars. Father was walking fast along the lonely road to Mudgee, but he was too late. About midnight they called Mother in. The old watchman, passing just then, cried, "Twelve o'clock and all's well!" I have often thought how well it was, for there has ever hung a cloud over our family.

Early in the morning after the funeral, Father took his maul and wedges and cross-cut and went up into the ridges to split rails. I heard the maul and wedges and the song of the saw until dusk. He was trying to work it out of him. After tea he walked to and fro, to and fro in the starlight, with his arms folded and his head down, but now and again he'd put his hands behind him and take a few turns looking up at the stars. I pace the room or the yard a lot nowadays.

When I was nine years old there happened a thing which was to cloud my whole life, to drive me into myself, and to be, perhaps, in a great measure responsible for my writing. I remember we children were playing in the dust one evening and all that night I had an excruciating ear-ache and was unspeakably sick on my stomach. Father kept giving me butter and sugar, "to bring it up", which it eventually did. It was the first and the last time I had the ear-ache. Next day I was noticeably deaf, and remained slightly so till I was fourteen, when I became as deaf as I am now. Before that my eyes were bad but my hearing was always very keen. I remember, one night, when I was in bed, Mother was telling a very pathetic story to some visitors three rooms away; when she came in to me she found me sobbing. I'd heard every word.

III.   The Selection and a Sketch of Grandfather

I don't know whether Father took up the selection because he had a liking for farming and believed in the chances or because the ground was on an old goldfield and he was a digger. He had been a sailor and had passed in navigation, he had also served in a ship-building yard, and was a good all round carpenter: he was clever at anything where tools were concerned. I know he had always a fancy for a vegetable garden and a few fruit trees; but our land was about the poorest round there, where selectors were shoved back amongst barren, stony ridges because of old land grants, or because the good land was needed to carry sheep. Our selection, about three hundred acres, lay round a little rocky, stony, scrubby, useless ridge, fronting the main road; the soil of the narrow sidings, that were not too steep for the plough, was grey and poor, and the gullies were full of waste heaps of clay from the diggers' holes. It was hopeless — only a lifetime of incessant bullocking might have made a farm of the place. I suppose it was the digger's instinct in Father — for a long time he was always "putting down a shaft" about the place in spare times, or thinking about putting it down. (He had two men on prospecting when he died.)

I'm not going to enter into details of grubbin', clearin', burnin' off, fencin', ploughin', etc. See "Settling on the Land" and "A Day on a Selection" in *While the Billy Boils*; and, for a description of the poorer class selection, see " 'Past Carin' ' " in *Joe Wilson and His Mates*. In addition to grubbin', etc., we had to reclaim land for ploughing by filling up the diggers' holes. The shafts were driven underneath, of course, so the whole of the waste heaps wouldn't go down. We used to "spread" the lighter dirt — and it didn't improve the poor land; and we carted the hard lumpy clay away to the boundary in barrows; some of it we used for making a dam. When I left the Old Bark School, I used to tail the "cattle" in the gullies and do a bit of "ring-barkin' ". The "cattle" were a few weedy stunted cows — one of them barren — and some steers, and were always straying. The elders were mischievous and demoralized the rest; some of them could get through, over or under our scraggy two-rail fence. Ditto the old grey horse — he'd get his fore-quarters over and slide. Then, when we got new cows one or two of them would be sure to fall down a digger's hole if we didn't watch sharp. A cow, and sometimes a horse, would be cropping the grass round the edge of the shaft, and sometimes, in wet weather, the shaft would fall in, or else the beast, turning round, would miscalculate and slide down. Then the cry of "cow in a hole" (it was "man in a hole" once or twice) and we'd run in all directions and scare up the male population of Pipeclay; and, provided the beast hadn't fallen head first and broken its neck or smothered, they'd rig a Spanish windlass and get it out, little the worse.

It was very scratchy farming as far as I was concerned, but then I was only a child. I had no heart in it — perhaps I realized by instinct that the case was hopeless. But Father stuck to it between building contracts. He used to walk from five to seven miles to work, at first, work twelve hours and walk home again. He'd insult anyone who offered him the loan of a riding horse — I never knew a man so obstinately independent as he was in those days. Then, between jobs, he made a spring cart, wheels and all — except the iron-work. He could make anything in wood. Then he bought our old grey horse, "Prince" — used to run in Cobb & Co's — I must tell you about Prince someday, and how he pulled up an hour on the Gulgong road, with a heavy spring-cart load of mails, in bad weather, when the coach broke down, but was never the same horse afterwards. Then, when Father worked in town he carted home a load of manure every night and spread it on the barren ground. And sometimes at night he'd burn off, and dig in the dam by moonlight. There had been a bullock camp on the level, and several acres where the old road had been were so hard that even a big bullock plough, which Father hired for the day, couldn't break up the ground. He broke it later on with charges of blasting powder! He trenched deep round the house and built frames and planted grape vines behind, and in front a rose bush and a slip of an ivy plant that had come from England in the early days. The last time I saw the place the house was a mass of vines. The mater talked of christening the farm "Arundel" after Father's birth-place in Norway, as soon as we got it ship-shape.

I remember the last questions at night would be, "Are you quite sure all the calves are in the pen?" "Are you quite sure the slip-rails are pegged?" And often at daylight the mater would cry, "Get up quick, the cows are getting away!" and one of us boys would turn out and run across the hard baked sods barefoot, or the frosty flats in winter — running hard so that the cold and the burrs wouldn't hurt so much — and head off the cows which had broken through the fence and were hurrying down the lanes after "Spot", their old wall-eyed ringleader, in the direction of a neighbour's wheat or lucerne paddock. Prince got very fat one drought and we couldn't make it out, until one morning a neighbour, getting up earlier than usual, saw Prince's rump sticking out of his haystack and hit it hard with a paling. Prince was very much surprised, and his condition and the mysterious hole in the stack were accounted for at the same time. I remember, often, on a bitter cold frosty morning, rooting up a camping cow and squatting with my bare, perishing feet on the warm spot where she'd been lying.

After we left the Old Bark School we went, for a month or so, to the Old Pipeclay School across the ridges. Curtis was the master. His first idea was to unlearn the Old Bark School scholars all that Tierney had taught them. I suppose the mater had fallen out with Tierney, but I used to go to him at night later on and get lessons in arithmetic and grammar. He'd improved in that branch.

At the Old Pipeclay School I worshipped pretty Lucy W———. We were both going into the fourth class when I left, but she used to go home in a different direction. My old sweetheart was Mary B ——— the tomboy of the Old Bark School, but one day we quarrelled and she said she wouldn't be my sweetheart any more. I think she made up to Fred Spencer for a while. Fred, by the way, was the Tom Sawyer of our school. Mary's sister Bertha, a prettier girl, began to look kindly on me, but I'd had enough of women. Childish recollections begin to crowd — recollections of child life and character — but there is no room for them here. It was Curtis, by the way, who first noticed that I was a solitary child. There were days, during play hour, when I liked to get away by myself; and once or twice he tried to draw me out, and asked me whether my school-mates had been annoying me. But it wasn't that — I couldn't explain what it was. Sometimes I'd run home ahead of the rest, and once or twice Mary came running after me to try to find out what was the matter, but she soon gave it up. It was while at this school that my companions first began to say I was "barmy".

The mother was ambitious. She used to scribble a lot of poetry and publish some in the local paper. There were nine or ten daughters in her family, most of them big women and all naturally intelligent and refined. Almost any one of them might have made a mark under other conditions. Their lots were cast in the rough early days, in big bark humpies where all things were rough and ready and mean and sordid and gipsy-like, and they were brought up surrounded by the roughest of rough crowds on the goldfields. (My diggers are idealized, or drawn from a few better class diggers, as my Bushmen are sketched from better class Bushmen.) Then amongst those left on the abandoned goldfields, the most unspeakably dreary, narrow and paltry minded of all communities.

The girls used to try to establish little schools, singing classes, etc. and humanize the place, but the horizon was altogether too narrow and hopeless, and, as they grew up,

they became embittered. But they had humour, a keen sense
of the ridiculous, and that saved them to a great extent.
Grandfather was a big strong dark handsome man, who
came from Kent with his family. Wavy black hair, worn
long, and profile Roman. His people were supposed to have
been gipsies and he was very gipsy-like in his habits. He had
sight like a blackfellow and was a first class Bushman of the
old school. He was a humorist of the loud-voiced order.
When he was sixty he could handle timber and knock out
palings and shingles with any young man. He had the head
of an intellectual man, a strong man, a leader of men, and
he couldn't read or write — a fact which he hid successfully
from many. He liked to camp by himself in the bush. *He*
never had no eddication, he'd say, and he didn't see what his
children wanted with it. He drank. At home he had been
known to smash all the crockery and bring home a string of
pint pots and a pile of tin plates and dump them on the
table. He was very mysterious and seldom did things like
other men. For instance, he'd go to Mudgee and buy a string
of boots for the family, but he wouldn't bring them home.
No — not he. He'd roar at one of the girls: "D'yer see that
shaller digger's hole up there on the sidin'?" "Yes, Father."
"Then go up there, yer'll find a piece of bark in the bottom
— lift it up and see what yer'll find." And the girls would
find the boots. Again, when they were all married and had
families, he'd visit them in turn, and most unexpectedly of
course, once in years. But he wouldn't come up to the door
and knock. No. In the morning the daughter or one of the
children would look out and see a big man standing at the
gate with his back to the house, or, more likely, leaning on a
fence across the road. Then "Why, there's father" or "Why,
there's Grandfather", and he'd be brought in. He'd be very
clean and have on a full new suit of tweed, with, maybe a
dandy pair of shoes and a little curl at the bottom of his
pants — but his old greasy hat:

"Father why don't you get another hat?"

What do I want with another hat? I hain't got two heads,
have I?"

He'd leave as unexpectedly as he came.

He nearly always shouted at the top of his voice, and it was
a big voice.

"Mr. Albury, why do you speak so loud?"

Grandfather, roaring: *"Because I want people to hear
me?"*

I've seen a man roll on the ground and shriek at something Grandfather said, and heard him, with a face as solemn as a judge's, tell that man to get up and not be a thundrin' jumpt-up fool.

Save for "thundrin' " or "jumpt'up" I never heard Grandfather swear. There's a legend to the effect that one day, in his young days, he swore so badly at his bullocks that he frightened himself; but I don't believe that.

I worked with him now and again in the mountains in the eighties, humping palings and rails out of gullies. He was taking care of an empty house and camping there. He "had the writin's" (a letter from the owner, authorizing him as caretaker). He had great faith in "writin's". (See "Uncle Abe", in "Buckolt's Gate", *Children of the Bush.*) An ordinary fire wouldn't do Grandfather, he'd pile on logs till he roasted us to the back of the room, and sometimes outside altogether. He was a good cook and very clean in camp; he'd polish up his tin-ware till he could shave in it. Saturday afternoon or Sunday morning he'd clean up. The furniture and things would be chucked out with great noise and clatter — the furniture was home-made and strong and could stand it. Then Grandfather would take off his boots, tuck up his trousers and arm himself with a broom and a mop. My business was to run to the tank and back as fast as I could with two buckets. We camped in an outhouse, and when the house was let he was asked to clean it out for the new tenant. It was a great cleaning — I'll never forget it. They say the house was damp all summer, but it was clean. He couldn't do things like an ordinary man. He was fond of dogs, little mongrel dogs, and he'd talk to them, and they seemed to understand. But if a strange dog came sneaking round Grandfather would lay for him. He wouldn't attack that dog in the ordinary way; he'd heave a chair, or table, or something equally handy. I remember a big hairy thievish dog used to come sneaking round. Grandfather laid for him. He had just finished making a picket gate and it stood inside the door. It was dark inside and broad moonlight in the yard, and when the dog sneaked into the yard he didn't see us. Suddenly Grandfather jumped up, seized the gate and hove it. It missed the dog by a hair, struck on one corner and smashed to smithereens. I never saw that dog again.

He was a great man in Mudgee in the early days. He cleared the main street and owned blocks of land in town. He lost them — drink of course. Amongst other things he was an undertaker. He buried many, and under all sorts of conditions — some in sheets of bark; and he was in great demand at burials. He usually had a coffin cut out roughly and stuck up over the tie-beams of the kitchen to season, and wait. The family hated this sort of thing. They say he generally had an eye on the prospective client too and cut his coffin accordingly.

Jones, the legitimate undertaker, made a palisading for a child's grave, gave it a coat of paint and stood it outside his shop to dry. Grandfather, coming along, vaulted into the palisading, took hold of each side, lifted it, and ran, with Jones out and after him. Grandfather ran up a blind lane, dropped the palisading and jumped the fence. Jones took his palisading back in a dray and nothing would convince him that Grandfather didn't want to steal it. The old man would suddenly go down on his knees in the middle of the street and stare hard at a stone till the floating population gathered round and put its hands on its knees and stared too. Then he'd get up and go away. And they'd stare harder after him than they had at the stone.

The last time I saw him in Sydney he'd bought some tools and a new carpenter's bag to carry them in. He put the handle of an adze through the loops of the bag and carried it across his back. Out of one side stuck an auger and out of the other the blade of a saw. He walked straight down the middle of George Street, towards Redfern railway station — the tram wasn't there then — and he walked fast. It was Saturday evening and the street was pretty full. Every few yards a passenger, coming in the opposite direction, would catch sight of the point of the saw or auger and duck just in time to save an eye or an ear. Heads were bobbing to right or left all the way. I saw no traces of anger on any of their faces — just mild startled surprise. Just such an expression as a man might wear who has nearly stumbled against a cart coming out of a lane. An uncle and I walked behind the old man all the way and enjoyed the show. One would have thought that he was absolutely unconscious of the mild sensation he was creating, but we knew the old man better than that.

I don't remember ever hearing Grandfather laugh. Little Jimmy Howlett (Nowlett in my books) the bullock-driver could throw some light on the subject. One day he was out looking for a bullock in the scrub just outside Mudgee, and had sat down to rest and smoke on a log on the edge of a little clearing about fifty yards from the road, when he saw Grandfather coming along. The old man seemed rather more mysterious than usual, and Jimmy watched him — he thought perhaps he had come to look for some timber. Grandfather glanced round, very cautiously, like a black-fellow, but he didn't see Jimmy. Then he started to laugh. He laughed till the tears ran down his cheeks. He put his hands on his hips and roared till he doubled up; then, when he recovered, he straightened himself, composed his face and went back whence he'd come. And thereafter it worried Jimmy a good deal at times, for he never could find out what Harry Albury was laughing at that day.

I have moods now, sometimes, when I feel inclined to go out of the world apiece and laugh. But then I am growing old. Father used to work with Grandfather as a young man, and there are many anecdotes. Father got on with him famously and I never met two characters more opposite in every way. Add to this the fact that Father was a total abstainer. Father used to say that the one thing he liked and admired the old man for above all else was that he'd never harp on a string — he'd say a thing and have done with it. Father, you must bear in mind, was married when he used to say this. I never heard the old man say an ill word of anybody. The worst things I remember of him were: 1st, he drank — but I drink too; 2nd, he would seldom sack a man for whom he had no further use — he'd wait for an excuse to have a row with him, and the man would leave bursting with indignation, and burning with a sense of injustice: but that was, in a way, in keeping with the old man's character; 3rd, he got nearly all his stringy-bark palings out of mountain ash: but that was due to: (a) the prejudice of his clients (who could never hope to live as long as that timber) in favour of stringy-bark, (b) the extreme scarcity of stringy-bark, (c) the prevalence of mountain ash; 4th, hens used to come round our camp for what they could pick up, and were encouraged, and often picked up more than they came for and left but the head: but then I was fond of poultry too, and the blame, if any, was on our gipsy ancestry. The old man usually had an old horse, bony and angular past description, popularly believed to be as old as himself, and locally known as "Old Albury" too. The old man fed the old horse well, but no power on earth could ever fatten him. (I've noticed that bosses who are extra fond of animals are usually hardest on their men.) I remember seeing the old man throwing out some corn he kept for the horse to a stray fowl. He explained that he was fattening that fowl up for Christmas. I asked if the hen belonged to him, and he said No, not exactly; but he thought it would about Christmas time. He bought a fowl occasionally, for the sake of appearances and to provide against accidents.

He had, as I said, the sight of a blackfellow, and would bring his heavy eyebrows together and peer at something in the distance, standing and looking for the moment just like a blackfellow and seeing as far.

I got on well with him and was, I think, the only one in the family who could get him to sing. He had a good voice and I used to read old songs to him and he'd get them line by line. Like most illiterate men he remembered nearly all he had ever seen or heard.

Supposed to be without sentiment, I discovered him to be a dumb poet, a poet of the trees, "the timber", and all living things amongst or in them. Supposed to be without affection, I know that in his old age, when the family was scattered and he alone, he made a long and useless journey just to have a look at the ruins of the church he was married in.

Granny was the daughter of an English clergyman; she came out to Australia as an immigrant and went into domestic service Penrith way, where she met Grandfather, who looked like a young god then, and married him for his looks. She went with him over the mountains and went through forty years of a rougher Bush life than you could imagine. She was good and well-meaning and old-fashioned — and helpless. The diggers on Pipeclay in its flush days once proposed subscribing to send my mother to England to have her voice trained, but Granny would not hear of it, for she had a horror of any of her children "becoming public".

IV.   Loneliness and a Trade

I was eleven or twelve when I first began to talk about being a writer some day; but I may have cherished the idea earlier. It exasperated Father, but Mother encouraged. Mother had a copy of Edgar Allan Poe's poetical works. I often heard her read "The Raven" aloud and the other short poems and I read them myself later on, over and over again. Not very healthy reading for a child, was it?

Home life, I might as well say here, was miserably unhappy, but it was fate — there was no one to blame. It was the result of one of those utterly impossible matches so common in Australia. I remember a child who, after a violent and painful scene, used to slip out in the dark and crouch down behind the pig-stye and sob as if his heart would break. And a big black mongrel dog who'd come round with slobbery sympathy. And the child would put his arms round the dog's neck and bury his wet white face in the shaggy hair. But that child had a stubborn spirit and would not kiss the rod.

Spencer had given up his selection to a man who was mining mad, and taken in exchange a little two acre freehold, up near the Old Bark School, at the foot of Sapling Gully — a piece of land which the man had prospected exhaustively and had sunk a good deal of money in. The tenant on Spencer's old selection was an Irishman named Page, and there was a feud between him and our family until we left. It was about a boundary fence, of course, with a stray bull thrown in. Page "didn't want to be onneigh-bourly", but "he'd be aven wud 'em some day". We bought a small secondhand harmonium, and Page got a barrel-organ next week. Both houses were close to the fence, and so sure as we started the organ of an evening Page would grind his hurdy-gurdy, and a digger across the road a concertina, and Fred Spencer would thump a kerosene tin in the still moonlight, and there would be music on Pipeclay. Page said that the hurdy-gurdy would go "rippin' wid him if he only had the noats".

One day, after our rooster and Page's rooster had crowed defiance at each other — each on the top of his own haystack — for several days, our bird went down, and got on Page's haystack and tackled the other fowl. We watched the fight until both birds fell down on the other side of the stack. We dared not go through the fence, but, some half-hour later, we heard Page's familiar "Insoide there — come out!" He had our rooster and [was] handling him gently. "Yere cock beat my cock!" he said, "but I bear no malice — 'twas a grand fight. There he is." And he set him down carefully.

We boys — the Spencers and we — used to annoy Page a good deal. "I'll tell the masther on ye!" he'd say. We used to like to run bare-foot along the moonlit road and plough up the thick white dust with boughs until we were enveloped in a dense cloud. Page had a score or so of turkeys and they roosted along the top rail of the fence in front of his place; and sometimes, as late as possible, we'd slip down and brush those turkeys from end to end with a bough, and they'd gobble, gobble, gobble, all down the line like a new musical instrument. And Page would come out, sometimes in his shirt, and then we'd vanish. In my memory my childhood, or boyhood, if I had any, went out with the gobble of those turkeys. There was a flicker when I got a horse of my own, and again when I got a gun, but it went dead out.

Page found our cattle in his wheat one morning, and I met him taking them to pound. I don't remember what I said to him, but he gave the cattle to me. He was at feud with all his neighbours, English, Irish, German, and Father, but the morning we were leaving the selection for good, he came up to the gate and shouted: "Insoide there, come out." We came out. "Here's some fruit," he said. " 'Tis a harrd worrld and it's little we have to be foightin' for. Shake hands and let bygones be bygones between us." The last time I heard of Page he was doing pick and shovel work at Prospect.

'Twas a hard world and it was little we had to be fighting each other for. There was Harry Spencer; few men worked harder and longer than he did, unless it was Father. He was a stern father, was Harry Spencer, but all his children turned out well; and he was a very kind husband. There was a split between the two families, by the way — over something a woman said another woman said — and we were forbidden to play with the Spencer children and they with us, so we had to meet privately, and if caught both sides were punished. The mother reckoned that the Spencer children led us astray. And Mrs. Spencer said that Charlie led Fred into mischief, and neighbours repeated. Well. Harry Spencer strained himself rolling heavy logs on a clearing contract on a neighbouring run, and was never quite well afterwards. Then he worked for wages in a claim in the petered-out Log Paddock, opposite our place. One morning he had breakfast, kissed his wife and the younger children, as was his custom when leaving home, and went to work. He sat down at a water-hole to wash a prospect — a dish of "wash-dirt" or gold-bearing clay — but had scarcely wetted the clay when he suddenly exclaimed, "Oh! my heart!" and fell backwards. A few minutes later Harry O'Brien came running up to our place and said, "Harry Spencer's just dead!"

I saw them bring him out of the paddock. Four of them carried him on a sheet of bark with two sticks under it to lift it. They took out the bottom rail of the slip-rails, but the top rail jambed, so the bearers stooped through with the bier. Away up the hot white road Mother was running through the dust like a mad woman, to Mrs. Spencer. 'Twas a hard little world and 'twas little we had to be fighting for.

I went for a few months to a Catholic school in Mudgee. I

don't know why I was sent there; but probably because my mater had become disgusted with our own churchmen as they were then. I remember one day, Pat Tovey, the coach driver, who was taking the mails out on a pack-horse because of the bad weather and flooded creeks, gave me a lift home on the pack-horse. He stayed to deliver a bag at a post office near our place kept by a bigoted Protestant family with whom our family were at feud.

"What are they sending that boy to a Catholic school for?" asked the post-mistress.

"Sure he's bein' educated for a priesht," said Pat: and a little further on he said, half to himself and half to me: "Let her put that in her pipe and shmoke it." Then he added with a chuckle, "It'll be all round the dishtrict be tomorrer mornin'."

I was given a weedy riding hack and used to ride to school. I usually milked six or seven cows and had to catch the horse before riding to school, and was never late that I remember. Some children had to rise before daylight and milk ten or fifteen cows in [the] bitter cold frosty morning before starting for school. I don't suppose there was ever such a collection of young fiends as were in the Catholic school in Mudgee when I went there. One had thrown a slate at the last master, who broke a blood vessel and died. Several masters had resigned, but the present one, Mr. Kevan, was a strong man and kept the young devils well in hand without the assistance of Father O'Donovan. His successor, a better scholar, a younger and cleverer man (who nevertheless said things like "Don't do that no more") had a tough fight but got the school under after using up two or three canes a day for a week or so. I got a sharp cut once by mistake, but, somehow, I didn't seem to mind. Of course, there were no girls in this school.

Father O'Donovan was a character and I liked him. He didn't mind the young men and boys of his flock touching their hats to him but he discouraged the habit in old men: "Oh, don't bother about that!" he'd say to a tottering ancient who'd suddenly recollect himself and take off his hat to the Father. Father O'Donovan would come into the yard, go softly behind a kneeling boy playing marbles, stoop, and take that boy by the shoulders. The boy would start to swear and blaspheme like a shearer in a rough shed, and the Father would lay him gently on his back and the nipper, still testifying, would look up into the Father's face. Then he'd stop swearing.

At other times the Father would come into school, make eyes at the boys behind the master's back, and one or two would laugh and be called out for punishment. Then the Father, with a face as solemn as a priest's, would beg them off. One day a boy said, "Please, Sir, Father O'Donovan was makin' eyes at me" — and he got it hot.

Father O'Donovan attended the Mudgee races, all three days, to look after the big "bhoys" of his flock, whom [he] corrected on occasion with a buggy whip. They say he always had a horse or two running, but this didn't prevent him from taking care of the boys.

The few Protestant pupils were sent out during prayers in the morning, but woe betide the Catholic boy who threw the Protestant boys' religion in [their faces], whether he fell into the hands of the schoolmaster afterwards or Father O'Donovan. "I'll have none of that sort of thing," said Father O'Donovan, with no softness in his voice. "I want that understood once for all."

Once or twice Mr. Kevan came and sat beside me, as I sat lonely and unhappy, by myself on a stool in the corner of the yard, and drew me out of myself and talked to me about poetry and Edgar Allan Poe. He'd heard something of Mother, I suppose.

I was tormented a good deal by the town boys, after school hours, and used to get to the paddock where I'd left my horse, and get off home as quickly as possible. I was called "Chummy" by some, and by others "Barmy Harry". Years before there had been another Barmy Henry in Sydney, a pale delicate shy and sensitive boy, carrying a tray of pastry on his head, to customers, for his master, a fancy baker, and mumbling verses to himself. It was the habit of "talkin' to hisself", as his companions thought he did, that won him the nickname and the reputation of being mad. Henry Kendall.

I read Dickens. Got him at the School of Arts in Mudgee and read *The Old Curiosity Shop* first I think. I have read Dickens over and over again and can read him now at any time. Next I read Marryat — *Jacob Faithful* and *Peter Simple*. I paid a visit to my mother's people at Wallerawang, and, on leaving, one of my aunts presented me with a volume of Bret Harte's, entitled *Some Folks,* and containing "Tennessee's Partner", "Mliss", etc. I read that book on the journey home and it fascinated me; it seemed to bring a new light, a new world into my life, and this with Dickens still fresh. But Dickens stayed by me and Bret Harte did not. I read *Don Quixote* before I was fourteen, but that was an accident — somebody had left the book at our place. I remember being greatly puzzled and worried about the loss and recovery of Sancho's ass. It was only the other day I read somewhere that Cervantes did not read his proofs and that it was doubtful if he had even read his copy. And oh! of course we read *Robbery Under Arms* when it first appeared in the *Sydney Mail* — Browne, by the way, touched an Australian sore when he described the Marsden family as being, the girls Catholics and the boys Protestants. We read *For the Term of His Natural Life* (as Marcus Clarke wrote it) in the *Australian Journal*. The introduction was, I think, equal to Dickens's style. The sight of the book with its mutilated chapters and melodramatic "prologue" exasperates me even now. And we read *Jack Harkaway* — I was going on for thirty before I read *Dead-wood Dick*, and then I used to read him to put me to sleep. And Mother used to recite Gordon from the *Australian Journal*. I liked tailing the cows amongst the gullies, for it gave me opportunities for reading — though I was supposed to do some ring-barking. But when I was about thirteen I went to work with Father.

V.   Father

I cannot say much of the English side of my family. They were supposed to have come of English gipsies and were hop pickers in Kent, and chicken lifters, for aught I know, and, further back, the Lord knows what else besides they had or hadn't been. They were a queer tribe, tall, dark and eccentric. The women most certainly descended from Eve, but the majority of the females of late generations had and always held to their own opinions as to the origin of men. The old man, grandfather, in his later years, would always rather camp alone in the Bush and split palings and shingles for tucker and an occasional spree than live in comfort with one of his married daughters; he had ten and most of them had married well. Grandchildren nine and ten on an average — as it was in his own days. He was a character, a hard case and a family mystery — he was too deep even for his own tribe. He went on a spree, few ever knew where, about once every six months, and never looked better than after a drinking bout. Maybe I was and am just as eccentric as he was. Anyway, I was always restless and a rover and used to think for years that the roving star was my lucky star.

On the other side I go back further than England, for my father came from Norway. He was, as I have said, a Norwegian sailor, a quarter master with a mate's certificate. He had served in a ship-building yard at home; he was a master of navigation. His father was a schoolmaster, all his brothers sailors, and they were all lost at sea. He deserted his ship at Melbourne — on a voyage from New York, or 'Frisco, I forget which — and ran away to the goldfields in the days of Ballarat and Bendigo. He found gold and lost it speculating in puddling machines, crushing mills, and duffers. He drifted into New South Wales with the gold rushes, came to Old Pipeclay, and got married. He was well educated in his own language, could understand and appreciate German poetry, knew French well enough to understand a Frenchman, was a good penman, and wrote good English. He was clever at all sorts of mechanical work, and the terror in mathematics of all the school-teachers in the district in his time. I don't believe that a kinder man in trouble or a gentler nurse in sickness ever breathed. I've known him to work hard all day and then sit up all night by a neighbour's sick child. He was very independent then, and had a strange way of seeming to drop the acquaintanceship of people he had helped. He was short and nuggety and fair, with blue eyes, brown hair, and a short dark-red beard, which turned rapidly grey towards the end (he died at fifty-four of heart disease). I am tall and dark. He was said to have been a very natty, or "dapper" little fellow in his single days, and the best dancer in the district. (He grew very different as I knew him.) He had an ear for music — I have none, nor for much else. His camp was a model, they said, his tent as neat as a cabin, and he had a little vegetable garden in front fenced in with stakes to keep out the eternal goats that went with all rushes, in carts and on foot, and haunted the dreary old thistle and burr infested diggings for years afterwards. I just remember the site of Father's last digger's camp on the siding on Pipeclay. Two half buried logs were still there to mark where the sides of the tent had been.

Grandfather kept a public house — and also had a saw-mill and bullock teams — on Pipeclay. There was a rough crowd — Irish of both parties. One, a bully, used to start a row, ask for five minutes' grace, and then put up his mate, a big-limbed, hard-muscled softy, to fight for him. One day they were in the bar and started playing up, while the second eldest Miss Albury was there. The bully commenced pulling down the boards of a partition between the bar and the rest of the house — a sort of loose boards in slots arrangement — to get at some real or imaginary enemy whom he thought to be behind there, I suppose. At last Miss Albury called in little Peter Larsen, who happened to be passing; the bully bluffed to the end, then put up his big mate as usual. A few minutes later the girl was getting the little Norwegian sailor a dish of water at the back to wash the blood off his hands. That's how all the trouble commenced, and it will only end with my line, I suppose.

I first became dimly aware of Father on Pipeclay, going somewhere with an axe on his shoulder. It seems as if it was late afternoon. We passed a place where there was a lot of thistles, horehound, and such weeds as grow on the sites of old sheep-yards. The yard must have been there before the diggings broke out. I next became — less dimly — aware of Father walking away from the hut on Gulgong with an axe over his shoulder. He was going for firewood. I was following behind. It was twilight and I distinctly remember the gleam of his moleskins, which seemed to loom large in the gathering darkness — probably because I was so small. He seemed always going somewhere in the evening with an axe over his shoulder, after work; later on, back at Pipeclay, it was axe and cross-cut saw — the latter awkward to carry and flapping and clanging — or a maul and a bag of wedges. I got at the other end of that cross-cut early, I remember (before I remember, it almost seems) but I do remember a big flinty white box long near "our house", that we had to cut up for firewood, and to get it out of the way. My brother was old enough for *me* to drag at the other end of the saw before that log ceased from troubling my Saturdays, holidays, and evenings, and haunting my dreams. Father had done a bit at the other end of Grandfather's saw in his time.

Father had taken up a bit of land at Pipeclay before Gulgong, and built a slab-and-bark house, and, when Gulgong petered out, he returned to it and took up more selections — forty-acre blocks that we called "front", "top", and "back runs"; it was on the base of barren ridges back amongst which the farmers were shoved because every yard of the rich, black-soil river flats and red-soil slopes beyond were old land grants, or squatters' runs, and were needed to carry cattle and sheep. But I fancy that Father took up this land mainly because it was on the old goldfield — the fever never quite dies out of a digger's blood until the day of his death. He was always prospecting or fossicking round with a pick, shovel, and gold-dish on Sundays and in spare hours: and, when he died, he had two men putting down shafts for him on shares and rations. He worked at building and carpentering in the little farming town of Mudgee five miles away, and, later on, when the new educational act of 1880 came into force, took contracts to build or repair the little schools which were dotted all over the Bush. And, between whiles, he'd work on the "farm", fencing, grubbing, and making a dam to catch the surface water, for there was no permanent water there, except in the deepest of the old shafts. The strip of possible land between the spur and the Government road was so narrow that every foot seemed precious, and the ground so hard where the old road had been that a big bullock plough failed to break it. Father tried blasting powder in it. I've seen him come home night after night after a hard day's work in town with a cart-load of stable manure to put on the "poor" grey soil; and after tea he'd drag or lever logs to burn out stumps, or dig in the tank by moonlight. ("Settling on the land" — *While the Billy Boils*) Father would tackle a big brute of a dead, iron-bark stump, that wouldn't burn or split, and was like cast-iron to chop. He'd dig a big hole round it, in the hardened clay, that wasn't much softer than the stump, and, kneeling in the hole, chop away at the flinty dead tap-root that tapered down from nearly the thickness of the stump to somewhere nearer the other side of the world, I think. He had to cut it through to get the stump out — for there was no tree to give purchase — and afterwards dig trenches part of a mile to trace the great surface roots (that had roots going down from them too) — and all the branch roots were big and tough enough to snap the cheap cast-iron plough-shares we used in those days. In addition we had to reclaim ground from the old diggings — fill the shafts with the worst of the waste-heaps, "spread" the stuff that came from near the surface, and cart the rest away to the dam or the edge of the selection: not much more than half would go back into the holes, because it had come from the "drives" underneath. Part of my childhood was used to shepherd the cows to keep them on the selection and the new ones out of the holes — they mostly died of "ploorer" afterwards. It was miserable, wretched, hopeless "farming", like a great deal of the scratching called farming in the dusty stumpy patches amongst the scrubby ridges down there. Home-life was unspeakably wretched. There seemed ever a curse over Grandfather's tribe and all it came in contact with. And perhaps an old boomeranging curse that came down the generations from a gipsy girl and a careless white scamp, for all I know. And in our case the curse from a bad match which was ever too common in the Bush. I remember, as a child, slipping round in the dark behind the pig-stye, or anywhere, to cry my heart out, and old Pedro, the dog, would come round with sympathic nose and tail, and I'd put my arms round his neck and bury my face in his rough hair, and have my cry out.

Yes, Pipeclay was a miserable little hell to me to the bitter end, and a trip to Grannie's at Wallerawang was the only glimpse of heaven my childhood ever knew. There was the railway line there, and water, and something more like God's country and scenery; and happy sympathetic children's society. But such a trip left me worse and more hopelessly in my own little hell afterwards.

I was sent to Sydney when I was between thirteen and fourteen to see if I could get anything done to my hearing. The first impressions of the old coach road, the railway journey, and first living in brick and two story houses have been written elsewhere: "The House that was Never Built" in the London-published *Children of the Bush,* and in other stories and sketches. I stayed with my grandpeople at Granville, who had shifted down from Wallerawang, and I remember some of Grannie's boarders, workmen at Clyde, expressing astonishment at the quiet way in which I took Sydney, my first trip on the harbour, and my first visit to the theatre; but I knew Sydney from childish recollections, descriptions, and pictures, and had got some idea of acting and scenery from a performance of *The Pirates of Penzance* by Charles Turner's company, I think, in the dilapidated old weatherboard theatre on Gulgong. The first play I saw in Sydney was old *Romany Rye,* and I always went to see it in after years while George Rignold's company played it. I say "see" because I never *heard* a play throughout and had to enquire beforehand — or after — and read the notices, or guess the plot and dialogue.

The boarders were a jolly lot, and one, Tom Punt, was the leading spirit. He used to gather the others round a fire outside of nights, and preside. He'd lead off in the perfect snuffle and whine, with "I know a boarding house — Not far away — etc." — or "I wish I had a few more bricks — To build my chimney higher —" and the rest of it, and get the choir in full swing, to Grannie's great disgust. It was scandalous. He was always in mischief, or skylarking, when he wasn't working or sleeping. He used to hide when Father O'D——— passed, I don't know why, and seemed afraid of Grandfather — probably because he recognized, by some strange instinct of the tribe, a veteran devil of his own sort and a greater one than himself. Now, though Grandfather could still earn good money amongst the timber on the mountains, and was no man for home, it pleased him to buy an old horse and cart and go into the vegetable hawking line, to the breathless scandal of Grannie and the girls and the unspeakable disgust of his youngest son. He used to start some time in the night and go to Sydney, Paddy's Market, once or twice a week for his "truck". One week he brought home several loads of pumpkins from somewhere close at hand in the scrub, but the source a mystery of course — he never went out nor returned twice in the same directions — and nowhere would suit him to stack those pumpkins save on the front verandah. He stacked them carefully in three or four piles, with the first rows of the square bases at the edge of the verandah and the apexes against the wall between the windows and doors, exactly like half pyramids cut by the wall. Grandfather finished on Saturday afternoon, while we were in Sydney, and he said it improved the look of the place — an oblong weatherboard house — and it certainly didn't add to its ugliness. Nothing can to that truly Australian style of architecture. He said the pumpkins would attract healthy, hard-working boarders. Well, he finished about dark, and was resting from his labours, with a pipe, when Tom Punt, skylarking round the house with one of the other boarders, stumbled on the first rows of pumpkins at the end of the verandah, and — Bump-bump-bump! Thump-thump-thump! Thump-bump-thump and Bump-thump-bump! — You'd have thought the pumpkins would never stop. Pumpkins from the first pile started the second and so on to the end of the verandah. Tom was hiding in the scrub; there were sounds of strong men trying not to laugh, and over it all Grandfather's voice inquiring for the thunderin' jumpt-up jack-ass who started his pumpkins. The incident filled my uncle and me so full of laughter that we had to go into the scrub too, to avoid appearing ridiculous — where smothered guffaws from close at hand didn't help us much. The thing kept us coughing in bed till after midnight, and when the bad colds eased a little a reference, from the back room, to thunderin' jumpt-up idiots, would set the whole house coughing again. But my boy-uncle and I saw Tom Punt's wicked foolery in a right and proper and religious light very early next morning, which was a frosty one, when we were turned out and set to work to help Grandfather re-stack those pumpkins before breakfast.

I went to Dr. Stanish, in Wynyard Square, on his pauper days, and he spoke to me and treated me like one, and did me no good — though, fortunately, no harm.

I got some house painting to do from Richie, the agricultural implement maker at Granville, at thirty shillings a week. Trade was booming then, and anyone who knew one end of a brush from another seemed sure of work. The slump came in the latter end of the eighties.

I took my first gun back to the Bush from Granville — a single, twist barrel, muzzle-loading shot-gun, to kill at fifty yards, for twelve and six. I sold it afterwards to an old schoolmate for five shillings who took it out of twist (and me out of winding) with a piece of emery paper and found it a very serviceable old American army rifle for kangaroos if he aimed high enough.

I also had my first portrait taken, a "gem" of the while-you-wait variety. Here it is:

(Portrait if I can get it)

Just before I went home Grannie shifted into a larger cottage close by, and Grandfather took the thing on his hands and impressed us all one Saturday afternoon. It was a great shifting and couldn't have been done quicker if there'd been a fire.

Back to Pipeclay in the height of the worst drought the district had ever suffered. Blazing heat that made Granite Ridge and the Peak seem molten masses turned out on the scrub. Blue-grey ragged bush and the ashes of a soil. We drove the few cows to the creek for water twice a day, through private property, and there was always trouble about alleged loitering and the slip-rails. The cows would lie in the shade for the rest of the day, and lived on the water, some wheaten chaff we had collected, and the native appletree boughs we lopped down in the "cool of the evening". Then — on the strength of the straw and wheaten chaff, I suppose — I was sent some miles to bring a wall-eyed steer and a barren heifer that were going as a gift to whosoever would come and fetch them. And they brought "the ploorer" amongst our cows. Then I used to bleed them by cutting their tails and ears in the sickening heat — and was often sick over the job — and inoculate them with a big needle and Berlin-wool dipped in calf lymph, and rouse them up and feed them, at the risk of my life, with slices of young pumpkin from a crop that had failed in Chinaman's garden (even Chinamen failed) and about half the cows, including the best milkers, died. At their last gasp they would often stagger up and charge.

Father got the contract to build the new school at Canadian Lead ("Th' Canadian" of the golden days), near Home Rule, between Mudgee and Gulgong, and [I] went there to work with him when I was about fourteen. It was "facing" and "shooting" stringy-bark flooring boards, rough from the mill, with saw-marks an eighth of an inch deep on the best sides of some of them. (No ready-faced tongued and grooved soft wood for us then.) I had to sharpen the smoothing plane every board or so; and I was always ready for Father's "Put the billy on Sonny," or "Ah well! — knock off Sonny." And on that job I learned to handle a paint brush. I picked up things rapidly and the greatest praise was for Father to say, "Well. I didn't know it was in you." A favourite expression of his was, "Take notice", no matter if it was only a bullocky making a bullock yoke in camp. Father reckoned the "natives", as the Australian-born whites were always called, the best he had seen at rough and ready carpentry and makeshifts — and he had worked on old sailing ships. But the life! The stifling tent in summer till part of the building was up, then a rough bunk; and work from sunrise till dark, and the billy and the frying-pan — steak and chops, and bacon — bacon, and steak and chops — potatoes sometimes for dinner, milkless tea. Except on Sunday when we found time to wash our shirts and socks and cook a bit. And the terrible dreariness and weariness and loneliness of it all, for Father grew more silent and given to brooding over his pipe at night. (He never drank, though I've seen him so worried and upset that he *couldn't* smoke.) But the loneliness, even in company, that led in the end to extreme sensitiveness and shyness. Even home was a relief. And then the craving for love, affection, even consideration from a quarter where there was none, the sympathy, love, even worship, wasted in a quarter where there was none. The strange child (for I was little more) who had been misunderstood, mocked, and tormented at school the few months he went there until the time was a very hell he seldom cared to look back to — until he'd say, while yet a child himself, that he "thought boys were very brutal and heartless"; whereat his ignorant elders would consider him to be, if not as mad as his schoolmates said he was, at least very "queer" and idiotic.

I worked about with Father on various jobs — sometimes at schools where I'd be always glad when the boys — many of them older than I – were safe in school, or gone home. They respected me now as something of a workman, I suppose, but I seemed strange and apart and was shy of them and avoided them on every possible occasion. And, remember, my deafness was but newly come upon me.

I remember looking ahead half hopefully for a change in the scenery as I approached [the] site of each new job; but — and it seemed fate — there was never a change — each hole in the scrub we worked in seemed wretcheder than the last.

And speaking of scenery, I once went, on a memorable occasion, to witness an alleged performance called *Dick Turpin and Tom King,* given by, and in aid of, an "amateur dramatic society" in the School of Arts, Mudgee; a noble pile with "an upstairs in it" in our Bush childhood days, which boasted — on every possible occasion — one piece of scenery, about the size of a large school map — or a little larger — and representing a small lake with mountains. This was hung out on every possible occasion — in almost every act that wasn't supposed to be inside a house and always referred to by the hero (the local poet), either in soliloquy and with windmill business as "What a magnificent scene! .... Here, I, in the midst of lonely grandeur —" etc.; or, in a love scene, with one arm engaged and the other working, "Here at last, my darling — you and I alone with nature in all her soul-inspiring—"and the rest of it. But the first sight of that scene (it was my first "play") took my breath away and roused my emotions.

Again, while working with Father on Gulgong, he took me to see Charles Turner's company give *The Pirates of Penzance.* Well, you know how much scenery that opera needed — and they travelled by coach — not Cobb & Co's either on that road, for the diggings were done. There was a lot of knocking before the curtain went up, but when it did I gasped, and though generally far too shy and sensitive to express my emotions, especially to Father, who was practical, I said, "Father! Father! — look at the scenery!" Someone laughed and it covered me with confusion and almost spoilt my enjoyment of the performance.

I wonder now how the incident affected Father, who had seen some of the grandest scenes in the old world and the new, and some of the best-staged plays of his day. And did he think of the dapper little sailor ashore for a run in European ports, in New York, 'Frisco, and the Lord knows where else.

Then the break-up of the drought and several good seasons. But we had rust in the wheat one season and "smut" the next: I remember we washed the wheat in tubs, skimming off the smut as it rose to the surface of the water, and we dried the grain on borrowed tarpaulins. I put in the last crop, or most of it. I had an old cart-horse and a light pot-bellied mare, with a stunted colt and filly as reserves. I had a good seat and it was a district of riders, but I never had a horse you could call a horse to ride — it was misery down to the old patched borrowed saddle. I was lucky to get both "plough-horses" started at once. Usually the heavier horse stumbled forward first and jerked the lighter one back onto the gear; then, as often as not, something would break and I'd fix it up with wire and clothes-line and try for another start. When both horses got off level they'd go at a sort of run, like two small boys with a tub of water, till one gave in. One day a clothes-line rein broke, or came loose, and they went into the scrub and in and out amongst the stumps and saplings. The old plough mark may be there yet: it looked like a piece of fancy steering by a very drunken ploughman.

The general result was plough-marks in the dust — I cannot call them furrows — but the crop grew that year. Reaping hooks were the fashion, but strippers were coming in — I don't remember the cradle.

The "break-up-of-the-drought" is as aggressively, resentfully, weirdly melancholy as anything else in the Bush — or in the world I think: as if it knew it wouldn't last and was useless. The dark grey blanket over all the world apparently; the dark, dismal, dripping, rotting, scrubby gullies; the blue-grey bush flats, the dead, ring-barked white trees standing naked and ghastly, and the dark ragged boughs about them, and on the ridges, wind-swept in an agony of hopelessness and melancholy. A rainy day in England or New Zealand is nothing to it; an English country white fog is a bright and cheerful thing and London "pea-soup" comforting compared to rain in the Bush.

Then came sunny days, and waving grass, and produce went down to nothing in the market; eggs weren't worth carrying into town, and we melted down the last lot of butter.

Then we sold everything which went well — except the farm, which didn't go at all, but was let to a tenant for a nominal rental and only sold in recent years.

I went to Rylstone to work with Father on small building

contracts — the rest of the family went to Sydney, and the railway was going on to Mudgee — to see what I could do.

Then the tent, the temporary galvanised iron shed to work under, the square boxes — of stone now — of four rooms and a passage with the corrugated iron roof, and days often so hot that you couldn't handle the snips if you left them on the roof in the sun: hot enough on the roads to raise blisters through your boots. And the smell of white lead and oil.

And the bag bunk, and the billy and frying-pan, and the blucher boots and cheap new stinking "moleskin" trousers for Sunday: and the loneliness and hopelessness until Father had only enough work to keep himself going and I was wanted in Sydney.

When work became slack at Kerridge's I went to Mount Victoria and worked with Father for a while, who built most of the town — save the few houses that were there in the old coaching days. Tent and hut and bunk and frying-pan and billy again. Poor Father had become closer and more "cantankerous" — though seldom so with me, and altogether careless of comfort and personal appearance. Steak, potatoes and bread and treacle. As far back as Canadian he had taken to working by candlelight and on Sunday when he could do it quietly, but now he had men working for him. I was told that he had an idea of going back to Norway before he died and taking at least his youngest son with him, leaving the rest provided for as well he could.

But now, in 'eighty-six, the dreaded age of twenty-one seemed rushing on me, all unprepared and unarmed to meet it and what was beyond. My deafness worried me more and more, so at last I managed to go to Melbourne to go to the eye and ear hospital there. And I managed to go saloon too, in little old *Wendouree* that left her weary rusty bones on the Oyster Bank years ago. It was glorious. We were a happy little party from the skipper down, and there was a nice natural girl who drew me out of myself a bit, and banished my shyness. The steward's surprising "Tea or coffee, Sir?" helped the good work and made an impression that I never forgot. I must have looked Bushy enough with my carpet bag and a few washed and mended clothes. I had a slop suit bought at a store on the mountains, and the cloth was like coarse corduroy dyed blue and the pants too bulky and short. I had a piece taken out of them somewhere, in Melbourne, and put onto the bottoms. I didn't know what to do with my hat, half the time, and used a knife for fish then and for years afterwards. But I never got sea-sick, either then or since.

I went to stay at a Mrs. Kelly's in West Melbourne, to whom I had a letter of recommendation from a young woman who boarded at our place in Sydney. I had about a week's board money left after I had done with the four-wheeler; it was my first experience with a cabman and it left me utterly demoralized, alone in a strange city at the door of my first boarding house. The rest was more or less a blank until I found myself in bed next morning at Mrs. Kelly's.

Mrs. Kelly kept a dingy little boarding house for superior tradesmen (mechanics) and inferior clerks and shopkeeper's assistants, with a precarious "traveller" in difficulties sandwiched in at times, a gentleman with a business in the city, and a young lady in a dress-makery — both permanent — and an occasional windfall. It was in a shabby dusty street of two-storied "terraces", the house one room and a passage wide and two deep, with a kitchen behind where Mrs. Kelly was supposed to sleep — if she slept at all — and a room over it sacred to the lady lodgers. Mrs. Kelly was a little elderly Irish woman, with one rusty, black best dress and shawl, a bonnet like an old cob-web in a corner, a pair of cloth "larstens", and a face like a small apple that had been left for a long time in the sunny window of a little lolly shop that was to let but never seemed to go. A seamed and smoked little old Judy doll, and she kept her boarding house very genteel to the bitter end.

The head boarder was a stout gentleman in a rusty walking coat with a mysterious business in town. He was a sort of combination of country newspaper proprietor, schoolmaster, and storekeeper, with the hoggish throat of a Yankee lecturer or quack medicine seller and showman, and he had the balcony room to himself. He was manager in the storeroom of a modest ironmongery, over the entire clerical staff — himself — and the lumper or storeman and the vanman.

Next was a stout lady, fair, fat and forty and decidedly haughty, a schoolmaster's wife or something, down on a holiday or something, whom they called "the Queen", and who used to sit on the paper at breakfast, and walk out of the room whenever a gentleman's clothes or laundry was mentioned. She monopolized the bathroom for an hour or so every Sunday morning, when the "gentlemen" wanted to use it. There was a rumour that she never had a bath at all in chilly weather, only made a splash, and wetted her hair so that she might have an excuse to sit in the sun in a dressing gown at the back window and dry it in public and for the rest that she only held the bathroom to aggravate her enemies, with whom were included all in the house save poor Mrs. Kelly — or else that she drank and smoked in there. At last, to get out of that (and to get her out of this) two choice spirits put cayenne pepper on a piece of wadding one Sunday morning, and lighted it softly and slipped it under the bathroom door.

Next there was the Queen's arch-enemy, Mr. Heckler, canvasser — or "commercial traveller", as Mrs. Kelly put it, who was always behind with her — who was doing nothing just then but trying his hand at everything and anything that looked hopeless enough and didn't require capital; he had a decent extra pair of pants and boots, a cheerful sanguine disposition, and a solid English portmanteau he wanted to sell for thirty shillings and advertised whenever he had one to spare. Both boots and pants went in advertising and cigarette tobacco before he sold that portmanteau. He pawned them.

There was a careless, easy-going young fellow named Tom Punt, who worked on the railway, and he, Heckler and I were room-mates in the room behind the ironmongery gentleman's. Heckler was keen on advertisements that offered him a means of making a livelihood in his spare time for nothing, and untiring in his hunting up of advertisers who had certainties or taught everything in three lessons of an hour each — and squeezing their intellects dry. In plain words, pumping them for all they were worth. And, from his advertisement reading and answering he got an idea, one of many to make his fortune. I was too young and green and unfinancial, so he took Punt into his confidence, convinced him, and took [him] into partnership, putting his name first in the firm for euphony. They swore me to secrecy and Punt bought and brought home some packets of hops and other things, according to Heckler's directions. Then they started to make something that would look and taste like Warner's Safe Cure. Bob — that was Heckler — argued and proved that Warner and many other great men rose from such small beginnings, till they, Punt & Heckler, saw world-spreading advertisements, posters, "branches", and fortunes in the future. They worked surreptitiously, and with closed door, and long after the shabby genteel establishment was supposed to have retired to rest — for Heckler was jealous of guarding his secret, and also sensitive on Mrs. Kelly's account. He surrounded the business with such an atmosphere of mystery that even the Queen was caught peeping and listening and hinting darkly to Mrs. Kelly. They brewed the stuff in a saucepan, kept it in bulk in the water jug, cooled it in the wash basin, and stored it in bottles, until they broke the jug — and something else — and the bottles began to go off in the small hours like a desperately resisted burglar arrest. Then Mrs. Kelly interfered. She said it wasn't genteel and Mr. Walker — the iron-mongrel — might object. And who was going to pay her for the bedroom things? Enthusiasm waned — at least as far as Tom was concerned, which was everything; he had a girl to take to amusements who couldn't wait for fortunes; so, in the end, Punt & Heckler's Only Cure went down the sink by night.

There was a decent young fellow from the country who was serving his time to the coach-building, and nearly out of it, and whose father paid his board. And last — she should have been first — there was a Miss Smith who worked in the dressmakery, and who, being rather left on her own hands, took me on, and tried to teach me how to walk with a woman, without getting in her way or my own, and to lift my hat to her friends when we met them, and see her chum into a bus when they parted on Saturday night, and other useful things. But I avoided fish in public for years.

I went to the Eye and Ear Hospital, then under Dr Grey, for a while, but they did little or no good. They said it was chronic catarrh or something and used to put an instrument shaped like a gas-blower's pipe up my nose, and turn it round inside my head with the point towards my ear and blow into it with an india-rubber bulb. I remember the students asking me which instruments the Doctor used and I'd show them.

But, whether it was the Eye and Ear Hospital, the change, the healthier and happier life, I went to the Theatre one night and heard the play better than any I'd ever been to. But then I got close, there was standing room only, and I edged down to the end of the first row of stalls. It was *The Silver King*, with Titheradge the King of Silver Kings, Maggie Knight, poor Phil Day, Sass (or Williamson) the "Spider", Olly Deering, Coombs' friend, "Mis-s-ter Hen-ery Kaw-w-kitt".

I got work at a railway truck factory close at hand and then at the tramway car and omnibus works way out miles beyond the Exhibition Buildings. I got thirty shillings there, or maybe thirty-five; I have no recollection of the place, except of a would-be bully I put down and a mighty buck nigger night watchman with awful rolling eyes, a dark lantern, a step like a cat's and a sudden guffaw like a graveyard eruption which, coming unexpectedly and out of place, might have scared anybody out of his wits. The sudden apparition would have been enough for any burglar, I reckon.

I had to get up very early again, but Mrs. Kelly was always up before me with a "bit-o'-breakfast" ready. When I worked nearer home she always asked in the hearing of the others:

"Ar-re ye goin' to *beesnis* this mornin', Mr. Lawson?" and "Will ye take yere *loonch* wid ye to beesnis this mornin', Mr. Lawson?" I was slinging sludge on railway trucks then, and doing some house-painting and kalsomining for the boss between whiles. "Sludge" was the contents of all the paint pots, emptied and scraped out into a drum, "boxed" and strained through coarse scrim.

She had an old basket perambulator, with a list to port, that went in circles if let go, like a lost bushman or a man in the dark, and she used to wheel it to the market on Saturday night for supplies.

"It belonged to me daughter Mr. Lawson — Her little boy, me grandson that died of diptheery. Dead an' gone — dead an' gone. An' miny's the time I've wheeled thim in it."

"So you had children, Mrs. Kelly?"

"Yes, yes — long years agone — long years agone."

"Dead, Mrs. Kelly?"

"Yes, save wan, an' grandchildren; father an' grandfather. An' the old perambulator reminds me of him; it goes just like him o' Saturday nights if he wasn't steered, especially whin it's loaded — an' it steered about the same. But — God bless you, an' God rest him — barrin' that I had no more trouble with him than I do wid the ould perambulator."

I used often to go with Mrs. Kelly to market on Saturday, in company with Miss Smith and the old perambulator, and wheel it home.

But I still "longed to rise" even when I was getting thirty or thirty-five shillings a week at the tramway and omnibus works — and I did rise, and this is how it came about:

I had long had an idea of learning to draw and sketch and being an artist, and I used to practise a bit now. I remember trying to make an enlarged drawing of a portrait of a gentleman Miss Smith said she was engaged to at one time, and who died, or went away, I forget which. Perhaps he went away and died, for he wasn't expected back. [I] used to say

that I'd practise, and study, and go on and on, till I got paid
for my work, and some day I'd go to Italy and Paris, and
study there, and be a great artist.

Now Bob Heckler, who still kept his eye out for likely
advertisements, was greatly interested — he was my artistic
adviser and critic, ready made and self elected, as most of
my critics are to this day — in an advertisement offering any
person with an artistic eye a certain and immediate opportunity of adding to their income by a few hours' easy work of
an evening. This was just the thing Bob wanted, for he was
an art critic now with no income at all, and all day to add to
it. He wanted some evenings off. So he went out after dinner
and returned at tea-time greatly excited. It seemed that he
had made my fortune and his too, for I was going to do the
work and he to canvass — we were going to take the business
off the advertiser's hands altogether just as soon as we had
got the full strength of it. So I had to go with him after tea.

It was a little weatherboard hutch in a mean street
behind Collingwood, and a worried canvasser — with a baby
under his arm, held just as he might hold a lose and
awkward portfolio while getting into a tram — opened the
door. He was tidy, in a washed tweed suit, and had the
mechanic's lines across his forehead. He said "Take the
child!" to a draggled anxious woman — his poor, stale and
unprofitable wife — and she took it and shooed a warren of
other clamorous little canvassers out into the kitchen. Then
he got two chairs and told us what he wanted. He was
travelling for a firm of photographers, and their artist, who
was an invalid, wanted someone to help touch up the
enlargements. He gave me some, to try my hand on the coat
lapels and edges, buttons, button-holes, trouser creases and
seems, etc. with a camel-hair brush and India ink.

My work was a dead failure — the artist had to wash it all
off, in fact. But it turned out that the photographer was a
gentleman's son, at Windsor, a sort of amateur photographer and mechanic, the artist, his friend, a cripple, also
a gentleman, and a widow's son; and they had an idea of
starting a business. The gentleman's son's father advanced
some money, they made their own frames, and, knowing I
was a carpenter and painter, they took me on at thirty
shillings a week and rented a little empty produce store near
the railway station, and I fitted it up. I was a natural born
carpenter and should have stuck to it. I was always great at
makeshifts and inventing ways and means on the spur of the
moment and could see a way to do a thing while a mechanic

with practical and technical training might be getting out the mechanical drawing implements. I might have made a first-class military engineer, provided I was never super-intended.

Well, I made the counter and dark-room, fitted the troughs, made trays or dishes with kauri sides and ends and glass bottoms, and even a camera for enlargements — sort of sliding or telescopic box arrangement of cedar and brass. And I painted, stained, and varnished the shop. But though I had an eye for invention, at fine work I never had the hand. I never could cut the mitres of the frames so neatly as the canvasser could. For the same reason I never could learn lining, fine decorating or signwriting in my trade. I think the mechanical genius helps and develops the poetical one, but the latter most certainly interferes with the former.

By the way there's a dinner waggon of my make in Harpenden, Hertfordshire, England, also a new kind of wardrobe, a hat-rack, and other things, polished, stained, and varnished, and not a nail in 'em, and likely to last longer than any of my other works.

I batched on the business premises at Windsor and we had a big vermilion sign with the firm's name in white letters. But N.S.F. loomed larger in the end, and I took twenty-five shillings, then a pound, and then fifteen. I did odd jobs round the gentleman's house, to help things along, but the children, little fairies, got awfully interested and addressed me as "man", and it pained me — though twenty-one was three years off yet — so I gave it best and came back to Sydney steerage to try to rise in something else.

But I don't want you to hold Bob Heckler too cheaply. Men like him have struck roads to fortune over and over and over again.

VI.   Sydney

I don't want to linger long over this chapter. We came to Sydney and I went to work at Hudson Brothers, railway carriage works, at Clyde, near Granville, amongst a rough crowd. I must have worked hard and well, for I got twenty-five shillings a week to start with and thirty a few months later. I was seventeen then. We lived in Phillip Street and I had an alarm clock on a tray or a sheet of tin to wake me, for I had been very deaf since I was fourteen. That alarm clock haunted me for years afterwards. I wrote it up

in "Arvie Aspinall's Alarm Clock" in *While the Billy Boils,*
and mentioned it lately in "The Last Review" (*When I Was
King*). Sometimes I'd wake with a start, thinking it had gone
and I had not heard it; and often I'd wake on Sunday or a
holiday morning thinking it was too good to be true. That
clock was the terror of my late boyhood — if I can be said to
have had any boyhood at all. I had to get up at five o'clock
to catch the workman's train from Redfern at six. I remember arriving on the platform one morning at five, having set
the alarm wrong — it had woke me at four. There were
times when I would have given my soul for another hour's
sleep. I used to make bread and milk over a little spirit lamp
before leaving home, but sometimes I'd be so weak and worn
out with overnight study and want of rest that I'd go out in
the yard and be ill before starting for Redfern. I walked
through Hyde Park, Elizabeth Street, and Belmore Park to
the railway station, and it was then that the faces in the
street first began to haunt me. The faces, and the wretched
rag-covered forms on the benches, and under them, and on
the grass. The loafers and the unemployed used to sleep
under the verandahs round the old central markets, and
under the eaves of the sheds on Circular Quay on wet nights.
(See " 'Dossing Out' and 'Camping' " in *While the Billy
Boils.*) But then if a deaf, uneducated Bush boy of seventeen, who had never learned a trade, could earn thirty
shillings a week in Sydney —.

I remember, one morning, seeing a horrible old bundle of
rags and bones, that had been a woman, struggle up from
the wet grass and, staggering, try to drink from an empty
bottle. I don't know why she sticks in my memory picture.

I was going to a night-school, trying for the matriculation
examination, and used to study in the train when I could
keep awake. There was a nasty guard who always woke me
about Homebush to look at my workman's ticket. I took
breakfast and "lunch" with me — bread and meat or bread
and butter — or whatever I could find in the safe at home.
The hardest part of the work was the "rubbing down". We
used to lead colour the carriages first and then put on many
coats of rough quick-drying filling, which, when it was hard
enough, we used to rub down to a surface. But I found it
harder in private carriage shops, later on, where the old
varnish was hard as flint, and had to be soaked with water
and soda for days. You see, if you don't rub through the old
cracks they will come through the new colour and varnish
after a while. On cold winter mornings at Clyde I used to get

warm water from one of the pipes. I remember the blood coming from my finger ends and trickling over the pumice stone. Then I used rag or an old glove. I was very willing, and so was Bob H———, a boy of my own age. The boss — a subcontractor — used to set us rubbing down two carriage doors (off their hinges) and urge us to race — strive to rouse our sporting instincts and keep up our enthusiasm. But Bob and I came to an arrangement after a while, when the boss got too enthusiastic.

The hands were mostly recruited from Birmingham and the North Country, and from Woolloomooloo. I was bushy, shy, different from other boys (and therefore "ratty") and suspected of being of the Sunday school sort, and therefore I was tormented by Hudson Brothers' larrikins: but, considering that, though I was extremely sensitive, I was not tortured to an unendurable extent, they could not have been such a bad push after all. Selfish parents say, "They are more to be pitied than you." I've seen the poor, pale, delicate victim and butt of brutal ignorance in many places since then. I always know him. I saw him last, in coarse clothes and heavy hob-nailed boots, in a hopeless English farm-labourers' village. And his face, figure, voice and manner told plainly of a gentleman blackguard and a silly village girl. I wondered how on earth they were going to make one of themselves of him, or drive the natural refinement out of him without killing him.

I usually got home about a quarter or half-past six, according to the workman's train, and went to a night school in Phillip Street about seven, where I first made acquaintance with English history: William the First, ten-sixty-six, William the Second, ten-eighty-seven, and so on. I went there three evenings a week for a couple of quarters, and on other nights to the School of Arts with an idea of learning Latin and drawing. I had tried the fiddle in the Bush, before I became too deaf. Someone said that Latin would improve my English. I told that to a snuffy old broken-down professor, when he asked me why I wanted to learn Latin, and he cackled a short, dusty broken-down old cackle — I don't know why. There were one or two like me there, and one or two chemists' apprentices.

I remember, one morning in the workshop, after having been tormented more than usual on the platform and in the train the evening before, I said that I would rise above them all yet; and my work mate, who was not a bad fellow, advised me not to let them hear me talking like that, or they'd chyack me worse than ever. They believed I was half ratty already, he said. About this time a boy in a workshop in Darling Harbour, tormented and ill-used to madness, struck another with a batten and killed him. This made a fiercely indignant impression on my mind, as also did the story in court on the minds of the Judge and jury, it would appear, for they acquitted him. "Arvie Aspinall", "Bill" in the "Visit of Condolence", "Two Boys at Grinder Brothers", and "Jones's Alley" (in *While the Billy Boils*) all came from my Hudson Brothers' days, but Hudson Brothers were not Grinders. If they had been they mightn't have failed. Their work was Australian. They imported the best mechanics they could get, treated and paid them well, went in for agricultural implement making, and were open to encourage "ideas". Their work for Australia deserves to be looked up a bit and credited to them.

My tormented days ended later, in another shop, when I took a tormentor by the throat and his nose bled. He arranged to meet me outside after knock off, but had to hurry home. I didn't know my physical strength.

I always had the longing for something better — something higher — something different anyhow — but always felt more or less the hollow hopelessness of attempting to rise higher; so I neglected no opportunity of learning my trade. I was painfully shy and extremely sensitive, sensitive about my deafness, my lack of education, my surroundings, my clothes, slimness and paleness, my "h's", handwriting, grammar, pronunciation (made worse by deafness) — everything almost. I was terribly shy of strange girls, and if a girl I knew took any notice of me I would reckon that she was only either pitying me or laughing at me. I am shy of women now, but in another way.

I remember having an idea, born of the notion that a change comes every seven years, that I would recover my hearing when I was twenty-one. I got first noticeably deaf at nine and as deaf as I am now when I was fourteen. And I used to swear, secretly, that if I did not get cured I would not live after twenty-one. And mind, I had none of the suspicious notions generally attributed to the deaf, and never *looked* deaf; nor do I ever remember being annoyed or taken advantage of on that account, except perhaps by friends and relatives. But if they did they fell into the habit naturally, and perhaps unconsciously, and were in every way excusable.

I went up to the University matriculation examination

twice, and failed. I don't remember being at all shy or sensitive on those occasions. On the last occasion I had a good sound patch in my trousers, and a pair of Father's boots on. All the other boys were well dressed, but I supposed they were more to be pitied than I was. I wished I'd had Father's head too, for his was a mathematical one. I couldn't hear the dictation, so I was taken into another room by an old man without teeth who dictated in Irish. I failed in everything save English history and English composition.

But that's a bit ahead. I seldom went out, Sundays or holidays, but either worked or studied. Later on I took to taking long walks at night and by lonely ways. Every penny of my wages, save ticket fares, went to help others. I paid for the night-schooling and bought my clothes with over-time money; and I washed and mended my own clothes. There was no starching for me in those days. And there was a dark cloud and plenty of trouble. I remember, in darkest days, when all days were dark, being sometimes undecided between home or work and the harbour. And later on, during a brief unemployed period, I saw the American Consul, and haunted the wharves in hopes of getting a ship to America or somewhere.

I was never afraid of physical work, never lazy — I never had the patience to loaf, and my mates often grumbled because they said I was working myself and them out of a job. I was a very quick brush-hand. But I thought what a glorious thing it would be to be able to give even a quarter of my time to study. Of course, I had the ridiculously exaggerated idea of the value of education and of my own ignorance. And it seemed getting too late fast, if, indeed, it were not too late already. I used to seek comfort in stories of self-taught men (my first school prize was entitled *Self-taught Men*) and instances of men who had risen after certain ages. It was a curious sort of self-deception, if it could be called self-deception. I was exquisitely self-conscious — it was a sort of insane analytical gymnastics most of the time. It was torture through the invulnerable ignorance and mad, unreasoning, and absolutely unnecessary selfishness of others, and self torture with it all. And one thing my body craved for and my soul longed for was another hour's sleep in the morning. Often I lay, dead tired and resting, and afraid to go to sleep lest it wouldn't seem half a moment before the harsh and grating alarm sounded. I went to work with a dry unrested feeling and weak and sick in the stomach from sheer weariness and worry.

But the Faces in the Street were passing all the time. The
worn faces and gaunt figures in the poor pitiful clothing.
Meeting me and passing, and catching up and passing, and
seeming to turn momentarily, hopelessly, fearfully, resentfully, appealingly, as though looking to me for help or
sympathy — or guidance — for something — I didn't know
what. And my face was one of them and not the least pale
and pinched nor my figure the least gaunt or meanly clad.

I used to meet the same back-wash and eddy of the stream
of life — the same debris of a people — mornings, and
evenings when the workman's train ran to time. I remember
one girl, or woman, another that sticks in a memory picture,
but she seems in her right place. Elder, or only grown-up
sister; anything between twenty and forty; unlovely, ungraceful — ugly and hard; sexually starved, or starved for
love no doubt on account of her ugliness, resentful and
ill-tempered; slaving to keep the home together; lot of
younger children; mother washing, serving, or cleaning
office, useless grown-up brother or two perhaps. Father
unemployed, drinking or dead. And they loyal to his
drunken memory. She belonged to a mean little circle of
Brethren and Sister (round a dear minister) no doubt, who
made mean, unscrupulous and snuffling use of her few spare
hours. You'll see her face over and over again in the little
Salvation Army street gatherings at night in all weathers.
Those were sweating times and days of long hours in
factories for girls. I used to meet her in Elizabeth Street
every evening about twenty past six. She carried an old fibre
bag like workmen carried their dinners in. She looked at
nothing but went straight on, and there was nothing but
dogged endurance in every jerky, wooden movement of her
most ungraceful walk. I used to meet her in the mornings
too, sometimes, when I happened to miss the first train. I
supposed she had an alarm clock too. But perhaps "mother"
had long been in the habit of getting up earlier than she did.
I saw her sometimes in Paddy's Market on Saturday nights
with a big basket and a brat or two — younger brothers and
sisters — and a woman who might have been her twin sister
in birth and circumstances, but was probably her mother.

Then I missed her. Maybe she went home ill one night
and grew worse before morning — feverish and then
delirious; and mother took the alarm clock away in case she
might drop asleep; and it never woke her any more in this
world. Or — here's another picture.

I used to haunt Paddy's Market — about the only place I

went to on Saturday night. One Saturday night I saw a
woman like what that girl might have been ten or fifteen
years older — if indeed she could have aged visibly any
more. The haggard draggled woman had Sunday's supplies
on one arm and a baby on the other. Cheap little workman's
boarding house, no doubt, with a young clerk or draper or
grocer out of work. Three or four children trailing. One
tugging at her draggle-tailed skirt (which was high in front
and long behind like a duckling's damp muddy tail, and
seemed to keep her up, like a duckling too) and the child
kept asking for something with unreasoning, maddening,
childish reiteration. The loads slip, first the living and then
the dead, and something falls from the pile on the basket.
Then, goaded by cruel, merciless, unrelenting circumstances, she turns on the toddler at her skirt and says:

"Be quiet! blarst yer! — Where am I to get hokey-pokey
money from?"

God help her! and where was she to get hokey-pokey
money from?

A brighter incident came along on the way home, and
from amongst my own poor people too. I saw a woman
sitting on a ledge, outside a theatre, with papers, and a
sleeping baby in an old shawl on a coat like something on a
shelf. But she was of the fresh cheerful sort, though she
looked poor and tired enough. I was moving towards her to
buy a paper when a bright little fellow ran between. "Paper,
sir! *News,* sir!", and seeing me hesitate, he said brightly,
briskly and most cheerfully: "It's alright mister! It's all the
same! — She's my mother."

His mother's mate.

[VII]

I worked at Hudson Bros.' branch work-shops at Wickham,
Newcastle, where I haunted the School of Arts, still with an
idea of learning before it was too late. I felt that I must take
up some branch of study or other, and it seemed getting too
late fast. I fretted, chafed, and nearly worried my soul-case
out about "wasted time". Shyness, deafness in a measure,
and the cruel early life and "training" had almost made me
a hypocrite. And extreme sensitiveness, together with a false
sense of physical weakness, led me or forced me to pander to
the vanity of ignorant bosses when I could. This last foreman
especially, who was a cur of the poodle species, a little man,

with a tremendous opinion of his "position", a set speech for every new hand containing cant about his employers, and very big feet that went straight ahead, or turned clumsily at right angles into pubs on Saturday nights. He had never been anything but a brush hand, and had never bossed a man — or even a crawler — before.

I was very green and very soft, and, because of the deafness, years behind my real age in worldly matters. Also all spirit and moral courage, if any had survived my childhood, had been bullied and ground out of me. This foreman half hurried, half bluffed me into boarding and lodging at his weatherboard humpy, where his missus always managed to get a skimpy, half cooked breakfast on the table a few minutes before the work-shop bell went. His name, was, of course, a name which is commonly supposed to be the commonest in the English language, and he looked it, right to his boots, which of course were "larstins".

There was another hand boarding with him, and we both must have been cowards (or perhaps it was because the other was an indifferent brush-hand) for we hung out till the bitter end. I sent home every penny I had, but was soon wanted at home, or my board money perhaps, for I came back to Sydney and worked at the Redfern branch shops, where, if I had not been so soft and willing, I might have worked all along and had my extra hour's sleep every morning. Nothing happened in those shops except that I helped paint some beams one morning which I found belonged to the Mount Rennie gallows.

I still longed for something better and never rested but worked things until I got into the office on trial as a clerk. My tribe wanted a gentleman, or the appearance of a gentleman, in the family, but they wanted every penny I could earn also. Something of the cad must have been instilled into my alleged being at this time, but, if so, I was soon cured. I couldn't write a simple business letter, I wasn't worth five shillings a week in the office, and so was sent into the timber yard to learn measuring up under a nasty jealous brute with a liver and a son he wanted there. I found that in practice I couldn't measure timber in separate pieces and slowly, with a slate, so I was set to work lumping it. My father could measure up a truck load of different sizes before men who were trained and paid to do it were done scratching their heads and staring at the stuff. Then they'd stare at him.

I appealed to the powers for another trial in the office,

but it was no use, so I resigned. Mr. Dean (of Clarke & Dean, the carriage painting contractors) wanted me to go back to Newcastle with him that night, but I wouldn't — for pride or something. Strange that I should get homesick in those days. The cure came very slowly. If Clarke or Dean ever read this book I want them to know that I have kindly recollections of them. Especially of Mr. Clarke, who was my immediate boss. Dean was at Redfern mostly.

It was on the first trip to Newcastle with Mr. Dean that I got my first breath of the ocean, and, as the steamer rose to the swell outside the heads I drew a breath as deep as the sea itself.

[VIII]

I worked about in various private shops and did a bit of house-painting too. I knew what it was, when I was out of work for a few days in winter, to turn out shivering and be down at the *Herald* office at four o'clock on bitter mornings, and be one of the haggard group striking matches and running them down the wanted columns on the damp sheets posted outside. I knew what it was to tramp long distances and be one of a hopeless crowd of applicants. I knew what it was to drift about the streets in shabby and patched clothes and feel furtive and criminal-like. I knew all that before I wrote "Faces in the Street" — before I was twenty. I knew what it was to go home to a cold, resentful, gloomy and unbelieving welcome, and blind unreasoning reproaches at the very least. And, above and beyond other unemployed, I knew what it was to know, later on, that all this was selfishly, brutally unnecesary. That all those weary and unspeakably dark and dreary years of trouble, toil, of longing for the world, and fearful, exquisite shyness of the world, of humiliation and heart-break were absolutely wasted, and the resultant years barren of good effects, reward, and even consideration, but pregnant with fierce hatred, lies, and slander and all the paltry petty annoyances born of a haunting consciousness in the minds (or hearts if they had any) of others — of a great wrong done.

I got on with old Mr. Kerridge, carriage builder of Castlereagh Street, and worked for him for about two years. It was a blessed relief, even in those dark days of little relief for me, for I had been working for a man in the same street whose name was remembered and hated by many, and

whose name and language had best be filled in by a Blank
here. Does anybody remember the second pilot that Mark
Twain worked under in *Life on the Mississippi* (not the
"Mississippi Pilot")? Well, that was the man — or his own
son. Blank had the horse face and a skin disease in addition.
I remember one of his employees, a trimmer, who rose in the
labour movement afterwards, who used to go home ill to his
young wife and family because of that Blank brute. He
seemed to hate me especially — because of my clean skin
and effeminate appearance probably. He used to call me a
"B———y woman!" "Come out from under that carriage
and let me see what yer doin', yer b———y ———g old
woman!" etc. He used to sack me every other day, but the
first evening or two he sent his little girl after me to tell me I
could come in the morning: so I got used to it and would
take no notice of his lurid sacks — work was cruelly scarce.
He kept me on until one morning there was nothing left to
do except clean up and sweep out the shop. He told me to do
that and then go home and go to bed for a ——— ———
———! woman, and come and see him in a week or two if I
could get no one else to take me on.

Old Mr. Kerridge was the opposite; he was an old
gentleman. He was a little old gentleman with snow white
hair and a white frill beard and was always in a hurry — an
old-fashioned, bird-like, pecking and jerky hurry. It was as
if he'd been wound up, like a busy mechanical toy, all the
first half of his life, and would never live long enough to run
down. And when he brushed up and put on a very tall hat to
go out on business, he looked like something rather special,
but soberly respectable, albeit a trifle dusty and rusty in
colour and springs, that had been turned out of Dickens's
workshop, and had stood over-long in the show-room.

But he stuck to the shop too much when he should have
been out looking after business. He had men who had been
with him for from twenty-five to thirty years, and they said
so too. He couldn't get out of the habit of working with his
men, whether it inconvenienced them or not, but was always
particularly careful to uphold the prestige and the alleged
dignity of his foremen — whom he always addressed as
foreman, and referred to as *the* foreman — though he had
three grown sons in the shop. Every Saturday morning he'd
have his two big retriever dogs in and lather them and hose
them and rub them down and dry them, just as if he was
washing down two buggies against time. But he was out of
date and the business went down — not for lack of honest

work. I had a reference from him which said that I was a steady, trustworthy, hard-working young man, and had worked for him for two years. He told me that I was never afraid of work. He must have been gone for years now. I remember him brushed up and tall-hatted to go to court on a civil case, and I cannot conceive his having gone to the highest court any other way if he had time. *Vale!* old-fashioned tradesman and gentleman.

My mother started to publish *The Dawn,* in Phillip Street, then *The Young Idea* and *Young Australia,* which last was sacrificed in later years and is alive now I believe. Later on I edited and helped print, wrap and post a paper called *The Republican,* with William Keep, one time Tommy Walker's manager, and a sort of adopted brother of mine — but that was later on.

It was mostly house-painting now, and odd jobs about.

One wet night I was coming home through Hyde Park from working late on a job at Paddington. Rain and wind and swept boughs and sickly gaslights on the wet asphalt; and poles and scaffolding about in preparation for the Jubilee celebrations. I had sent a couple of attempts on the subject to the *Bulletin,* and had got encouragement in Answers to Correspondents. And now the idea of "Sons of the South" or "Song of the Republic" came. I wrote it and screwed up courage to go down to the *Bulletin* after hours, intending to drop the thing into the letter box, but, just as I was about to do so, or rather making up my mind as to whether I'd shove it in, or take it home and have another look at the spelling and the dictionary, the door opened suddenly and a haggard woman stood there. And I shoved the thing into her hand and got away round the corner, feeling something like a person who had been nearly caught on the premises under suspicious circumstances and was not safe yet by any means.

I watched the Answers to Correspondents column as hundreds have watched it since — they'll understand. Here is the reply:

(Get An's to Corr.)

I hadn't the courage to go near the *Bulletin* office again, but used to lie awake at night and get up very early and slip down to the nearest news-agent's on Thursday mornings, to have a peep at the *Bulletin,* in fear and trembling and half furtively as if the news-agent — another hard-life woman, by the way — named Mrs. Furlong would guess my secret.

At last, sick with disappointment, I went to the office and saw Mr. Archibald, who seemed surprised, encouraged me a lot and told me that they were holding the "Song of a Republic" over for a special occasion — Eight Hours Day.

It has never been printed in any of my books, so I give it here: not because of any literary merit, but because it was my first song and sincere — written by a Bush boy who was a skinny city work-boy in patched pants and blucher boots, struggling on the edge of the unemployed gulf — and written twenty years ago in Australia in high toady days.

("Song of the Republic")

Then I wrote "The Wreck of the Derry Castle" — strange theme for a Bush boy; and on another rainy night, from a dark dreary gully behind our camp at Mount Victoria — where I had gone to paint for Father — I got the idea of the lines to "Golden Gully" at Pipeclay. It was published in the Christmas *Bulletin*, 1887. It has never been reprinted, and, as it might be useful to show how I had brought the atmosphere of weird melancholy from the heart of the Bush, I print it here:

("Golden Gully")

I wrote "The Watch on the Kerb" — lines to a street girl — and one or two other attempts which I have forgotten; and then — about then — I wrote what I always considered my first song, and superior to "Faces in the Street"; it certainly was more lyrical. I can't remember writing it or where I got the idea from; it must have been composed quickly, and perhaps half unconsciously, as was "Faces in the Street". And as was everything of a popular kind ever written that was worth reading; in spite of Byron's clever and catchy bluffing saying that he wished he had the art of easy reading, which would be easy writing. Hard writing makes hard reading. Is *Don Juan* easy reading? It's like a dray coming down a long gully by a rough track where the only easy places are the bogs.

The song I speak of was published in the *Bulletin* as the "Song of the Outcasts", and went through the United States as "The Army of the Rear". And that was nearly twenty years ago. I print it here in a book for the first time, to show I was in deadly earnest, anyway.

("Army of the Rear")

I would like to say here, while I think of it — out of place, and before I forget — that there are a great many old rhymes of mine, printed, but lost or forgotten, which may turn up when I am not likely to. I burnt my scrap books and old MSS. in London (in the yard of the house where Micawber and David Copperfiled lived, by the way) to get rid of the worry of them; and I'm sorry for it now, for much was political and had an historical value, if nothing else. Much of the stuff contained truer history than Australia is ever likely to see. This can be taken as an advertisement for copies of my old songs, not in the books, which will be gratefully received. They were published over the names of Joe Swallow, and Cervus Wright, and Henry Lawson in the old *Truth, Boomerang, Town and Country Journal, Echo,* etc.

Another rainy night on Petersham platform. I don't remember what I was doing there unless I had been out late to see about a job. The sickly gaslamps again, the wet shining asphalt, the posters on the mean brick walls close at hand, the light glistening on the enamelled iron notice saying "Second Class Wait Here", and I alone and tired as usual and cold with a shoddy overcoat coarse as sacking and warm as [a] refrigerator. But it was here I struck the keynote, or the key-line, of "Faces in the Street".

It all seems very tame now. I thought that, when I came to writing about having my first verses accepted and seeing them in print, I would rise to the occasion without effort, but I haven't. I can't even remember the emotions that such things gave rise to. I only remember that I didn't worry any more about my surroundings, and "rising", and the School of Arts, after "Faces in the Street". I just went on painting and helping with the *Republican*. It all seems very tame now, but I couldn't have felt tame then, nor could the flood of emotions have been so, that swelled for years and, pent beyond the poor tortured soul's endurance, broke bounds in a burst of red republicanism — found vent in "Song of the Outcasts", "Faces in the Street", and other songs of freedom.

[IX] *"The Republican"*

The life of *The Republican* ("Cambaroora Star" in *When the World was Wide*) was a tragical farce now I come to look back at it. We got hold of a little old printing press that had been over the mountains in the early days — and Keep had been a draper in London. He was a weed then, but with the vitality, energy and blind self confidence of a dozen fat men.

He's getting stout and young now at forty-five. We had to
turn the press by hand and it ran like a dray most of the
time; we had to feed and fly by hand, too — when the press
was going. The bed was uneven and worm-eaten and the
types old and new, so there was always a great deal of
digging out and pasting on round the cylinder. I could never
tell when the machine was likely to go wrong, or shy, or why
it went right at times at all. Keep had an inventive mind. We
got some old roller moulds with the press and once he
invented some new roller composition, out of treacle and
stuff I think and in hot weather those rollers would bring the
flies and pick up loose type. The paper was illustrated,
mind, with portraits, that came out black or blank or half
and half, or smudged according to Keep's cheerful digging
or pasting on the cylinder. But he'd get 'em right in time or
at least recognisable as being intended to represent portraits. Then the letter-press would begin to disappear here
and there, and there would be more pasting. Then there'd
be a break-down or smash-up somewhere and Keep would
go round briskly and cheerfully in front of the machine,
behind it and under it, and squeeze between it and the wall,
with a couple of spanners and a screw-wrench for odd nuts
and screw up a nut here and loosen one there, and try her
again, until at last, by some accident, or wonderful combination of accidents incomprehensible to me, he'd get her
going all right. Then we'd wire in as if afraid of our lives to
give her time to think about playing up again. I've known
that press to print from two to three hundred sheets (it was
one side only) without a break-down or smash-up. Then,
towards the end, Keep would get excited, and, if it were a
hot night, peel to his pants and shirt and rustle up every
damaged or soiled sheet of paper from the floor and put it
through. I believe if such a contingency had arisen to make
it seem necessary, he would have put his shirt and pants
through too, rather than disappoint two of our subscribers.
The subscribers were few enough in number but most
enthusiastic, and Rasmussen's ad. was our mainstay. Keep
used to buy damaged lots of paper, of different colours and
sizes, from fires and old stock, and he'd cut the larger sheets
to size with a carving knife. We used to soak the paper in a
tub of water the night before going to press.

The night after we'd fold, wrap (there wasn't much
folding) and carry the papers to the post in the early hours in
a clothes basket; and, before daylight we'd have a public
breakfast at the old coffee stall outside the *Herald* office

where Keep would argue politics and freethought and other things with cabmen and others. Occasionally a fresh policeman would bail us up and enquire about the basket. Little incidents like this cheered Keep and made him happy, and if that policeman would wait he'd try to bring him to his way of thinking.

When things were tight Keep would get a billet as clerk or something and put his wages into the *Republican* and the other two little ventures. He would tackle anything, and generally succeeded — went on the platform once, for the first time in his life, and at five minutes' notice, and gave a lecture, when he was managing for Tommy Walker and Walker fell ill.

When things looked up, we'd hire in a labouring man to turn the press.

We shifted that old machine about a good deal, on account of the rent and because of other circumstances, and Keep always took it to pieces and put it together again as careully as he would have taken a baby to pieces and put it together again — had that been possible, without spoiling the baby, and had Keep been called upon to do it.

We had an office in the top of a building in George Street once; a long narrow room with a window back and front, and got a small, pedal hand-bill press, a cutter and a small wirer, and then Keep was happy. As we got on he bought a net hammock and slung it there and slept in the office — to be on the spot all the time I suppose. Perhaps he dreamed of special editions.

Well, one Sunday morning he'd cleaned up and set fire to a lot of waste paper in the fireplace, and was pottering happily and lovingly round the old press with a screw-wrench, getting ready for the monthly fray, when he should be again in holts with her, when there was a crash below and a tremendous clattering and bumping on the stairs, and Keep got [to] the front window quick, thinking that part of the building was collapsing. Then the door burst open and several big helmeted firemen burst in, and Keep, looking out dazedly, saw two fire engines in the street, and more coming, and the opposite side was lined with stupid upturned faces and gaping mouths. He had left both windows open, and the wind had blown the smoke from the waste paper through the front one.

I came in a little later, when things had cooled down a bit, and Keep said, with a sickly sort of smile, that I always missed all the fun. But he soon recovered, and, on one of the firemen returning — for the address, or something they had forgotten in their indignation — Keep cornered him, got him vacantly interested in the machinery, then the paper, and actually got, by easy stages, to talking *Progress and Poverty* and Henry George with him.

We rechristened the *Republican* the *Nationaliser* against my convictions, and eventually dropped it just as it was getting a little lighter to our shoulders.

Keep is a great breeder of Persian cats now, and goes to church on Sunday.

[X] *Father's Death*

I was on a scaffold, kalsomining or painting a ceiling at the Deaf, Dumb and Blind Institution, Sydney, on New Year's Eve, eighteen-eighty-eight when my brother brought a telegram from Mount Victoria to say that my father had died that morning. He had just completed a row of cottages called the Sanitorium, and was working at his old friend Mr. Rienits' school — "The School", Mount Victoria. He had several men working for him, but still worked and lived as hard as ever. He was camping in a room of one of the new cottages, and the night before his death he had two or three young fellows up to see him who used to discuss Henry George's *Progress and Poverty* and other democratic subjects with him, and always got onto mathematics. But my first story, "His Father's Mate", had just been published in the Christmas *Bulletin* and Father was still full of this. About the first thing he would ask, they told me, when a newcomer dropped in, was "Have you seen my son Henry's story in the Sydney *Bulletin?*" "And he said [it] in a voice for all the world to hear," said an old mate of mine, "though he was a quiet man." One, a Bob Evans, a bit of an artist, traced Father's shadow in profile on the wall that evening, and I transferred it afterwards on oiled paper.

Next morning, they told me, he went down to work at the school building as usual, and though he complainted of "feeling queer" — "quare", poor Father would say, putting his hand to his side — he returned to the cottages for a keg or small drum of white lead, instead of letting one of the men go for it. He carried that down, and, feeling "very queer", started for home again. One of his men, a Swede — he mostly had a Swede or Norwegian with him at that time — either went back to the cottages with him or was working there. About half way Father must have felt worse, for he began to run. When he reached the new cottages he told Fred Olsen, the Swede, that he didn't think this could last long and that he had better go for the doctor; so Fred ran for Dr. Morgan, who said he would come as soon as he was dressed and had a cup of tea. Then Father told Fred to run for his friend, Constable Brassington — old Lucknow man retired years ago — he had something to tell him. The Constable came at once, but got there too late. Father was sitting dead on his bunk, beside his table, leaning back against the wall. He had got a mustard plaster on his chest under his flannel and still had his hands pressed to it.

The doctor told me it was heart disease, and an old thing. I reached Mount Victoria by the midnight train when bonfires were blazing and rockets going up. Some said it was the only time they had ever seen him rest.

I painted the cottages where Father had left the painting unfinished, did one or two other jobs on the Mount, and, there being no work there, and things in Sydney being very bad, I went steerage to Western Australia and struck Albany while the new town was being built, and shortly after responsible government had been granted. There were three master painters there and no hands — except a stranded sailor or two.

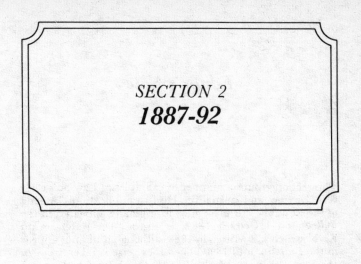

SECTION 2
1887-92

Editor's Note

This section groups a number of examples of Lawson's early verse, fiction, and journalism. His first publication, "A Song of the Republic", is printed as it originally appeared in the *Bulletin* on 1 October 1887, as also is "The Watch on the Kerb" which was written in 1888, although it did not appear in the *Bulletin* until 1890. The other verse is taken from *In the Days When the World Was Wide*, except for "Freedom on the Wallaby" from *For Australia*. "The City Bushman", which appeared originally in the *Bulletin* in 1892 titled "In Answer to 'Banjo' and Otherwise", formed part of the famous (if factitious) "debate" between Lawson and Paterson in the columns of the *Bulletin*. For an account of the *Bulletin* and Lawson's estimation of its importance in developing an Australian literature see the extract from "The Sydney *Bulletin*" included in the last section.

"A Neglected History" is an editorial piece he wrote for the *Republican* (4 April 1888), and with "The New Religion" from the *Albany Observer* of 15 July 1890 (written when Lawson was in Western Australia working as a labourer for some, months in 1890) reveals the social and political ideas he espoused as a young radical.

The texts of the early short stories and sketches are taken from *While the Billy Boils* ("A Day on a Selection"), *Over the Sliprails* ("Two Boys at Grinder Bros.'") and *The Country I Come From* ("The Drover's Wife" and "The Bush Undertaker"). These pieces show Lawson's emergence as a writer from his first appearance in print in 1887 until his trip to Bourke in late 1892 and early 1893.

A SONG OF THE REPUBLIC

Sons of the South, awake! arise!
　　Sons of the South, and do.
Banish from under your bonny skies
Those old-world errors and wrongs and lies.
Making a hell in a Paradise
　　That belongs to your sons and you.

Sons of the South, make choice between
　　(Sons of the South, choose true),
The Land of Morn and the Land of E'en,
The Old Dead Tree and the Young Tree Green,
The Land that belongs to the lord and the Queen,
　　And the Land that belongs to you.

Sons of the South, *your* time will come –
　　Sons of the South, 'tis near –
The "Signs of the Times", in their language dumb,
Fortell it, and ominous whispers hum
Like sullen sounds of a distant drum,
　　In the ominous atmosphere.

Sons of the South, aroused at last!
　　Sons of the South are few!
But your ranks grow longer and deeper fast,
And ye shall swell to an army vast,
And free from the wrongs of the North and Past
　　The land that belongs to you.

FACES IN THE STREET

They lie, the men who tell us in a loud decisive tone
That want is here a stranger, and that misery's unknown;
For where the nearest suburb and the city proper meet
My window-sill is level with the faces in the street –
　　　　Drifting past, drifting past,
　　　　To the beat of weary feet –
While I sorrow for the owners of those faces in the street.

And cause I have to sorrow, in a land so young and fair,
To see upon those faces stamped the marks of Want and
　　　　Care;
I look in vain for traces of the fresh and fair and sweet
In sallow, sunken faces that are drifting through the street—

Drifting on, drifting on,
To the scrape of restless feet;
I can sorrow for the owners of the faces in the street.

In hours before the dawning dims the starlight in the sky
The wan and weary faces first begin to trickle by,
Increasing as the moments hurry on with morning feet,
Till like a pallid river flow the faces in the street—
Flowing in, flowing in,
To the beat of hurried feet—
Ah! I sorrow for the owners of those faces in the street.

The human river dwindles when 'tis past the hour of eight,
Its waves go flowing faster in the fear of being late;
But slowly drag the moments, whilst beneath the dust and
heat
The city grinds the owners of the faces in the street—
Grinding body, grinding soul,
Yielding scarce enough to eat—
Oh! I sorrow for the owners of the faces in the street.

And then the only faces till the sun is sinking down
Are those of outside toilers and the idlers of the town,
Save here and there a face that seems a stranger in the street,
Tells of the city's unemployed upon his weary beat—
Drifting round, drifting round,
To the tread of listless feet—
Ah! My heart aches for the owner of that sad face in the
street.

And when the hours on lagging feet have slowly dragged
away,
And sickly yellow gaslights rise to mock the going day,
Then flowing past my window like a tide in its retreat,
Again I see the pallid stream of faces in the street—
Ebbing out, ebbing out,
To the drag of tired feet,
While my heart is aching dumbly for the faces in the street.

And now all blurred and smirched with vice the day's sad
pages end,
For while the short "large hours" toward the longer "small
hours" trend,
With smiles that mock the wearer, and with words that half
entreat,
Delilah pleads for custom at the corner of the street—
Sinking down, sinking down,
Battered wreck by tempests beat—
A dreadful, thankless trade is hers, that Woman of the
Street.

But, ah! to dreader things than these our fair young city
     comes,
For in its heart are growing thick the filthy dens and slums,
Where human forms shall rot away in sties for swine unmeet,
And ghostly faces shall be seen unfit for any street—
        Rotting out, rotting out,
        For the lack of air and meat—
In dens of vice and horror that are hidden from the street.

I wonder would the apathy of wealthy men endure
Were all their windows level with the faces of the Poor?
Ah! Mammon's slaves, your knees shall knock, your
     hearts in terror beat,
When God demands a reason for the sorrows of the street,
        The wrong things and the bad things
        And the sad things that we meet
In the filthy lane and alley, and the cruel, heartless street.

I left the dreadful corner where the steps are never still,
And sought another window overlooking gorge and hill;
But when the night came dreary with the driving rain and
     sleet,
They haunted me — the shadows of those faces in the street,
        Flitting by, flitting by,
        Flitting by with noiseless feet,
And with cheeks but little paler than the real ones in the
     street.

Once I cried: "Oh, God Almighty! if Thy might doth still
     endure,
"Now show me in a vision for the wrongs of Earth a cure."
And, lo! with shops all shuttered I beheld a city's street,
And in the warning distance heard the tramp of many feet,
        Coming near, coming near,
        To a drum's dull distant beat,
And soon I saw the army that was marching down the street.

Then, like a swollen river that has broken bank and wall,
The human flood came pouring with the red flags over all,
And kindled eyes all blazing bright with revolution's heat,
And flashing swords reflecting rigid faces in the street.
        Pouring on, pouring on,
        To a drum's loud threatening beat,
And the war-hymns and the cheering of the people in the
     street.

And so it must be while the world goes rolling round its
     course,
The warning pen shall write in vain, the warning voice grow
     hoarse,

But not until a city feels Red Revolution's feet
Shall its sad people miss awhile the terrors of the street—
  The dreadful everlasting strife
  For scarcely clothes and meat
In that pent track of living death — the city's cruel street.

THE WATCH ON THE KERB

Night-lights are falling;
  Girl of the street,
Go to your calling
  If you would eat.
Lamplight and starlight
  And moonlight superb,
Bright hope is a farlight,
  So watch on the kerb.

    Watch on the kerb,
    Watch on the kerb;
Hope is a farlight, then watch on the kerb.

Comes a man; call him—
  Gone! he is vext;
Curses befall him,
  Wait for the next!
Fair world and bright world,   .
  Life still is sweet—
Girl of the night-world,
  Watch on the street.

Dreary the watch is;
  Moon sinks from sight,
Gas only blotches
  Darkness with light;
Never, oh never,
  Let courage go down;
Keep from the river,
  Oh, Girl of the Town!

ANDY'S GONE WITH CATTLE

Our Andy's gone to battle now
  'Gainst Drought, the red marauder;
Our Andy's gone with cattle now
  Across the Queensland border.

He's left us in dejection now;
   Our hearts with him are roving.
It's dull on this selection now,
   Since Andy went a-droving.

Who now shall wear the cheerful face
   In times when things are slackest?
And who shall whistle round the place
   When Fortune frowns her blackest?

Oh, who shall cheek the squatter now
   When he comes round us snarling?
His tongue is growing hotter now
   Since Andy cross'd the Darling.

The gates are out of order now,
   In storms the "riders" rattle;
For far across the border now
   Our Andy's gone with cattle.

Poor Aunty's looking thin and white;
   And Uncle's cross with worry;
And poor old Blucher howls all night
   Since Andy left Macquarie.

Oh, may the showers in torrents fall,
   And all the tanks run over;
And may the grass grow green and tall
   In pathways of the drover;

And may good angels send the rain
   On desert stretches sandy;
And when the summer comes again
   God grant 'twill bring us Andy.

A Neglected History

We must admit that the Centennial celebrations in Sydney were not wholly useless. The glorious occasion called forth from every daily, weekly and monthly periodical, every advertising medium, twopenny calendar, and centennial keepsake, a more or less complete history of Australian progress during the past 100 years. The youngsters in our schools, and Australians generally, had thus for the first time the salient facts regarding the history of Australia thrust before them.

If this is Australia, and not a mere outlying suburb of England: if we really are the nucleus of a nation and not a mere handful of expatriated people dependent on an English Colonial Secretary for guidance and tuition, it behoves us to educate our children to a knowledge of the country they call their own.

It is a matter of public shame that while we have now commemorated our hundredth anniversary, not one in every ten children attending Public schools throughout the colonies is acquainted with a single historical fact about Australia.

The children are taught more of the meanest state in Europe than of the country they are born and bred in, despite the singularity of its characteristics, the interest of its history, the rapidity of its advance, and the stupendous promise of its future.

They can conjure with the name of Captain Cook; they are aware that he sailed into Botany Bay, and they have some indistinct theories regarding him, but of the men who in the past fought for the freedom of our constitution as it is, they scarcely know the names.

It is of course desirable that they should be familiar with the features of European history, but that they should at the same time be so grossly unacquainted with their native land is an obvious anomaly.

Select almost any Australian schoolboy from one of the higher classes and you will find that he can glibly recite the names of the English sovereigns from the Conqueror to Victoria, with the dates of their ascension. He can then give you their relationship to each other, and the principal events and noteworthy persons of each reign, with a rapidity that runs clear away from elocution and transmutes the English language into a kind of lightning gibberish. If you ask for geographical information he can quote, without drawing breath, the rivers, mountains and towns in Europe, and can then run through the counties and towns of England, repeating such names as Kent, Surrey, Sussex, Berkshire, Hampshire, Wiltshire, etc., with a great relish. But if you ask him what town in Australia was formerly called Bendigo, or where Port Phillip settlement was, he becomes bashfully silent, and if you follow this by inquiries as to the Black War in Tasmania, or ask him the causes which led to the Fight of Vinegar Hill, he will come to the conclusion that you are "greening" him, and will leave with an injured air.

Of the gradual separation of one colony from another, of the differences still existing in their constitutions, and of the men and influences which have made them what they are he knows nothing. His knowledge of the natural history and geographical features of Australia he picks up chiefly from the talk of his associates, and the information he casually encounters in the newspapers.

It is quite time that our children were taught a little more about their country, for shame's sake. Are they always to be "Colonials" and not "Australians"?

It may be urged that the early history of Australia is for the most part better left unknown; but for that reason are all the bright spots, the clean pages, the good deeds, and the noble names, to be left unremembered too?

There is apparently quite another reason why Australian history may not claim a place in the school's curriculum. It is considered necessary that a loyal spirit should be instilled into the minds of the rising generation: an attachment to a mother land which they have never seen: a "home" which should remain always dearer to them than the place of their birth and childhood. This object might be considerably retarded if the children learned how the mother land cradled and nursed the nation they belonged to, and the measure of gratitude and respect they owe her for her tender guardianship: if they knew how the present Australian aristocracy (so loyal and sceptre loving) arose, and whence they came; how the Old New South Wales convict slave-holders and tyrants tried to drag Victoria into the sewer while she made efforts for liberty; how the same worthies tried to divert a convict stream into the northern settlement (now Queensland) that they might reap the benefit of convict labour; if the noble efforts of Lang resulted in the freedom of the mother colony, and lastly how Australian honour and interests were sold right and left for mammon.

If all these things, and much more that might and would become apparent, were taught, Australian school children might develope a spirit totally at variance with the wishes of Australian Groveldom.

They might form a low admiration for the thirty digger patriots, who on that eventful December morning in 1854 died in the Eureka Stockade to gain a juster government for their country and to baulk the first "try on" of what was no less than convict government in a free colony. They might also learn to love the blue flag with the white cross, that bonny "Flag of the Southern Cross," which only rose once, but rose to mark the brightest spot in Australian history, and to give a severe check to that high-handed government which is only now gaining ground again.

They might acquire a preference for some national and patriotic song of their own homes and their own appointed rulers, rather than to stand in a row and squeal, in obedience to custom and command, "God Save our Gracious Queen".

In their present state of blissful compulsory ignorance they cannot perceive the foolishness of singing praises of the graciousness of their condescending magnate, a ruler at the further end of the world who, knowing as little of them and their lives and aspirations as they know of her, is nevertheless their sovereign and potentate, and who is sometimes benevolent enough to send them a brief cable message judiciously filtered through her own appointed underling and deputy.

When the school children of Australia are told more truths about their own country, and fewer lies about the virtues of Royalty, the day will be near when we can place our own national flag in one of the proudest places among the ensigns of the world.

THE ROARING DAYS

The night too quickly passes
   And we are growing old,
So let us fill our glasses
   And toast the Days of Gold;
When finds of wondrous treasure
   Set all the South ablaze,
And you and I were faithful mates
   All through the roaring days!

Then stately ships came sailing
   From every harbour's mouth,
And sought the land of promise
   That beaconed in the South;
Then southward streamed their streamers
   And swelled their canvas full
To speed the wildest dreamers
   E'er borne in vessel's hull.

Their shining Eldorado,
   Beneath the southern skies,
Was day and night for ever
   Before their eager eyes.
The brooding bush, awakened,
   Was stirred in wild unrest,
And all the year a human stream
   Went pouring to the West.

The rough bush roads re-echoed
   The bar-room's noisy din,
When troops of stalwart horsemen
   Dismounted at the inn.
And oft the hearty greetings
   And hearty clasp of hands
Would tell of sudden meetings
   Of friends from other lands;
When, puzzled long, the new-chum
   Would recognize at last,
Behind a bronzed and bearded skin,
   A comrade of the past.

And when the cheery camp-fire
   Explored the bush with gleams,
The camping-grounds were crowded
   With caravans of teams;
Then home the jests were driven,
   And good old songs were sung,
And choruses were given
   The strength of heart and lung.

Oh, they were lion-hearted
   Who gave our country birth!
Oh, they were of the stoutest sons
   From all the lands on earth!

Oft when the camps were dreaming,
   And fires began to pale,
Through rugged ranges gleaming
   Would come the Royal Mail.
Behind six foaming horses,
   And lit by flashing lamps,
Old "Cobb and Co.'s," in royal state,
   Went dashing past the camps.

Oh, who would paint a goldfield,
   And limn the picture right,
As we have often seen it
   In early morning's light;
The yellow mounds of mullock
   With spots of red and white,
The scattered quartz that glistened
   Like diamonds in light;
The azure line of ridges,
   The bush of darkest green,
The little homes of calico
   That dotted all the scene.

I hear the fall of timber
   From distant flats and fells,
The pealing of the anvils
   As clear as little bells,
The rattle of the cradle,
   The clack of windlass-boles,
The flutter of the crimson flags
   Above the golden holes.

Ah, then our hearts were bolder,
   And if Dame Fortune frowned
Our swags we'd lightly shoulder
   And tramp to other ground.
But golden days are vanished,
   And altered is the scene;
The diggings are deserted,
   The camping-grounds are green;
The flaunting flag of progress
   Is in the West unfurled,
The mighty bush with iron rails
   Is tethered to the world.

THE TEAMS

A cloud of dust on the long white road,
   And the teams go creeping on
Inch by inch with the weary load;
And by the power of the green-hide goad
   The distant goal is won.

With eyes half-shut to the blinding dust,
   And necks to the yokes bent low,
The beasts are pulling as bullocks must;
And the shining tires might almost rust
   While the spokes are turning slow.

With face half-hid 'neath a broad-brimmed hat
   That shades from the heat's white waves,
And shouldered whip with its green-hide plait,
The driver plods with a gait like that
   Of his weary, patient slaves.

He wipes his brow, for the day is hot,
   And spits to the left with spite;
He shouts at "Bally", and flicks at "Scot",
And raises dust from the back of "Spot",
   And spits to the dusty right.

He'll sometimes pause as a thing of form
   In front of a settler's door,
And ask for a drink, and remark "It's warm,"
Or say "There's signs of a thunder-storm;"
   But he seldom utters more.

But the rains are heavy on roads like these;
   And, fronting his lonely home,
For weeks together the settler sees
The teams bogged down to the axletrees,
   Or ploughing the sodden loam.

And then when the roads are at their worst,
   The bushman's children hear
The cruel blows of the whips reversed
While bullocks pull as their hearts would burst,
   And bellow with pain and fear.

And thus with little of joy or rest
   Are the long, long journeys done;
And thus— 'tis a cruel war at the best—
Is distance fought in the mighty West,
   And the lonely battles won.

The New Religion

I am glad to see that the workmen of Albany are beginning to form branch unions here because I think that the surest and the shortest road to the great social reformation of the future lies through trades unionism.

No doubt if a simple-minded writer attempted in this enlightened year to explain the objects of trades unionism he would be referred to his aged grandmother as a fitting pupil to undergo a course of instruction in the art of sucking eggs; but at the same time there are many, perhaps thousands, of intelligent people who hold altogether wrong ideas regarding trades unionism and its objects. As an instance of this, I once heard a gentleman say that trades unionism was an evil and unnatural thing because it was a formation of brotherhoods antagonistic to the formation of a universal brotherhood. I never thought that an intelligent man could get such a mighty grip on the bull's tail.

It is true that unions are formed for protection against unprincipled labour as well as unprincipled capital, but if man is selfish and unphilanthropic enough to go in opposition to the principles of labour unionism so long as it is to his interest to do so he must abide by the consequences. The fault is his and not the union's. Every workman should bear in mind that self-denial in the individual is quite as essential to social reformation as it is to individual reformation.

In the "Mississippi Pilot" Mark Twain tells the story of the rise of the Pilots' Union on the Mississippi River. The promoters of this union were boycotted from the first, and it was only after great perseverance and self-denial that they were in a position to cope with their opponents. Then the tables turned rapidly, and the other party were soon in a position similar to that occupied by the unionists at the outset. Many of the old pilots held out to the bitter end with a courage worthy of a more philanthropic cause, and when they were at last compelled by necessity to seek admission to the union fold they were obliged to pay entrance fees of sufficient size to have swallowed up all the profits of their selfishness, even had they been in constant employment up to that time. In fact, it was with the greatest difficulty that some of these bitter spirits were got into the union at all. Perhaps these stringent measures were necessary under the circumstances, and considering that this was in the early days of the rise of trades unionism; but our unions of today are not obliged to adopt such measures and it is not their policy to do so. Trades unionism is not "a formation of brotherhoods antagonistic to the formation of a universal brotherhood", as my friend remarked. Trades unionism really aims at the abolition of all unions and class distinctions and when this is accomplished it will be no longer necessary for men to combine against their fellow-men.

Trades unionism is a new and grand religion; it recognizes no creed, sect, language or nationality; it is a universal religion — it spreads from the centres of European civilization to the youngest settlements on the most remote portions of the earth: it is open to all and will include all — the Atheist, the Christian, the Agnostic, the Unitarian, the Socialist, the Conservative, the Royalist, the Republican, the black, and the white, and a time will come when all the "ists","isms",etc., will be merged and lost in one great "ism" — the unionism of labour.

There is something grand in the rise and progress of trades unionism; it is like a great green vine growing steadily round the world and bearing fruit in all its branches. There is no branch union so small or remote that it does not contribute strength to the grand union, and there is no branch so insignificant and unimportant as not to be able to depend upon the assistance of the main unions in a good cause.

I have seen the unions from Townsville to Adelaide stand up as one man, and demand justice for some small branch union. I have seen the stern-faced unionists of Sydney gather in thousands (forming a meeting that had to be divided into three portions) and stand for five long hours arranging plans of campaign and subscribing funds to carry them out, simply because a body of men, whom they had never seen and who were separated from them by fifteen thousand miles of sea, sought their assistance against a bitter wrong. I refer to the great dock labourers' strike, and I must add, in justice to the outsiders, that many rich and influential gentlemen in Sydney, and many workmen outside the unions, worked like unionists on this occasion.

Of course, we all know that there is one great flaw in the theory of universal brotherhood. It is where the Chinaman comes in. The Chinaman is a kind of gigantic eastern question, which will take a deal of solving. There will be no difficulty in including the progressive "Jap" in the scheme, and the American negro is already a man and brother. The American Indian, the African and South Sea savage, and the aboriginals of Australia will soon in the course of civilization become extinct, and so relieve the preachers of universal brotherhood of all anxiety on their account. The Chinaman remains to be dealt with. Whether he is the going man; the descendant of a people who once ruled the old world and were crowded into the East by the spread of European civilization, we do not know; whether he is (God forbid it) the coming man time alone can tell. But our time won't tell it, and the Chinese question is, I fear, one of the problems which we must leave to our children to solve. The Chinese nation is an unnatural, and as far as we know, an unprecedented growth on the history of the world, and in all schemes for the furtherance of the universal brotherhood we must leave the Chinaman out of the question altogether; or at least until we can understand him better.

For my part I think a time will come eventually when the Chinaman will have to be either killed or cured — probably the former — it would be advisable for the world to wait further (Chinese) developments before taking decisive action in the matter. In the meantime we will have plenty of work to do by way of civilizing ourselves. I think the European nations should have left the Chinaman alone in the first place.

The woman's question is another bugbear with trades unionists, and one which places them in a very delicate position. The position of the unions with regard to female labour is often misunderstood even by unionists themselves. It is not, as some advocates of woman's rights think, a question of trades unionism against woman, but the old question in a new guise — of trades unionism against cheap labour. It is all very well to say that it is a woman's place to keep house, and a man's place to keep her: but I know for a fact that many poor women in cities are obliged to go out and work by the day in order to feed a large family of small children and a lazy or drunken husband. Something must be done in this matter, either Adam must be compelled to keep

Eve in comfort in return for her domestic services or Eve must be allowed to earn her living by working at such trades as are most suited to her strength. Of course under the existing social conditions Adam is not always able to keep Eve and himself in comfort, and so they both starve, or live in a state of starvation. But this is one of the evils for the cure of which trades unions exist.

I think, if I may venture an opinion on the subject, women should be allowed to work at such trades as are suited to her, but she should be required to learn the trade thoroughly, and not work for less than the union standard of wages. In order to do this she would have to be received into the union in the first place as an apprentice. I think this would do more towards keeping female labour within proper limits than any offensive measures could do.

But the female labour question is one that cannot be disposed of in a few lines, and, with the editor's permission I would like to devote some future article to the question.

In the meantime I would be glad if some Western writer would start a controversy on the subject, for the woman question will have to be dealt with sooner or later in Western Australia.

MIDDLETON'S ROUSEABOUT

Tall and freckled and sandy,
    Face of a country lout;
This was the picture of Andy,
    Middleton's Rouseabout.

Type of a coming nation,
    In the land of cattle and sheep,
Worked on Middleton's station,
    "Pound a week and his keep."

On Middleton's wide dominions
    Plied the stockwhip and shears;
Hadn't any opinions,
    Hadn't any "idears."

Swiftly the years went over,
    Liquor and drought prevailed;
Middleton went as a drover,
    After his station had failed.

Type of a careless nation,
    Men who are soon played out,
Middleton was:— and his station
    Was bought by the Rouseabout.

Flourishing beard and sandy,
    Tall and robust and stout;
This is the picture of Andy,
    Middleton's Rouseabout.

Now on his own dominions
    Works with his overseers;
Hasn't any opinions,
    Hasn't any "idears."

FREEDOM ON THE WALLABY

Our fathers toiled for bitter bread
    While idlers thrived beside them;
But food to eat and clothes to wear
    Their native land denied them.
They left their native land in spite
    Of royalties' regalia,
And so they came, or if they stole
    Were sent out to Australia.

They struggled hard to make a home,
   Hard grubbing 'twas and clearing.
They weren't troubled much with toffs
   When they were pioneering;
And now that we have made the land
   A garden full of promise,
Old greed must crook his dirty hand
   And come to take it from us.

But Freedom's on the Wallaby,
   She'll knock the tyrants silly,
She's going to light another fire
   And boil another billy.
We'll make the tyrants feel the sting
   Of those that they would throttle;
They needn't say the fault is ours
   If blood should stain the wattle.

A Day on a Selection

The scene is a small New South Wales Western selection, the holder whereof is native-English. His wife is native-Irish. Time, Sunday, about 8 a.m. A used-up-looking woman comes from the slab-and-bark house, turns her face towards the hillside, and shrieks:

"T-o-o-m-*may!*"

No response, and presently she draws a long breath and screams again:

"*Tom* m-a-a-y!"

A faint echo comes from far up the siding where Tommy's presence is vaguely indicated by half-a-dozen cows moving slowly — very slowly — down towards the cow-yard.

The woman retires. Ten minutes later she come out again and screams:

"*Tom*my!!"

"Y-e-e-a-a-s-s-!" very passionately and shrilly.

"Ain't you goin" to bring those cows down today?"

"Y-e-e-a-a-s-s-s! — carn't yer see I'm comin'?"

A boy is seen to run wildly along the siding and hurl a missile at a feeding cow; the cow runs forward a short distance through the trees, and then stops to graze again while the boy stirs up another milker.

An hour goes by.

The rising Australian generation is represented by a thin, lanky youth of about fifteen. He is milking. The cow-yard is next the house, and is mostly ankle-deep in slush. The boy drives a dusty, discouraged-looking cow into the bail, and pins her head there; then he gets tackle on to her right hind-leg, hauls it back, and makes it fast to the fence. There are eleven cows, but not one of them can be milked out of the bail — chiefly because their teats are sore. The selector does not know what makes the teats sore, but he had an unquestioning faith in a certain ointment, recommended to him by a man who knows less about cows than he does himself, which he causes to be applied at irregular intervals — leaving the mode of application to the discretion of his son. Meanwhile the teats remain sore.

Having made the cow fast, the youngster cautiously takes hold of the least sore teat, yanks it suddenly, and dodges the cow's hock. When he gets enough milk to dip his dirty hands in, he moistens the teats, and things go on more smoothly. Now and then he relieves the monotony of his occupation by squirting at the eye of a calf which is dozing in the adjacent pen. Other times he milks into his mouth. Every time the cow kicks, a burr or a grass-seed or a bit of something else falls into the milk, and the boy drowns these things with a well-directed stream — on the principle that what's out of sight is out of mind.

Sometimes the boy sticks his head into the cow's side, hangs on by a teat, and dozes, while the bucket, mechanically gripped between his knees, sinks lower and lower till it rests on the ground. Likely as not he'll doze on until his mother's shrill voice startles him with an enquiry as to whether he intends to get that milking done today; other times he is roused by the plunging of the cow, or knocked over by a calf which has broken through a defective panel in the pen. In the latter case the youth gets tackle on to the calf, detaches its head from the teat with the heel of his boot, and makes it fast somewhere. Sometimes the cow breaks or loosens the leg-rope and gets her leg into the bucket and then the youth clings desperately to the pail and hopes she'll get her hoof out again without spilling the milk. Sometimes she does, more often she doesn't — it depends on the strength of the boy and the pail and on the strategy of the former. Anyway, the boy will lamb the cow down with a jagged yard shovel, let her out, and bail up another.

When he considers that he has finished milking he lets the cows out with their calves and carries the milk down to the dairy, where he has a heated argument with his mother, who — judging from the quantity of milk — has reason to believe that he has slummed some of the milkers. This he indignantly denies, telling her she knows very well the cows are going dry.

The dairy is built of rotten box bark — though there is plenty of good stringy bark within easy distance — and the structure looks as if it wants to lie down and is only prevented by three crooked props on the leaning side; more props will soon be needed in the rear for the dairy shows signs of going in that direction. The milk is set in dishes made of kerosene tins, cut in halves, which are placed on bark shelves fitted round against the walls. The shelves are not level and the dishes are brought to a comparatively horizontal position by means of chips and bits of bark, etc, inserted under the lower sides. The milk is covered by soiled sheets of old newspapers supported on sticks laid across the dishes. This protection is necessary, because the box bark in the roof has crumbled away and left fringed holes — also because the fowls roost up there. Sometimes the paper sags, and the cream may have to be scraped off an article on Dairy Farming.

The selector's wife removes the newspapers, and reveals a thick, yellow layer of rich cream, plentifully peppered with dust that has drifted in somehow. She runs a dirty forefinger round the edges of the cream to detach it from the tin, wipes her finger in her mouth, and skims. If the milk and cream are very thick she rolls the cream over like a pancake with her fingers, and lifts it out in sections. The thick milk is poured into a slop-bucket, for the pigs and calves, the dishes are "cleaned" — by the aid of a dipper full of warm water and a rag — and the wife proceeds to set the morning's milk. Tom holds up the doubtful-looking rag that serves as a strainer while his mother pours in the milk. Sometimes the boy's hand gets tired and he lets some of the milk run over, and gets into trouble; but it doesn't matter much, for the straining-cloth has several sizeable holes in the middle.

The door of the dairy faces the dusty road and is off its hinges and has to be propped up. The prop is missing this morning, and Tommy is accused of having been seen chasing old Poley with it at an earlier hour. He never see'd the damn prop, never chased no cow with it, and wants to know what's the use of always accusing him. He further complains that he's always blamed for everything. The pole is not forthcoming, and so an old dray is backed against the door to keep it in position. There is more trouble about a cow that is lost, and hasn't been milked for two days. The boy takes the cows up to the paddock slip-rails and lets the top rail down: the lower rail fits rather tightly and some exertion is required to free it, so he makes the animals jump that one. Then he "poddies" — hand-feeds — the calves which have been weaned too early. He carries the skim-milk to the yard in a bucket made out of an oil-drum — sometimes a kerosene tin — seizes a calf by the nape of the neck with his left hand, inserts the dirty forefinger of his right into its mouth, and shoves its head down into the milk. The calf sucks, thinking it has a teat, and pretty soon it butts violently — as calves do to remind their mothers to let down the milk — and the boy's wrist gets barked against the jagged edge of the bucket. He welts that calf in the jaw, kicks it in the stomach, tries to smother it with its nose in the milk, and finally dismisses it with the assistance of the calf rope and a shovel, and gets another. His hand feels sticky and the cleaned finger makes it look as if he wore a filthy, greasy glove with the forefinger torn off.

The selector himself is standing against a fence talking to a neighbour. His arms rest on the top rail of the fence, his chin rests on his hands, his pipe rests between his fingers, and his eyes rest on a white cow that is chewing her cud on the opposite side of the fence. The neighbour's arms rest on the top rail also, his chin rests on his hands, his pipe rests between his fingers, and his eyes rest on the cow. They are talking about that cow. They have been talking about her for three hours. She is chewing her cud. Her nose is well up forward, and her eyes are shut. She lets her lower jaw fall a little, moves it to one side, lifts it again, and brings it back into position with a springing kind of jerk that has almost a visible recoil. Then her jaws stay perfectly still for a moment, and you would think she had stopped chewing. But she hasn't. Now and again a soft, easy, smooth-going swallow passes visibly along her clean, white throat and disappears. She chews again, and by-and-by she loses consciousness and forgets to chew. She never opens her eyes. She is young and in good condition; she has had enough to eat, the sun is just properly warm for her, and — well if an animal can be really happy, she ought to be.

Presently the two men drag themselves away from the fence, fill their pipes, and go to have a look at some rows of forked sticks, apparently stuck in the ground for some purpose. The selector calls these sticks fruit-trees, and he calls the place "the orchard". They fool round these wretched sticks until dinner-time, when the neighbour says he must be getting home. "Stay and have some dinner! Man alive! Stay and have some dinner!" says the selector; and so the friend stays.

It is a broiling hot day in summer, and the dinner consists of hot roast meat, hot baked potatoes, hot cabbage, hot pumpkin, hot peas, and burning-hot plum-pudding. The family drinks on an average four cups of tea each per meal. The wife takes her place at the head of the table with a broom to keep the fowls out, and at short intervals she interrupts the conversation with such exclamations as "Shoo! shoo!" "Tommy, can't you see that fowl? Drive it out!" The fowls evidently pass a lot of their time in the house. They mark the circle described by the broom, and take care to keep two or three inches beyond it. Every now and then you see a fowl on the dresser amongst the crockery, and there is great concern to get it out before it breaks something. While dinner is in progress two steers get into the wheat through a broken rail which has been spliced with stringy bark, and a calf or two break into the vineyard. And yet this careless Australian selector, who is too shiftless to put up a decent fence, or build a decent house and who knows little or nothing about farming, would seem by his conversation to have read up all the great social and political questions of the day. Here are some fragments of conversation caught at the dinner-table. Present — the Selector, the Missus, the neighbour, Corney George — nicknamed "Henry George" — Tommy, Jackey, and the younger children. The spaces represent interruptions by the fowls and children: —

Corney George (continuing conversation): "But Henry George says, in 'Progress and Poverty', he says ——"

Missus (to the fowls): "Shoo! Shoo!"

Corney: "He says ——"

Tom: "Marther, jist speak to this Jack."

Missus (to Jack): "If you can't behave yourself, leave the table."

Tom: "He says in Progress and ——"

Missus: "Shoo!"

Neighbour: "I think 'Lookin' Backwards' is more ——"

Missus: "Shoo! Shoo! Tom, carn't you see that fowl?"

Selector: "Now I think 'Caesar's Column ' is more likely ——. Just look at ——"

Missus: "Shoo! Shoo!"

Selector: "Just look at the French Revolution."

Corney: "Now, Henry George ——"

Tom: "Marther! I seen a old-man kangaroo up on ——"

Missus: "Shut up! Eat your dinner an' hold your tongue. Carn't you see someone's speakin'? "

Selector: "Just look at the French ——"

Missus (to the fowls): "Shoo! Shoo!" (turning suddenly and unexpectedly on Jacky): "Take your fingers out of the sugar! — Blarst yer! that I should say such a thing."

Neighbour: "But 'Lookin' Back'ards' ——"

Missus: "There you go, Tom! Didn't I say you'd spill that

tea? Go away from the table!"

Selector: "I think 'Caesar's Column' is the only natural ——"

Missus: "Shoo! Shoo!" She loses patience, gets up and fetches a young rooster with the flat of the broom, sending him flying into the yard; he falls with his head towards the door and starts in again. Later on the conversation is about Deeming.

Selector: "There's no doubt the man's mad ——"

Missus: "Deeming! That Windsor wretch! Why, if I was in the law I'd have him boiled alive! Don't tell me he didn't know what he was doing! Why. I'd have him ——"

Corny: "But, Missus, you ——"

Missus (to the fowls): "Shoo! Shoo!"

Two Boys at Grinder Bros.'

Five or six half-grown larrikins sat on the cemented sill of the big window of Grinder Bros.' Railway Coach Factory waiting for the work bell, and one of the number was Bill Anderson — known as "Carstor Hoil" — a young terror of fourteen or fifteen.

"Here comes Balmy Arvie," exclaimed Bill as a pale, timid-looking little fellow rounded the corner and stood against the wall by the door. "How's your parents, Balmy?"

The boy made no answer; he shrank closer to the entrance. The first bell went.

"What yer got for dinner, Balmy? Bread 'n' treacle?" asked the young ruffian; then for the edification of his chums he snatched the boy's dinner bag and emptied its contents on the pavement.

The door opened. Arvie gathered up his lunch, took his time-ticket, and hurried in.

"Well, Balmy," said one of the smiths as he passed, "what do you think of the boat race?"

"I think," said the boy, goaded to reply, "that it would be better if young fellows of this country didn't think so much about racin' an' fightin'."

The questioner stared blankly for a moment, then laughed suddenly in the boy's face, and turned away. The rest grinned.

"Arvie's getting balmier than ever," guffawed young Bill.

"Here, Carstor Hoil," cried one of the smiths' strikers, "how much oil will you take for a chew of terbaccer?"

"Teaspoonful?"

"No, two."

"All right; let's see the chew, first."

"Oh, you'll get it. What yer frighten' of?... Come on, chaps, 'n' see Bill drink oil."

Bill measured out some machine oil and drank it. He got

the tobacco, and the others got what they called "the fun of seein' Bill drink oil!"

The second bell rang, and Bill went up to the other end of the shop, where Arvie was already at work sweeping shavings from under a bench.

The young terror seated himself on the end of this bench, drummed his heels against the leg, and whistled. He was in no hurry, for his foreman had not yet arrived. He amused himself by lazily tossing chips at Arvie, who made no protest for a while. "It would be — better — for this country," said the young terror, reflectively and abstractedly, cocking his eye at the whitewashed roof beams and feeling behind him on the bench for a heavier chip — "it would be better — for this country — if young fellers didn't think so much about — about — racin' — *and* fightin'."

"You let me alone," said Arvie.

"Why, what'll you do?" exclaimed Bill, bringing his eye down with feigned surprise. Then, in an indignant tone, "I don't mind takin' a fall out of yer, now, if yer like."

Arvie went on with his work. Bill tossed all the chips within reach, and then sat carelessly watching some men at work, and whistling the "Dead March". Presently he asked:

"What's yer name, Balmy?"

No answer.

"Carn't yer answer a civil question? I'd soon knock the sulks out of yer if I was yer father."

"My name's Arvie; you know that."

"Arvie what?"

"Arvie Aspinal."

Bill cocked his eye at the roof and thought a while and whistled; then he said suddenly:

"Say, Balmy, where d'yer live?"

"Jones' Alley."

"What?"

"Jones' Alley."

A short, low whistle from Bill. "What house?"

"Number Eight."

"Garn! What yer giv'nus?"

"I'm telling the truth. What's there funny about it? What do I want to tell you a lie for?"

"Why, we lived there once, Balmy. Old folks livin'?"

"Mother is; father's dead."

Bill scratched the back of his head, protruded his under lip, and reflected.

"I say, Arvie, what did yer father die of?"

"Heart disease. He dropped down dead at his work."

Long, low, intense whistle from Bill. He wrinkled his forehead and stared up at the beams as if he expected to see something unusual there. After a while he said, very impressively: "So did mine."

The coincidence hadn't done striking him yet; he wrestled with it for nearly a minute longer. Then he said:

"I suppose yer mother goes out washin'?"

"Yes."

"N' cleans offices?"

"Yes."

"So does mine. Any brothers 'n' sisters?"

"Two — one brother 'n' one sister."

Bill looked relieved — for some reason.

"I got nine," he said. "Your's younger'n you?"

"Yes."

"Lot of bother with the landlord?"

"Yes, a good lot."

"Had any bailiffs in yet?"

"Yes, two."

They compared notes a while longer, and tailed off into a silence which lasted three minutes and grew awkward towards the end.

Bill fidgeted about on the bench, reached round for a chip, but recollected himself. Then he cocked his eye at the roof once more and whistled, twirling a shaving round his fingers the while. At last he tore the shaving in two, jerked it impatiently from him, and said abruptly:

"Look here, Arvie! I'm sorry I knocked over yer barrer yesterday."

"Thank you."

This knocked Bill out the first round. He rubbed round uneasily on the bence, fidgeted with the vise, drummed his fingers, whistled, and finally thrust his hands in his pockets and dropped on his feet.

"Look here, Arvie!" he said in low, hurried tones. "Keep close to me goin' out tonight, 'n' if any of the other chaps touches yer or says anything to yer I'll hit'em!"

Then he swung himself round the corner of a carriage "body" and was gone.

Arvie was late out of the shop that evening. His boss was a sub-contractor for the coach-painting, and always tried to find twenty minutes' work for his boys just about five or ten minutes before the bell rang. He employed boys because they were cheap and he had a lot of rough work, and they could get under floors and "bogies" with their pots and brushes, and do all the "priming" and paint the trucks. His name was Collins, and the boys were called "Collins' Babies". It was a joke in the shop that he had a "weaning" contract. The boys were all "over fourteen", of course, because of the Education Act. Some were nine or ten — wages from five shillings to ten shillings. It didn't matter to Grinder Brothers so long as the contracts were completed and the dividends paid. Collins preached in the park every Sunday. But this has nothing to do with the story.

When Arvie came out it was beginning to rain and the hands had all gone except Bill, who stood with his back to a verandah-post, spitting with very fair success at the ragged toe of one boot. He looked up, nodded carelessly at Arvie, and then made a dive for a passing lorry, on the end of which he disappeared round the next corner, unsuspected by the driver, who sat in front with his pipe in his mouth and a bag over his shoulders.

Arvie started home with his heart and mind pretty full, and a stronger, stranger aversion to ever going back to the shop again. This new, unexpected, and unsought-for friendship embarrassed the poor lonely child. It wasn't welcome.

But he never went back. He got wet going home, and that night he was a dying child. He had been ill all the time, and Collins was one "baby" short next day.

The Drover's Wife

The two-roomed house is built of round timber, slabs, and stringy bark, and floored with split slabs. A big bark kitchen standing at one end is larger than the house itself, verandah included.

Bush all round — bush with no horizon, for the country is flat. No ranges in the distance. The bush consists of stunted, rotten native apple trees. No undergrowth. Nothing to relieve the eye save the darker green of a few sheoaks which are sighing above the narrow, almost waterless creek. Nineteen miles to the nearest sign of civilization — a shanty on the main road.

The drover, an ex-squatter, is away with sheep. His wife and children are left here alone.

Four ragged, dried-up-looking children are playing about the house. Suddenly one of them yells: "Snake! Mother, here's a snake!"

The gaunt, sun-browned bushwoman dashes from the kitchen, snatches her baby from the ground, holds it on her left hip, and reaches for a stick.

"Where is it?"

"Here! gone into the wood-heap!" yells the eldest boy — a sharp-faced, excited urchin of eleven. "Stop there, mother! I'll have him. Stand back! I'll have the beggar!"

"Tommy, come here, or you'll be bit. Come here at once when I tell you, you little wretch!"

The youngster comes reluctantly, carrying a stick bigger than himself. Then he yells, triumphantly:

"There it goes — under the house!" and darts away with club uplifted. At the same time the big, black, yellow-eyed dog-of-all-breeds, who has shown the wildest interest in the proceedings, breaks his chain and rushes after that snake. He is a moment late, however, and his nose reaches the crack in the slabs just as the end of its tails disappears.

Almost at the same moment the boy's club comes down and skins the aforesaid nose. Alligator takes small notice of this, and proceeds to undermine the building; but he is subdued after a struggle and chained up. They cannot afford to lose him.

The drover's wife makes the children stand together near the dog-house while she watches for the snake. She gets two small dishes of milk and sets them down near the wall to tempt it to come out; but an hour goes by and it does not show itself.

It is near sunset, and a thunderstorm is coming. The children must be brought inside. She will not take them into the house, for she knows the snake is there, and may at any moment come up through the cracks in the rough slab floor; so she carries several armfuls of firewood into the kitchen, and then takes the children there. The kitchen has no floor — or, rather, an earthen one — called a "ground floor" in this part of the bush. There is a large, roughly made table in the centre of the place. She brings the children in, and makes them get on this table. They are two boys and two girls — mere babies. She gives them some supper, and then, before it gets dark, she goes into the house, and snatches up some pillows and bedclothes — expecting to see or lay her hand on the snake any minute. She makes a bed on the kitchen table for the children, and sits down beside it to watch all night.

She has an eye on the corner, and a green sapling club laid in readiness on the dresser by her side, together with her sewing basket and a copy of the *Young Ladies' Journal*. She has brought the dog into the room.

Tommy turns in, under protest, but says he'll lie awake all night and smash that blinded snake.

His mother asks him how many times she has told him not to swear.

He has his club with him under the bedclothes, and Jacky protests:

"Mummy! Tommy's skinnin' me alive wif his club. Make him take it out."

Tommy: "Shet up, you little ———! D'yer want to be bit with the snake?"

Jacky shuts up.

"If yer bit," says Tommy, after a pause, "you'll swell up, an' smell, an' turn red an' green an' blue all over till yer bust. Won't he, mother?"

"Now then, don't frighten the child. Go to sleep," she says.

The two younger children go to sleep, and now and then Jacky complains of being "skeezed". More room is made for him. Presently Tommy says: "Mother! listen to them (adjective) little 'possums. I'd like to screw their blanky necks."

And Jacky protests drowsily:

"But they don't hurt us, the little blanks!"

Mother: "There, I told you you'd teach Jacky to swear." But the remark makes her smile. Jacky goes to sleep.

Presently Tommy asks:

"Mother! Do you think they'll ever extricate the (adjective) kangaroo?"

"Lord! How am I to know, child? Go to sleep."

"Will you wake me if the snake comes out?"

"Yes. Go to sleep."

Near midnight. The children are all asleep and she sits there still, sewing and reading by turns. From time to time she glances round the floor and wall-plate, and whenever she hears a noise she reaches for the stick. The thunderstorm comes on, and the wind, rushing through the cracks in the slab wall, threatens to blow out her candle. She places it on a sheltered part of the dresser and fixes up a newspaper to protect it. At every flash of lightning, the cracks between the slabs gleam like polished silver. The thunder rolls, and the rain comes down in torrents.

Alligator lies at full length on the floor, with his eyes turned towards the partition. She knows by this that the snake is there. There are large cracks in that wall opening under the floor of the dwelling-house.

She is not a coward, but recent events have shaken her nerves. A little son of her brother-in-law was lately bitten by a snake, and died. Besides, she has not heard from her husband for six months, and is anxious about him.

He was a drover, and started squatting here when they were married. The drought of 18 — ruined him. He had to sacrifice the remnant of his flock and go droving again. He intends to move his family into the nearest town when he comes back, and, in the meantime, his brother, who keeps a shanty on the main road, comes over about once a month with provisions. The wife has still a couple of cows, one horse, and a few sheep. The brother-in-law kills one of the sheep occasioally, gives her what she needs of it, and takes the rest in return for other provisions.

She is used to being left alone. She once lived like this for eighteen months. As a girl she built the usual castles in the air; but all her girlish hopes and aspirations have long been dead. She finds all the excitement and recreation she needs in the *Young Ladies' Journal,* and, Heaven help her! takes a pleasure in the fashion-plates.

Her husband is an Australian, and so is she. He is careless, but a good enough husband. If he had the means he would take her to the city and keep her there like a princess. They are used to being apart, or at least she is. "No use fretting," she says. He may forget sometimes that he is married; but if he has a good cheque when he comes back he will give most of it to her. When he had money he took her to the city several times — hired a railway sleeping compartment, and put up at the best hotels. He also bought her a buggy, but they had to sacrifice that along with the rest.

The last two children were born in the bush — one while her husband was bringing a drunken doctor, by force, to attend to her. She was alone on this occasion, and very weak. She had been ill with a fever. She prayed to God to send her assistance. God sent Black Mary — the "whitest" gin in all the land. Or, at least, God sent "King Jimmy" first, and he sent Black Mary. He put his black face round the door-post, took in the situation at a glance, and said cheerfully: "All right, Missis — I bring my old woman, she down alonga creek."

One of her children died while she was here alone. She rode nineteen miles for assistance, carrying the dead child.

It must be near one or two o'clock. The fire is burning low. Alligator lies with his head resting on his paws, and watches the wall. He is not a very beautiful dog to look at, and the light shows numerous old wounds where the hair will not grow. He is afraid of nothing on the face of the earth or under it. He will tackle a bullock as readily as he will tackle a flea. He hates all other dogs — except kangaroo-dogs — and has a marked dislike to friends or relations of the family. They seldom call, however. He sometimes makes friends with strangers. He hates snakes and has killed many, but he will be bitten some day and die; most snake-dogs end that way.

Now and then the bushwoman lays down her work and watches, and listens, and thinks. She thinks of things in her own life, for there is little else to think about.

The rain will make the grass grow, and this reminds her how she fought a bush fire once while her husband was away. The grass was long, and very dry, and the fire

threatened to burn her out. She put on an old pair of her
husband's trousers and beat out the flames with a green
bough, till great drops of sooty perspiration stood out on her
forehead and ran in streaks down her blackened arms. The
sight of his mother in trousers greatly amused Tommy, who
worked like a little hero by her side, but the terrified baby
howled lustily for his "mummy". The fire would have
mastered her but for four excited bushmen who arrived in
the nick of time. It was a mixed-up affair all round; when
she went to take up the baby he screamed and struggled
convulsively, thinking it was a "black man"; and Alligator,
trusting more to the child's sense than his own instinct,
charged furiously, and (being old and slightly deaf) did not
in his excitement at first recognize his mistress's voice, but
continued to hang on to the moleskins until choked off by
Tommy with a saddle-strap. The dog's sorrow for his
blunder, and his anxiety to let it be known that it was all a
mistake, was as evident as his ragged tail and a twelve-inch
grin could make it. It was a glorious time for the boys; a day
to look back to, and talk about, and laugh over for many
years.

She thinks how she fought a flood during her husband's
absence. She stood for hours in the drenching downpour,
and dug an overflow gutter to save the dam across the creek.
But she could not save it. There are things that a bushwoman cannot do. Next morning the dam was broken, and
her heart was nearly broken too, for she thought how her
husband would feel when he came home and saw the result
of years of labour swept away. She cried then.

She also fought the *pleuro-pneumonia* — dosed and bled
the few remaining cattle, and wept again when her two best
cows died.

Again, she fought a mad bullock that besieged the house
for a day. She made bullets and fired at him through cracks
in the slabs with an old shotgun. He was dead in the
morning. She skinned him and got seventeen-and-six for the
hide.

She also fights the crows and eagles that have designs on
her chickens. Her plan of campaign is very original. The
children cry "Crows, mother!" and she rushes out and aims a
broomstick at the birds as though it were a gun, and says,
"Bung!" The crows leave in a hurry; they are cunning, but a
woman's cunning is greater.

Occasionally a bushman in the horrors, or a villainous-
looking sundowner, comes and nearly scares the life out of

her. She generally tells the suspicious-looking stranger that her husband and two sons are at work below the dam, or over at the yard, for he always cunningly inquires for the boss.

Only last week a gallows-faced swagman — having satisfied himself that there were no men on the place — threw his swag down on the verandah, and demanded tucker. She gave him something to eat; then he expressed his intention of staying for the night. It was sundown then. She got a batten from the sofa, loosened the dog, and confronted the stranger, holding the batten in one hand and the dog's collar with the other. "Now you go!" she said. He looked at her and at the dog, said "All right, mum," in a cringing tone, and left. She was a determined-looking woman, and Alligator's yellow eyes glared unpleasantly — besides, the dog's chawing-up apparatus greatly resembled that of the reptile he was named after.

She has few pleasures to think of as she sits here alone by the fire, on guard against a snake. All days are much the same to her; but on Sunday afternoon she dresses herself, tidies the children, smartens up baby, and goes for a lonely walk along the bush-track, pushing an old perambulator in front of her. She does this every Sunday. She takes as much care to make herself and the children look smart as she would if she were going to do the block in the city. There is nothing to see, however, and not a soul to meet. You might walk for twenty miles along this track without being able to fix a point in your mind, unless you are a bushman. This is because of the everlasting, maddening sameness of the stunted trees — that monotony which makes a man long to break away and travel as far as trains can go, and sail as far as ships can sail — and further.

But this bushwoman is used to the loneliness of it. As a girl-wife she hated it, but now she would feel strange away from it.

She is glad when her husband returns, but she does not gush or make a fuss about it. She gets him something good to eat, and tidies up the children.

She seems contented with her lot. She loves her children, but has no time to show it. She seems harsh to them. Her surroundings are not favourable to the development of the "womanly" or sentimental side of nature.

It must be near morning now; but the clock is in the dwelling-house. Her candle is nearly done; she forgot that she was out of candles. Some more wood must be got to keep the fire up, and so she shuts the dog inside and hurries round to the wood-heap. The rain has cleared off. She seizes a stick, pulls it out, and — crash! the whole pile collapses.

Yesterday she bargained with a stray blackfellow to bring her some wood, and while he was at work she went in search of a missing cow. She was absent an hour or so, and the native black made good use of his time. On her return she was so astonished to see a good heap of wood by the chimney, that she gave him an extra fig of tobacco, and praised him for not being lazy. He thanked her, and left with head erect and chest well out. He was the last of his tribe and a King; but he had built that wood-heap hollow.

She is hurt now, and tears spring to her eyes as she sits down again by the table. She takes up a handkerchief to wipe the tears away, but pokes her eyes with her bare fingers instead. The handkerchief is full of holes, and she finds that she has put her thumb through one, and her forefinger through another.

This makes her laugh, to the surprise of the dog. She has a keen, very keen, sense of the ridiculous; and some time or other she will amuse bushmen with the story.

She has been amused before like that. One day she sat down "to have a good cry," as she said — and the old cat rubbed against her dress and "cried too." Then she had to laugh.

It must be near daylight. The room is very close and hot because of the fire. Alligator still watches the wall from time to time. Suddenly he becomes greatly interested; he draws himself a few inches nearer the partition, and a thrill runs through his body. The hair on the back of his neck begins to bristle, and the battle-light is in his yellow eyes. She knows what this means, and lays her hand on the stick. The lower end of one of the partition slabs has a large crack on both sides. An evil pair of small, bright, bead-like eyes glisten at one of these holes. The snake — a black one — comes slowly out, about a foot, and moves its head up and down. The dog lies still, and the woman sits as one fascinated. The snake comes out a foot further. She lifts her stick, and the reptile, as though suddenly aware of danger, sticks his head in through the crack on the other side of the slab, and hurries to get his tail round after him. Alligator springs, and his jaws come together with a snap. He misses, for his nose is large and the snake's body down in the angle formed by the slabs and the floor. He snaps again as the tail comes round. He has the snake now, and tugs it out eighteen inches. Thud, thud comes the woman's club on the ground. Alligator pulls again. Thud, thud Alligator gives another pull and he has the snake out — a black brute, five feet long. The head rises to dart about, but the dog has the enemy close to the neck. He is a big, heavy dog, but quick as a terrier. He shakes the snake as though he felt the original curse in common with mankind. The eldest boy wakes up, seizes his stick, and tries to get out of bed, but his mother forces him back with a grip of iron. Thud, thud — the snake's back is broken in several places. Thud, thud — its head is crushed, and Alligator's nose skinned again.

She lifts the mangled reptile on the point of her stick, carries it to the fire, and throws it in; then piles on the wood, and watches the snake burn. The boy and dog watch, too. She lays her hand on the dog's head, and all the fierce, angry light dies out of his yellow eyes. The younger children are quieted, and presently go to sleep. The dirty-legged boy stands for a moment in his shirt, watching the fire. Presently he looks up at her, sees the tears in her eyes, and, throwing his arms round her neck, exclaims:

"Mother, I won't never go drovin'; blast me if I do!"

And she hugs him to her worn-out breast and kisses him; and they sit thus together while the sickly daylight breaks over the bush.

The Bush Undertaker

"Five bob!"

The old man shaded his eyes and peered through the dazzling glow of that broiling Christmas Day. He stood just within the door of a slab-and-bark hut situated upon the bank of a barren creek; sheep-yards lay to the right, and a low line of bare brown ridges formed a suitable background to the scene.

"Five Bob!" shouted he again; and dusty sheep-dog rose wearily from the shaded side of the hut and looked inquiringly at his master, who pointed towards some sheep which were straggling from the flock.

"Fetch 'em back," he said confidently.

The dog went off, and his master returned to the interior of the hut.

"We'll yard 'em early," he said to himself; "the super won't know. We'll yard 'em early, and have the arternoon to ourselves."

"We'll get dinner," he added, glancing at some pots on the fire, "I cud do a bit of doughboy, an' that theer boggabri 'll eat like tater-marrer along of the salt meat." He moved one of the black buckets from the blaze. "I likes to keep it jist on the sizzle," he said in explanation to himself; "hard bilin' makes it tough — I'll keep it jist a-simmerin'."

Here his soliloquy was interrupted by the return of the dog.

"All right, Five Bob," said the hatter, "dinner'll be ready dreckly. Jist keep yer eye on the sheep till I calls yer; keep 'em well rounded up, an' we'll yard 'em afterwards and have a holiday."

This speech was accompanied by a gesture evidently intelligible, for the dog retired as though he understood English, and the cooking proceeded.

"I'll take a pick an' shovel with me an' root up that old

blackfellow," mused the shepherd, evidently following up a recent train of thought; "I reckon it'll do now. I'll put in the spuds."

The last sentence referred to the cooking, the first to a blackfellow's grave about which he was curious.

"The sheep's a-campin'," said the soliloquizer, glancing through the door. "So me an' Five Bob'll be able to get our dinner in peace. I wish I had just enough fat to make the pan siss; I'd treat myself to a leather-jacket; but it took three weeks' skimmin' to get enough for them theer doughboys."

In due time the dinner was dished up; and the old man seated himself on a block, with the lid of a gin-case across his knees for a table. Five Bob squatted opposite with the liveliest interest and appreciation depicted on his intelligent countenance.

Dinner proceeded very quietly, except when the carver paused to ask the dog how some tasty morsel went with him, and Five Bob's tail declared that it went very well indeed.

"Here y'are, try this," cried the old man, tossing him a large piece of doughboy. A click of Five Bob's jaws and the dough was gone.

"Clean into his liver!" said the old man with a faint smile.

He washed up the tinware in the water the duff had been boiled in, and then, with the assistance of the dog, yarded the sheep.

This accomplished, he took a pick and shovel and an old sack, and started out over the ridge, followed, of course, by his four-legged mate. After tramping some three miles he reached a spur, running out from the main ridge. At the extreme end of this, under some gum trees, was a little mound of earth, barely defined in the grass, and indented in the centre as all blackfellows' graves were.

He set to work to dig it up, and sure enough, in about half-an-hour he bottomed on payable dirt.

When he had raked up all the bones, he amused himself by putting them together on the grass and by speculating as to whether they had belonged to black or white, male or female. Failing, however, to arrive at any satisfactory conclusion, he dusted them with great care, put them in the bag, and started for home.

He took a short cut this time over the ridge and down a gully which was full of ring-barked trees and long white grass. He had nearly reached its mouth when a great greasy black iguana clambered up a sapling from under his feet and looked fightable.

"Dang the jumpt-up thing!" cried the old man. "It gin me a start!"

At the foot of the sapling he espied an object which he at first thought was the blackened carcass of a sheep, but on closer examination discovered to be the body of a man; it lay with its forehead resting on its hands, dried to a mummy by the intense heat of the western summer.

"Me luck's in for the day and no mistake!" said the shepherd, scratching the back of his head, while he took stock of the remains. He picked up a stick and tapped the body on the shoulder; the flesh sounded like leather. He turned it over on its side; it fell flat on its back like a board, and the shrivelled eyes seemed to peer up at him from under the blackened wrists.

He stepped back involuntarily, but, recovering himself, leant on his stick and took in all the ghastly details.

There was nothing in the blackened features to tell aught of name or race, but the dress proclaimed the remains to be those of a European. The old man caught sight of a black bottle in the grass, close beside the corpse. This set him thinking. Presently he knelt down and examined the soles of the dead man's Blucher boots, and then, rising with an air of conviction, exclaimed: "Brummy! by gosh! — busted up at last!"

"I tole yer so, Brummy," he said impressively, addressing the corpse, "I allers told yer as how it 'ud be — an' here y'are, you thundering jumpt-up cuss-o'-God fool. Yer cud earn mor'n any man in the colony, but yer'd lush it all away. I allers sed as how it 'ud end, an' now yer kin see fur y'self."

"I spect yer was a-comin' t' me t' get fixt up an' set straight agin; then yer was agoin' to swear off, same as yer allers did; an' here y'are, an' now I expect I'll have t' fix yer up for the last time an' make yer decent, for 'twon't do t' leave yer a-lyin' out here like a dead sheep."

He picked up the corked bottle and examined it. To his great surprise it was nearly full of rum.

"Well, this gits me," exclaimed the old man; "me luck's in, this Christmas, an' no mistake. He must a' got the jams early in his spree, or he wouldn't be a-making for me with near a bottleful left. Howsomenever, here goes."

Looking round, his eyes lit up with satisfaction as he saw some waste bits of bark which had been left by a party of strippers who had been getting bark there for the stations. He picked up two pieces, one about four and the other six feet long, and each about two feet wide, and brought them over to the body. He laid the longest strip by the side of the corpse, which he proceeded to lift on to it.

"Come on, Brummy," he said, in a softer tone than usual, "yer ain't as bad as yer might be, considerin' as it must be three good months since yer slipped yer wind. I spect it was the rum as preserved yer. It was the death of yer when yer was alive, an' now yer dead, it preserved yer like — like a mummy."

Then he placed the other strip on top, with the hollow side downwards — thus sandwiching the defunct between the two pieces — removed the saddle strap, which he wore for a belt, and buckled it round one end, while he tried to think of something with which to tie up the other.

"I can't take any more strips off my shirt," he said, critically examining the skirts of the old blue overshirt he wore. "I might get a strip or two more off, but it's short enough already. Let's see; how long have I been awearin' of that shirt? Oh, I remember, I bought it jist two days afore Five Bob was pupped. I can't afford a new shirt jist yet; howsomenever, seein' it's Brummy, I'll jist borrow a couple more strips and sew 'em on agen when I git home."

He up-ended Brummy, and placing his shoulder against the middle of the lower sheet of bark, lifted the corpse to a horizontal position; then taking the bag of bones in his hand, he started for home.

"I ain't a-spendin' sech a dull Christmas arter all," he reflected, as he plodded on; but he had not walked above a hundred yards when he saw a black iguana sidling into the grass by the side of the path.

"That's another of them theer dang things!" he exclaimed. "That's two I've seed this mornin'."

Presently he remarked: "Yer don't smell none too sweet, Brummy. It must 'a' been jist about the middle of shearin' when yer pegged out. I wonder who got yer last cheque? Shoo! theer's another black gohanner — theer must be a flock on 'em."

He rested Brummy on the ground while he had another pull at the bottle, and, before going on, packed the bag of bones on his shoulder under the body, but he soon stopped again.

"The thunderin' jumpt-up bones is all skew-whift," he said. "'Ole on, Brummy, an' I'll fix 'em;" and he leaned the dead man against a tree while he settled the bones on his shoulder, and took another pull at the bottle.

About a mile further on he heard a rustling in the grass to

the right, and, looking round, saw another iguana gliding off sideways, with its long snaky neck turned towards him.

This puzzled the shepherd considerably, the strangest part of it being that Five Bob wouldn't touch the reptile, but slunk off with his tail down when ordered to "sick 'em."

"Theer's sothin' comic about them theer gohanners," said the old man at last. "I've seed swarms of grasshoppers an' big mobs of kangaroos, but dang me if ever I seed a flock of black gohanners afore!"

On reaching the hut the old man dumped the corpse against the wall, wrong end up, and stood scratching his head while he endeavoured to collect his muddled thoughts; but he had not placed Brummy at the correct angle, and, consequently, that individual fell forward and struck him a violent blow on the shoulder with the iron toes of his Blucher boots.

The shock sobered him. He sprang a good yard, instinctively hitching up his moleskins in preparation for flight; but a backward glance revealed to him the true cause of this supposed attack from the rear. Then he lifted the body, stood it on its feet against the chimney, and ruminated as to where he should lodge his mate for the night, not noticing that the shorter sheet of bark had slipped down on the boots and left the face exposed.

"I spect I'll have ter put yer into the chimney trough for the night, Brummy," said he, turning round to confront the corpse. "Yer can't expect me to take yer into the hut, though I did it when yer was in a worse state than —— Lord!"

The shepherd was not prepared for the awful scrutiny that gleamed on him from those empty sockets; his nerves received a shock, and it was some time before he recovered himself sufficiently to speak.

"Now look a-here, Brummy," said he, shaking his finger severely at the delinquent, "I don't want to pick a row with yer; I'd do as much for yer an' more than any other man, an' well yer knows it; but if yer starts playin' any of yer jumpt-up pranktical jokes on me, and a scarin' of me after a-humpin' of yer 'ome, by the 'oly frost I'll kick yer to jim-rags, so I will."

This admonition delivered, he hoisted Brummy into the chimney trough, and with a last glance towards the sheep-yards, he retired to his bunk to have, as he said, a snooze.

He had more than a "snooze", however, for when he woke it was dark, and the bushman's instinct told him it must be nearly nine o'clock.

He lit a slush lamp and poured the remainder of the rum into a pannikin; but, just as he was about to lift the draught to his lips, he heard a peculiar rustling sound overhead, and put the pot down on the table with a slam that spilled some of the precious liquor.

Five Bob whimpered, and the old shepherd, though used to the weird and dismal, as one living alone in the bush must necessarily be, felt the icy breath of fear at his heart.

He reached hastily for his old shot-gun, and went out to investigate. He walked round the hut several times and examined the roof on all sides, but saw nothing. Brummy appeared to be in the same position.

At last, persuading himself that the noise was caused by 'possums or the wind, the old man went inside, boiled his billy, and after composing his nerves somewhat with a light supper and a meditative smoke, retired for the night. He was aroused several times before midnight by the same mysterious sound overhead, but, though he rose and examined the roof on each occasion by the light of the rising moon, he discovered nothing.

At last he determined to sit up and watch until daybreak, and for this purpose took up a position on a log a short distance from the hut, with his gun laid in readiness across his knee.

After watching for about an hour, he saw a black object coming over the ridge-pole. He grabbed his gun and fired. The thing disappeared. He ran round to the other side of the hut, and there was a great black iguana in violent convulsions on the ground.

Then the old man saw it all. "The thunderin' jumpt-up thing has been a-havin' o' me," he exclaimed. "The same cuss-o'-God wretch has a-follered me 'ome, an' has been a-havin' its Christmas dinner off of Brummy, an' a-hauntin' o' me into the bargain, the jumpt-up tinker!"

As there was no one by whom he could send a message to the station, and the old man dared not leave the sheep and go himself, he determined to bury the body the next afternoon, reflecting that the authorities could disinter it for inquest if they pleased.

So he brought the sheep home early, and made arrangements for the burial by measuring the outer casing of Brummy and digging a hole according to those dimensions.

"That 'minds me," he said, "I never rightly knowed Brummy's religion, blest if ever I did. Howsomenever, there's one thing sartin — none o' them theer pianer-

fingered parsons is a-goin' ter take the trouble ter travel out
inter this God-for-gotten part to hold sarvice over him, seein'
as how his last cheque's blued. But as I've got the fun'ral
arrangements all in me own hands, I'll do jestice to it, and
see that Brummy has a good comfortable buryin' — and
more's unpossible."

"It's time yer turned in, Brum," he said, lifting the body
down.

He carried it to the grave and dropped it into one corner
like a post. He arranged the bark so as to cover the face,
and, by means of a piece of clothes-line, lowered the body
to a horizontal position. Then he threw in an armful of gum
leaves, and then, very reluctantly, took the shovel and
dropped in a few shovelfuls of earth.

"An' this is the last of Brummy," he said, leaning on his
spade and looking away over the tops of the ragged gums on
the distant range.

This reflection seemed to engender a flood of memories,
in which the old man became absorbed. He learned heavily
upon his spade and thought.

"Arter all," he murmured sadly, "arter all — it were
Brummy."

"Brummy," he said at last, "it's all over now; nothin'
matters now — nothin' didn't ever matter, nor — nor don't.
You uster say as how it 'ud be all right termorrer" (pause);
"termorrer's come, Brummy — come fur you — it ain't
come fur me yet, but — it's a-comin'."

He threw in some more earth.

"Yer don't remember, Brummy, an' mebbe yer don't want
to remember — *I* don't want to remember — but — well,
but, yer see that's where yer got the pull on me."

He shovelled in some more earth and paused again.

The dog rose, with ears erect, and looked anxiously first at
his master, and then into the grave.

"Theer oughter be somethin' sed," muttered the old man;
"'tain't right to put 'im under like a dog. There oughter to
be some sort o' sarmin." He sighed heavily in the listening
silence that followed this remark, and proceeded with his
work. He filled the grave to the brim this time, and
fashioned the mound carefully with his spade. Once or twice
he muttered the words, "I am the rassaraction." As he laid
the tools quietly aside, and stood at the head of the grave, he
was evidently trying to remember the something that ought
to be said. He removed his hat, placed it carefully on the
grass, held his hands out from his sides and a little to the

front, drew a long deep breath, and said with a solemnity that greatly disturbed Five Bob, "Hashes ter hashes, dus ter dus, Brummy, — an' — an' in hopes of a great an' gerlorious rassaraction!"

He sat down on a log near by, rested his elbows on his knees and passed his hand wearily over his forehead — but only as one who was tired and felt the heat; and presently he rose, took up the tools, and walked back to the hut.

And the sun sank again on the grand Australian bush — the nurse and tutor of eccentric minds, the home of the weird, and of much that is different from things in other lands.

THE CITY BUSHMAN

It was pleasant up the country, City Bushman, where you
    went,
For you sought the greener patches and you travelled like a
    gent;
And you curse the trams and buses and the turmoil and the
    push,
Though you know the squalid city needn't keep you from
    the bush;
But we lately heard you singing of the "plains where shade
    is not,"
And you mentioned it was dusty— "all was dry and all was
    hot."

True, the bush "hath moods and changes" —and the bushman
    hath 'em, too,
For he's not a poet's dummy — he's a man, the same as you;
But his back is growing rounder — slaving for the absentee—
And his toiling wife is thinner than a country wife should be
For we noticed that the faces of the folks we chanced to
    meet
Should have made a greater contrast to the faces in the
    street;
And, in short, we think the bushman's being driven to the
    wall,
And it's doubtful if his spirit will be "loyal thro' it all."

Though the bush has been romantic and it's nice to sing
    about,
There's a lot of patriotism that the land could do without—
Sort of BRITISH WORKMAN nonsense that shall perish in
    the scorn
Of the drover who is driven and the shearer who is shorn,
Of the struggling western farmers who have little time for
    rest,
And are ruined on selections in the sheep-infested West;
Droving songs are very pretty, but they merit little thanks
From the people of a country in possession of the Banks.

And the "rise and fall of seasons" suits the rise and fall of
    rhyme,
But we know that western seasons do not run on schedule
    time;
For the drought will go on drying while there's anything to
    dry,

Then it rains until you'd fancy it would bleach the sunny
       sky—
Then it pelters out of reason, for the downpour day and
       night
Nearly sweeps the population to the Great Australian Bight.
It is up in Northern Queensland that the seasons do their
       best,
But it's doubtful if you ever saw a season in the West;
There are years without an autumn or a winter or a spring,
There are broiling Junes, and summers when it rains like
       anything.

In the bush my ears were opened to the singing of the bird,
But the "carol of the magpie" was a thing I never heard.
Once the beggar roused my slumbers in a shanty, it is true,
But I only heard him asking, "Who the blanky blank are
       you?"
And the bell-bird in the ranges — but his "silver chime" is
       harsh
When it's heard beside the solo of the curlew in the marsh.

Yes, I heard the shearers singing "William Riley", out of
       tune,
Saw 'em fighting round a shanty on a Sunday afternoon,
But the bushman isn't always "trapping brumbies in the
       night",
Nor is he for ever riding when "the morn is fresh and
       bright",
And he isn't always singing in the humpies on the run—
And the camp fire's "cheery blazes" are a trifle over-done;
We have grumbled with the bushmen round the fire on
       rainy days,
When the smoke would blind a bullock and there wasn't any
       blaze,
Save the blazes of our language, for we cursed the fire in
       turn
Till the atmosphere was heated and the wood began to burn.
Then we had to wring our blueys which were rotting in the
       swags,
And we saw the sugar leaking through the bottoms of the
       bags,
And we couldn't raise a chorus, for the toothache and the
       cramp,
While we spent the hours of darkness draining puddles round
       the camp.

Would you like to change with Clancy — go a-droving? tell
    us true,
For we rather think that Clancy would be glad to change
    with you,
And be something in the city; but 'twould give your muse a
    shock
To be losing time and money through the foot-rot in the
    flock,
And you wouldn't mind the beauties underneath the starry
    dome
If you had a wife and children and a lot of bills at home.

Did you ever guard the cattle when the night was inky-black,
And it rained, and icy water trickled gently down your back
Till your saddle-weary backbone fell a-aching to the roots
And you almost felt the croaking of the bull-frog in your
    boots—
Sit and shiver in the saddle, curse the restless stock and
    cough
Till a squatter's irate dummy cantered up to warn you off?
Did you fight the drought and pleuro when the "seasons"
    were asleep,
Felling sheoaks all the morning for a flock of starving sheep,
Drinking mud instead of water — climbing trees and lopping
    boughs
For the broken-hearted bullocks and the dry and dusty cows?

Do you think the bush was better in the "good old droving
    days",
When the squatter ruled supremely as the king of western
    ways,
When you got a slip of paper for the little you could earn,
But were forced to take provisions from the station in
    return —
When you couldn't keep a chicken at your humpy on the
    run,
For the squatter wouldn't let you — and your work was
    never done;
When you had to leave the missus in a lonely hut forlorn
While you "rose up Willy Riley" — in the days ere you were
    born?

Ah! we read about the drovers and the shearers and the like
Till we wonder why such happy and romantic fellows strike.
Don't you fancy that the poets ought to give the bush a rest
Ere they raise a just rebellion in the over-written West?

Where the simple-minded bushman gets a meal and bed and
    rum
Just by riding round reporting phantom flocks that never
    come;
Where the scalper — never troubled by the "war-whoop of
    the push"—
Has a quiet little billet — breeding rabbits in the bush;
Where the idle shanty-keeper never fails to make a draw,
And the dummy gets his tucker through provisions in the
    law;
Where the labour-agitator — when the shearers rise in might—
Makes his money sacrificing all his substance for The Right;
Where the squatter makes his fortune, and "the seasons rise
    and fall",
And the poor and honest bushman has to suffer for it all;
Where the drovers and the shearers and the bushmen and the
    rest
Never reach the Eldorado of the poets of the West.

And you think the bush is purer and that life is better there,
But it doesn't seem to pay you like the "squalid street and
    square".
Pray inform us, City Bushman, where you read, in prose or
    verse,
Of the awful "city urchin who would greet you with a curse".
There are golden hearts in gutters, though their owners lack
    the fat,
And we'll back a teamster's offspring to outswear a city brat.
Do you think we're never jolly where the trams and buses
    rage?
Did you hear the gods in chorus when "Ri-tooral" held the
    stage?
Did you catch a ring of sorrow in the city urchin's voice
When he yelled for Billy Elton, when he thumped the floor
    for Royce?
Do the bushmen, down on pleasure, miss the everlasting stars
When they drink and flirt and so on in the glow of private
    bars?

You've a down on "trams and buses", or the "roar" of 'em,
    you said
And the "filthy, dirty attic", where you never toiled for
    bread.
(And about that self-same attic — Lord! wherever have you
    been?
For the struggling needlewoman mostly keeps her attic clean.)
But you'll find it very jolly with the cuff-and-collar push,
And the city seems to suit you, while you rave about the bush.

You'll admit that Up-the-Country, more especially in drought,
Isn't quite the Eldorado that the poets rave about,
Yet at times we long to gallop where the reckless bushman
     rides
In the wake of startled brumbies that are flying for their
     hides;
Long to feel the saddle tremble once again between our
     knees
And to hear the stockwhips rattle just like rifles in the
     trees!
Long to feel the bridle-leather tugging strongly in the hand
And to feel once more a little like a native of the land.
And the ring of bitter feeling in the jingling of our rhymes
Isn't suited to the country nor the spirit of the times.
Let us go together droving, and returning, if we live,
Try to understand each other while we reckon up the div.

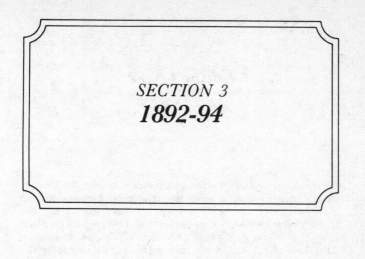

SECTION 3
1892-94

Editor's Note

This section, mainly stories and sketches, shows the impact of the trip to Bourke and the tramp to Hungerford on Lawson's imagination. The letter to Aunt Emma is from Colin Roderick's edition of the letters. The preface to *Short Stories in Verse and Prose* and "Some Popular Australian Mistakes" (*Bulletin*, 18 November 1893) are taken from the original sources. The texts for the stories and sketches are: *While the Billy Boils* ("Hungerford", "That There Dog O' Mine", "In a Wet Season", " 'Dossing Out' and 'Camping' "); *The Country I Come From* ("The Union Buries Its Dead", "Stiffner and Jim (Thirdly, Bill)"). *In the Days When the World Was Wide* provides the text of "Australian Bards and Bush Reviewers".

Late in 1893 Lawson went to New Zealand where he worked as a labourer for six months. "Stiffner and Jim (Thirdly, Bill)" was written there. *Short Stories in Verse and Prose* published by his mother late in 1894 included " 'Rats' ", "The Drover's Wife", "The Union Buries Its Dead", and "The Bush Undertaker". The version of " 'Rats' " from *While the Billy Boils* printed here omitted a final paragraph which appeared in Lawson's first book. This paragraph from *Short Stories in Prose and Verse* has been added in parenthesis to show how a "sketch" could be transformed by an ironic twist at the end into a "story", and how the disturbing implications of the sketch are lost in the factitiously well made story version. The first-published ending to "That There Dog of Mine" (given in Colin Roderick's *Commentaries* on the prose) reverses this process, turning the familiar, sentimental version given here into a macabre sketch.

Letter to Aunt Emma
(Mrs. Brooks)

Hungerford,
Queensland.
16th January 1893.

Dear Aunt,

I found your letter in the Post Office of this God-Forgotten town. I carried my swag nearly two hundred miles since I last wrote to you, and I am now camped on the Queensland side of the border — a beaten man. I start back tomorrow — 140 miles by the direct road — and expect to reach Bourke in nine days. My mate goes on to Thargomindah. No work and very little to eat; we lived mostly on Johnny cakes and cadged a bit of meat here and there at the miserable stations. Have been three days without sugar. Once in Bourke I'll find the means of getting back to Sydney — never to face the bush again. I got an offer to go over and edit a New Zealand paper and wrote to say that I doubted my ability to edit but would take a place on the staff. They seemed anxious to get me, and asked me to state my own terms. Simpson is negotiating with 'em. You can have no idea of the horrors of the country out here. Men tramp and beg and live like dogs. It is two months since I slept in what you can call a bed. We walk as far as we can — according to the water — and then lie down and roll ourselves in our blankets. The flies start at daylight and we fight them all day till dark — then mosquitoes start. We carry water in bags. Got bushed on a lignum plain Sunday before last and found the track at four o'clock in the afternoon — then tramped for four hours without water and reached a government dam. My mate drank nearly all night. But it would take a year to tell you all about my wanderings in the wilderness.

It would not be so bad if it was shearing season — then, at

least we'd be sure of tucker. But the experience will help me to live in the city for the next year or so. So much for myself.

I'm real glad to hear that you are still at North Shore (you may expect me there within the next six months — as soon as I get a few decent clothes). Sorry Don is dead.

I'm writing on an old tin and my legs ache too much to let me sit any longer. I've always tried to write cheerful letters so you'll excuse this one. Will tell you all about it when I get down.

And now for a lonely walk of 140 miles. Will write from Bourke.

> Your affectionate nephew,
> Henry Lawson

P.S. I'm going off the track to try and get a few weeks' work on a Warrego station. Will write from there if successful.

Hungerford

One of the hungriest cleared roads in New South Wales runs to within a couple of miles of Hungerford, and stops there; then you strike through the scrub to the town. There is no distant prospect of Hungerford — you don't see the town till you are quite close to it, and then two or three white-washed galvanized-iron roofs start out of the mulga.

They say that a past Ministry commenced to clear the road from Bourke, under the impression that Hungerford was an important place, and went on, with the blindness peculiar to Governments, till they got to within two miles of the town. Then they ran short of rum and rations, and sent a man on to get them, and make enquiries. The member never came back, and two more were sent to find him — or Hungerford. Three days later the two returned in an exhausted condition, and submitted a motion of want-of-confidence, which was lost. Then the whole House went on and was lost also. Strange to relate, that Government was never missed.

However, we found Hungerford and camped there for a day. The town is right on the Queensland border, and an interprovincial rabbit-proof fence — with rabbits on both sides of it — runs across the main street.

This fence is a standing joke with Australian rabbits — about the only joke they have out there, except the memory of Pasteur and poison and inoculation. It is amusing to go a little way out of town, about sunset, and watch them crack Noah's Ark rabbits jokes about that fence, and burrow under and play leap-frog over till they get tired. One old buck rabbit sat up and nearly laughed his ears off at a joke of his own about that fence. He laughed so much that he couldn't get away when I reached for him. I could hardly eat him for laughing. I never saw a rabbit laugh before; but I've seen a possum do it.

Hungerford consists of two houses and a humpy in New South Wales, and five houses in Queensland. Characteristically enough, both the pubs are in Queensland. We got a glass of sour yeast at one and paid sixpence for it — we had asked for English ale.

The post-office is in New South Wales, and the police-barracks in Bananaland. The police cannot do anything if there's a row going on across the street in New South Wales, except to send to Brisbane and have an extradition warrant applied for; and they don't do much if there's a row in Queensland. Most of the rows are across the border, where the pubs are.

At least, I believe that's how it is, though the man who told me might have been a liar. Another man said he was a liar, but then *he* might have been a liar himself — a third person said he was one. I heard that there was a fight over it, but the man who told me about the fight might not have been telling the truth.

One part of the town swears at Brisbane when things go wrong, and the other part curses Sydney.

The country looks as though a great ash-heap had been spread out there, and mulga scrub and firewood planted — and neglected. The country looks just as bad for a hundred miles round Hungerford, and beyond that it gets worse — a blasted, barren wilderness that doesn't even howl. If it howled it would be a relief.

I believe that Burke and Wills found Hungerford, and it's a pity they did; but, if I ever stand by the graves of the men who first travelled through this country, when there were neither roads nor stations, nor tanks, nor bores, nor pubs, I'll — I'll take my hat off. There were brave men in the land in those days.

It is said that the explorers gave the district its name chiefly because of the hunger they found there, which has remained there ever since. I don't know where the ford comes in — there's nothing to ford, except in flood-time. Hungerthirst would have been better. The town is supposed to be situated on the banks of a river called the Paroo, but we saw no water there, except what passed for it in a tank. The goats and sheep and dogs and the rest of the population drink there. It is dangerous to take too much of that water in a raw state.

Except in flood-time you couldn't find the bed of the river without the aid of a spirit level and a long straight-edge. There is a Custom-house against the fence on the northern side. A pound of tea often costs six shillings on that side, and you can get a common lead pencil for fourpence at the rival store across the street in the mother province. Also, a small loaf of sour bread sells for a shilling at the humpy afore-mentioned. Only about sixty per cent of the sugar will melt.

We saw one of the storekeepers give a deadbeat swagman five shillings' worth of rations to take him on into Queensland. The storekeepers often do this, and put it down on the loss side of their books. I hope the recording angel listens, and puts it down on the right side of his book.

We camped on the Queensland side of the fence, and after tea had a yarn with an old man who was minding a mixed flock of goats and sheep; and we asked him whether he thought Queensland was better than New South Wales, or the other way about.

He scratched the back of his head, and thought awhile, and hesitated like a stranger who is going to do you a favour at some personal inconvenience.

At last, with the bored air of a man who has gone through the same performance too often before, he stepped deliberately up to the fence and spat over it into New South Wales. After which he got leisurely through and spat back on Queensland.

"That's what *I* think of the blanky colonies!" he said.

He gave us time to become sufficiently impressed; then he said.:

"And if I was at the Victorian and South Australian border I'd do the same thing."

He let that soak into our minds, and added: "And the same with West Australia — and — and Tasmania." Then he went away.

The last would have been a long spit — and he forgot Maoriland.

We heard afterwards that his name was Clancy, and he had that day been offered a job droving at "twenty-five shillings a week and find your own horse". Also find your own horse-feed and tobacco and soap and other luxuries, at station price. Moreover, if you lost your own horse you would have to find another, and if that died or went astray you would have to find a third — or forfeit your pay and return on foot. The boss drover agreed to provide flour and mutton — when such things were procurable.

Consequently, Clancy's decidedly unfavourable opinion of the colonies.

My mate and I sat down on our swags against the fence to

talk things over. One of us was very deaf. Presently a black
tracker went past and looked at us, and returned to the pub.
Then a trooper in Queensland uniform came along and
asked us what the trouble was about, and where we came
from and were going, and where we camped. We said we
were discussing private business, and he explained that he
thought it was a row, and came over to see. Then he left us,
and later on we saw him sitting with the rest of the
population on a bench under the hotel verandah. Next
morning we rolled up our swags and left Hungerford to the
North-West.

That There Dog O' Mine

Macquarie the shearer had met with an accident. To tell the truth, he had been in a drunken row at a wayside shanty, from which he had escaped with three fractured ribs, a cracked head, and various minor abrasions. His dog, Tally, had been a sober but savage participator in the drunken row. and had escaped with a broken leg. Macquarie afterwards shouldered his swag and staggered and struggled along the track ten miles to the Union Town Hospital. Lord knows how he did it. He didn't exactly know himself. Tally limped behind all the way, on three·legs.

The doctors examined the man's injuries and were surprised at his endurance. Even doctors are surprised sometimes — though they don't always show it. Of course they would take him in, but they objected to Tally. Dogs were not allowed on the premises.

"You will have to turn that dog out," they said to the shearer, as he sat on the edge of a bed.

Macquarie said nothing.

"We cannot allow dogs about the place, my man," said the doctor in a louder tone, thinking the man was deaf.

"Tie him up in the yard then."

"No. He must go out. Dogs are not permitted on the grounds."

Macquarie rose slowly to his feet, shut his agony behind his set teeth, painfully buttoned his shirt over his hairy chest, took up his waistcoat, and staggered to the corner where the swag lay.

"What are you going to do?" they asked.

"You ain't going to let my dog stop?"

"No. It's against the rules. There are no dogs allowed on the premises."

He stooped and lifted his swag, but the pain was too great, and he leaned back against the wall.

"Come, come now! man alive!" exclaimed the doctor, impatiently. "You must be mad. You know you are not in a fit state to go out. Let the wardsman help you to undress."

"No!" said Macquarie. "No. If you won't take my dog in you don't take me. He's got a broken leg and wants fixing up just — just as much as — as I do. If I'm good enough to come in, he's good enough — and — and better."

He paused awhile, breathing painfully, and then went on.

"That — that there old dog of mine has follered me faithful and true, these twelve long hard and hungry years. He's about — about the only thing that ever cared whether I lived or fell and rotted on the cursed track."

He rested again; then he continued: "That — that there dog was pupped on the track," he said, with a sad sort of a smile. "I carried him for months in a billy can, and afterwards on my swag when he knocked up... And the old slut — his mother — she'd foller along quite contented — and sniff the billy now and again — just to see if he was all right... She follered me for God knows how many years. She follered me till she was blind — and for a year after. She follered me till she could crawl along through the dust no longer, and — and then I killed her, because I couldn't leave her behind alive!"

He rested again.

"And this here old dog," he continued, touching Tally's upturned nose with his knotted fingers, "this here old dog has follered me for — for ten years; through floods and droughts, through fair times and — and hard — mostly hard; and kept me from going mad when I had no mate nor money on the lonely track; and watched over me for weeks when I was drunk — drugged and poisoned at the cursed shanties; and saved my iife more'n once, and got kicks and curses very often for thanks; and forgave me for it all; and — and fought for me. He was the only living thing that stood up for me against that crawling push of curs when they set onter me at the shanty back yonder — and he left his mark on some of 'em too; and — and so did I."

He took another spell.

Then he drew in his breath, shut his teeth hard, shouldered his swag, stepped into the doorway, and faced round again.

The dog limped out of the corner and looked up anxiously.

"That there dog," said Macquarie to the Hospital staff in general, "is a better dog than I'm a man — or you too, it seems — and a better Christian. He's been a better mate to me than I ever was to any man — or any man to me. He's watched over me; kep' me from getting robbed many a time; fought for me; saved my life and took drunken kicks and curses for thanks — and forgave me. He's been a true, straight, honest, and faithful mate to me — and I ain't going to desert him now. I ain't going to kick him out in the road with a broken leg. I — Oh, my God! my back!"

He groaned and lurched forward, but they caught him, slipped off the swag, and laid him on a bed.

Half and hour later the shearer was comfortably fixed up. "Where's my dog?" he asked, when he came to himself.

"Oh, the dog's all right," said the nurse, rather impatiently. "Don't bother. The doctor's setting his leg out in the yard."

Some Popular Australian Mistakes

1. An Australian mirage does not look like water; it looks too dry and dusty.

2. A plain is not necessarily a wide, open space covered with waving grass or green sward, like a prairie (the prairie isn't necessarily that way either, but that's an American mistake, not an Australian one); it is either a desert or a stretch of level country covered with wretched scrub.

3. A river is not a broad, shining stream with green banks and tall, dense eucalypti walls; it is more often a string of muddy water-holes — "a chain of dry water-holes," someone said.

4. There are no "mountains" out West; only ridges on the floors of hell.

5. There are no forests; only mongrel scrubs.

6. Australian poetical writers invariably get the coastal scenery mixed up with that of "Out Back."

7. An Australian Western homestead is not an old-fashioned, gable-ended, brick-and-shingle building with avenues and parks; and the squatter doesn't live there either. A Western station, at best, is a collection of slab and galvanized-iron sheds and humpies, and is the hottest, driest, dustiest, and most God-forsaken hole you could think of; the manager lives there — when compelled to do so.

8. The manager is not called the "super.;" he is called the "overseer" — which name fits him better.

9. Station-hands are not noble, romantic fellows; they are mostly crawlers to the boss — which they have to be. Shearers — the men of the West — despise station-hands.

10. Men tramping in search of a "shed" are not called "sundowners" or "swaggies;" they are "trav'lers."

11. A swag is not generally referred to as a "bluey" or "Matilda" — it is *called* a "swag".

12. No bushman thinks of "going on the wallaby" or "walking Matilda", or "padding the hoof"; he goes on the track — when forced to't.

13. You do not "hump bluey" — you simply "carry your swag".

14. You do not stow grub — you "have some tucker, mate".

15. (Item for our Australian artists). A traveller rarely, if ever, carries a stick; it suggests a common suburban loafer, back-yards, clothes-lines, roosting fowls, watch-dogs, blind men, sewer-pipes, and goats eating turnip-parings.

16. (For Artists). No traveller out-back carries a horse-collar swag — it's too hot; and the swag is not carried by a strap passed round the chest, but round *one* shoulder. The nose (tucker) bag hangs over the other shoulder and balances the load nicely — when there's anything in the bag.

17. It's not glorious and grand and free to be on the track. Try it.

18. A shearing-shed is not what city people picture it to be — if they imagine it at all; it is perhaps the most degrading hell on the face of this earth. Ask any better-class shearer.

19. An Australian lake is not a lake; it is either a sheet of brackish water or a patch of dry sand.

20. Least said about shanties the better.

21. The poetical bushman does not exist; the majority of the men out-back now are from the cities. The real native out-back bushman is narrow-minded, densely ignorant, invulnerably thick-headed. How could he be otherwise?

22. The blackfellow is a fraud. A white man *can* learn to throw the boomerang as well as an aborigine — even better. A blackfellow is *not* to be depended on with regard to direction, distance, or weather. A blackfellow once offered to take us to better water than that at which we were camping. He said it was only half-a-mile. We rolled up our swags and followed him and his gin five miles through the scrub to a mud-hole with a dead bullock in it. Also, he said that it would rain that night; and it didn't rain there for six months. Moreover, he threw a boomerang at a rabbit and lamed one of his dogs — of which he had about 150.

23, etc. Half the bushmen are *not* called "Bill", nor the other half "Jim". We knew a shearer whose name was Reginald! Jim doesn't tell pathetic yarns in bad doggerel in a shearer's hut — if he did, the men would tap their foreheads and wink.

In conclusion. We wish to Heaven that Australian writers would leave off trying to make a paradise out of the Out Back Hell; if only out of consideration for the poor, hopeless, half-starved wretches who carry swags through it and look in vain for work — and ask in vain for tucker very often. What's the good of making a heaven of a hell when by describing it as it really is, we might do some good for the lost souls there?

The Union Buries
Its Dead

While out boating one Sunday afternoon on a billabong across the river, we saw a young man on horseback driving some horses along the bank. He said it was a fine day, and asked if the water was deep there. The joker of our party said it was deep enough to drown him, and he laughed and rode farther up. We didn't take much notice of him.

Next day a funeral gathered at a corner pub and asked each other in to have a drink while waiting for the hearse. They passed away some of the time dancing jigs to a piano in the bar parlour. They passed away the rest of the time sky-larking and fighting.

The defunct was a young union labourer, about twenty-five, who had been drowned the previous day while trying to swim some horses across a billabong of the Darling.

He was almost a stranger in town, and the fact of his having been a union man accounted for the funeral. The police found some union papers in his swag, and called at the General Labourers' Union Office for information about him. That's how we knew. The secretary had very little information to give. The departed was a "Roman", and the majority of the town were otherwise — but unionism is stronger than creed. Drink, however, is stronger than union-ism; and, when the hearse presently arrived, more than two-thirds of the funeral were unable to follow. They were too drunk.

The procession numbered fifteen, fourteen souls following the broken shell of a soul. Perhaps not one of the fourteen possessed a soul any more than the corpse did — but that doesn't matter.

Four or five of the funeral, who were boarders at the pub borrowed a trap which the landlord used to carry passengers to and from the railway station. They were strangers to us who were on foot, and we to them. We were all strangers to the corpse.

A horseman, who looked like a drover just returned from a big trip, dropped into our dusty wake and followed us a few hundred yards, dragging his pack-horse behind him, but a friend made wild and demonstrative signals from a hotel verandah — hooking at the air in front with his right hand and jobbing his left thumb over his shoulder in the direction of the bar — so the drover hauled off and didn't catch up to us any more. He was a stranger to the entire show.

We walked in twos. There were three twos. It was very hot and dusty; the heat rushed in fierce dazzling rays across every iron roof and light-coloured wall that was turned to the sun. One or two pubs closed respectfully until we got past. They closed their bar doors and the patrons went in and out through some side or back entrance for a few minutes. Bushmen seldom grumble at an inconvenience of this sort, when it is caused by a funeral. They have too much respect for the dead.

On the way to the cemetery we passed three shearers sitting on the shady side of a fence. One was drunk — very drunk. The other two covered their right ears with their hats, out of respect for the departed — whoever he might have been — and one of them kicked the drunk and muttered something to him.

He straightened himself up, stared, and reached helplessly for his hat, which he shoved half off and then on again. Then he made a great effort to pull himself together — and succeeded. He stood up, braced his back against the fence, knocked off his hat, and remorsefully placed his foot on it — to keep it off his head till the funeral passed.

A tall, sentimental drover, who walked by my side, cynically quoted Byronic verses suitable to the occasion — to death — and asked with pathetic humour whether we thought the dead man's ticket would be recognized "over yonder". It was a G.L.U. ticket, and the general opinion was that it would be recognized.

Presently my friend said:

"You remember when we were in the boat yesterday, we saw a man driving some horses along the bank?"

"Yes."

He nodded at the hearse and said:

"Well, that's him."

I thought awhile.

"I didn't take any particular notice of him," I said. "He said something, didn't he?"

"Yes; said it was a fine day. You'd have taken more notice if you'd known that he was doomed to die in the hour, and that those were the last words he would say to any man in this world."

"To be sure," said a full voice from the rear. "If ye'd known that, ye'd have prolonged the conversation."

We plodded on across the railway line and along the hot, dusty road which ran to the cemetery, some of us talking about the accident, and lying about the narrow escapes we had had ourselves. Presently some one said:

"There's the Devil."

I looked up and saw a priest standing in the shade of the tree by the cemetery gate.

The hearse was drawn up and the tail-boards were opened. The funeral extinguished its right ear with its hat as four men lifted the coffin out and laid it over the grave. The priest — a pale, quiet young fellow — stood under the shade of a sapling which grew at the head of the grave. He took off his hat, dropped it carelessly on the ground, and proceeded to business. I noticed that one or two heathens winced slightly when the holy water was sprinkled on the coffin. The drops quickly evaporated, and the little round black spots they left were soon dusted over; but the spots showed, by contrast, the cheapness and shabbiness of the cloth with which the coffin was covered. It seemed black before; now it looked a dusky grey.

Just here man's ignorance and vanity made a farce of the funeral. A big, bull-necked publican, with heavy, blotchy features, and a supremely ignorant expression, picked up the priest's straw hat and held it about two inches over the head of his reverence during the whole of the service. The father, be it remembered, was standing in the shade. A few shoved their hats on and off uneasily, struggling between their disgust for the living and their respect for the dead. The hat had a conical crown and a brim sloping down all round like a sunshade, and the publican held it with his great red claw spread over the crown. To do the priest justice, perhaps he didn't notice the incident. A stage priest or parson in the same position might have said, "Put the hat down, my friend; is not the memory of our departed brother worth more than my complexion?" A wattlebark layman might have expressed himself in stronger language, none the less to the point. But my priest seemed unconscious of what was going on. Besides, the publican was a great and important pillar of the Church. He couldn't, as an ignorant and conceited ass, lose such a good opportunity of asserting his faithfulness and importance to his Church.

The grave looked very narrow under the coffin, and I drew a breath of relief when the box slid easily down. I saw a coffin get stuck once, at Rookwood, and it had to be yanked out with difficulty, and laid on the sods at the feet of the heartbroken relations, who howled dismally while the grave-diggers widened the hole. But they don't cut contracts so fine in the West. Our grave-digger was not altogether bowelless, and, out of respect for that human quality described as "feelin's", he scraped up some light and dusty soil and threw it down to deaden the fall of the clay lumps on the coffin. He also tried to steer the first few shovelfuls gently down against the end of the grave with the back of the shovel turned outwards, but the hard, dry Darling River clods rebounded and knocked all the same. It didn't matter much — nothing does. The fall of lumps of clay on a stranger's coffin doesn't sound any different from the fall of the same things on an ordinary wooden box — at least I didn't notice anything awesome or unusual in the sound; but, perhaps, one of us — the most sensitive — might have been impressed by being reminded of a burial of long ago, when the thump of every sod jolted his heart.

I have left out the wattle — because it wasn't there. I have also neglected to mention the heart-broken old mate, with his grizzled head bowed and great pearly drops streaming down his rugged cheeks. He was absent — he was probably "Out Back". For similar reasons I have omitted reference to the suspicious moisture in the eyes of a bearded bush ruffian named Bill. Bill failed to turn up, and the only moisture was that which was induced by the heat. I have left out the "sad Australian sunset" because the sun was not going down at the time. The burial took place exactly at mid-day.

The dead bushman's name was Jim, apparently; but they found no portraits, nor locks of hair, nor any love letters, nor anything of that kind in his swag — not even a reference to his mother; only some papers relating to union matters. Most of us didn't know the name till we saw it on the coffin; we knew him as "that poor chap that got drowned yesterday".

"So his name's James Tyson," said my drover acquaintance, looking at the plate.

"Why! Didn't you know that before?" I asked.

"No; but I knew he was a union man."

It turned out, afterwards, that J.T. wasn't his real name — only "the name he went by".

Anyhow he was buried by it, and most of the "Great Australian Dailies" have mentioned in their brevity columns that a young man named James John Tyson was drowned in a billabong of the Darling last Sunday.

We did hear, later on, what his real name was; but if we ever chance to read it in the "Missing Friends Column", we shall not be able to give any information to heart-broken Mother or Sister or Wife, nor to any one who could let him hear something to his advantage — for we have already forgotten the name.

"Rats"

"Why, there's two of them, and they're having a fight! Come on."

It seemed a strange place for a fight — that hot, lonely, cotton-bush plain. And yet not more than half-a-mile ahead there were apparently two men struggling together on the track.

The three travellers postponed their smoke-ho! and hurried on. They were shearers — a little man and a big man, known respectively as "Sunlight" and "Macquarie", and a tall, thin, young jackeroo whom they called "Milky".

"I wonder where the other man sprang from? I didn't see him before," said Sunlight.

"He muster bin layin' down in the bushes," said Macquarie. "They're goin' at it proper, too. Come on! Hurry up and see the fun!"

They hurried on.

"It's a funny-lookin' feller, the other feller," panted Milky. "He don't seem to have no head. Look! he's down — they're both down! They must ha' clinched on the ground. No! they're up an' at it again... Why, good Lord! I think the other's a woman!"

"My oath! so it is!" yelled Sunlight. "Look! the brute's got her down again! He's kickin' her! Come on, chaps; come on, or he'll do for her!"

They dropped swags, water-bags and all, and raced forward; but presently Sunlight, who had the best eyes, slackened his pace and dropped behind. His mates glanced back at his face, saw a peculiar expression there, looked ahead again, and then dropped into a walk.

They reached the scene of the trouble, and there stood a little withered old man by the track, with his arms folded close up under his chin; he was dressed mostly in calico patches; and half-a-dozen corks, suspended on bits of string from the brim of his hat, dangled before his bleared optics to scare away the flies. He was scowling malignantly at a stout, dumpy swag which lay in the middle of the track.

"Well, old Rats, what's the trouble," asked Sunlight.

"Oh, nothing, nothing," answered the old man, without looking round. "I fell out with my swag, that's all. He knocked me down, but I've settled him."

"But look here," said Sunlight, winking at his mates, "we saw you jump on him when he was down. That ain't fair, you know."

"But you didn't see it all," cried Rats, getting excited. "He hit *me* down first! And, look here, I'll fight him again for nothing, and you can see fair play."

They talked awhile; then Sunlight proposed to second the swag, while his mate supported the old man, and after some persuasion, Milky agreed, for the sake of the lark, to act as time-keeper and referee.

Rats entered into the spirit of the thing; he stripped to the waist, and while he was getting ready the travellers pretended to bet on the result.

Macquarie took his place behind the old man, and Sunlight up-ended the swag. Rats shaped and danced round; then he rushed, feinted, ducked, retreated, darted in once more, and suddenly went down like a shot on the broad of his back. No actor could have done it better; he went down from that imaginary blow as if a cannon-ball had struck him in the forehead.

Milky called time, and the old man came up, looking shaky. However, he got in a tremendous blow which knocked the swag into the bushes.

Several rounds following with varying success.

The men pretended to get more and more excited, and betted freely; and Rats did his best. At last they got tired of the fun, Sunlight let the swag lie after Milky called time, and the jackeroo awarded the fight to Rats. They pretended to hand over the stakes, and then went back for their swags, while the old man put on his shirt.

Then he calmed down, carried his swag to the side of the track, sat down on it and talked rationally about bush matters for awhile; but presently he grew silent and began to feel his muscles and smile idiotically.

"Can you len' us a bit o'meat?" said he suddenly.

They spared him half-a-pound; but he said he didn't want it all, and cut off about an ounce, which he laid on the end of his swag. Then he took the lid off his billy and produced a fishing-line. He baited the hook, threw the line across the track, and waited for a bite. Soon he got deeply interested in the line, jerked it once or twice, and drew it in rapidly. The bait had been rubbed off in the grass. The old man regarded the hook disgustedly.

"Look at that!" he cried, "I had him, only I was in such a hurry. I should ha' played him a little more."

Next time he was more careful, he drew the line in warily, grabbed an imaginary fish and laid it down on the grass. Sunlight and Co. were greatly interested by this time.

"Wot yer think o' that?" asked Rats. "It weighs thirty pound if it weighs an ounce! Wot per think o' that for a cod? The hook's half-way down his blessed gullet?"

He caught several cod and a bream while they were there, and invited them to camp and have tea with him. But they wished to reach a certain shed next day, so — after the ancient had borrowed about a pound of meat for bait — they went on, and left him fishing contentedly.

But first Sunlight went down into his pocket and came up with half-a-crown, which he gave to the old man, along with some tucker. "You'd best push on to the water before dark, old chap," he said, kindly.

When they turned their heads again, Rats was still fishing: but when they looked back for the last time before entering the timber, he was having another row with his swag; and Sunlight reckoned that the trouble arose out of some lies which the swag had been telling about the bigger fish it caught.

[And late that evening a little withered old man with no corks round his hat and with a humorous twinkle, instead of a wild glare in his eyes called at a wayside shanty, had several drinks, and entertained the chaps with a yarn about the way in which he had "had" three "blanky fellers" for some tucker and "half a caser" by pretending to be "Barmy".]¹

1. See Editor's Note to section 3.

In a Wet Season

It was raining — "general rain".

The train left Bourke, and then there began the long, long agony of scrub and wire fence, with here and there a natural clearing, which seemed even more dismal than the funereal "timber" itself. The only thing which might seem in keeping with one of these soddened flats would be the ghost of a funeral — a city funeral with plain hearse and string of cabs — going very slowly across from the scrub on one side to the scrub on the other. Sky like a wet, grey blanket; plains like dead seas, save for the tufts of coarse grass sticking up out of the water; scrub indescribably dismal — everything damp, dark, and unspeakably dreary.

Somewhere along here we saw a swagman's camp — a square of calico stretched across a horizontal stick, some rags steaming on another stick in front of a fire, and two billies to the leeward of the blaze. We knew by instinct that there was a piece of beef in the larger one. Small, hopeless-looking man standing with his back to the fire, with his hands behind him, watching the train; also, a damp, sorry-looking dingo warming itself and shivering by the fire. The rain had held up for a while. We saw two or three similar camps further on, forming a temporary suburb of Byrock.

The population was on the platform in old overcoats and damp, soft felt hats; one trooper in a waterproof. The population looked cheerfully and patiently dismal. The local push had evidently turned up to see off some fair enslavers from the city, who had been up-country for the cheque season, now over. They got into another carriage. We were glad when the bell rang.

The rain recommenced. We saw another swagman about a mile on struggling away from the town, through mud and water. He did not seem to have heart enough to bother about trying to avoid the worst mud-holes. There was a low-spirited dingo at his heels, whose sole object in life was seemingly to keep his front paws in his master's last footprint. The traveller's body was bent well forward from the hips up; his long arms — about six inches through his coat sleeves — hung by his sides like the arms of a dummy, with a billy at the end of one and a bag at the end of the other; but his head was thrown back against the top end of the swag, his hat-brim rolled up in front, and we saw a ghastly, beardless face which turned neither to the right nor the left as the train passed him.

After a long while we closed our book, and, looking through the window, saw a hawker's turn-out which was too sorrowful for description.

We looked out again while the train was going slowly, and saw a teamster's camp: three or four waggons covered with tarpaulins which hung down in the mud all round and suggested death. A long, narrow man, in a long, narrow, shoddy overcoat and a damp felt hat, was walking quickly along the road past the camp. A sort of cattle-dog glided silently and swiftly out from under a waggon, "heeled" the man, and slithered back without explaining. Here the scene vanished.

We remember stopping — for an age it seemed — at half-a-dozen straggling shanties on a flat of mud and water. There was a rotten weatherboard pub, with a low, dripping verandah, and three wretchedly forlorn horses hanging, in the rain, to a post outside. We saw no more, but we knew that there were several apologies for men hanging about the rickety bar inside — or round the parlour fire. Streams of cold, clay-coloured water ran in all directions, cutting fresh gutters, and raising a yeasty froth whenever the water fell a few inches. As we left, we saw a big man in an overcoat riding across a culvert; the tails of the coat spread over the horse's rump, and almost hid it. In fancy still we saw him — hanging up his weary, hungry, little horse in the rain, and swaggering into the bar; and we almost heard someone say, in a drawling tone: "Ello, Tom! 'Ow are yer poppin' up?"

The train stopped (for about a year) within a mile of the next station. Trucking-yards in the foreground, like any other trucking-yards along the line; they looked drearier than usual, because the rain had darkened the posts and rails. Small plain beyond, covered with water and tufts of grass. The inevitable, God-forgotten "timber", black in the distance; dull, grey sky and misty rain over all. A small, dark-looking flock of sheep was crawling slowly in across the flat from the unknown, with three men on horse-back

zig-zagging patiently behind. The horses just moved — that
was all. One man wore an oilskin, one an old tweed
overcoat, and the third had a three-bushel bag over his head
and shoulders.

Had we returned an hour later, we should have seen the
sheep huddled together in a corner of the yards, and the
three horses hanging up outside the local shanty.

We stayed at Nyngan — which place we refrain from
sketching — for a few hours, because the five trucks of cattle
of which we were in charge were shunted there, to be taken
on by a very subsequent goods train. The Government allows
one man to every five trucks in a cattle-train. We shall pay
our fare next time, even if we have not a shilling left over
and above. We had haunted local influence at Comanava-
drink, for two long, anxious, heart-breaking weeks ere we
got the pass; and we had put up with all the indignities, the
humiliation — in short, had suffered all that poor devils
suffer whilst besieging Local Influence. We only thought of
escaping from the bush.

The pass said that we were John Smith, drover, and that
we were available for return by ordinary passenger-train
within two days, we think — or words in that direction.
Which didn't interest us. We might have given the pass away
to an unemployed in Orange, who wanted to go Out Back,
and who begged for it with tears in his eyes; but we didn't
like to injure a poor fool who never injured us — who was an
entire stranger to us. He didn't know what Out Back meant.

Local Influence had given us a kind of note of introduction to be delivered to the cattle-agent at the yards that
morning; but the agent was not there — only two of his
satellites, a cockney colonial-experience man, and a scrub-
town clerk, both of whom we kindly ignore. We got on
without the note, and at Orange we amused ourself by
reading it. It said:

"Dear Old Man, — Please send this beggar on; and I hope
he'll be landed safely at Orange — or — or wherever the
cattle go. — Yours, —."

We had been led to believe that the bullocks were going to
Sydney. We took no further interest in those cattle.

After Nyngan the bush grew darker and drearier, and the
plains more like ghastly oceans; and here and there the
"dominant note of Australian scenery" was accentuated, as
it were, by naked, white, ring-barked trees standing in the
water and haunting the ghostly surroundings.

We spent that night in a passenger compartment of a van

which had been originally attached to old No. 1 engine.
There was only one damp cushion in the whole concern. We
lent that to a lady who travelled for a few hours in the other
half of the next compartment. The scats were about nine
inches wide and sloped in at a sharp angle to the bare
matchboard wall, with a bead on the outer edge; and as the
cracks had become well caulked with the grease and dirt of
generations, they held several gallons of water each. We
scuttled one, rolled ourself in a rug, and tried to sleep; but
all night long overcoated and comfortered bushmen would
get in, let down all the windows, and then get out again at
the next station. Then we would wake up frozen and shut
the windows.

We dozed off again and woke at daylight, and recognized
the ridgy gum-country between Dubbo and Orange. It
didn't look any drearier than the country further west —
because it couldn't. There is scarcely a part of the country
out west which looks less inviting or more horrible than any
other part.

The weather cleared, and we had sunlight for Orange,
Bathurst, the Blue Mountains, and Sydney. They deserve it;
also as much rain as they need.

"Dossing Out" and "Camping"

At least two hundred poor beggars were counted sleeping out on the pavements of the main streets of Sydney the other night — grotesque bundles of rags lying under the verandahs of the old Fruit Markets and York-street shops, with their heads to the wall and their feet to the gutter. It was raining and cold that night, and the unemployed had been driven in from Hyde Park and the bleak Domain — from dripping trees, damp seats, and drenched grass — from the rain, and cold, and the wind. Some had sheets of old newspapers to cover them — and some hadn't. Two were mates, and they divided a *Herald* between them. One had a sheet of brown paper, and another (lucky man!) had a bag — the only bag there. They all shrank as far into their rags as possible — and tried to sleep. The rats seemed to take them for rubbish, too, and only scampered away when one of the outcasts moved uneasily, or coughed, or groaned — or when a policeman came along.

One or two rose occasionally and rooted in the dust-boxes on the pavement outside the shops — but they didn't seem to get anything. They were feeling "peckish", no doubt, and wanted to see if they could get something to eat before the corporation carts came along. So did the rats.

Some men can't sleep very well on an empty stomach — at least, not at first; but it mostly comes with practice. They often sleep for ever in London. Not in Sydney as yet — so we say.

Now and then one of our outcasts would stretch his cramped limbs to ease them — but the cold soon made him huddle again. The pavement must have been hard on the men's "points", too; they couldn't dig holes nor make soft places for their hips, as you can in camp out back. And then, again, the stones had nasty edges and awkward slopes, for the pavements were very uneven.

The Law came along now and then, and had a careless

glance at the unemployed in bed. They didn't look like sleeping beauties. The Law appeared to regard them as so much rubbish that ought not to have been placed there, and for the presence of which somebody ought to be prosecuted by the Inspector of Nuisances. At least, that was the expression the policeman had on his face.

And so Australian workmen lay at two o'clock in the morning in the streets of Sydney, and tried to get a little sleep before the traffic came along and took their bed.

The idea of sleeping out might be nothing to bushmen, not even an idea; but "dossing out" in the city and "camping" in the bush are two very different things. In the bush you can light a fire, boil your billy, and make some tea — if you have any; also fry a chop (there are no sheep running round in the city). You can have a clean meal, take off your shirt and wash it, and wash yourself — if there's water enough — and feel fresh and clean. You can whistle and sing by the camp fire, and make poetry, and breathe fresh air, and watch the everlasting stars that keep the mateless traveller from going mad as he lies in his lonely camp on the plains. Your privacy is even more perfect than if you had a suite of rooms at the Australia; you are at the mercy of no policeman; there's no one to watch you but God — and He won't move you on. God watches the "dossers-out", too, in the city, but He doesn't keep them from being moved on or run in.

With the city unemployed the case is entirely different. The city outcast cannot light a fire and boil a billy — even if he has one — he'd be run in at once for attempting to commit arson, or create a riot, or on suspicion of being a person of unsound mind. If he took off his shirt to wash it, or went in for a swim, he'd be had up for indecently exposing his bones — and perhaps he'd get flogged. He cannot whistle or sing on his pavement bed at night, for, if he did, he'd be violently arrested by two great policemen for riotous conduct. He doesn't see many stars, and he's generally too hungry to make poetry. He only sleeps on the pavement on sufferance, and when the policeman finds the small hours hang heavily on him, he can root up the unemployed with his big foot and move him on — or arrest him for being around with the intention to commit a felony; and, when the wretched "dosser" rises in the morning, he cannot shoulder his swag and take the track — he must cadge a breakfast at some back gate or restaurant, and then sit in the park or walk round and round, the same old hopeless round, all day. There's no prison like the city for a poor man.

Nearly every man the traveller meets in the bush is about as dirty and ragged as himself, and just about as hard up; but in the city nearly every man the poor unemployed meets is a dude, or at least, well dressed, and the unemployed *feels* dirty and mean and degraded by the contrast — and despised.

And he can't help feeling like a criminal. It may be imagination, but every policeman seems to regard him with suspicion, and this is terrible to a sensitive man.

We once had the key of the street for a night. We don't know how much tobacco we smoked, how many seats we sat on, or how many miles we walked before morning. But we do know that we felt like a felon, and that every policeman seemed to regard us with a suspicious eye; and at last we began to squint furtively at every trap we met, which, perhaps, made him more suspicious, till finally we felt bad enough to be run in and to get six months' hard.

Three winters ago a man, whose name doesn't matter, had a small office near Elizabeth Street, Sydney. He was an hotel broker, debt collector, commission agent, canvasser, and so on, in a small way — a very small way — but his heart was big. He had a partner. They batched in the office, and did their cooking over a gas lamp. Now, every day the man-whose-name-doesn't-matter would carefully collect the scraps of food, add a slice or two of bread and butter, wrap it all up in a piece of newspaper, and, after dark, step out and leave the parcel on a ledge of the stonework outside the building in the street. Every morning it would be gone. A shadow came along in the night and took it. This went on for many months, till at last one night the man-whose-name-doesn't-matter forgot to put the parcel out, and didn't think of it till he was in bed. It worried him, so that at last he had to get up and put the scraps outside. It was midnight. He felt curious to see the shadow, so he waited until it came along. It wasn't his long-lost brother, but it was an old mate of his.

Let us finish with a sketch: —

The scene was Circular Quay, outside the Messageries sheds. The usual number of bundles of misery — covered more or less with dirty sheets of newspaper — lay along the wall under the ghastly glare of the electric light. Time — shortly after midnight. From among the bundles an old man sat up. He cautiously drew off his pants, and then stood close to the wall, in his shirt, tenderly examining the seat of the trousers. Presently he shook them out, folded them with great care, wrapped them in a scrap of newspaper, and laid them down where his head was to be. He had thin, hairy legs and a long grey beard. From a bundle of rags he extracted another pair of pants, which were all patches and tatters, and into which he engineered his way with great caution. Then he sat down, arranged the paper over his knees, laid his old ragged grey head back on his precious Sunday-go-meetings — and slept.

AUSTRALIAN BARDS AND BUSH REVIEWERS

While you use your best endeavour to immortalize in verse
The gambling and the drink which are your country's
    greatest curse,
While you glorify the bully and take the spieler's part—
You're a clever southern writer, scarce inferior to Bret Harte.

If you sing of waving grasses when the plains are dry as
    bricks,
And discover shining rivers where there's only mud and sticks;
If you picture "mighty forests" where the mulga spoils the
    view—
You're superior to Kendall, and ahead of Gordon too.

If you swear there's not a country like the land that gave
    you birth,
And its sons are just the noblest and most glorious chaps on
    earth;
If in every girl a Venus your poetic eye discerns,
You are gracefully referred to as the "young Australian
    Burns".

But if you should find that bushmen — spite of all the poets
    say—
Are just common brother-sinners, and you're quite as good as
    they—
You're a drunkard, and a liar, and a cynic, and a sneak,
Your grammar's simply awful and your intellect is weak.

Stiffner and Jim
(Thirdly, Bill)

We were tramping down in Canterbury, Maoriland, at the time, swagging it — me and Bill — looking for work on the new railway line. Well, one afternoon, after a long, hot tramp, we comes to Stiffner's Hotel — between Christchurch and that other place — I forget the name of it — with throats on us like sun-struck bones, and not the price of a stick of tobacco.

We had to have a drink, anyway, so we chanced it. We walked right into the bar, handed over our swags, put up four drinks, and tried to look as if we'd just drawn our cheques and didn't care a curse for any man. We looked solvent enough, as far as swagmen go. We were dirty and haggard and ragged and tired-looking, and that was all the more reason why we might have our cheques all right.

This Stiffner was a hard customer. He'd been a spieler, fighting man, bush parson, temperance preacher, and a policeman, and a commercial traveller, and everything else that was damnable; he'd been a journalist, and an editor; he'd been a lawyer, too. He was an ugly brute to look at, and uglier to have a row with — about six-foot-six, wide in proportion, and stronger than Donald Dinnie.

He was meaner than a gold-field Chinaman, and sharper than a sewer rat: he wouldn't give his own father a feed, nor lend him a sprat — unless some safe person backed the old man's IOU.

We knew that we needn't expect any mercy from Stiffner; but something had to be done, so I said to Bill:

"Something's got to be done, Bill! What do you think of it?"

Bill was mostly a quiet young chap, from Sydney, except when he got drunk — which was seldom — and then he was a lively customer from all round. He was cracked on the subject of spielers. He held that the population of the world was divided into two classes — one was spielers and the other was mugs. He reckoned that he wasn't a mug. At first I thought that he was a mug. He used to say that a man had to do it these times; that he was honest once and a fool, and was robbed and starved in consequence by his friends and relations; but now he intended to take all that he could get. He said that you either had to have or be had; that men were driven to be sharps, and there was no help for it.

Bill said:

"We'll have to sharpen our teeth, that's all, and chew somebody's lug."

"How?" I asked.

There was a lot of navvies at the pub, and I knew one or two by sight, so Bill says:

"You know one or two of these mugs. Bite one of their ears."

So I took aside a chap that I knowed and bit his ear for ten bob, and gave it to Bill to mind, for I thought it would be safer with him than with me.

"Hang on to that," I says, "and don't lose it for your natural life's sake, or Stiffner'll stiffen us."

We put up about nine bob's worth of drinks that night — me and Bill — and Stiffner didn't squeal: he was too sharp. He shouted once or twice.

By-and-by I left Bill and turned in, and in the morning when I woke up there was Bill sitting alongside of me, and looking about as lively as the fighting kangaroo in London in fog time. He had a black eye and eighteen-pence. He'd been taking down some of the mugs.

"Well, what's to be done now?" I asked. "Stiffner can smash us both with one hand, and if we don't pay up he'll pound our swags and cripple us. He's just the man to do it. He loves a fight even more than he hates being had."

"There's only one thing to be done, Jim," says Bill, in a tired, disinterested tone that made me mad.

"Well, what's that?" I said.

"Smoke!"

"Smoke be damned," I snarled, losing my temper. "You know dashed well that our swags are in the bar, and we can't smoke without them."

"Well, then," says Bill, "I'll toss you to see who's to face the landlord."

"Well, I'll be blessed!" I says. "I'll see you further first. You have got a front. You mugged that stuff away, and you'll have to get us out of the mess."

It made him wild to be called a mug, and we swore and growled at each other for a while; but we daren't speak loud enough to have a fight, so at last I agreed to toss up for it, and I lost.

Bill started to give me some of his points, but I shut him up quick.

"You've had your turn, and made a mess of it," I said. "For God's sake give me a show. Now, I'll go into the bar and ask for the swags, and carry them out on to the verandah and then go back to settle up. You keep him talking all the time. You dump the two swags together, and smoke like sheol. That's all you've got to do."

I went into the bar, got the swags from the missus, carried them out on to the verandah, and then went back.

Stiffner came in.

"Good morning!"

"Good morning, sir," says Stiffner.

"It'll be a nice day, I think?"

"Yes, I think so. I suppose you are going on?"

"Yes, we'll have to make a move today." Then I hooked carelessly on to the counter with one elbow, and looked dreamy-like out across the clearing, and presently I gave a sort of sigh and said: "Ah, well! I think I'll have a beer."

"Right you are! Where's your mate?"

"Oh, he's round at the back. He'll be round directly; but ain't drinking this morning."

Stiffner laughed that nasty empty laugh of his. He thought Bill was whipping the cat.

"What's yours, boss?" I said.

"Thankee! . . . Here's luck!"

"Here's luck!"

The country was pretty open round there — the nearest timber was better than a mile away, and I wanted to give Bill a good start across the flat before the go-as-you-can commenced; so I talked for a while, and while we were talking I thought I might as well go the whole hog — I might as well die for a pound as a penny, if I had to die; and if I hadn't I'd have the pound to the good, anyway, so to speak. Anyhow, the risk would be about the same, or less, for I might have the spirit to run harder the more I had to run for — the more spirits I had to run for, in fact, as it turned out — so I says:

"I think I'll take one of them there flasks of whisky to last us on the road."

"Right y'are," says Stiffner. "What'll yer have — a small one or a big one?"

"Oh, a big one, I think — if I can get it into my pocket."

"It'll be a tight squeeze" he said, and he laughed.

"I'll try," I said. "Bet you two drinks I'll get it in."

"Done!" he says. "The top inside coat pocket, and no tearing."

It was a big bottle, and all my pockets were small; but I got it into the pocket he'd betted against. It was a tight squeeze, but I got it in.

Then we both laughed, but his laugh was nastier than usual, because it was meant to be pleasant, and he'd lost two drinks; and my laugh wasn't easy — I was anxious as to which of us would laugh next.

Just then I noticed something, and an idea struck me — about the most up-to-date idea that ever struck me in my life. I noticed that Stiffner was limping on his right foot this morning, so I said to him:

"What's up with your foot?" putting my hand in my pocket.

"Oh, it's a crimson nail in my boot," he said. "I thought I got the blanky thing out this morning; but I didn't."

There just happened to be an old bag of shoemaker's tools in the bar, belonging to an old cobbler who was lying dead drunk on the verandah. So I said, taking my hand out of my pocket again:

"Lend us the boot, and I'll fix it in a minute. That's my old trade."

"Oh, so you're a shoemaker," he said. "I'd never have thought it."

He laughs one of his useless laughs that wasn't wanted, and slips off the boot — he hadn't laced it up — and hands it across the bar to me. It was an ugly brute — a great thick, iron-bound, boiler-plated navvy's boot. It made me feel sore when I looked at it.

I got the bag and pretended to fix the nail; but I didn't.

"There's a couple of nails gone from the sole," I said. "I'll put 'em in if I can find any hobnails, and it'll save the sole," and I rooted in the bag and found a good long nail, and shoved it right through the sole on the sly. He'd been a bit of a sprinter in his time, and I thought it might be better for me in the near future if the spikes of his running-shoes were inside.

"There, you'll find that better, I fancy," I said, standing the boot on the bar counter, but keeping my hand on it in an absent-minded kind of way. Presently I yawned and stretched myself, and said in a careless way:

"Ah, well! How's the slate?"

He scratched the back of his head and pretended to think.

"Oh, well, we'll call it thirty bob."

Perhaps he thought I'd slap down two quid.

"Well," I says, "and what will you do supposing we don't pay you?"

He looked blank for a moment. then he fired up and gasped and choked once or twice; and then he cooled down suddenly and laughed his nastiest laugh — he was one of those men who always laugh when they're wild — and said in a nasty, quiet tone:

"You thundering, jumped-up crawlers! If you don't (something) well part up I'll take your swags and (something) well kick your gory pants so you won't be able to sit down for a month — or stand up either!"

"Well, the sooner you begin the better," I said; and I chucked the boot into a corner and bolted.

He jumped the bar counter, got his boot, and came after me. He paused to slip the boot on — but he only made one step, and then gave a howl and slung the boot off and rushed back. When I looked round again he'd got a slipper on, and was coming — and gaining on me, too. I shifted scenery pretty quick the next five minutes. But I was soon pumped. My heart began to beat against the ceiling of my head, and my lungs all choked up in my throat. When I guessed he was getting within kicking distance I glanced round so's to dodge the kick. He let out; but I shied just in time. He missed fire, and the slipper went about twenty feet up in the air and fell in a waterhole.

He was done then, for the ground was stubbly and stony. I seen Bill on ahead pegging out for the horizon, and I took after him and reached for the timber for all I was worth, for I'd seen Stiffner's missus coming with a shovel — to bury the remains, I suppose; and those two were a good match — Stiffner and his missus, I mean.

Bill looked round once, and melted into the bush pretty soon after that. When I caught up he was about done; but I grabbed my swag and we pushed on, for I told Bill that I'd seen Stiffner making for the stables when I'd last looked round; and Bill thought that we'd better get lost in the bush as soon as ever we could, and stay lost, too, for Stiffner was a man that couldn't stand being had.

The first thing that Bill said when we got safe into camp was: "I told you that we'd pull through all right. You need never be frightened when you're travelling with me. Just take my advice and leave things to me, and we'll hang out all right. Now —"

But I shut him up. He made me mad.

"Why, you —! What the sheol did *you* do?"

"Do?" he says. "I got away with the swags, didn't I? Where'd they be now if it wasn't for me?"

Then I sat on him pretty hard for his pretensions, and paid him out for all the patronage he'd worked off on me, and called him a mug straight, and walked round him, so to speak, and blowed, and told him never to pretend to me again that he was a battler.

Then, when I thought I'd licked him into form, I cooled down and soaped him up a bit; but I never thought that he had three climaxes and a crisis in store for me.

He took it all pretty cool; he let me have my fling, and gave me time to get breath; then he leaned languidly over on his right side, shoved his left hand down into his left trouser pocket, and brought up a boot-lace, a box of matches, and nine-and-six.

As soon as I got the focus of it I gasped:

"Where the deuce did you get that?"

"I had it all along," he said, "but I seen at the pub that you had the show to chew a lug, so I thought we'd save it — nine-and-sixpences ain't picked up every day."

Then he leaned over on his left, went down into the other pocket, and came up with a piece of tobacco and half-a-sovereign. My eyes bulged out.

"Where the blazes did you get that from?" I yelled.

"That," he said, "was the half-quid you give me last night. Half-quids ain't to be thrown away these times; and, besides, I had a down on Stiffner, and meant to pay him out; I reckoned that if we wasn't sharp enough to take him down we hadn't any business to be supposed to be alive. Anyway I guessed we'd do it; and so we did — and got a bottle of whisky into the bargain."

Then he leaned back, tired-like, against the log, and dredged his upper left-hand waistcoat pocket, and brought up a sovereign wrapped in a pound-note. Then he waited for me to speak; but I couldn't. I got my mouth open, but couldn't get it shut again.

"I got that out of the mugs last night, but I thought that we'd want it, and might as well keep it. Quids ain't so easily picked up nowadays; and, besides, we need stuff mor'n Stiffner does, and so —"

"And did he know you had the stuff?" I gasped.

"Oh yes, that's the fun of it. That's what made him so excited. He was in the parlour all the time I was playing. But we might as well have a drink!"

We did. I wanted it.

Bill turned in by-and-by, and looked like a sleeping innocent in the moonlight. I sat up late, and smoked, and thought hard, and watched Bill, and turned in, and thought till near daylight, and then went to sleep, and had a nightmare about it. I dreamed I chased Stiffner forty miles to buy his pub, and that Bill turned out to be his nephew.

Bill divvied up all right, and gave me half-a-crown over, but I didn't travel with him long after that. He was a decent young fellow as far as chaps go, and a good mate as far as mates go; but he was too far ahead for a peaceful, easy-going chap like me. It would have worn me out in a year to keep up to him.

Preface to
Short Stories in Prose and Verse

This is an attempt to publish, in Australia, a collection of sketches and stories at a time when everything Australian, in the shape of a book, must bear the imprint of a London publishing firm before our critics will condescend to notice it, and before the "reading public" will think it worth its while to buy nearly so many copies as will pay for the mere cost of printing a presentable volume.

The Australian writer, until he gets a "London hearing", is only accepted as an imitator of some recognized English or American author; and, so soon as he shows signs of coming to the front, he is labelled "The Australian Southey", "The Australian Burns", or "The Australian Bret Harte", and, lately, "The Australian Kipling". Thus, no matter how original he may be, he is branded, at the very start, as a plagiarist, and by his own country, which thinks, no doubt, that it is paying him a compliment and encouraging him, while it is really doing him a cruel and an almost irreparable injury.

But, mark! So soon as the Southern writer goes "home" and gets some recognition in England, he is "So-and-So, the well-known Australian author whose work has attracted so much attention in London lately"; and we first hear of him by cable, even though he might have been writing at his best for ten years in Australia.

The same paltry spirit tried to dispose of the greatest of modern short story writers as "The Californian Dickens", but America wasn't built that way — neither was Bret Harte!

"To illustrate the above growl: a Sydney daily paper, reviewing the *Bulletin's Golden Shanty* when the first edition came out, said of my story, "His Father's Mate", that it stood out distinctly as an excellent specimen of that kind of writing which Bret Harte set the world imitating in vain, and, being "full of local colour, it was no unworthy copy of the great master." That critic evidently hadn't studied the "great master" any more than he did my yarn, or Australian goldfield life.

Then he spoke of another story as also having the "Californian flavour". For the other writers I can say that I feel sure they could point out their scenery, and name, or, in some cases, introduce "the reader" to their characters in the flesh. The first seventeen years of my life was spent on the goldfields, and, therefore, I didn't need to go back, in imagination, to a time before I was born, and to a country I had never seen, for literary material.

This pamphlet — I can scarcely call it a volume — contains some of my earliest efforts, and they are sufficiently crude and faulty. They have been collected and printed hurriedly, with an eye to Xmas, and without experienced editorial assistance, which last, I begin to think, was sadly necessary.

However, we all hope to do better in future, and I shall have more confidence in my first volume of verse, which will probably be published some time next year. The stories and sketches were originally written for the *Bulletin*, *Worker*, *Truth*, *Antipodean Magazine*, and the Brisbane *Boomerang*, which last was one of the many Australian publications which were starved to death because they tried to be original, to be honest, to pay for and encourage Australian literature, and, above all, to be Australian, while the "high average intelligence of the Australians" preferred to patronize thievish imported rags of the "Faked-Bits" order.

SECTION 4
1894-99

Editor's Note

The work in this section shows Lawson consolidating his reputation in fiction and verse from the publication of his first book until his departure for London. In 1896 Lawson married, went to Perth and in the following year to New Zealand where he was the teacher at a Native School. He returned to Australia early in 1898. In 1900 with his wife and two children he left for London.

The sources for the texts here are: *While the Billy Boils* ("Remailed", "Going Blind", "The Geological Spieler"); *On the Track* ("Mr. Smellingscheck", "An Oversight of Steelman's", "The Iron Bark Chip"); *Over the Sliprails* ("They Wait on the Wharf in Black"); *In the Days When the World Was Wide* ("The Star of Australasia", "Past Carin'"); *Verses Popular and Humorous* ("Reedy River", "But What's the Use", "The Uncultured Rhymer", "Second Class Wait Here"); the *Bulletin*, 1899 ("'Pursuing Literature' in Australia" and "Crime in the Bush") and Colin Roderick's edition of the *Letters* for those to Robertson and Beauchamp.

Remailed

There is an old custom prevalent in Australasia — and other parts, too, perhaps, for that matter — which, we think, deserves to be written up. It might not be an "honoured" custom from a newspaper manager's or proprietor's point of view, or from the point of view (if any) occupied by the shareholders on the subject; but, nevertheless, it is a time-honoured and a good old custom. Perhaps, for several reasons, it was more prevalent amongst diggers than with the comparatively settled bushmen of today — the poor, hopeless, wandering swaggy doesn't count in the matter, for he has neither the wherewithal nor the opportunity to honour the old custom; also his movements are too sadly uncertain to permit of his being honoured by it. We refer to the remailing of newspapers and journals from one mate to another.

Bill gets his paper and reads it through conscientiously from beginning to end by candle or slush-lamp as he lies on his back in the hut or tent with his pipe in his mouth; or, better still, on a Sunday afternoon as he reclines on the grass in the shade, in all the glory and comfort of a clean pair of moleskins and socks and a clean shirt. And when he has finished reading the paper — if it is not immediately bespoke — he turns it right side out, folds it, and puts it away where he'll know where to find it. The paper is generally bespoke in the following manner:

"Let's have a look at that paper after you, Bill, when yer done with it," says Jack.

And Bill says:

"I just promised it to Bob. You can get it after him."

And, when it is finally lent, Bill says:

"Don't forget to give that paper back to me when yer done with it. Don't let any of those other blanks get holt of it, or the chances are I won't set eyes on it again."

But the other blanks get it in their turn after being referred to Bill. "You must ask Bill," says Jack to the next blank, "I got it from him." And when Bill gets his paper back finally — which is often only after much bush grumbling, accusation, recrimination, and denial — he severely and carefully re-arranges the pages, folds the paper, and sticks it away up over a rafter, or behind a post or batten, or under his pillow where it will be safe. He wants that paper to send to Jim.

Bill is but an indifferent hand at folding, and knows little or nothing about wrappers. He folds and re-folds the paper several times and in various ways, but the first result is often the best, and is finally adopted. The parcel looks more ugly than neat; but Bill puts a weight upon it so that it won't fly open, and looks round for a piece of string to tie it with. Sometimes he ties it firmly round the middle, sometimes at both ends; at other times he runs the string down inside the folds and ties it that way, or both ways, or all the ways, so as to be sure it won't come undone — which it doesn't as a rule. If he can't find a piece of string long enough, he ties two bits together, and submits the result to a rather severe test; and if the string is too thin, or he has to use thread, he doubles it. Then he worries round to find out who has got the ink, or whether anyone has seen anything of the pen; and when he gets them, he writes the address with painful exactitude on the margin of the paper, sometimes in two or three places. He has to think a moment before he writes; and perhaps he'll scratch the back of his head afterwards with an inky finger, and regard the address with a sort of mild, passive surprise. His old mate Jim was always plain Jim to him, and nothing else; but, in order to reach Jim, this paper has to be addressed to —

> MR. JAMES MITCHELL,
> c/o J.W. Dowell, Esq.,
> Munnigrubb Station.

and so on. "Mitchell" seems strange — Bill couldn't think of it for the moment — and so does "James".

And, a week or so later, over on Coolgardie, or away up in Northern Queensland, or bush-felling down in Maoriland, Jim takes a stroll up to the post office after tea on mail night. He doesn't expect any letters, but there might be a paper from Bill. Bill generally sends him a newspaper. They seldom write to each other, these old mates.

There were points, of course, upon which Bill and Jim

couldn't agree — subjects upon which they argued long and loud and often in the old days; and it sometimes happens that Bill comes across an article or a paragraph which agrees with and, so to speak, barracks for a pet theory of his as against one held by Jim; and Bill marks it with a chuckle and four crosses at the corners — and an extra one at each side perhaps — and sends it on to Jim; he reckons it'll rather corner old Jim. The crosses are not over ornamental nor artistic, but very distinct; Jim sees them from the reverse side of the sheet first, maybe, and turns it over with interest to see what it is. He grins a good-humoured grin as he reads — poor old Bill is just as thick-headed and obstinate as ever — just as far gone on his old fad. It's rather rough on Jim, because he's too far off to argue; but, if he's very earnest on the subject, he'll sit down and write, using all his old arguments to prove that the man who wrote that rot was a fool. This is one of the few things which will make them write to each other. Or else Jim will wait till he comes across a paragraph in another paper which barracks for his side of the argument, and, in his opinion, rather knocks the stuffing out of Bill's man; then he marks it with more and bigger crosses and a grin, and sends it along to Bill. They are both democrats — these old mates generally are — and at times one comes across a stirring article or poem, and marks it with approval and sends it along. Or it may be a good joke, or the notice of the death of an old mate. What a wave of feeling and memories a little par can take through the land!

Jim is a sinner and a scoffer, and Bill is an earnest, thorough, respectable old freethinker, and consequently they often get a War Cry or a tract sent inside their exchange — somebody puts it in for a joke.

Long years agone — long years agone Bill and Jim were "sweet" on a rose of the bush — or a lily of the goldfields — call her Lily King. Bill and Jim both courted her at the same time, and quarrelled over her — fought over her, perhaps — and were parted by her for years. But that's all bygones. Perhaps she loved Bill, perhaps she loved Jim — perhaps both; or, maybe, she wasn't sure which. Perhaps she loved neither, and was only "stringing them on". Anyway, she didn't marry either the one or the other. She married another man — call him Jim Smith. And so, in after years, Bill comes across a paragraph in a local paper, something like the following: —

> On July 10th, at her residence, Eureka Cottage, Ballarat-street, Tally Town, the wife of James Smith of twins (boy and girl); all three doing well.

And Bill marks it with a loud chuckle and big crosses, and sends it along to Jim. Then Bill sits and thinks and smokes, and thinks till the fire goes out, and quite forgets all about putting that necessary patch on his pants.

And away down on Auckland gumfields, perhaps, Jim reads the par with a grin; then grows serious, and sits and scrapes his gum by the flickering firelight in a mechanical manner, and — thinks. His thoughts are far away in the back years — faint and far, far and faint. For the old, lingering, banished pain returns, and hurts a man's heart like the false wife who comes back again, falls on her knees before him, and holds up her trembling arms and pleads with swimming, upturned eyes, which are eloquent with the love she felt too late.

It is supposed to be something to have your work published in an English magazine, to have it published in book form, to be flattered by critics and reprinted throughout the country press, or even to be cut up well and severely. But, after all, now we come to think of it, we would almost as soon see a piece of ours marked with big inky crosses in the soiled and crumbled rag that Bill or Jim gets sent him by an old mate of his — the paper that goes thousands of miles scrawled all over with smudgy addresses and tied with a piece of string.

Going Blind

I met him in the Full-and-Plenty Dining Rooms. It was a cheap place in the city, with good beds upstairs let at one shilling per night — "Board and residence for respectable single men, fifteen shillings per week." I was a respectable single man then. I boarded and resided there. I boarded at a greasy little table in the greasy little corner under the fluffy little staircase in the hot and greasy little dining-room or restaurant down stairs. They called it dining-rooms, but it was only one room, and there wasn't half enough room in it to work your elbows when the seven little tables and forty-nine chairs were occupied. There was not room for an ordinary-sized steward to pass up and down between the tables; but our waiter was not an ordinary-sized man — he was a living skeleton in miniature. We handed the soup, and the "roast beef one", and "roast lamb one", "corn beef and cabbage one", "veal and stuffing one", and the "veal and pickled pork", one — or two, or three, as the cast might be — and the tea and coffee, and the various kinds of puddings — we handed them over each other, and dodged the drops as well as we could. The very hot and very greasy little kitchen was adjacent, and it contained the bathroom and other conveniences, behind screens of whitewashed boards.

I resided upstairs in a room where there were five beds and one wash-stand; one candle-stick, with a very short bit of soft yellow candle in it; the back of a hair-brush, with about a dozen bristles in it; and half a comb — the big-tooth end — with nine and a half teeth at irregular distances apart.

He was a typical bushman, not one of those tall, straight, wiry, brown men of the West, but from the old Selection Districts, where many drovers came from, and of the old bush school; one of those slight active little fellows whom we used to see in cabbage-tree hats, Crimean shirts, strapped trousers, and elastic-side boots — "larstins", they called them. They could dance well; sing indifferently, and mostly through their noses, the old bush songs; play the concertina horribly; and ride like — like — well, they *could* ride.

He seemed as if he had forgotten to grow old and die out with this old colonial school to which he belonged. They *had* careless and forgetful ways about them. His name was Jack Gunther, he said, and he'd come to Sydney to try to get something done to his eyes. He had a portmanteau, a carpet bag, some things in a three-bushel bag, and a tin box. I sat besides him on his bed, and struck up an acquaintance, and he told me all about it. First he asked me would I mind shifting round to the other side, as he was rather deaf in that ear. He'd been kicked on the side of the head by a horse, he said, and had been a little dull o'hearing on that side ever since.

He was as good as blind. "I can see the people near me," he said, "but I can't make out their faces. I can just make out the pavement and the houses close at hand, and all the rest is a sort of white blur." He looked up: "That ceiling is a kind of white, ain't it? And this," tapping the wall and putting his nose close to it, "is a sort of green, ain't it?" The ceiling might have been whiter. The prevalent tints of the wall-paper had originally been blue and red, but it was mostly green enough now — a damp, rotten green; but I was ready to swear that the ceiling was snow and that the walls were as green as grass if it would have made him feel more comfortable. His sight began to get bad about six years before, he said; he didn't take much notice of it at first, and then he saw a quack, who made his eyes worse. He had already the manner of the blind — the touch in every finger, and even the gentleness in his speech. He had a boy down with him — a "sorter cousin of his", and the boy saw him round. "I'll have to be sending that youngster back," he said, "I think I'll send him home next week. He'll be picking up and learning too much down here."

I happened to know the district he came from, and we would sit by the hour and talk about the country, and chaps by the name of this and chaps by the name of that — drovers mostly, whom we had met or had heard of. He asked me if I'd ever heard of a chap by the name of Joe Scott — a big sandy-complexioned chap, who might be droving; he was his brother, or, at least, his half-brother, but he hadn't heard of him for years; he'd last heard of him at Blackall, in Queensland; he might have gone overland to Western Australia with Tyson's cattle to the new country.

We talked about grubbing and fencing and digging and droving and shearing — all about the bush — and it all came back to me as we talked. "I can see it all now," he said once, in an abstracted tone, seeming to fix his helpless eyes on the wall opposite. But he didn't see the dirty blind wall, nor the dingy window, nor the skimpy little bed, nor the greasy washstand: he saw the dark blue ridges in the sunlight, the grassy sidings and flats, the creek with clumps of sheoak here and there, the course of the willow-fringed river below, the distant peaks and ranges fading away into a lighter azure, the granite ridge in the middle distance, and the rocky rises, the stringy-bark and the apple-tree flats, the scrubs, and the sunlit plains — and all. I could see it, too — plainer than ever I did.

He had done a bit of fencing in his time, and we got talking about timber. He didn't believe in having fencing-posts with big butts; he reckoned it was a mistake. "You see," he said, "the top of the butt catches the rain water and makes the post rot quicker. I'd back posts without any butt at all to last as long or longer than posts with 'em — that's if the fence is well put up and well rammed." He had supplied fencing stuff, and fenced by contract, and — well, you can get more posts without butts out of a tree than posts with them. He also objected to charring the butts. He said it only made more work, and wasted time — the butts lasted longer without being charred.

I asked him if he'd ever got stringy-bark palings or shingles out of mountain ash, and he smiled a smile that did my heart good to see, and said he had. He had also got them out of various other kinds of trees.

We talked about soil and grass, and gold-digging, and many other things which came back to one like a revelation as we yarned.

He had been to the hospital several times. "The doctors don't say they can cure me," he said, "they say they might be able to improve my sight and hearing, but it would take a long time — anyway, the treatment would improve my general health. They know what's the matter with my eyes," and he explained it as well as he could. "I wish I'd seen a good doctor when my eyes first began to get weak; but young chaps are always careless over things. It's harder to get cured of anything when you're done growing."

He was always hopeful and cheerful. "If the worst comes to the worst," he said, "there's things I can do where I come from. I might do a bit o' wool-sorting, for instance. I'm a pretty fair expert. Or else when they're weeding out I could help. I'd just have to sit down and they'd bring the sheep to me, and I'd feel the wool and tell them what it was — being blind improves the feeling, you know."

He had a packet of portraits, but he couldn't make them out very well now. They were sort of blurred to him, but I described them and he told me who they were. "That's a girl o' mine," he said, with reference to one — a jolly, good-looking bush girl. "I got a letter from her yesterday. I managed to scribble something, but I'll get you, if you don't mind, to write something more I want to put in on another piece of paper, and address an envelope for me."

Darkness fell quickly upon him now — or, rather, the "sort of white blur" increased and closed in. But his hearing was better, he said, and he was glad of that and still cheerful. I thought it natural that his hearing should improve as he went blind.

One day he said that he did not think he would bother going to the hospital any more. He reckoned he'd get back to where he was known. He'd stayed down too long already, and the "stuff" wouldn't stand it. He was expecting a letter that didn't come. I was away for a couple of days, and when I came back he had been shifted out of the room and had a bed in an angle of the landing on top of the staircase, with the people brushing against him and stumbling over his things all day on their way up and down. I felt indignant, thinking that — the house being full — the boss had taken advantage of the bushman's helplessness and good nature to put him there. But he said that he was quite comfortable. "I can get a whiff of air here," he said.

Going in next day I thought for a moment that I had dropped suddenly back into the past and into a bush dance, for there was a concertina going upstairs. He was sitting on the bed, with his legs crossed, and a new cheap concertina on his knee, and his eyes turned to the patch of ceiling as if it were a piece of music and he could read it. "I'm trying to knock a few tunes into my head," he said, with a brave smile, "in case the worst comes to the worst." He tried to be cheerful, but seemed worried and anxious. The letter hadn't come. I thought of the many blind musicians in Sydney, and I thought of the bushman's chance, standing at a corner swanking a cheap concertina, and I felt very sorry for him.

I went out with a vague idea of seeing someone about the matter, and getting something done for the bushman — of

bringing a little influence to his assistance; but I suddenly
remembered that my clothes were worn out, my hat in a
shocking state, my boots burst, and that I owed for a week's
board and lodging, and was likely to be thrown out at any
moment myself; and so I was not in a position to go where
there was influence.

When I went back to the restaurant there was a long,
gaunt, sandy-complexioned bushman sitting by Jack's side.
Jack introduced him as his brother, who had returned
unexpectedly to his native district, and had followed him to
Sydney. The brother was rather short with me at first, and
seemed to regard the restaurant people — all of us, in fact
— in the light of spielers, who wouldn't hesitate to take
advantage of Jack's blindness if he left him a moment; and
he looked ready to knock down the first man who stumbled
against Jack, or over his luggage — but that soon wore off.
Jack was going to stay with Joe at the Coffee Palace for a few
weeks, and then go back up country, he told me. He was
excited and happy. His brother's manner towards him was as
if Jack had just lost his wife, or boy, or someone very dear to
him. He would not allow him to do anything for himself, nor
try to — not even lace up his boots. He seemed to think that
he was thoroughly helpless, and when I saw him pack up
Jack's things, and help him at the table, and fix his tie and
collar with his great brown hands, which trembled all the
time with grief and gentleness, and make Jack sit down on
the bed whilst he got a cab and carried the traps down to it,
and take him downstairs as if he were made of thin glass,
and settle with the landlord — then I knew that Jack was all
right.

We had a drink together — Joe, Jack, the cabman, and I.
Joe was very careful to hand Jack the glass, and Jack made a
joke about it for Joe's benefit. He swore he could see a glass
yet, and Joe laughed, but looked extra troubled the next
moment.

I felt their grips on my hand for five minutes after we
parted.

The Geological Spieler

> There's nothinig so interesting as Geology, even to common and ignorant people, especially when you have a bank or the side of a cutting, studded with fossil fish and things and oysters that were stale when Adam was fresh to illustrate by. (*Remark made by Steelman, professional wanderer, to his pal and pupil, Smith.*)

The first man that Steelman and Smith came up to on the last embankment, where they struck the new railway line, was a heavy, gloomy, labouring man with bow-yangs on and straps round his wrists. Steelman bade him the time of day and had a few words with him over the weather. The man of mullick gave it as his opinion that the fine weather wouldn't last, and seemed to take a gloomy kind of pleasure in that reflection; he said there was more rain down yonder, pointing to the south-east, than the moon could swallow up — the moon was in its first quarter, during which time it is popularly believed in some parts of Maoriland that the south-easter is most likely to be out on the wallaby and the weather bad. Steelman regarded that quarter of the sky with an expression of gentle remonstrance mingled as it were with a sort of fatherly indulgence, agreed mildly with the labouring man, and seemed lost for a moment in a reverie from which he roused himself to enquire cautiously after the boss. There was no boss, it was a co-operative party. That chap standing over there by the dray in the end of the cutting was their spokesman — their representative: they called him Boss, but that was only his nickname in camp. Steelman expressed his thanks and moved on towards the cutting, followed respectfully by Smith.

Steelman wore a snuff-coloured sac suit, a wide-awake hat, a pair of professional-looking spectacles, and a scientific expression; there was a clerical atmosphere about him, strengthened however by an air as of unconscious dignity and superiority, born of intellect and knowledge. He carried a black bag, which was an indispensable article in his profession in more senses than one. Smith was decently dressed in sober tweed and looked like a man of no account, who was mechanically devoted to his employer's interests, pleasures, or whims, whatever they may have been.

The boss was a decent-looking young fellow with a good face — rather solemn — and a quiet manner.

"Good day, sir," said Steelman.

"Good day, sir," said the Boss.

"Nice weather this."

"Yes, it is, but I'm afraid it won't last."

"I am afraid it will not by the look of the sky down there," ventured Steelman.

"No, I go mostly by the look of our weather prophet," said the Boss with a quiet smile, indicating the gloomy man.

"I suppose bad weather would put you back in your work?"

"Yes, it will; we didn't want any bad weather just now."

Steelman got the weather question satisfactorily settled; then he said:

"You seem to be getting on with the railway."

"Oh, yes, we are about over the worst of it."

"The worst of it?" echoed Steelman, with mild surprise: "I should have thought you were just coming into it" and he pointed to the ridge ahead.

"Oh, our section doesn't go any further than that pole you see sticking up yonder. We had the worst of it back there across the swamps — working up to our waists in water most of the time, in mid-winter too — and at eighteenpence a yard."

"That was bad."

"Yes, rather rough. Did you come from the terminus?"

"Yes, I sent my baggage on in the brake."

"Commercial traveller, I suppose," asked the Boss, glancing at Smith, who stood a little to the rear of Steelman, seeming interested in the work.

"Oh no," said Steelman, smiling — "I am — well — I'm a geologist; this is my man here," indicating Smith. "(You may put down the bag, James, and have a smoke.) My name is Stoneleigh — you might have heard of it."

The Boss said "oh", and then presently he added "indeed", in an undecided tone.

There was a pause — embarrassed on the part of the Boss

— he was silent not knowing what to say. Meanwhile Steelman studied his man and concluded that he would do.

"Having a look at the country, I suppose?" asked the Boss presently.

"Yes," said Steelman; then after a moment's reflection: "I am travelling for my own amusement and improvement, and also in the interest of science, which amounts to the same thing. I am a member of the Royal Geological Society — vice-president in fact of a leading Australian branch;" and then, as if conscious that he had appeared guilty of egotism, he shifted the subject a bit. "Yes. Very interesting country this — very interesting indeed. I should like to make a stay here for a day or so. Your work opens right into my hands. I cannot remember seeing a geological formation which interested me so much. Look at the face of that cutting, for instance. Why! you can almost read the history of the geological world from yesterday — this morning as it were — beginning with the super-surface on top and going right down through the different layers and stratas — through the vanished ages — right down and back to the prehistorical — to the very primeval or fundamental geological formations!" And Steelman studied the face of the cutting as if he could read it like a book, with every layer or stratum a chapter, and every streak a note of explanation. The Boss seemed to be getting interested, and Steelman gained confidence and proceeded to identify and classify the different "stratas and layers", and fix their ages, and describe the conditions and politics of Man in their different times, for the Boss's benefit.

"Now," continued Steelman, turning slowly from the cutting, removing his glasses, and letting his thoughtful eyes wander casually over the general scenery — "now the first impression that this country would leave on an ordinary intelligent mind — though maybe unconsciously, would be as of a new country — new in a geological sense; with patches of an older geological and vegetable formation cropping out here and there; as for instance that clump of dead trees on that clear alluvial slope there, that outcrop of lime-stone, or that timber yonder," and he indicated a dead forest which seemed alive and green because of the parasites. "But the country is old — old; perhaps the oldest geological formation in the world is to be seen here, as is the oldest vegetable formation in Australia. I am not using the words old and new in an ordinary sense, you understand, but in a geological sense."

The Boss said, "I understand," and that geology must be a very interesting study.

Steelman ran his eye meditatively over the cutting again, and turning to Smith said,

"Go up there, James, and fetch me a specimen of that slaty out-crop you see there — just above the coeval strata."

It was a stiff climb and slippery, but Smith had to do it, and he did it.

"This," said Steelman, breaking the rotten piece between his fingers, "belongs probably to an older geological period than its position would indicate — a primitive sandstone level perhaps. It position on that layer is no doubt due to volcanic upheavals — such disturbances, or rather the results of such disturbances, have been and are the cause of the greatest trouble to geologists — endless errors and controversy. You see we must study the country, not as it appears now, but as it would appear had the natural geological growth been left to mature undisturbed; we must restore and reconstruct such disorganized portions of the mineral kingdom, if you understand me."

The Boss said he understood.

Steelman found an opportunity to wink sharply and severely at Smith, who had been careless enough to allow his features to relapse into a vacant grin.

"It is generally known even amongst the ignorant that rock grows — grows from the outside — but the rock here, a specimen of which I hold in my hand, is now in the process of decomposition; to be plain it is rotting — in an advanced stage of decomposition — so much so that you are not able to identify it with any geological period or formation, even as you may not be able to identify any other extremely decomposed body."

The Boss blinked and knitted his brow, but had the presence of mind to say: "Just so."

"Had the rock on that cutting been healthy — been alive, as it were — you would have had your work cut out; but it is dead and has been dead for ages perhaps. You find less trouble in working it than you would ordinary clay or sand, or even gravel, which formations together are really rock in embryo — before birth as it were."

The Boss's brow cleared.

"The country round here is simply rotting down — simply rotting down."

He removed his spectacles, wiped them, and wiped his face; then his attention seemed to be attracted by some stones at his feet. He picked one up and examined it.

"I shouldn't wonder," he mused, absently, "I shouldn't wonder if there is alluvial gold in some of these creeks and gullies, perhaps tin or even silver, quite probably antimony."

The boss seemed interested.

"Can you tell me if there is any place in this neighbourhood where I could get accommodation for myself and my servant for a day or two?" asked Steelman presently. "I should very much like to break my journey here."

"Well, no," said the Boss. "I can't say I do — I don't know of any place nearer than Pahiatua, and that's seven miles from here."

"I know that," said Steelman reflectively, "but I fully expected to have found a house of accommodation of some sort on the way, else I would have gone on in the van."

"Well," said the Boss. "If you like to camp with us for tonight, at least, and don't mind roughing it, you'll be welcome, I'm sure."

"If I was sure that I would not be putting you to any trouble, or interfering in any way with your domestic economy ——"

"No trouble at all," interrupted the Boss. "The boys will be only too glad, and there's an empty whare where you can sleep. Better stay. It's going to be a rough night."

After tea Steelman entertained the Boss and a few of the more thoughtful members of the party with short chatty lectures on geology and other subjects.

In the meantime Smith, in another part of the camp, gave selections on a tin whistle, sang a song or two, contributed, in his turn, to the sailor yarns, and ensured his popularity for several nights at least. After several draughts of something that was poured out of a demijohn into a pint pot, his tongue became loosened, and he expressed an opinion that geology was all bosh, and said if he had half his employer's money he'd be dashed if he would go rooting round in the mud like a blessed old ant-eater; he also irreverently referred to his learned boss as "Old Rocks" over there. He had a pretty easy billet of it though, he said, taking it all round, when the weather was fine; he got a couple of notes a week and all expenses paid, and the money was sure; he was only required to look after the luggage and arrange for accommodation, grub out a chunk of rock now and then, and (what perhaps was the most irksome of his duties) he had to appear interested in old rocks and and clay.

Towards midnight Steelman and Smith retired to the unoccupied whare which had been shown them, Smith carrying a bundle of bags, blankets, and rugs, which had been placed at their disposal by their good-natured hosts. Smith lit a candle and proceeded to make the beds. Steelman sat down, removed his specs and scientific expression, placed the glasses carefully on a ledge close at hand, took a book from his bag, and commenced to read. The volume was a cheap copy of Jules Verne's *Journey to the Centre of the Earth*. A little later there was a knock at the door. Steelman hastily resumed the spectacles, together with the scientific expression, took a note-book from his pocket, opened it on the table, and said "Come in." One of the chaps appeared with a billy of hot coffee, two pint pots, and some cake. He said he thought you chaps might like a drop of coffee before you turned in, and the boys had forgot to ask you to wait for it down in the camp. He also wanted to know whether Mr. Stoneleigh and his man would be all right and quite comfortable for the night, and whether they had blankets enough. There was some wood at the back of the whare and they could light a fire if they liked.

Mr. Stoneleigh expressed his thanks and his appreciation of the kindness shown him and his servant. He was extremely sorry to give them any trouble.

The navvy; a serious man, who respected genius or intellect in any shape or form, said that it was no trouble at all, the camp was very dull and the boys were always glad to have some one come round. Then, after a brief comparison of opinions concerning the probable duration of the weather which had arrived, they bade each other good night, and the darkness swallowed the serious man.

Steelman turned into the top bunk on one side and Smith took the lower on the other. Steelman had the candle by his bunk, as usual; he lit his pipe for a final puff before going to sleep, and held the light up for a moment so as to give Smith the full benefit of a solemn, uncompromising wink. The wink was silently applauded and dutifully returned by Smith. Then Steelman blew out the light, lay back, and puffed at his pipe for a while. Presently he chuckled, and the chuckle was echoed by Smith; by-and-bye Steelman chuckled once more, and then Smith chuckled again. There was silence in the darkness, and after a bit Smith chuckled twice. Then Steelman said:

"For God's sake give her a rest, Smith, and give a man a show to get some sleep."

Then the silence in the darkness remained unbroken.

The invitation was extended next day, and Steelman sent Smith on to see that his baggage was safe. Smith stayed out of sight for two or three hours, and then returned and reported all well.

They stayed on for several days. After breakfast and when the men were going to work Steelman and Smith would go out along the line with the black bag and poke round amongst the "layers and stratas" in sight of the works for a while, as an evidence of good faith; then they'd drift off casually into the bush, camp in a retired and sheltered spot, and light a fire when the weather was cold, and Steelman would lie on the grass and read and smoke and lay plans for the future and improve Smith's mind until they reckoned it was about dinner time. And in the evening they would come home with the black bag full of stones and bits of rock, and Steelman would lecture on those minerals after tea.

On about the fourth morning Steelman had a yarn with one of the men going to work. He was a lanky young fellow with a sandy complexion, and seemingly harmless grin. In Australia he might have been regarded as a "Cove" rather than a "chap", but there was nothing of the "bloke" about him. Presently the cove said:

"What do you think of the Boss, Mr. Stoneleigh? He seems to have taken a great fancy for you, and he's fair gone on geology."

"I think he is a very decent fellow indeed, a very intelligent young man. He seems very well read and well informed."

"You wouldn't think he was a University man," said the cove.

"No, indeed! Is he?"

"Yes. I thought you knew!"

Steelman knitted his brows. He seemed slightly disturbed for the moment. He walked on a few paces in silence and thought hard.

"What might have been his special line?" he asked the cove.

"Why, something the same as yours. I thought you knew. He was reckoned the best — what do you call it? — the best minrologist in the country. He had a first-class billet in the Mines Department, but he lost it — you know — the booze."

"I think we will be making a move, Smith," said Steelman, later on, when they were private. "There's a little too much intellect in this camp to suit me. But we haven't done so bad anyway. We've got three days' good board and lodging with entertainments and refreshments thrown in." Then he said to himself: "We'll stay for another day anyway. If those beggars are having a lark with us, we're getting the worth of it anyway, and I'm not thin-skinned. They're the mugs and not us, anyhow it goes, and I can take them down before I leave."

But on the way home he had a talk with another man whom we might set down as a "chap".

"I wouldn't have thought the Boss was a college man," said Steelman to the chap.

"A what?"

"A University man — University education."

"Why! Who's been telling you that?"

"One of your mates."

"Oh, he's been getting at you, why: it's all the Boss can do to write his own name. Now that lanky sandy cove with the birth-mark grin — it's him that's had the college education."

"I think we'll make a start to-morrow," said Steelman to Smith in the privacy of their whare. "There's too much humour and levity in this camp to suit a serious scientific gentleman like myself."

An Oversight of
Steelman's

Steelman and Smith — professional wanderers — were making back for Wellington, down through the wide and rather dreary-looking Hutt Valley. They were broke. They carried their few remaining belongings in two skimpy, amateurish-looking swags. Steelman had fourpence left. They were very tired and very thirsty — at least Steelman was, and he answered for both. It was Smith's policy to feel and think just exactly as Steelman did. Said Steelman:

"The landlord of the next pub is not a bad sort. I won't go in — he might remember me. You'd best go in. You've been tramping round in the Wairarapa district for the last six months, looking for work. You're going back to Wellington now, to try and get on the new corporation works just being started there — the sewage works. You think you've got a show. You've got some mates in Wellington, and they're looking out for a chance for you. You did get a job last week on a sawmill at Silverstream, and the boss sacked you after three days and wouldn't pay you a penny. That's just his way. I know him — at least a mate of mine does. I've heard of him often enough. He name's Cowman. Don't forget the name, whatever you do. The landlord here hates him like poison; he'll sympathize with you. Tell him you've got a mate with you; he's gone ahead — took a short cut across the paddocks. Tell him you've got only fourpence left, and see if he'll give you a drop in a bottle. Says you: "Well, boss, the fact is we've only got fourpence, but you might let us have a drop in a bottle;" and very likely he'll stand you a couple of pints in a gin-bottle. You can fling the coppers on the counter, but the chances are he won't take them. He's not a bad sort. Beer's fourpence a pint out here, same's in Wellington. See that gin-bottle lying there by the stump; get it, and we'll take it down to the river with us and rinse it out."

They reached the river bank.

"You'd better take my swag — it looks more decent," said Steelman. "No, I'll tell you what we'll do: we'll undo both swags and make them into one — one decent swag, and I'll cut round through the lanes and wait for you on the road ahead of the pub."

He rolled up the swag with much care and deliberation and considerable judgment. He fastened Smith's belt round one end of it, and the handkerchiefs round the other, and made a towel serve as a shoulder-strap.

"I wish we had a canvas-bag to put it in," he said, "or a cover of some sort. But never mind. The landlord's an old Australian bushman, now I come to think of it; the swag looks Australian enough, and it might appeal to his feelings, you know — bring up old recollections. But you'd best not say you come from Australia, because he's been there, and he'd soon trip you up. He might have been where you've been, you know, so don't try to do too much. You always do mug-up the business when you try to do more than I tell you. You might tell him your mate came from Australia — but no, he might want you to bring me in. Better stick to Maoriland. I don't believe in too much ornamentation. Plain lies are the best."

"What's the landlord's name?" asked Smith.

"Never mind that. You don't want to know that. You are not supposed to know him at all. It might look suspicious if you called him by his name, and lead to awkward questions; then you'd be sure to put your foot into it."

"I could say I read it over the door."

"Bosh. Travellers don't read the names over the doors when they go into pubs. You're an entire stranger to him. Call him 'boss'. Say 'Good day, boss,' when you go in, and swing down your swag as if you're used to it. Ease it down like this. Then straighten yourself up, stick your hat back, and wipe your forehead, and try to look as hearty and independent and cheerful as you possibly can. Curse the Government, and say the country's done. It don't matter what Government it is, for he's always against it, I never knew a real Australian that wasn't. Say that you're thinking about trying to get over to Australia, and then listen to him talking about it — and try to look interested, too! Get that damned stone-deaf expression off your face! . . . He'll run Australia down most likely (I never knew an Othersider that had settled down over here who didn't). But don't you make any mistake and agree with him, because, although successful Australians over here like to run their own country down, there's very few of them that care to hear anybody else do it . . . . Don't come away as soon as you get your beer. Stay and listen to him for a while, as if you're interested in his yarning, and give him time to put you on to a job, or offer you one. Give him a chance to ask how you and your mate are off for tobacco or tucker. Like as not he'll sling you half-a-crown when you come away — that is, if you work it all right. Now try to think of something to say to him, and make yourself a bit interesting — if you possibly can. Tell him about the fight we saw back at the pub the other day. He might know some of the chaps. This is a sleepy hole, and there ain't much news knocking round . . . . I wish I could go in myself, but he's sure to remember *me*. I'm afraid he got left the last time I stayed there (so did one or two others); and, besides, I came away without saying good-bye to him, and he might feel a bit sore about it. That's the worst of travelling on the old road. Come on now, wake up!"

"Bet I'll get a quart," said Smith, brightening up, "and some tucker for it to wash down."

"If you don't," said Steelman, "I'll stoush you. Never mind the bottle; fling it away. It doesn't look well for a traveller to go into a pub with an empty bottle in his hand. A real swagman never does. It looks much better to come out with a couple of full ones. That's what you've got to do. Now, come along."

Steelman turned off into a lane, cut across the paddocks to the road again, and waited for Smith. He hadn't long to wait.

Smith went on towards the public-house, rehearsing his part as he walked — repeating his "lines" to himself, so as to be sure of remembering all that Steelman had told him to say to the landlord, and adding, with what he considered appropriate gestures, some fancy touches of his own, which he determined to throw in in spite of Steelman's advice and warning. "I'll tell him (this) — I'll tell him (that). Well, look here, boss, I'll say, you're pretty right and I quite agree with you as far as that's concerned, but," etc. And so, murmuring and mumbling to himself, Smith reached the hotel. The day was late, and the bar was small, and low, and dark. Smith walked in with all the assurance he could muster, eased down his swag in a corner in what he no doubt considered the true professional style, and, swinging round to the bar, said in a loud voice which he intended to be cheerful, independent, and hearty:

"Good-day, boss!"

But it wasn't a "boss". It was about the hardest-faced old woman that Smith had ever seen. The pub had changed hands.

"I — I beg your pardon, missus," stammered poor Smith.

It was a knock-down blow for Smith. He couldn't come to time. He and Steelman had had a landlord in their minds all the time, and laid their plans accordingly; the possibility of having a she — and one like this — to deal with, never entered into their calculations. Smith had no time to reorganize, even if he had had the brains to do so, without the assistance of his mate's knowledge of human nature.

"I — I beg your pardon, missus," he stammered.

Painful pause. She sized him up.

"Well, what do you want?"

"Well, missus — I — the fact is — will you give me a bottle of beer for fourpence?"

"Wha — what?"

"I mean — The fact is, we've only got fourpence left, and — I've got a mate outside, and you might let us have a quart or so, in a bottle, for that. I mean — anyway, you might let us have a pint. I'm very sorry to bother you, missus."

But she couldn't do it. No. Certainly not. Decidedly not. All her drinks were sixpence. She had her license to pay, and the rent, and a family to keep. It wouldn't pay out there — it wasn't worth her while. It wouldn't pay the cost of carting the liquor out, etc. etc.

"Well, missus," poor Smith blurted out at last, in sheer desperation, "give me what you can in a bottle for this. I've — I've got a mate outside." And he put the four coppers on the bar.

"Have you got a bottle:"

"No — but —"

"If I give you one, will you bring it back? You can't expect me to give you a bottle as well as a drink."

"Yes, mum; I'll bring it back directly."

She reached out a bottle from under the bar, and very deliberately measured out a little over a pint and poured it into the bottle, which she handed to Smith without a cork.

Smith went his way without rejoicing. It struck him forcibly that he should have saved the money until they reached Petone, or the city, where Steelman would be sure to get a decent drink. But how was he to know? He had chanced it, and lost; Steelman might have done the same. What troubled Smith most was the thought of what Steelman would say; he already heard him, in imagination, saying: "You're a mug, Smith — Smith, you *are* a mug."

But Steelman didn't say much. He was prepared for the worst by seeing Smith come along so soon. He listened to his story with an air of gentle sadness, even as a stern father might listen to the voluntary confession of a wayward child; then he held the bottle up to the fading light of departing day, looked through it (the bottle), and said:

"Well — it ain't worth while dividing it."

Smith's heart shot right down through a hole in the sole of his left boot into the hard road.

"Here, Smith," said Steelman, handing him the bottle, "drink it, old man; you want it. It wasn't altogether your fault; it was an oversight of mine. I didn't bargain for a woman of that kind, and, of course *you* couldn't be expected to think of it. Drink it! Drink it down, Smith. I'll manage to work the oracle before this night is out."

Smith was forced to believe his ears, and, recovering from his surprise, drank.

"I promised to take back the bottle," he said, with the ghost of a smile.

Steelman took the bottle by the neck and broke it on the fence.

"Come on, Smith; I'll carry the swag for a while."

And they tramped on in the gathering starlight.

Letters to George Robertson

No address.
[Perth]
9th September 1896.

I didn't get note of 3rd inst. posted. Am very well pleased with book. Have noticed several errors — as in "Lizzie shoved" instead of "shovel" in "Unfinished Love Story", "dread of daily resurrection" instead of "daily dread, etc." in "Jones's Alley", but nothing very awful.

Don't take any notice of Stephen's complaints in *Bulletin* reviews. *It was I who suggested to him the order of selection which he now suggests as his own.* He and the *Bulletin* know that we had to abandon our original plan of selection because the *Bulletin held the sketches which were to complete series and would not put them through.* I notice with astonishment that I am accused of *imitating Bulletin humourists*! Stephens has only been there two years. I have written for them for ten. Am writing to *Bulletin* and other papers about this.

I've just done a hard day's painting and don't feel well, so you mustn't expect a very coherent letter. I like that "For Auld Lang Syne" as well as any, but am doubtful about "Bogg of Geebung" and one or two others. *We must* have English edition perfect and with a preface. The sentiment in "Arvie Aspinal's Alarm Clock" is not "deliberately manufactured", as Stevens (that's how he spells his name, I think) says: it is true to life. The alarm clock was mine and "Grinder Bros" are Hudson Bros — keep this private. "Bogg of Geebung" was built on a par in a Queensland paper.

Don't take any notice of S. or his kind of literary old women. Keep on as you are going and let me keep on as I'm going. We've made the thing a success and they can't get round that. Why, the cock-sure *Bulletin* said, "the author who publishes in Australia does himself a cruel and (almost) irreparable injury"!!!!?? Whoop! Am writing for the *Mail* and will get a good review. You might send a book to *Geraldton Express*.

Try to get "Free Selector's Daughter" and "Incident at Stiffners" from *Truth* files. Mind you, I think Steven's idea, or rather mine, of a novel, or something connected, is right, and I can do it. What do you think of working up "The Tale of a Tank" or something in that line (I gave you the outline of it, I think) and letting the held-over yarns and sketches be worked in or told incidentally by characters. By the way, I'm at work on a story — an autobiography, really — of selection diggings and vagabond life. There will be a lot of that "Unfinished Love Story" style in it.

> Write soon,
> H.L.

> 91 Redfern Street,
> Redfern.
> n.d. [January 1897]

Dear Robertson,

There are several things I wish to speak to you about, but we have no opportunity for conversation in the shop in business hours. I think the best thing we could do would be to hurry out a second volume of prose in a cheaper form. It would perhaps create a demand for the first. I cannot understand why *While the Billy Boils* didn't go better. It had twice the praise and notice of the other — but you can't tell what the public will go for. I feel confident that the prose will sell eventually. The sketches you have in hand, including "Darling River Sketches", which contain many entirely new pictures, would give the second volume a brighter tone than the first: see "The Mystery of Dave Regan", for instance. "The Ventriloquial Rooster" and others in the *Bulletin* would help to brighten up the book and the characters of Steelman and Mitchell would be developed and the series completed. The whole prose business is in an unfinished state at present. I saw Archibald today, who made me a definite promise *re* prose in hand. That tale, "The Free Selector's Daughter", would do for the second book (if we can get it) what "The Drover's Wife" did for the first, and "An Incident at Stiffners". "Thin Lips and False Teeth" would develop the "Unfinished Love Story". The verse on hand would take more time for revision, and be the cause of more worry, advice, hope, despair, blue-lights, rows, and consequently beer, than I could stand at present, or until after I have pulled myself together in New Zealand. I'm afraid that neither you nor Mr Angus can realize the amount of brain-work I expended on the last volume. Compare the old copy, proofs and revises. "Lawson was a most exacting and (I forget what) author. He corrected and re-wrote his verse till all was blue." Melbourne paper.

It's one thing to point out a weak verse and another thing to strengthen it.

You mustn't take notice of the drivel to the effect that I should write a long novel — anything in fact save what I *have* written. That was originally one man's idea. If I had published a novel, they would have said that it was jerky and disconnected and I should try my hand at short stories and sketches. My line is writing short stories and sketches in prose and verse. I'm not a novelist. You will find a man to write you an Australian novel soon enough. If you were a builder, would you set the painters to do the carpentering? My mother holds strong opinions on this subject, and I thoroughly agree with it. Probably if I published a novel now it would fall flat and squelch both of us, though I won't say that a decent one mightn't come to me yet.

The poem is dragging along very slowly, but I'll get it through. It's the "philosophy" in it that makes the work so heavy. If I only dealt with three dummies and the Bank robbery incident, I could rattle it off in no time — and perhaps it would go just as well. My writing developed very slowly — on account of my deafness mostly — and I think I tackled the long poem too suddenly.

Stephens has offered to publish extracts from poem in advance and give me some preliminary puffs, if you don't mind. He asked me if you would object.

Yours truly,
HENRY LAWSON

91 Redfern Street,
Redfern.
[February 1897]

Dear Robertson,

When I spoke to you *re* sketches yesterday morning I thought you didn't want sketches and it would only waste your time and mine bringing them in. The merit or worthlessness, acceptance or rejection of the last sketch had nothing to do with it. That was for *you* to decide. I spoke without any ill feeling whatever. I'm very sorry that you adopted such a tone in reply to me in the presence of Mr Angus; and you can't blame me for resenting it.

If you think that I consider myself ill-treated otherwise by you, or am likely to give anyone that impression, you make a great mistake. If you think that I am trying to make a convenience of your firm, you make a greater mistake (I know from Mr. Maccallum that you have not got your money back for the books, and I'm just as anxious that you should as you are yourself.) And if you think that I am always ready to put aside my self-respect for the sake of a few shillings, you make the greatest mistake of all. You don't understand me yet. Something has disagreed with you, during the past week, in connection with my work or books; and, if I am making a mistake now, it is because you did not tell me straight what it was, instead of meeting me with black looks and short words.

Yours truly,
HENRY LAWSON

REEDY RIVER

Ten miles down Reedy River
    A pool of water lies,
And all the year it mirrors
    The changes in the skies,
And in that pool's broad bosom
    Is room for all the stars;
Its bed of sand has drifted
    O'er countless rocky bars.

Around the lower edges
    There waves a bed of reeds,
Where water rats are hidden
    And where the wild duck breeds;
And grassy slopes rise gently
    To ridges long and low,
Where groves of wattle flourish
    And native bluebells grow.

Beneath the granite ridges
    The eye may just discern
Where Rocky Creek emerges
    From deep green banks of fern;
And standing tall between them,
    The grassy sheoaks cool
The hard, blue-tinted waters
    Before they reach the pool.

Ten miles down Reedy River
    One Sunday afternoon,
I rode with Mary Campbell
    To that broad bright lagoon;
We left our horses grazing
    Till shadows climbed the peak,
And strolled beneath the sheoaks
    On the banks of Rocky Creek.

Then home along the river
    That night we rode a race,
And the moonlight lent a glory
    To Mary Campbell's face;
And I pleaded for my future
    All thro' that moonlight ride,
Until our weary horses
    Drew closer side by side.

Ten miles from Ryan's crossing
    And five below the peak,

I built a little homestead
    On the banks of Rocky Creek;
I cleared the land and fenced it
    And ploughed the rich red loam,
And my first crop was golden
    When I brought Mary home.

Now still down Reedy River
    The grassy sheoaks sigh,
And the waterholes still mirror
    The pictures in the sky;
And over all for ever
    Go sun and moon and stars,
While the golden sand is drifting
    Across the rocky bars;

But of the hut I builded
    There are no traces now.
And many rains have levelled
    The furrows of the plough;
And my bright days are olden,
    For the twisted branches wave
And the wattle blossoms golden
    On the hill by Mary's grave.

BUT WHAT'S THE USE

But what's the use of writing "bush"—
    Though editors demand it—
For city folk, and farming folk,
    Can never understand it.
They're blind to what the bushman sees
    The best with eyes shut tightest,
Out where the sun is hottest and
    The stars are most and brightest.

The crows at sunrise flopping round
    Where some poor life has run down;
The pair of emus trotting from
    The lonely tank at sundown,
Their snaky heads well up, and eyes
    Well out for man's manoeuvres,
And feathers bobbing round behind
    Like fringes round improvers.

The swagman tramping 'cross the plain;
   Good Lord, there's nothing sadder,
Except the dog that slopes behind
   His master like a shadder;
The turkey-tail to scare the flies,
   The water-bag and billy;
The nose-bag getting cruel light,
   The traveller getting silly.

The plain that seems to Jackaroos
   Like gently sloping rises,
The shrubs and tufts that's miles away
   But magnified in sizes;
The track that seems arisen up
   Or else seems gently slopin',
And just a hint of kangaroos
   Way out across the open.

The joy and hope the swagman feels
   Returning, after shearing,
Or after six months' tramp Out Back,
   He strikes the final clearing.
His weary spirit breathes again,
   His aching legs seem limber
When to the East across the plain
   He spots the Darling Timber!

But what's the use of writing "bush"
   Though editors demand it—
For city folk and cockatoos,
   They do not understand it.
They're blind to what the whaler sees
   The best with eyes shut tightest,
Out where Australia's widest, and
   The stars are most and brightest.

THE STAR OF AUSTRALASIA

We boast no more of our bloodless flag, that rose from a
   nation's slime;
Better a shred of a deep-dyed rag from the storms of the
   olden time.
From grander clouds in our "peaceful skies" than ever were
   there before
I tell you the Star of the South shall rise — in the lurid
   clouds of war.

It ever must be while blood is warm and the sons of men
    increase;
For ever the nations rose in storm, to rot in a deadly peace.
There comes a point that we will not yield, no matter if
    right or wrong,
And man will fight on the battle-field while passion and
    pride are strong—
So long as he will not kiss the rod, and his stubborn spirit
    sours,
And the scorn of Nature and curse of God are heavy on
    peace like ours.

There are boys out there by the western creeks, who hurry
    away from school
To climb the sides of the breezy peaks or dive in the shaded
    pool,
Who'll stick to their guns when the mountains quake to the
    tread of a mighty war,
And fight for Right or a Grand Mistake as men never
    fought before;
When the peaks are scarred and the sea-walls crack till the
    furthest hills vibrate,
And the world for a while goes rolling back in a storm of
    love and hate.

There are boys today in the city slum and the home of
    wealth and pride
Who'll have one home when the storm is come, and fight for
    it side by side,
Who'll hold the cliffs 'gainst the armoured hells that batter a
    coastal town,
Or grimly die in a hail of shells when the walls come crashing
    down.
And many a pink-white baby girl, the queen of her home
    today,
Shall see the wings of the tempest whirl the mist of our
    dawn away—
Shall live to shudder and stop her ears to the thud of the
    distant gun,
And know the sorrow that has no tears when a battle is lost
    and won—
As a mother or wife in the years to come, will kneel, wild-
    eyed and white,
And pray to God in her darkened home for the "men in the
    fort tonight".

But, oh! if the cavalry charge again as they did when the
    world was wide,

Twill be grand in the ranks of a thousand men in that
  glorious race to ride
And strike for all that is true and strong, for all that is
  grand and brave,
And all that ever shall be, so long as man has a soul to save.
He must lift the saddle, and close his "wings", and shut his
  angels out,
And steel his heart for the end of things, who'd ride with a
  stockman scout,
When the race they ride on the battle track, and the
  waning distance hums,
And the shelled sky shrieks or the rifles crack like stockwhip
  amongst the gums—
And the "straight" is reached and the field is "gapped" and
  the hoof-torn sward grows red
With the blood of those who are handicapped with iron and
  steel and lead;
And the gaps are filled, though unseen by eyes, with the
  spirit and with the shades
Of the world-wide rebel dead who'll rise and rush with the
  Bush Brigades.

All creeds and trades will have soldiers there — give every
  class its due—
And there'll be many a clerk to spare for the pride of the
  jackeroo.
They'll fight for honour and fight for love, and a few will
  fight for gold,
For the devil below and for God above, as our fathers fought
  of old;
And some half-blind with exultant tears, and some stiff-
  lipped, stern-eyed,
For the pride of a thousand after-years and the old eternal
  pride;
The soul of the world they will feel and see in the chase and
  the grim retreat—
They'll know the glory of victory — and the grandeur of
  defeat.

The South will wake to a mighty change ere a hundred years
  are done
With arsenals west of the mountain range and every spur its
  gun.
And many a rickety son of a gun, on the tides of the future
  tossed,
Will tell how battles were really won that History says were
  lost,
Will trace the field with his pipe, and shirk the facts that are
  hard to explain,

As grey old mates of the diggings work the old ground over
    again—
How "this was our centre, and this a redoubt, and that was
    a scrub in the rear,
"And this was the point where the guards held out, and the
    enemy's lines were here."

They'll tell the tales of the nights before and the tales of the
    ship and fort
Till the sons of Australia take to war as their fathers took to
    sport,
Their breath come deep and their eyes grow bright at the
    tales of our chivalry,
And every boy will want to fight, no matter what cause it
    be—
When the children run to the doors and cry: "Oh, mother,
    the troops are come!"
And every heart in the town leaps high at the first loud thud
    of the drum.
They'll know, apart from its mystic charm, what music is at
    last,
When, proud as a boy with a broken arm, the regiment
    marches past.
And the veriest wreck in the drink-fiend's clutch, no
    matter how low or mean,
Will feel, when he hears the march, a touch of the man that
    he might have been.

And fools, when the fiends of war are out and the city skies
    aflame,
Will have something better to talk about than an absent
    woman's shame,
Will have something nobler to do by far than jest at a
    friend's expense,
Or blacken a name in a public bar or over a backyard fence.
And this you learn from the libelled past, though its
    methods were somewhat rude—
A nation's born where the shells fall fast, or its lease of life
    renewed.
We in part atone for the ghoulish strife, and the crimes of
    the peace we boast,
And the better part of a people's life in the storm comes
    uppermost.

The self-same spirit that drives the man to the depths of
    drink and crime
Will do the deeds in the heroes' van that live till the end of
    time.
The living death in the lonely bush, the greed of the selfish
    town,

And even the creed of the outlawed push is chivalry—
    upside down.
'Twill be while ever our blood is hot, while ever the world
    goes wrong,
The nations rise in a war, to rot in a peace that lasts too
    long.
And southern nation and southern state, aroused from their
    dream of ease,
Must sign in the Book of Eternal Fate their stormy histories.

Mr. Smellingscheck

I met him in a sixpenny restaurant — "All meals, 6d. — Good beds, 1s." That was before sixpenny restaurants rose to a third-class position, and became possibly respectable places to live in, through the establishment, beneath them, of fourpenny hash-houses (good beds, 6d.), and, beneath *them* again, of *three*-penny "dining-rooms — *clean* beds, 4d."

There were five beds in our apartment, the head of one against the foot of the next, and so on round the room, with a space where the door and washstand were. I chose the bed the head of which was near the foot of his, because he looked like a man who took his bath regularly. I should like, in the interests of sentiment, to describe the place as a miserable, filthy, evil-smelling garret; but I can't — because it wasn't. The room was large and airy; the floor was scrubbed and the windows cleaned at least once a week, and the beds kept fresh and neat, which is more — a good deal more — than can be said of many genteel private boarding-houses. The lodgers were mostly respectable unemployed, and one or two — fortunate men! — in work; it was the casual boozer, the professional loafer, and the occasional spieler — the one-shilling-bed-men — who made the place objectionable, not the hard-working people who paid ten pounds a week for the house; and, but for the one-night lodgers and the big gilt black-and-red bordered and "shaded" "6d." in the window — which made me glance guiltily up and down the street, like a burglar about to do a job, before I went in — I was pretty comfortable there.

They called him "Mr. Smellingscheck", and treated him with a peculiar kind of deference, the reason for which they themselves were doubtless unable to explain or even understand. The haggard woman who made the beds called him "Mr. Smell-'is-check". Poor fellow! I didn't think, by the

look of him, that he'd smelt his cheque, or anyone else's, or
that anyone else had smelt his, for many a long day. He was
a fat man, slow and placid. He looked like a typical
monopolist who had unaccountably got into a suit of clothes
belonging to a Domain unemployed, and hadn't noticed, or
had entirely forgotten, the circumstance in his business cares
— if such a word as care could be connected with such a
calm, self-contained nature. He wore a suit of cheap slops of
some kind of shoddy "tweed". The coat was too small and
the trousers too short, and they were drawn up to meet the
waistcoat — which they did with painful difficulty, now and
then showing, by way of protest, two pairs of brass buttons
and the ends of the brace-straps; and they seemed to blame
the irresponsive waistcoat or the wearer for it all. Yet he
never gave way to assist them. A pair of burst elastic-sides
were in full evidence, and a rim of cloudy sock, with a hole
in it, showed at every step.

But he put on his clothes and wore them like — like a
gentleman. He had two white shirts, and they were both
dirty. He'd lay them out on the bed, turn them over, regard
them thoughtfully, choose that which appeared to his calm
understanding to be the cleaner, and put it on, and wear it
until it was unmistakably dirtier than the other; then he'd
wear the other till it was dirtier than the first. He managed
his three collars the same way. His handkerchiefs were
washed in the bathroom, and dried, without the slightest
disguise, in the bedroom. He never hurried in anything. The
way he cleaned his teeth, shaved, and made his toilet almost
transformed the place, in my imagination, into a gentleman's dressing-room.

He talked politics and such things in the abstract —
always in the abstract — calmly in the abstract. He was an
old-fashioned Conservative of the Sir Leicester Deadlock
style. When he was moved by an extra shower of aggressive
democratic cant — which was seldom — he defended
Capital, but only as if it needed no defence, and as if its
opponents were merely thoughtless, ignorant children whom
he condescended to set right because of their inexperience
and for their own good. He stuck calmly to his own order —
the order which had dropped him like a foul thing when the
bottom dropped out of his boom, whatever that was. He
never talked of his misfortunes.

He took his meals at the little greasy table in the dark
corner downstairs, just as if he were dining at the Exchange.
He had a chop — rather well-done — and a sheet of the
Herald for breakfast. He carried two handkerchiefs; he used

one for a handkerchief and the other for a table-napkin, and sometimes folded it absently and laid it on the table. He rose slowly, putting his chair back, took down his battered old green hat, and regarded it thoughtfully — as though it had just occurred to him in a calm, casual way that he'd drop into his hatter's, if he had time, on his way down town, and get it blocked, or else send the messenger round with it during business hours. He'd draw his stick out from behind the next chair, plant it, and, if you hadn't quite finished your side of the conversation, stand politely waiting until you were done. Then he'd look for a suitable reply into his hat, put it on, give it a twitch to settle it on his head — as gentlemen do a "chimney-pot" — step out into the gangway, turn his face to the door, and walk slowly out on to the middle of the pavement — looking more placidly well-to-do than ever. The saying is that clothes make a man, but *he* made his almost respectable just by wearing them. Then he'd consult his watch — (he stuck to the watch all through, and it seemed a good one — I often wondered why he didn't pawn it); then he'd turn slowly, right turn, and look down the street. Then slowly back, left-about turn, and take a cool survey in that direction, as if calmly undecided whether to take a cab and drive to the Exchange, or (as it was a very fine morning, and he had half an hour to spare) walk there and drop in at his club on the way. He'd conclude to walk. I never saw him go anywhere in particular, but he walked and stood as if he could.

Coming quietly into the room one day, I surprised him sitting at the table with his arms lying on it and his face resting on them. I heard something like a sob. He rose hastily, and gathered up some papers which were on the table; then he turned round, rubbing his forehead and eyes with his forefinger and thumb, and told me that he suffered from — something, I forget the name of it, but it was a well-to-do ailment. His manner seemed a bit jolted and hurried for a minute or so, and then he was himself again. He told me he was leaving for Melbourne next day. He left while I was out, and left an envelope downstairs for me. There was nothing in it except a pound note.

I saw him in Brisbane afterwards, well-dressed, getting out of a cab at the entrance of one of the leading hotels. But his manner was no more self-contained and well-to-do than it had been in the old sixpenny days — because it couldn't be. We had a well-to-do whisky together, and he talked of things in the abstract. He seemed just as if he'd met me in the Australia.

THE UNCULTURED RHYMER TO HIS
CULTURED CRITICS

Fight through ignorance, want, and care—
    Through the griefs that crush the spirit;
Push your way to a fortune fair,
    And the smiles of the world you'll merit.
Long, as a boy, for the chance to learn—
    For the chance that Fate denies you;
Win degrees where the Life-lights burn,
    And scores will teach and advise you.

My cultured friends! you have come too late
    With your bypath nicely graded;
I've fought thus far on my track of Fate,
    And I'll follow the rest unaided.
Must I be stopped by a college gate
    On the track of Life encroaching?
Be dumb to Love, and be dumb to Hate,
    For the lack of a college coaching?

You grope for Truth in a language dead—
    In the dust 'neath tower and steeple!
What know you of the tracks we tread?
    And what know you of our people?
"I must read this, and that, and the rest,"
    And write as the cult expects me?—
I'll read the book that may please me best,
    And write as my heart directs me!

You were quick to pick on a faulty line
    That I strove to put my soul in:
Your eyes were keen for a "dash" of mine
    In the place of a semi-colon—
And blind to the rest. And is it for such
    As you I must brook restriction?
"I was taught too little?" I learnt too much
    To care for a pedant's diction!

Must I turn aside from my destined way
    For a task your Joss would find me?
I come with strength of the living day,
    And with half the world behind me;
I leave you alone in your cultured halls
    To driven and croak and cavil:
Till your voice goes further than college walls,
    Keep out of the tracks we travel!

They Wait on the Wharf
in Black

"Seems to me that honest, hard-working men seem to accumulate the heaviest swags of trouble in this world." — Steelman.

Told By Mitchell's Mate

We were coming back from West Australia, steerage — Mitchell, the Oracle, and I. I had gone over saloon, with a few pounds in my pocket. Mitchell said this was a great mistake — I should have gone over steerage with nothing but the clothes I stood upright in, and come back saloon with a pile. He said it was a very common mistake that men made, but, as far as his experience went, there always seemed to be a deep-rooted popular prejudice in favour of going away from home with a few pounds in one's pocket and coming back stumped; at least amongst rovers and vagabonds like ourselves — it wasn't so generally popular or admired at home, or in the places we came back to, as it was in the places we went to. Anyway it went, there wasn't the slightest doubt that our nearest and dearest friends were, as a rule, in favour of our taking away as little as we could possibly manage with, and coming back with a pile, whether we came back saloon or not; and that ought to settle the matter as far as any chap that had the slightest consideration for his friends or family was concerned.

There was a good deal of misery, underneath, coming home in that steerage. One man had had his hand crushed and amputated out Coolgardie way, and the stump had mortified, and he was being sent to Melbourne by his mates. Some had lost their money, some a couple of years of their life, some their souls; but none seemed to have lost the heart to call up the quiet grin that southern rovers, vagabonds, travellers for "graft" or fortune, and professional wanderers wear in front of it all. Except one man — an elderly eastern digger — he had lost his wife in Sydney while he was away.

They sent him a wire to the Boulder Soak, or somewhere out back of White Feather, to say that his wife was seriously ill; but the wire went wrong, somehow, after the manner of telegrams not connected with mining, on the lines of "the Western". They sent him a wire to say that his wife was dead, and that reached him all right — only a week late.

I can imagine it. He got the message at dinner-time, or when they came back to the camp. His mate wanted him to sit in the shade, or lie in the tent, while he got the billy boiled. "You must brace up and pull yourself together, Tom, for the sake of the youngsters." And Tom for long intervals goes walking up and down, up and down, by the camp — under the brassy sky or the gloaming — under the brilliant star-clusters that hang over the desert plain, but never raising his eyes to them; kicking a tuft of grass or a hole in the sand now and then, and seeming to watch the progress of the track he is tramping out. The wife of twenty years was with him — though two thousand miles away — till that message came.

I can imagine Tom sitting with his mates round the billy, they talking in quiet, subdued tones about the track, the departure of coaches, trains and boats — arranging for Tom's journey East, and the working of the claim in his absence. Or Tom lying on his back in his bunk, with his hands under his head and his eyes fixed on the calico above — thinking, thinking, thinking. Thinking, with a touch of his boyhood's faith perhaps; or wondering what he had done in his long, hard-working married life, that God should do this thing to him now, of all times.

"You'd best take what money we have in the camp, Tom; you'll want it all ag'in' the time you get back from Sydney, and we can fix it up arterwards. . . . There's a couple o' clean shirts o' mine — you'd best take 'em — you'll want 'em on the voyage. . . . You might as well take them there new pants o' mine, they'll only dry-rot out here — and the coat, too, if you like — it's too small for me, anyway. You won't have any time in Perth, and you'll want some decent togs to land with in Sydney."

"I wouldn't 'a' cared so much if I'd 'a' seen the last of her," he said, in a quiet, patient voice, to us one night by the rail. "I would 'a' liked to have seen the last of her."

"Have you been long in the West?"

"Over two years. I made up to take a run across last Christmas, and have a look at 'em. But I couldn't very well get away when "exemption-time" came. I didn't like to leave the claim."

"Do any good over there?"

"Well, things brightened up a bit the last month or two. I had a hard pull at first; landed without a penny, and had to send back every shilling I could rake up to get things straightened up a bit at home. Then the oldest boy fell ill, and then the baby. I'd reckoned on bringing 'em over to Perth or Coolgardie when the cool weather came, and having them somewheres near me, where I could go and have a look at 'em now and then, and look after them."

"Going back to the West again?"

"Oh, yes. I must go for the sake of the youngsters. But I don't seem to have much heart in it." He smoked awhile. "Over twenty years we struggled along together — the missus and me — and it seems hard that I couldn't see the last of her. It's rough on a man."

"The world is damned rough on a man sometimes," said Mitchell, "most especially when he least deserves it."

The digger crossed his arms on the rail like an old "cocky" at the fence in the cool of the evening, yarning with an old crony.

"Mor'n twenty years she stuck to me and struggled along by my side. She never give in. I'll swear she was on her feet till the last, with her sleeves tucked up — bustlin' round . . . And just when things was brightening and I saw a chance of giving her a bit of a rest and comfort for the end of her life. . . . I thought of it all only t'other week when things was clearing up ahead; and the last "order" I sent over I set to work and wrote her a long letter, putting all the good news and encouragement I could think of into it. I thought how that letter would brighten up things at home, and how she'd read it round. I thought of lots of things that a man never gets time to think of while his nose is kept to the grindstone. And she was dead and in her grave, and I never knowed it."

Mitchell dug his elbow into my ribs and made signs for the matches to light his pipe.

"An' yer never knowed," reflected the Oracle.

"But I always had an idea when there was trouble at home," the digger went on presently, in his quiet, patient tone. "I always knowed; I always had a kind of feeling that way — I felt it — no matter how far I was away. When the youngsters was sick I knowed it, and I expected the letter that come. About a fortnight ago I had a feeling that way when the wife was ill. The very stars out there on the desert by the Boulder Soak seemed to say: 'There's trouble at home. Go home. There's trouble at home.' But I never dreamed what that trouble was. One night I did make up my mind to start in the morning, but when the morning come I hadn't an excuse, and was ashamed to tell my mates the truth. They might have thought I was going ratty, like a good many go out there." Then he broke off with a sort of laugh, as if it just struck him that we might think he was a bit off his head, or that his talk was getting uncomfortable for us. "Curious, ain't it?" he said.

"Reminds me of a case I knowed, —" commenced the Oracle, after a pause.

I could have pitched him overboard; but that was a mistake. He and the old digger sat on the for'ard hatch half the night yarning, mostly about queer starts, and rum go's, and curious cases the Oracle had knowed, and I think the Oracle did him a lot of good somehow, for he seemed more cheerful in the morning.

We were overcrowded in the steerage, but Mitchell managed to give up his berth to the old digger without letting him know it. Most of the chaps seemed anxious to make a place at the first table and pass the first helpings of the dishes to the "old cove that had lost his missus".

They all seemed to forget him as we entered the Heads; they had their own troubles to attend to. They were in the shadow of the shame of coming back hard up, and the grins began to grow faint and sickly. But I didn't forget him. I wish sometimes that I didn't take so much notice of things.

There was no mistaking them — the little group that stood apart near the end of the wharf, dressed in cheap black. There was the eldest single sister — thin, pale, and haggard-looking — that had had all the hard worry in the family till her temper was spoilt, as you could see by the peevish, irritable lines in her face. She had to be the mother of them all now, and had never known, perhaps, what it was to be a girl or a sweetheart. She gave a hard, mechanical sort of smile when she saw her father, and then stood looking at the boat in a vacant, hopeless sort of way. There was the baby, that he saw now for the first time, crowing and jumping at the sight of the boat coming in; there was the eldest boy, looking awkward and out of place in his new slop-suit of black, shifting round uneasily, and looking anywhere but at his father. But the little girl was the worst, and a pretty little girl she was, too; she never took her streaming eyes off her father's face the whole time. You could see that her little heart was bursting, and with pity for him. They were too far apart to speak to each other as yet. The boat seemed a cruel long long time swinging alongside — I wished they'd hurry up. He'd brought his traps up early, and laid 'em on the deck under the rail; he stood very quiet with his hands behind him, looking at his children. He had a strong, square workman's face, but I could see his chin and mouth quivering under the stubbly, iron-grey beard, and the lump working in his throat; and one strong hand gripped the other very tight behind, but his eyelids never quivered — only his eyes seemed to grow more and more sad and lonesome. These are the sort of long, cruel moments when a man sits or stands very tight and quiet and calm-looking, with his whole past life going whirling through his brain, year after year, and over and over again. Just as the digger seemed about to speak to them he met the brimming eyes of his little girl turned up to his face. He looked at her for a moment, and then turned suddenly and went below as if pretending to go down for his things. I noticed that Mitchell — who hadn't seemed to be noticing anything in particular — followed him down. When they came on deck again we were right alongside.

"'Ello, Nell!" said the digger to the eldest daughter.

"'Ello, father!" she said, with a sort of gasp, but trying to smile.

"'Ello, Jack, how are you getting on?"

"All right, father," said the boy, brightening up, and seeming greatly relieved.

He looked down at the little girl with a smile that I can't describe, but didn't speak to her. She still stood with quivering chin and mouth and great brimming eyes up-turned, full of such pity as I never saw before in a child-face — pity for him.

"You can get ashore now," said Mitchell; "see, they've got the gangway out aft."

Presently I saw Mitchell with the portmanteau in his hand, and the baby on his arm, steering them away to a quiet corner of the shed at the top of the wharf. The digger had the little girl in his arms, and both hers were round his neck, and her face hidden on his shoulder.

When Mitchell came back, he leant on the rail for a while by my side, as if it was a boundary fence out back, and there was no hurry to break up camp and make a start.

"What did you follow him below that time for, Mitchell?" I asked presently, for want of something better to say.

Mitchell looked at me out of the corners of his eyes.

"I wanted to score a drink!" he said. "I thought he wanted one and wouldn't like to be a Jimmy Woodser."

"Pursuing Literature" in Australia

In the first fifteen years of my life I saw the last of the Roaring Days on Gulgong goldfield, N.S.W. I remember the rush as a boy might his first and only pantomime. "On our selection" I tailed cows amongst the deserted shafts in the gullies of a dreary old field that was abandoned ere Gulgong "broke out". I grubbed, ring-barked, and plough-ed in the scratchy sort of way common to many "native-born" selectors round there; helped fight pleuro and drought; and worked on building contracts with "Dad", who was a carpenter. Saw selectors slaving their lives away in dusty holes amongst the barren ridges: saw one or two carried home, in the end, on a sheet of bark; the old men worked till they died. Saw how the gaunt selectors' wives lived and toiled. Saw older sons stoop-shouldered old men at thirty. Noted, in dusty patches in the scrubs, the pile of chimney-stones, a blue-gum slab or two, and the remains of the fence — the ultimate result of ten years', fifteen years', and twenty years' hard, hopeless graft by strong men who died like broken-down bullocks further out. And all the years miles and miles of rich black soil flats and chocolate slopes lay idle, because of old-time grants, or because the country carried sheep — for the sake of an extra bale of wool and an unknown absentee. I watched old fossickers and farmers reading *Progress and Poverty* earnestly and arguing over it Sunday aftenoons. And I wished that I could write.

The droughts of the early Eighties, coming with the pleuro, the rabbits, crop and vine-diseases and other trou-bles, burst a lot of us round there. Some old selectors did pick-and-shovel work in the city, or drove drays, while their wives took in washing. I worked for subcontractors in coach-factories, painting; tramped the cities in search of work; saw the haggard little group in front of the board outside the *Herald* office at 4 o'clock in the morning, striking matches to run down the "Wanted" columns; saw the slums and the poor — and wished that I could write, or paint.

I heard Tommy Walker, and Collins, and the rest of 'em and, of course, a host of Yankee free-thought and socialistic lecturers. I wore the green in fancy, gathered at the rising of the moon, charged for the fair land of Poland, and dreamed of dying on the barricades to the roar of the "Marseillaise" — for the Young Australian Republic. Then came the unexpected and inexplicable outburst of popular feeling (or madness) — called then the Republican riots — in '87, when the Sydney crowd carried a disloyal amendment on the Queen's Jubilee, and cheered, at the Town Hall, for an "Australian Republic". And I had to write then — or burst. The *Bulletin* saved me from bursting.

"Youth: the first four lines are the best. Try again." *Answers to Correspondents, Bulletin,* June 18, 1887.

The first four lines were printed. I haven't felt so excited over a thing since. The fire blazed too fiercely to last; but it burned for ten years.

"H.L.: Will publish your 'Song of the Republic'."

I was up at daylight every publishing morning and down to the earliest news-agent's, but "The Song of the Republic" was held over for a special occasion — Eight Hours' Day (Oct. 1887). Democracy and Unionism were alive those times, and Eight Hours' Day was called "The Carnival of Labour".

I was a coach painter's improver at 5s per day, with regular work, and only needed to practise "lining", or tracing, to be master of the trade. I helped write, machine, and publish a flyblister called the *Republican*. I wrote some verses called "The Song of the Outcasts", or "The Army of the Rear"; also "Golden Gully", "The Wreck of the Derry Castle", and one or two others (rejected). I took the parcel down to the old *Bulletin* office, in Pitt-street, after dusk, intending to slip it surreptitiously into the letter-box; but the char-woman, broom in hand, opened the door suddenly, and gave me a start. I thrust the screed into her hands and made off.

In Dec., '87, I was coach-painting at Windsor, Melb., for 6s a day, when I got *my* first Xmas *Bulletin*. I tore it open, tremblingly; glanced through it, to make sure I was there; and hid it in a hearse I was "rubbing-down" — for the boss was a fierce Wesleyan. I rubbed hard with the pumice-

stone till my heart didn't thump so much, and I felt calmer.
I stole glances, behind the hearse, at "Golden Gully" and
"The Wreck of the Derry Castle", and the kindly editorial
note to the effect that I was a mere lad (aged 19), earning a
living, under difficulties, at house-painting, and that my
education was as yet unfinished (N.B. — I couldn't spell),
and that my talent spoke for itself in the following poem. I
was in print, and in the Xmas number of a journal I had
worshipped, and devoured every inch of, for years. I felt
strong and proud enough to clean pigstyes, if need be, for a
living for the rest of my natural life — provided the *Bulletin*
went on publishing the poetry. Varnish on old hearses is
hard as flint; but I made a good job of that one, and a quick
job — for I "rubbed down" on air if I didn't walk on it. It
was the shortest eight hours' graft I ever did.

When house-painting on Mt. Victoria early in '88 (8s a
day — trade was good then) I got my first cheque, £1 7s
from the *Bulletin*. It was totally unexpected, for, being in
constant work and getting what I thought such a grand
outlet for my thoughts and feelings, I hadn't dreamed of
receiving payment for literary work — which might be a
hard fact for the present cashier of the *Bulletin* to swallow.
But before that I had written and worked, and I have
written and worked since, for Australian unionism and
Democracy — for nothing. I had a strong, deep-down
feeling against taking money for anything I wrote in the
interest of "the Cause" I believed in; and I felt red-hot
about —

> I hate the wrongs I read about! I hate the wrongs I see!
> The marching of that Army is as music unto me!
>
> — "The Army of the Rear", '87.

And I went a bit mad over —

> We'll make the tyrant feel the strength
> Of those that they would throttle!
> They need not say the fault is ours
> If blood should stain the wattle!
>
> — "Freedom on the Wallaby", '92.

But I believed what I wrote was true.

When out of graft awhile in Sydney I helped turn the old
Republican machine, and wrote "Faces in the Street", for
which I received a guinea. Along in these times I wrote bush
ballads for the *T. and C. Journal*, but only got an occasional

half-sovereign. I tried "Tom" Butler of the *Freeman's Journal,* of whom I have kindly recollections. He told me when I first saw him that they didn't pay for poetry, but I might bring something round to him; and if it was fairly good and suitable for his readers, he would see what he could do. I wrote a few bush rhymes for him; whenever I brought one round he reminded me that they didn't pay for verse — except, perhaps, at Xmas, and by special arrangement, or for special stuff; and whenever he wrote me a cheque he never failed to draw my attention to the fact that the *Freeman's Journal* didn't pay for poetry. The *T. and C.* proprietary treated me a little better later on — but only took Xmas matter; and, when I got "finally" hard-up in Sydney, contributed £1 towards my fare to Maoriland.

But it was before that — in '89 — that I went to Albany, W.A. I painted; and wrote articles at a penny a line for a local paper. Came back, and hung out for the best part of '90 in a third-rate hash-house in Sydney, where I got some good "copy"! Up-country again, and started house-painting at 8s or 9s a day, with every prospect of a good run of work; but one day, as I was painting a ceiling, I got a telegram to say that Brisb. *Boomerang* offered £2 per week and a position on the staff. I was doubtful of my abilities, and wired to an old friend in Sydney for advice. He advised accept; so I accepted.

It was the first, the last, and only chance I got in journalism. I wrote pars, sketches, and verse for six months for the £2; and barracked, spare times, for Democracy, in the Brisbane *Worker,* for nothing. I got very fond of the work, and was with difficulty kept out of the office on Sundays, publishing days, Saturday afternoons, and other holidays. I might have been an experienced journalist today, with a good "screw" and no ambition, but the *Boomerang* "ghost" was fading fast. We hashed up a couple of columns of pars from the country papers every week, with the names of the papers attached — to curry favour with the country press; and I conceived an idea of *rhyming* this "Country Crumbs" column, and having it set as prose, and kept two columns a week going for a couple of months. You can rhyme anything if you stare at it long enough between whiles of walking up and down and scratching your head.

Perhaps the "Country Crumbs" in prosy rhyme had the same effect on the readers as at first on the comps; anyway the spectre grew less and less discernible, and deputations of comps went up oftener to the sanctum to discuss the inadvisability of their taking shares in the paper in part-payment of wages. A piece I wrote, called the "Cambaroora Star", was the *Boomerang's* own epitaph.

I came south, steerage, with £2. It wasn't the first time I went saloon and came back steerage, so to speak. I got as far as Bathurst once, during an unemployed period, and came back in charge of the guard.

I hung out (with difficulty) in a restaurant in Sydney, getting an occasional guinea from the *Bulletin,* and painting for nigger-driving bosses at 5s a day. Hard times had come to Sydney, and it it took a good, all-round tradesman to be sure of seven or even six "bob" and fairly constant graft. When the trade failed me I used to write a column of red-hot socialistic and libellous political rhymes for *Truth.* I still believed in revolutions, and the spirit of righteousness upheld me. *Truth's* "ghost" was eccentric, and the usual rates for outside contributions were from 5s upwards; but John Norton gave me 15s to £1, for special stuff. He cursed considerably; and there were times when it wasn't advisable to curse back; but he saw that I, and one or two other poor devils of scribblers on their uppers, were paid — even before the comps; I haven't forgotten it.

Toward the end of '92 I got £5 and a railway ticket from the *Bulletin* and went to Bourke. Painted, picked-up in a shearing-shed, and swagged it for six months; then came back to Sydney "in charge of five trucks of cattle". Bourke people will understand that dodge. (Most of my hard-up experiences are in my published books, diguised but not exaggerated.)

Most of the matter in *While the Billy Boils* (and some of what my reviewers considered the best) was written for Syd. *Worker* for 12s 6d a column. During one of the frequent interregnums I edited the *Worker* a while gratis, on the understanding that I should get the permanent editorship — for "the Cause" didn't loom so big in my eyes as it used to, and I was only then beginning to find out that others had not been quite so enthusiastic as I was. But that mysterious inner circle, the trustees and their friends, brought an editor from another province.

Towards the end of '93 I landed in Wellington with a pound in my pocket — just in time to see the women vote for the first time. Got a little painting to do now and then, and a guinea (5s "out of the editor's pocket", I understood) from the *NZ Mail* for a 1½ col. rhyme called "For'ard". And I wrote some steerage sketches at the rate of 5s a

col. Did a three-months unemployed "perish", and then
went with a mate to a sawmill in the Hutt Valley, for a boss
who had contracted to supply the mill with logs. We two
bullocked in a rough, wet gully for a fortnight — felling
trees, making a track for the bullocks, and "jacking" logs to
it over stumps and boulders. But we were soft and inex-
perienced, and at the end of the fortnight the boss said we
weren't bushmen — which, strange to say, hurt me more
than any adverse criticism on my literary work could have
done at the time. The boss had no cash; and my mate was
only restrained from violence by the fact that he was a big
man and the boss a little one. He gave us each an order for
our wages on the owner of the sawmill in Wellington, and,
as we had no money for railway fares, we "tramped it" —
twenty miles, without tucker or tobacco. Those orders have
not been cashed yet.

I house-painted a bit; then got on with a ganging
lineman on a telegraph line in South Island. It was hard
graft at first, through rough country, in the depth of winter,
and camping-out all the time — humping poles some times
where the trace-horses couldn't go. The boss was a bit of
a driver, with a fondness for "hazing" the gang when his liver
went wrong; but it's better to be driven to the benefit of your
muscles, general health, and consequent happiness, than to
be brain-sweated in the city to the danger of your reason
through brooding over it. In four or five months I was too
healthy to read or write, or bother about it, or anything, or
to hate anybody except the cook when "duff" didn't even-
tuate at reasonable intervals. But there came a letter from
the *Worker* people to say that a *Daily Worker* had been
successfully floated, and there was a place for me on it. I
said, "Get behind me, Literature!" but she didn't; so I threw
up the billet, and caught a steamer that touched the coast to
deliver poles. I arrived in Sydney three days after the *Daily
Worker* went bung.

After a deal of shuffling humbug, I was put on the *Weekly
Worker* as "provincial editor", but in a month I received a
notice, alleged to come from the trustees, to the effect that,
on account of the financial position of the Workers' Union,
they were regretfully obliged to dispense with my services —
"for the present, at least". No one was responsible for the
Daily Worker, nor for the thousand pounds sunk in it, nor the
crowded staff, exorbitant "screws" and gross mismanage-
ment of the *Weekly Worker,* nor for me — except, perhaps,
the "last committee".

House-painting was dead; clerical work was always out of the question — I couldn't add a column of figures without hanging on like grim death till I got to the top, and two trips with poor results utterly demoralized me. Deafness stoof in the way of a possible Government billet.

My two books published by Angus and Robertson, *In the Days When the World was Wide* and *While the Billy Boils*, are advertised as in their seventh thousand and eighth thousand respectively. The former is sold to the public at 5s; the latter has been sold in various editions at from 5s to 2s 6d. My total receipts from these books have been something over £200; and I have sold the entire rights. The books represent the cream of twelve years' literary work. I estimate my whole literary earnings during that period at £700.

I went to W.A. again, painted houses, and wrote a little for the *Western Mail* people — who, by the way, didn't treat me so badly. Came back, went to Maoriland again, and taught school. I had a wife by this time. When I came back to Sydney last year there were three in the party.

Up to a couple of years ago the *Bulletin* paid me at the fixed rate of a guinea a column; but advances written off and special prices for special matter brought it nearer 30s per col. all through. The only thing I have to complain about with regard to the *Bulletin* is that the paper is unable to publish the sketches and stories within resonable time. Some of mine published lately were written and paid for as far back as '91. While the publication of "W.B.B." was being arranged for, the *Bulletin* held some stories and sketches which were to complete the "Steelman" and "Mitchell" series; and, as the *Bulletin* could not rush them through, an idea of having the matter arranged with an eye to sequence had to be abandoned. Which explains the apparently haphazard appearance of the order of the stories and sketches in the volume, and will be responsible for the same thing in my next prose volume — which will contain some *introductory* sketches to others in "W.B.B.".

There are, perhaps, a score of Australian writers known to the *Bulletin*, and most of them little more than lads, who could write better stuff than has been appearing in the shoal of popular English magazines lately (no offence intended); but they have no scope, and, as far as I can see, no hope of future material encouragement from the "great" and wealthy Australasian weeklies and dailies, only one or two of which (excepting the *Sunday Times*) that I know of have, up to date, offered even the most niggardly assistance to purely Australian writers, and this only after the *Bulletin* had introduced them and established their Australian reputations. Many papers, notably in Maoriland, clip their racy Australian sketches from the *Bulletin;* and in at least one of these offices that I know, and have a hearty contempt for, it would be thought an act of charity to offer a hard-up *Bulletin* writer 5s per col.; while in another it would be a mark of special favour to offer him a chair. I have stood (and walked up and down and boiled over) for two hours in the passage outside the office of a paper which has been "clipping" my work for years, and this because they knew I was hard up and wanted them to pay for a contribution by way of a change.

Meanwhile, our best Australian artists and writers are being driven to England and America — where the leaders are making their mark, and a decent living; and the rest would follow in a lump if *they* got the show.

The work of some of those who have gone brightened Australia for years, yet no one asked how they lived, and no one, in all the wide Australias, stood up and asked whether a native-born artist or writer went aboard the boat with a decent suit to his back, or a five-pound note in his pocket. And they talk about our "cheap", "unhealthy" or "affected pessimism!" The fools!

A last word for myself. I don't know about the merit or value of my work; all I know is that I started a shy, ignorant lad from the Bush, under every disadvantage arising from poverty and lack of education, and with the extra disadvantage of partial deafness thrown in. I started with implicit faith in human nature, and a heart full of love for Australia, and hatred for wrong and injustice. I taught myself a trade — the first years in Sydney I rose at five o'clock in the morning to go to work with a rough crowd in the factory of a hard taskmaster; and learnt the little I did at a night-school; and I worked even then, before I could write, for a cause I believed in. I sought out my characters and studied them; I wrote of nothing that I had not myself seen or experienced; I wrote and re-wrote painfully, and believed that every line was true and for the right. I kept steady and worked hard for seven years, and that work met with appreciation in Australia and a warm welcome in London. When desperately hard up and with a wife to provide for, I at last was forced to apply to the Govt. for temporary work. I was kept hanging about the office for weeks; and when, as a last resource, I applied for a railway-pass for a month to enable me to find work in the country and gather new material for literary work, I did not receive a reply. I was obliged to seek the means of earning bread and butter from the Govt. of a province (M.L.) in whose people's interests I had never written a line.

My advice to any young Australian writer whose talents have been recognized, would be to go steerage, stow away, swim, and seek London, Yankeeland, or Timbuctoo — rather than stay in Australia till his genius turned to gall, or beer. Or, failing this — and still in the interests of human nature and literature — to study elementary anatomy, especially as applies to the cranium, and then shoot himself carefully with the aid of a looking-glass.

Crime in the Bush

The average city man's ignorance concerning the nearer bush — to say nothing of "Out-Back" — and the human life therein, is greater even than the average new-chum's, for the new-chum usually takes pains to collect information concerning the land of his exile, adoption, or hope. To the city mind the drovers, the shearers, the station-hands, the "cockies" or farmers, the teamsters, and even the diggers, all belong to one and the same class, and are accepted in the street under the general term of "bushies" — and no questions asked. The city mind is too much occupied by the board-and-lodging or rent problems, etc., to have any but the vaguest ideas concerning the unique conditions of the life that lies beyond the cities. And, in return, the Sydney or Melbourne man is regarded Out-Back as a jackeroo or new-chum — little or no distinction being made between the Australian-born "green-hand" and the newly-arrived cockney; which is just. But it is with the farmer or "cockie" class that the writer is here chiefly concerned, for it is mostly in the so-called "settled" districts that are committed the crimes which seem so brutally senseless or motiveless to city people.

The shearer is a social animal at his worst; he is often a city bushman — i.e., a man who has been through and round and between the provinces by rail and boat. Not unfrequently he is an English public school man and a man of the world; so even the veriest Out-Back bushie, whose metropolis is Bourke, is brought in touch with outside civilization. But there are hundreds of out-of-the-way places in the nearer bush of Australia — hidden away in unheard-of "pockets" in the ranges; on barren creeks (abandoned by pioneering farmers and pastoralists "moving up country" half a century ago); up at the ends of long, dark gullies, and away out on God-forsaken "box", native-apple, or stringy-

bark flats — where families live for generations in mental
darkness almost inconceivable in this enlightened age and
country. They are often in a worse condition mentally than
savages to the manner born; for natural savages have a social
law, a social intercourse — perhaps more or less inadequate,
but infinitely better than none at all. Some of these families
live from one year's end to another without seeing a face
except the face of somebody of their own class, and that of
an occasional stranger whose character or sanity must at
least be doubtful, to explain his presence in such places.
Some of these families are descended from a convict of the
worst type on one side or the other, perhaps on both; and, if
not born criminals, are trained in shady ways from childhood. Conceived and bred under the shadow of exile,
hardship, or "trouble", the sullen, brooding spirit which
enwraps their lonely bush-buried homes will carry further
their moral degradation. You may sometimes see a dray or
spring-cart, of antiquated pattern, dragging wearily and
unnoticed into the "township", and containing a woman,
haggard and spiritless-looking, or hard and vicious-faced —
or else a sullen, brooding man — who sells produce for tea,
flour, and sugar, and goes out again within the hour,
without, perhaps, having exchanged half-a-dozen words
with anyone. This is the only hint conveyed to the outer
fringe of God's country — and wasted on apathetic neighbours — of the existence of such a people.

These places need to be humanized. There are things
done in the bush (where large families, and sometimes
several large families, pig together in ignorance in badly-
partitioned huts) known well to neighbours; or to school-
teachers — mere lads, going through their martyrdom in
such places — and to girl-teachers too, God forgive us! — or
even to the police; things which would make a strong man
shudder. Clean-minded people shrink from admitting the
existence of such things, until one, bolder than the rest, and
with the certainty of having his or her good name connected
with, perhaps, one of the dirtiest cases known to police
annals, speaks up for the sake of outraged nature and
reason, and "horrifies" Australia. But too often the infor-
mant is one of the brooding, unhealthy-minded ruck who
speaks up only from motives of envy or revenge.

We want light on these places. We have the crime of the
Dederers — the two brothers who killed their father and
burnt the body as they would have burned a log, and yet
seemed quite unconscious of having done anything out of

the common. To those who know the conditions under which many families like the Dederers exist in Australia, their crime is neither inexplicable nor particularly astounding. The Dederers, if I remember rightly, were reported as never having been even to the nearest "township" in their dark lives. No doubt they were incapable of expressing, in any sort of language, bush or otherwise, what they felt; if, indeed, they felt anything.

Such dark ignorance is especially dangerous because it is ape-like in its "emotions", in its likes and dislikes. There are families in the bush with the male members of whom an intelligent and experienced bushman would never trust himself alone — if he had reason to be satisfied with the natural shape of the back of his head; nor yet with the female members — if he valued his neck and the *post mortem* memory of him. You might be mates with a man in the bush for months, and be under the impression that you are on the best of terms with him, or even fancy that he has a decided liking for you, and yet he might brood over some fancied slight or injury — something you have said or done, or haven't said or done — anything, in fact, that might suggest itself to an ignorant, morose, and vindictive nature — until his alleged mind is in such a diseased condition that he is capable of turning on you any moment of the day or night and doing you to death.

So the respectable farmer — too outspoken and careless, perhaps, but good-hearted, and never dreaming of the existence of an enemy — turning to slumber again after the "cock-crow" hitch in his sleep, hears a furtive whistle and the clatter of retreating hoofs on slanting slip-rails, and thinks it is some over-late or early neighbours passing through; but starts wide enough awake next time to see the glare, sniff the smoke, and hear the roar and crackle of fire, and, rushing out, white-faced and with heart standing still, finds a shed or stack — the stack of unthreshed wheat, perhaps — in flames. The crime of arson used to be very, very common in Australia — and no "land laws" or "wrongs of Ireland" to explain its prevalence. Such malice is terrifying to those who have seen what it is capable of. You never know when you are safe, no matter how carefully you guard your words, looks, or actions; and the only remedy — for the application of which the law would promptly hang you — would be to sit up nights with a gun with a chalked sight, until you got a glimpse of your ape-minded and unprovoked enemy, and then carefully shoot him.

There are places in Australia where the existence of the evil-eye and of witches is believed in; and where national, religious, and clan hatreds, which perhaps have died out in the old-world countries from which they came, are preserved in their original intensity; where is all the ignorant suspicion and distrust of a half-savage peasantry. The police, whose duty it is to collect returns for harmless agricultural statistics, can tell you of the difficulty they experience — and not in such out-of-the-way localities either — and of the obstacles thrown in their way when trying to obtain the barest reliable information. "Experienced great difficulty in obtaining information from land-holders"; "Declines to supply necessary information"; "Still refuses," etc., are common on the margins and "remark" spaces of returned and re-returned schedule-forms. Perhaps the cruellest of all the bad sights of the bush is the case of the child born to a family with which it has nothing in common mentally (possibly physically) — the "throw-back" to original and better stock — whose bright mind is slowly but surely warped to madness by the conditions of life under which the individual is expected to be contented and happy. Such warped natures are often responsible for the worst sexual crimes. There are brutally selfish parents in the bush who regard and work their children as slaves — and worse. Any experienced bush school-teacher could bear me out in this, with heartrending stories of child slavery and ill-treatment almost past belief. I remember the case of a boy who attended night-school with me for a few months in the bush. His parents sent him under pressure of "public opinion". He had to work from daylight until after dark, and do the work of a man — or be starved and beaten to it. He was nineteen, and an idiot. But some people said that he was only an adopted son.

Democratic Maoriland, with its natural and geographical advantages over Australia, is yet not free from the dark spot I refer to. I have known three white children at a Maori (native) school who belonged to a family of (originally) seventeen children. Two or three of the family were alleged to be the children of the eldest unmarried daughter. Of the three who attended school, two girls and a boy, the boy was over fourteen; the girls eight and nine. The boy was ignorant even of the existence of an alphabet. He had the face of a weazened, vicious little old man; and a good deal of the nature. The girls' faces were little masks of what their mother's might have been were she twenty or thirty years older. Both parents looked younger and fresher than the children. Boy and girls rose at daylight, cooked their parents' breakfast (bacon, eggs, etc.), carried it into them, had a meal of bread and fat, and, when necessary, went into the bush to cut and get together a load of firewood. And the girls were eight and nine. The boy's physical development was naturally abnormal, but his head didn't seem to belong to his body. Sons can be over-worked, starved, stunted mentally, and otherwise cruelly treated to such an extent that they are capable of turning upon and killing a brutish parent — just as savage slaves will, when they get the chance, kill their savage masters.

Then there is the unprovoked, unpremeditated, passionless, and almost inexplicable bush murder, when two mates have lived together in the bush for years, until they can pass days and weeks without exchanging a word, or noticing anything unusual in the circumstance — till the shadow of the over-hanging, brooding ridge, or the awful monotony of the horizonless plain, deadens and darkens the mind of one so that the very presence of his mate, perhaps, becomes a constant source of vague but haunting irritation. Then, one day, being behind the other with an axe or an adze to his hand, he suddenly, but dispassionately, smashes his skull, and is afterwards utterly unable to account for his action except by the muttered explanations that he "had to do it", or "something made me do it". Bush loneliness has the same sort of influence on the blackfellow alone with whites — as instance the latest reported crime committed by a blackfellow, who afterwards expressed sorrow for killing the "poor old man", but couldn't understood why he did it — unless it was because the white man, having stooped to drink, was in "such a good position for killing".

Such crimes as those just instanced, and worse, might be described as the ultimate result of a craving for variety — for something better or brighter, perhaps, but, anyway, something *different* — the protest of the outraged nature of the black or white savage against the — to him — unnatural conditions.

Respectability only intensifies the awful monotony of these wretched bush townships — till the women are forced to watch for dirt and holes in a neighbour's washing hung out on the line, and men to gossip and make mischief like women. Short-comings in a neighbour are talked about and exaggerated — and invented. Even a tragedy is secretly welcomed — notwithstanding the fact that the whole community is supposed, in double-column head-lines, to be horrified. Careless remarks are caught up, disturbed and magnified. No respectable girl can leave the township on an innocent visit without something discreditable being discovered to be connected with her departure from the wretched hole. City spielers attach themselves to local pubs and prey with little or no disguise on idiotic cheque-men; bush larrikins — who are becoming more contemptible and cowardly than their city prototypes — openly boast of their "successes", and give the girl's name. And both classes are accepted as commonplace — the community never dreams of giving them an hour's start to get out of reach of *men*, or stand the penalty.

Then there is the miserable bush feud which arises (perhaps started generations ago — the original cause forgotten) over a stray bull, a party fence, a girl, a practical joke, a misunderstanding, or a fancied slight — anything or nothing; and is brooded over by men who have little else to think about in the brooding bush. There is the threat to "pull yer" and have satisfaction — the miserable court-case and cross-action brought on the paltriest pretences that ever merited the disgust of a magistrate — intensifying hatreds to a murderous degree. And "friends" aid and abet and fan the hell-fire in men's hearts, till at last birth is given to the spirit that sneaks out after dark and cuts a neighbour's wire-fences, or before daylight and stands a gate ajar, or softly lets down the rails that a neighbour's own cattle may get into his crop or garden, destroying the result of months of weary toil and taking the food out of his children's mouths. The spirit that shoots or hamstrings horses grazing under the star-light; that sets a match to stack or shed.

Mischief breeds mischief; malice, malice; and the tongues of the local hags applaud and chorus, and damn and exaggerate and lie, until the wretched hole is ripe for a "horror". Then the Horror comes.

The Iron-Bark Chip

Dave Regan and party — bush-fencers, tank-sinkers, rough carpenters, etc. — were finishing the third and last culvert of their contract on the last section of the new railway line, and had already sent in their vouchers for the completed contract, so that there might be no excuse for extra delay in connection with the cheque.

Now it had been expressly stipulated in the plans and specifications that the timber for certain beams and girders was to be iron-bark and no other, and Government inspectors were authorized to order the removal from the ground of any timber or material they might deem inferior, or not in accordance with the stipulations. The railway contractor's foreman and inspector of sub-contractors was a practical man and a bushman, but he had been a timber-getter himself; his sympathies were bushy, and he was on winking terms with Dave Regan. Besides, extended time was expiring, and the contractors were in a hurry to complete the line. But the Government inspector was a reserved man who poked round on his independent own and appeared in lonely spots at unexpected times — with apparently no definite object in life — like a grey kangaroo bothered by a new wire fence, but unsuspicious of the presence of humans. He wore a grey suit, rode, or mostly led, an ashen-grey horse; the grass was long and grey, so he was seldom spotted until he was well within the horizon and bearing leisurely down on a party of sub-contractors, leading his horse.

Now iron-bark was scarce and distant on those ridges, and another timber, similar in appearance, but much inferior in grain and "standing" quality, was plentiful and close at hand. Dave and party were "about full of" the job and place, and wanted to get their cheque and be gone to another "spec" they had in view. So they came to reckon they'd get the last girder from a handy tree, and have it

squared, in place, and carefully and conscientiously tarred
before the inspector happened along, if he did. But they
didn't. They got it squared, and ready to be lifted into its
place; the kindly darkness of tar was ready to cover a fraud
that took four strong men with crowbars and levers to shift;
and now (such is the regular cussedness of things) as the
fraudulent piece of timber lay its last hour on the ground,
looking and smelling, to their guilty imaginations like
anything but iron-bark, they were aware of the Government
inspector drifting down upon them obliquely, with something of the atmosphere of a casual Bill or Jim who had
dropped out of his easy-going track to see how they were
getting on, and borrow a match. They had more than half
hoped that, as he had visited them pretty frequently during
the progress of the work, and knew how near it was to
completion, he wouldn't bother coming any more. But it's
the way with the Government. You might move heaven and
earth in vain endeavour to get the "Guvermunt" to flutter an
eyelash over something of the most momentous importance
to yourself and mates and the district — even to the country;
but just when you are leaving authority severely alone, and
have strong reasons for not wanting to worry or interrupt it,
and not desiring it to worry about you, it will take a fancy
into its head to come along and bother.

"It's always the way!" muttered Dave to his mates. "I knew
the beggar would turn up! . . . . . And the only cronk log
we've had, too!" he added, in an injured tone. "If this had 'a'
been the only blessed iron-bark in the whole contract, it
would have been all right . . . . Good-day, sir!" (to the
inspector). "It's hot?"

The inspector nodded. He was not of an impulsive nature.
He got down from his horse and looked at the girder in an
abstracted way; and presently there came into his eyes a
dreamy, far-away, sad sort of expression, as if there had
been a very sad and painful occurrence in his family, way
back in the past, and that piece of timber in some way
reminded him of it and brought the old sorrow home to him.
He blinked three times, and asked, in a subdued tone:

"Is that iron-bark?"

Jack Bentley, the fluent liar of the party, caught his
breath with a jerk and coughed, to cover the gasp and gain
time. "I — iron-bark? Of course it is! I thought you would
know iron-bark, mister." (Mister was silent.) "What else
d'yer think it is?"

The dreamy, abstracted expression was back. The inspector, by-the-way, didn't know much about timber, but he had a great deal of instinct, and went by it when in doubt.

"L — look here, mister!" put in Dave Regan, in a tone of innocent puzzlement and with a blank bucolic face. "B — but don't the plans and specifications say iron-bark? Ours does, anyway. I — I'll git the papers from the tent and show yer, if yer like."

It was not necessary. The inspector admitted the fact slowly. He stopped, and with an absent air picked up a chip. He looked at it abstractedly for a moment, blinked his threefold blink; then, seeming to recollect an appointment, he woke up suddenly and asked briskly:

"Did this chip come off that girder?"

Blank silence. The inspector blinked six times, divided in threes, rapidly, mounted his horse, said "Day," and rode off.

Regan and party stared at each other.

"Wha — what did he do that for?" asked Andy Page, the third in the party.

"Do what for, you fool?" enquired Dave.

"Ta — take that chip for?"

"He's taking it to the office!" snarled Jack Bentley.

"What — what for? What does he want to do that for?"

"To get it blanky well analyzed! You ass! Now are yer satisifed?" And Jack sat down hard on the timber, jerked out his pipe, and said to Dave, in a sharp, toothache tone:

"Gimmiamatch!"

"We — well! what are we to do now?" enquired Andy, who was the hardest grafter, but altogether helpless, hopeless, and useless in a crisis like this.

"Grain and varnish the bloomin' culvert!" snapped Bentley.

But Dave's eyes, that had been ruefully following the inspector, suddenly dilated. The inspector had ridden a short distance along the line, dismounted, thrown the bridle over a post, laid the chip (which was too big to go in his pocket) on top of it, got through the fence, and was now walking back at an angle across the line in the direction of the fencing party, who had worked up on the other side, a little more than opposite the culvert.

Dave took in the lay of the country at a glance and thought rapidly.

"Gimme an iron-bark chip!" he said suddenly.

Bentley, who was quick-witted when the track was shown him, as is a kangaroo dog (Jack ran by sight, not scent), glanced in the line of Dave's eyes, jumped up, and got a chip about the same size as that which the inspector had taken.

Now the "lay of the country" sloped generally to the line from both sides, and the angle between the inspector's horse, the fencing party, and the culvert was well within a clear concave space; but a couple of hundred yards back from the line and parallel to it (on the side on which Dave's party worked their timber) a fringe of scrub ran to within a few yards of a point with would be about in line with a single tree on the cleared slope, the horse, and the fencing party.

Dave took the iron-bark chip, ran along the bed of the water-course into the scrub, raced up the siding behind the bushes, got safely, though without breathing, across the exposed space, and brought the tree into line between him and the inspector, who was talking to the fencers. Then he began to work quickly down the slope towards the tree (which was a thin one), keeping it in line, his arms close to his sides, and working, as it were, down the trunk of the tree, as if the fencing party were kangaroos and Dave was trying to get a shot at them. The inspector, by-the-bye, had a habit of glancing now and then in the direction of his horse, as though under the impression that it was flighty and restless and inclined to bolt on opportunity. It was an anxious moment for all parties concerned — except the inspector. They didn't want *him* to be perturbed. And, just as Dave reached the foot of the tree, the inspector finished what he had to say to the fencers, turned, and started to walk briskly back to his horse. There was a thunderstorm coming. Now was the critical moment — there were certain prearranged signals between Dave's party and the fencers which might have interested the inspector, but none to meet a case like this.

Jack Bentley gasped, and started forward with an idea of intercepting the inspector and holding him for a few minutes in bogus conversation. Inspirations come to one at a critical moment, and it flashed on Jack's mind to send Andy instead. Andy looked as innocent and guileless as he was, but was uncomfortable in the vicinity of "funny business", and must have an honest excuse. "Not that that mattered," commented Jack afterwards; "it would have taken the inspector ten minutes to get at what Andy was driving at, whatever it was."

"Run, Andy! Tell him there's a heavy thunderstorm coming and he'd better stay in our humpy till it's over. Run! Don't stand staring like a blanky fool. He'll be gone!"

Andy started. But just then, as luck would have it, one of

the fencers started after the inspector, hailing him as "Hi, mister!" He wanted to be set right about the survey or something — or to pretend to want to be set right — from motives of policy which I haven't time to explain here.

That fencer explained afterwards to Dave's party that he "seen what you coves was up to," and that's why he called the inspector back. But he told them that after they had told their yarn — which was a mistake.

"Come back, Andy!" cried jack Bentley.

Dave Regan slipped round the tree, down on his hands and knees, and made quick time through the grass which, luckily, grew pretty tall on the thirty or forty yards of slope between the tree and the horse. Close to the horse, a thought struck Dave that pulled him up, and sent a shiver along his spine and a hungry feeling under it. The horse would break away and bolt! But the case was desperate. Dave ventured an interrogatory "Cope, cope, cope?" The horse turned its head wearily and regarded him with a mild eye, as if he'd expected him to come, and come on all fours, and wondered what had kept him so long; then he went on thinking. Dave reached the foot of the post; the horse obligingly leaning over on the other leg. Dave reared head and shoulders cautiously behind the post, like a snake; his hand went up twice, swiftly — the first time he grabbed the inspector's chip, and the second time he put the iron-bark one in its place. He drew down and back, and scuttled off for the tree like a gigantic tailless "goanna".

A few minutes later he walked up to the culvert from along the creek, smoking hard to settle his nerves.

The sky seemed to darken suddenly; the first great drops of the thunderstorm came pelting down. The inspector hurried to his horse, and cantered off along the line in the direction of the fettlers' camp.

He had forgotten all about the chip, and left it on top of the post!

Dave Regan sat down on the beam in the rain and swore comprehensively.

PAST CARIN'

Now up and down the siding brown
    The great black crows are flyin',
And down below the spur, I know,
    Another "milker's" dyin';
The crops have withered from the ground,
    The tank's clay bed is glarin',
But from my heart no tear nor sound,
    For I have gone past carin'—
            Past worryin' or carin',
            Past feelin' aught or carin';
            But from my heart no tear nor sound,
            For I have gone past carin'.

Through Death and Trouble, turn about,
    Through hopeless desolation,
Through flood and fever, fire and drought,
    And slavery and starvation;
Through childbirth, sickness, hurt, and blight,
    And nervousness an' scarin',
Through bein' left alone at night,
    I've got to be past carin'.
            Past botherin' or carin',
            Past feelin' and past carin';
            Through city cheats and neighbours' spite,
            I've come to be past carin'.

Our first child took, in days like these,
    A cruel week in dyin',
All day upon her father's knees,
    Or on my poor breast lyin';
The tears we shed — the prayers we said
    Were awful, wild -- despairin'!
I've pulled three through, and buried two
    Since then — and I'm past carin'.
            I've grown to be past carin',
            Past worryin' and wearin';
            I've pulled three through and buried two
            Since then, and I'm past carin'.

'Twas ten years first, then came the worst,
    All for a dusty clearin',
I thought, I thought my heart would burst
    When first my man went shearin';
He's drovin' in the great North-west,
    I don't know how he's farin';
For I, the one that loved him best,
    Have grown to be past carin'.

I've grown to be past carin'
Past lookin' for or carin';
The girl that waited long ago,
Has lived to be past carin'.

My eyes are dry, I cannot cry,
    I've got no heart for breakin',
But where it was in days gone by,
    A dull and empty achin'.
My last boy ran away from me,
    I know my temper's wearin',
But now I only wish to be
    Beyond all signs of carin'.
        Past wearyin' or carin',
        Past feelin' and despairin';
        And now I only wish to be
        Beyond all signs of carin'.

SECOND CLASS WAIT HERE

On suburban railway stations — you may see them as you
        pass—
There are signboards on the platforms saying, "Wait here
        second class";
And to me the whirr and thunder and the cluck of running
        gear
Seem to be for ever saying, saying "Second class wait here"—
        "Wait here second class,
        "Second class wait here".
Seem to be for ever saying, saying "Second class wait here".

And the second class were waiting in the days of serf and
        prince,
And the second class are waiting — they've been waiting
        ever since.
There are gardens in the background, and the line is bare and
        drear,
Yet they wait beneath a signboard, sneering "Second class
        wait here".

I have waited oft in winter, in the mornings dark and damp,
When the asphalt platform glistened underneath the lonely
        lamp.
Ghastly on the brick-faced cutting "Sellum's Soap" and
        "Blower's Beer";
Ghastly on enamelled signboards with their "Second class
        wait here".

And the others seemed like burglars, slouched and muffled
    to the throats,
Standing round apart and silent in their shoddy overcoats,
And the wind among the wires, and the poplars bleak and
    bare,
Seemed to be for ever snarling, snarling "Second class wait
    there".

Out beyond the further suburb, 'neath a chimney stack
    alone,
Lay the works of Grinder Brothers, with a platform of their
    own;
And I waited there and suffered, waited there for many a
    year,
Slaved beneath a phantom signboard, telling our class to wait
    here.

Ah! a man must feel revengeful for a boyhood such as mine.
God! I hate the very houses near the workshop by the line;
And the smell of railway stations, and the roar of running
    gear,
And the scornful-seeming signboards, saying "Second class
    wait here".

There's a train with Death for driver, which is ever going
    past,
And there are no class compartments, and we all must go at
    last
To the long white jasper platform with an Eden in the rear;
And there won't be any signboards, saying "Second class wait
    here".

Letter to Earl Beauchamp

North Sydney.
19th January 1900.

Dear Lord Beauchamp,

I heard that you had spoken kindly of my books — "When the World Was Wide" and "While the Billy Boils" — and as you take an interest in art and literature, I thought, as a last resource, I would confide in you and ask you to help me. The manly and independent spirit you have shown since you came to govern the colony helped to decide me. The attached article, "Pursuing Literature", speaks for itself. All that I can say is that it is true and takes the widest possible view of the situation. The English reviews and correspondence in last part of scrap-book — if you will kindly glance at it — will explain my present position in the literary world (I must apologize for the appearance of scrap-book, which is not very presentable; it has knocked round in camps.)

The position of purely Australian literature is altogether hopeless in Australia — there is no market. The oldest and wealthiest Daily in Australia fills its columns with matter clipped from English and American magazines. The usual answer to would-be Australian contributors is, "Very sorry, Mr. So-and-So, but we have already exceeded our allowance for outside contributions." Nothing "goes" well here that does not come from or through England.

I have recently been obliged to sell, or, rather, sacrifice two more books in Australia, and both are larger and contain better class work than my first two. I would have waited until these books came out before writing to you, but there has been a delay in the printing. I send you specimens of the work I am doing now for £1 per column. I have been contributing to a Sydney daily, but the war news has crowded me out. I have to sell for £1 per column work that is honestly worth five.

I have never been in a position to wait until my work got home, found a market, and the money got back. I have had splendid reviews in the leading English literary journals, and letters from most of the publishers, but am tied down here because I can scarcely make a living, let alone money to go home or to keep me while I did good work and got it on the English market. I am, because of the prices paid literary men here, obliged to publish rubbish — or, at least, good ideas in a hurried and mutilated form — and, because of the reputation I have gained in Australia, I am forced to sign hurried work — else I couldn't get it published at all. That's the cruellest part of the business.

In short, I am wasting my work, wasting my life, spoiling the reputation I have gained, and wearing out my brains and heart here in Australia. If I were single I would find my way to England somehow; but I am married, have one child, and another one due this month, so I am tied hopelessly. We live comfortably on £2 per week, and it takes me all my time to make that with my pen.

I am sure that I could, in six months, command my own prices in London — but how am I to get there? In order to succeed it would be necessary for me to be in London a few months to learn the ropes. We cannot deal at this distance, as it takes 9 months at least to correspond with two magazines in succession. Or if I could have 12 months out here clear of financial worry, to do my best work and get it home, I would, I feel sure, raise myself out of this grinding, sordid life which is killing my work and me.

I send you a book by Barcroft Boake, a young Australian who, if he had lived, would have been our leading poet. While his best work was being published he hanged himself in the scrub, down Botany way — for the same reasons that I want to raise myself out of this hole of a place.

I will not appeal to the country. I can see nothing before me but years of hack-work, of sacrificing my books as soon as written — and before it — and in the end perhaps a big name in London and a chance to go there, and fancy prices, *when I have written myself out* — it was the case with Louis Becke. And all this for the want of a hundred pounds or so at the start. I have been obliged to sell all my rights as you will see by enclosed agreement — which you will kindly cause to be returned with scrap-book — everything except perhaps my soul; our newspaper proprietors would buy that if they could make anything on it.

I — how shall I put this? Will you help me out of the miserable hole I am in? I heard you were rich. All my friends are as poor as myself. I know none of our scrubby aristocracy, nor do I wish to know them. Will you — say — send me enough to hang out here for a year independent of the Australian Press — or go home? I could go in about April, but could not leave my wife behind. And I'm sure that within two years I could win fame and fortune in London and repay you. If you cannot help me, kindly destroy this. It is the first letter of this kind I have ever written in my life, and will be the last.

Yours truly,
HENRY LAWSON

Tried very hard to go as War correspondent with contingent; but could not get paper to pay expenses.

SECTION 5
1899-1901

Editor's Note

Lawson left for London in April 1900 and returned to Australia in May 1902. The stories in this section are selected from *Joe Wilson's Mates*, published by Blackwood while he was in England, hence the notes explaining Australian usage.

The Loaded Dog

Dave Regan, Jim Bently, and Andy Page were sinking a shaft at Stony Creek in search of a rich gold quartz reef which was supposed to exist in the vicinity. There is always a rich reef supposed to exist in the vicinity; the only questions are whether it is ten feet or hundreds beneath the surface, and in which direction. They had struck some pretty solid rock, also water which kept them baling. They used the old-fashioned blasting-powder and time-fuse. They'd make a sausage or cartridge of blasting-powder in a skin of strong calico or canvas, the mouth sewn and bound round the end of the fuse; they'd dip the cartridge in melted tallow to make it water-tight, get the drill-hole as dry as possible, drop in the cartridge with some dry dust, and wad and ram with stiff clay and broken brick. Then they'd light the fuse and get out of the hole and wait. The result was usually an ugly pot-hole in the bottom of the shaft and half a barrow-load of broken rock.

There was plenty of fish in the creek, fresh-water bream, cod, cat-fish, and tailers. The party were fond of fish, and Andy and Dave of fishing. Andy would fish for three hours at a stretch if encouraged by a "nibble" or a "bite" now and then — say once in twenty minutes. The butcher was always willing to give meat in exchange for fish when they caught more than they could eat; but now it was winter, and these fish wouldn't bite. However, the creek was low, just a chain of muddy water-holes, from the hole with a few bucketfuls in it to the sizeable pool with an average depth of six or seven feet, and they could get fish by baling out the smaller holes or muddying up the water in the larger ones till the fish rose to the surface. There was the cat-fish, with spikes growing out of the sides of its head, and if you got pricked you'd know it, as Dave said. Andy took off his boots, tucked up his trousers, and went into a hole one day to stir up the mud with his feet, and he knew it. Dave scooped one out with his hand and got pricked, and he knew it too; his arm swelled, and the pain throbbed up into his shoulder, and down into his stomach too, he said, like a toothache he had once, and kept him awake for two nights — only the toothache pain had a "burred edge", Dave said.

Dave got an idea.

"Why not blow the fish up in the big water-hole with a cartridge?" he said. "I'll try it."

He thought the thing out and Andy Page worked it out. Andy usually put Dave's theories into practice if they were practicable, or bore the blame for the failure and the chaffing of his mates if they weren't.

He made a cartridge about three times the size of those they used in the rock. Jim Bently said it was big enough to blow the bottom out of the river. The inner skin was of stout calico; Andy stuck the end of a six-foot piece of fuse well down in the powder and bound the mouth of the bag firmly to it with whipcord. The idea was to sink the cartridge in the water with the open end of the fuse attached to a float on the surface, ready for lighting. Andy dipped the cartridge in melted bees'-wax to make it water-tight. "We'll have to leave it some time before we light it," said Dave, "to give the fish time to get over their scare when we put it in, and come nosing round again; so we'll want it well water-tight."

Round the cartridge Andy, at Dave's suggestion, bound a strip of sail canvas — that they used for making water-bags — to increase the force of the explosion, and round that he pasted layers of stiff brown paper — on the plan of the sort of fireworks we called "gun-crackers". He let the paper dry in the sun, then he sewed a covering of two thicknesses of canvas over it, and bound the thing from end to end with stout fishing-line. Dave's schemes were elaborate, and he often worked his inventions out to nothing. The cartridge was rigid and solid enough now — a formidable bomb; but Andy and Dave wanted to be sure. Andy sewed on another layer of canvas, dipped the cartridge in melted tallow, twisted a length of fencing-wire round it as an afterthought, dipped it in tallow again, and stood it carefully against a tent-peg, where he'd know where to find it, and wound the fuse loosely round it. Then he went to the camp-fire to try some potatoes which were boiling in their jackets in a billy, and to see about frying some chops for dinner. Dave and Jim were at work in the claim that morning.

They had a big black young retriever dog — or rather an overgrown pup, a big, foolish, four-footed mate, who was always slobbering round them and lashing their legs with his heavy tail that swung round like a stock-whip. Most of his head was usually a red, idiotic, slobbering grin of appreciation of his own silliness. He seemed to take life, the world, his two-legged mates, and his own instinct as a huge joke. He'd retrieve anything: he carted back most of the camp rubbish that Andy threw away. They had a cat that died in hot weather, and Andy threw it a good distance away in the scrub; and early one morning the dog found the cat, after it had been dead a week or so, and carried it back to camp, and laid it just inside the tent-flaps, where it could best make its presence known when the mates should rise and begin to sniff suspiciously in the sickly smothering atmosphere of the summer sunrise. He used to retrieve them when they went in swimming; he'd jump in after them, and take their hands in his mouth, and try to swim out with them, and scratch their naked bodies with his paws. They loved him for his good-heartedness and his foolishness, but when they wished to enjoy a swim they had to tie him up in camp.

He watched Andy with great interest all the morning making the cartridge, and hindered him considerably, trying to help; but about noon he went off to the claim to see how Dave and Jim were getting on, and to come home to dinner with them. Andy saw them coming, and put a panful of mutton-chops on the fire. Andy was cook today; Dave and Jim stood with their backs to the fire, as Bushmen do in all weathers, waiting till dinner should be ready. The retriever went nosing round after something he seemed to have missed.

Andy's brain still worked on the cartridge; his eye was caught by the glare of an empty kerosene-tin lying in the bushes, and it struck him that it wouldn't be a bad idea to sink the cartridge packed with clay, sand, or stones in the tin, to increase the force of the explosion. He may have been all out, from a scientific point of view, but the notion looked all right to him. Jim Bently, by the way, wasn't interested in their "damned silliness". Andy noticed an empty treacle-tin — the sort with the little tin neck or spout soldered on to the top for the convenience of pouring out the treacle — and it struck him that this would have made the best kind of cartridge-case: he would only have had to pour in the powder, stick the fuse in through the neck, and cork and seal it with bees'-wax. He was turning to suggest this to Dave, when Dave glanced over his shoulder to see how the chops were doing — and bolted. He explained afterwards that he thought he heard the pan spluttering extra, and looked to see if the chops were burning. Jim Bently looked behind and bolted after Dave. Andy stood stock-still, staring after them.

"Run, Andy! run!" they shouted back at him. "Run!!! Look behind you, you fool!" Andy turned slowly and looked, and there, close behind him, was the retriever with the cartridge in his mouth — wedged into his broadest and silliest grin. And that wasn't all. The dog had come round the fire to Andy, and the loose end of the fuse had trailed and waggled over the burning sticks into the blaze; Andy had slit and nicked the firing end of the fuse well, and now it was hissing and spitting properly.

Andy's legs started with a jolt; his legs started before his brain did, and he made after Dave and Jim. And the dog followed Andy.

Dave and Jim were good runners — Jim the best — for a short distance; Andy was slow and heavy, but he had the strength and the wind and could last. The dog leapt and capered round him, delighted as a dog could be to find his mates, as he thought, on for a frolic. Dave and Jim kept shouting back, "Don't foller us! don't foller us, you coloured fool!" but Andy kept on, no matter how they dodged. They could never explain, any more than the dog, why they followed each other, but so they ran, Dave keeping in Jim's track in all its turnings, Andy after Dave, and the dog circling round Andy — the live fuse swishing in all directions and hissing and spluttering and stinking. Jim yelling to Dave not to follow him, Dave shouting to Andy to go in another direction — to "spread out", and Andy roaring at the dog to go home. Then Andy's brain began to work, stimulated by the crisis: he tried to get a running kick at the dog, but the dog dodged; he snatched up sticks and stones and threw them at the dog and ran on again. The retriever saw that he'd made a mistake about Andy, and left him and bounded after Dave. Dave, who had the presence of mind to think that the fuse's time wasn't up yet, made a dive and a grab for the dog, caught him by the tail, and as he swung round snatched the cartridge out of his mouth and flung it as far as he could: the dog immediately bounded after it and retrieved it. Dave roared and cursed at the dog, who seeing that Dave was offended, left him and went after Jim, who was well ahead. Jim swung to a sapling and went up it like a native bear; it was a young sapling, and Jim couldn't safely get more than ten or twelve feet from the ground. The dog laid the cartridge, as carefully as if it was a kitten, at the foot of the sapling, and capered and leaped and whooped joyously round under Jim. The big pup reckoned that this was part of the lark — he was all right now — it was Jim who was out for a spree. The fuse sounded as if it were going a mile a minute. Jim tried to climb higher and the sapling bent and cracked. Jim fell on his feet and ran. The dog swooped on the cartridge and followed. It all took but a very few moments. Jim ran to a digger's hole, about ten feet deep, and dropped down into it — landing on soft mud — and was safe. The dog grinned sardonically down on him, over the edge, for a moment, as if he thought it would be a good lark to drop the cartridge down on Jim.

"Go away, Tommy," said Jim feebly, "go away."

The dog bounded off after Dave, who was the only one in sight now; Andy had dropped behind a log, where he lay flat on his face, having suddenly remembered a picture of the Russo-Turkish war with a circle of Turks lying flat on their faces (as if they were ashamed) round a newly-arrived shell.

There was a small hotel or shanty on the creek, on the main road, not far from the claim. Dave was desperate, the time flew much faster in his stimulated imagination than it did in reality, so he made for the shanty. There were several casual Bushmen on the verandah and in the bar; Dave rushed into the bar, banging the door to behind him. "My dog!" he gasped, in reply to the astonished stare of the publican, "the blanky retriever — he's got a live cartridge in his mouth — —"

The retriever, finding the front door shut against him, had bounded round and in by the back way, and now stood smiling in the doorway leading from the passage, the cartridge still in his mouth and the fuse spluttering. They burst out of that bar. Tommy bounded first after one and then after another, for, being a young dog, he tried to make friends with everybody.

The Bushmen ran round corners, and some shut themselves in the stable. There was a new weather-board and corrugated-iron kitchen and wash-house on piles in the back-yard, with some women washing clothes inside. Dave and the publican bundled in there and shut the door — the publican cursing Dave and calling him a crimson fool, in hurried tones, and wanting to know what the hell he came here for.

The retriever went in under the kitchen, amongst the piles, but, luckily for those inside, there was a vicious yellow mongrel cattle-dog sulking and nursing his nastiness under there — a sneaking, fighting, thieving canine, whom neighbours had tried for years to shoot or poison. Tommy saw his danger — he'd had experience from this dog — and started out and across the yard, still sticking to the cartridge. Half-way across the yard the yellow dog caught him and nipped him. Tommy dropped the cartridge, gave one terrified yell, and took to the Bush. The yellow dog followed him to the fence and then ran back to see what he had dropped.

Nearly a dozen other dogs came from round all the corners and under the buildings — spidery, thievish, cold-blooded kangaroo-dogs, mongrel sheep- and cattle-dogs, vicious black and yellow dogs — that slip after you in the dark, nip your heels, and vanish without explaining — and yapping, yelping small fry. They kept at a respectable distance round the nasty yellow dog, for it was dangerous to go near him when he thought he had found something which might be good for a dog to eat. He sniffed at the cartridge twice, and was just taking a third cautious sniff when ——

It was very good blasting powder — a new brand that Dave had recently got up from Sydney; and the cartridge had been excellently well made. Andy was very patient and painstaking in all he did, and nearly as handy as the average sailor with needles, twine, canvas, and rope.

Bushmen say that that kitchen jumped off its piles and on again. When the smoke and dust cleared away, the remains of the nasty yellow dog were lying against the paling fence of the yard looking as if he had been kicked into a fire by a horse and afterwards rolled in the dust under a barrow, and finally thrown against the fence from a distance. Several saddle-horses, which had been "hanging-up" round the verandah, were galloping wildly down the road in clouds of dust, with broken bridle-reins flying; and from a circle round the outskirts, from every point of the compass in the scrub, came the yelping of dogs. Two of them went home, to the place where they were born, thirty miles away, and reached it the same night and stayed there; it was not till towards evening that the rest came back cautiously to make inquiries. One was trying to walk on two legs, and most of 'em looked more or less singed; and a little, singed, stumpy-tailed dog, who had been in the habit of hopping the back half of him along on one leg, had reason to be glad that he'd saved up the other leg all those years, for he needed it now.

There was one old one-eyed cattle-dog round that shanty for years afterwards, who couldn't stand the smell of a gun being cleaned. He it was who had taken an interest, only second to that of the yellow dog, in the cartridge. Bushmen said that it was amusing to slip up on his blind side and stick a dirty ramrod under his nose: he wouldn't wait to bring his solitary eye to bear — he'd take to the Bush and stay out all night.

For half an hour or so after the explosion there were several Bushmen round behind the stable who crouched, doubled up, against the wall, or rolled gently on the dust, trying to laugh without shrieking. There were two white women in hysterics at the house, and a half-caste rushing aimlessly round with a dipper of cold water. The publican was holding his wife tight and begging her between her squawks, to "hold up for my sake, Mary, or I'll lam the life out of ye".

Dave decided to apologize later on, "when things had settled a bit", and went back to camp. And the dog that had done it all, "Tommy", the great, idiotic mongrel retriever, came slobbering round Dave and lashing his legs with his tail, and trotted home after him, smiling his broadest, longest, and reddest smile of amiability, and apparently satisfied for one afternoon with the fun he'd had.

Andy chained the dog up securely, and cooked some more chops, while Dave went to help Jim out of the hole.

And most of this is why, for years afterwards, lanky, easy-going Bushmen, riding lazily past Dave's camp, would cry, in a lazy drawl and with just a hint of the nasal twang —

"'El-lo, Da-a-ve! How's the fishin' getting on, Da-a-ve?"

Telling Mrs. Baker

Most Bushmen who hadn't "known Bob Baker to speak to", had "heard tell of him". He'd been a squatter, not many years before, on the Macquarie River in New South Wales, and had made money in the good seasons, and had gone in for horse-racing and racehorse-breeding, and long trips to Sydney, where he put up at swell hotels and went the pace. So after a pretty severe drought, when the sheep died by thousands on his runs, Bob Baker went under, and the bank took over his station and put a manager in charge.

He'd been a jolly, open-handed, popular man, which means that he'd been a selfish man as far as his wife and children were concerned, for they had to suffer for it in the end. Such generosity is often born of vanity, or moral cowardice, or both mixed. It's very nice to hear the chaps sing "For he's a jolly good fellow", but you've mostly got to pay for it twice — first in company, and afterwards alone. I once heard the chaps singing that I was a jolly good fellow, when I was leaving a place and they were giving me a send-off. It thrilled me, and brought a warm gush to my eyes; but, all the same, I wished I had half the money I'd lent them, and spent on 'em, and I wished I'd used the time I'd wasted to be a jolly good fellow.

When I first met Bob Baker he was a boss-drover on the great north-westen route, and his wife lived at the township of Solong on the Sydney side. He was going north to new country round by the Gulf of Carpentaria, with a big mob of cattle, on a two years' trip; and I and my mate, Andy M'Culloch, engaged to go with him. We wanted to have a look at the Gulf Country.

After we had crossed the Queensland border it seemed to me that the Boss was too fond of going into wayside shanties and town pubs. Andy had been with him on another trip, and he told me that the Boss was only going this way lately.

Andy knew Mrs. Baker well, and seemed to think a deal of
her. "She's a good little woman," said Andy. "One of the
right stuff. I worked on their station for a while when I was a
nipper, and I know. She was always a damned sight too good
for the Boss, but she believed in him. When I was coming
away this time she says to me, "Look here, Andy, I'm afraid
Robert is drinking again. Now I want you to look after him
for me, as much as you can — you seem to have as much
influence with him as any one. I want you to promise me
that you'll never have a drink with him."

"And I promised," said Andy, "and I'll keep my word."
Andy was a chap who could keep his word, and nothing else.
And, no matter how the Boss persuaded, or sneered, or
swore at him, Andy would never drink with him.

It got worse and worse: the Boss would ride on ahead and
get drunk at a shanty, and sometimes he'd be days behind
us; and when he'd catch up to us his temper would be just
about as much as we could stand. At last he went on a
howling spree at Mulgatown, about a hundred and fifty
miles north of the border, and, what was worse, he got in
tow with a flash barmaid there — one of those girls who are
engaged, by the publicans up country, as baits for cheque-
men.

He went mad over that girl. He drew an advance cheque
from the stock-owner's agent there, and knocked that down;
then he raised some more money somehow, and spent that
   mostly on the girl.

We did all we could. Andy got him along the track for a
couple of stages, and just when we thought he was all right,
he slipped us in the night and went back.

We had two other men with us, but had the devil's own
bother on account of the cattle. It was a mixed-up job all
round. You see it was all big runs round there, and we had
to keep the bullocks moving along the route all the time, or
else get into trouble for trespass. The agent wasn't going to
go to the expense of putting the cattle in a paddock until the
Boss sobered up; there was very little grass on the route or
the travelling-stock reserves or camps, so we had to keep
travelling for grass.

The world might wobble and all the banks go bung, but
the cattle have to go through — that's the law of the
stock-routes. So the agent wired to the owners, and, when he
got their reply, he sacked the Boss and sent the cattle on in
charge of another man. The new Boss was a drover coming
south after a trip; he had his two brothers with him, so he

didn't want me and Andy; but, anyway, we were full up of this trip, so we arranged, between the agent and the new Boss, to get most of the wages due to us — the Boss had drawn some of our stuff and spent it.

We could have started on the back track at once, but, drunk or sober, mad or sane, good or bad, it isn't Bush religion to desert a mate in a hole; and the Boss was a mate of ours; so we stuck to him.

We camped on the creek, outside the town, and kept him in the camp with us as much as possible, and did all we could for him.

"How could I face his wife if I went home without him?" asked Andy, "or any of his old mates?"

The Boss got himself turned out of the pub. where the barmaid was, and then he'd hang round the other pubs, and get drink somehow, and fight, and get knocked about. He was an awful object by this time, wild-eyed and gaunt, and he hadn't washed or shaved for days.

Andy got the constable in charge of the police station to lock him up for a night, but it only made him worse: we took him back to the camp next morning, and while our eyes were off him for a few minutes he slipped away into the scrub, stripped himself naked, and started to hang himself to a leaning tree with a piece of clothes-line rope. We got to him just in time.

Then Andy wired to the Boss's brother Ned, who was fighting the drought, the rabbit-pest, and the banks, on a small station back on the border. Andy reckoned it was about time to do something.

Perhaps the Boss hadn't been quite right in his head before he started drinking — he had acted queer some time, now we came to think of it; maybe he'd got a touch of sunstroke or got brooding over his troubles — anyway he died in the horrors within the week.

His brother Ned turned up on the last day, and Bob thought he was the devil, and grappled with him. It took the three of us to hold the Boss down sometimes.

Sometimes, towards the end, he'd be sensible for a few minutes and talk about his "poor wife and children"; and immediately afterwards he'd fall a-cursing me, and Andy, and Ned, and calling us devils. He cursed everything; he cursed his wife and children, and yelled that they were dragging him down to hell. He died raving mad. It was the worst case of death in the horrors of drink that I ever saw or heard of in the Bush.

Ned saw to the funeral: it was very hot weather, and men have to be buried quick who die out there in the hot weather — especially men who die in the state the Boss was in. Then Ned went to the public-house where the barmaid was and called the landlord out. It was a desperate fight: the publican was a big man, and a bit of a fighting man; but Ned was one of those quiet, simple-minded chaps who will carry a thing through to death when they make up their minds. He gave that publican nearly as good a thrashing as he deserved. The constable in charge of the station backed Ned, while another policeman picked up the publican. Sounds queer to you city people, doesn't it?

Next morning we three started south. We stayed a couple of days at Ned Baker's station on the border, and then started on our three-hundred-mile ride down-country. The weather was still very hot, so we decided to travel at night for a while, and left Ned's place at dusk. He parted from us at the homestead gate. He gave Andy a small packet, done up in canvas, for Mrs. Baker, which Andy told me contained Bob's pocket-book, letters, and papers. We looked back, after we'd gone a piece along the dusty road, and saw Ned still standing by the gate; and a very lonely figure he looked. Ned was a bachelor. "Poor old Ned," said Andy to me. "He was in love with Mrs. Bob Baker before she got married, but she picked the wrong man — girls mostly do. Ned and Bob were together on the Macquarie, but Ned left when his brother married, and he's been up in these God-forsaken scrubs ever since. Look, I want to tell you something, Jack: Ned has written to Mrs. Bob to tell her that Bob died of fever, and everything was done for him that could be done, and that he died easy — and all that sort of thing. Ned sent her some money, and she is to think that it was the money due to Bob when he died. Now I'll have to go and see her when we get to Solong; there's no getting out of it, I'll have to face her — and you'll have to come with me."

"Damned if I will!" I said.

"But you'll have to," said Andy. "You'll have to stick to me; you're surely not crawler enough to desert a mate in a case like this? I'll have to lie like hell — I'll have to lie as I never lied to a woman before; and you'll have to back me and corroborate every lie."

I'd never seen Andy show so much emotion.

"There's plenty of time to fix up a good yarn" said Andy. He said no more about Mrs. Baker, and we only mentioned the Boss's name casually, until we were within about a day's ride of Solong; then Andy told me the yarn he'd made up about the Boss's death.

"And I want you to listen, Jack," he said, "and remember every word — and if you can fix up a better yarn you can tell me afterwards. Now it was like this: the Boss wasn't too well when he crossed the border. He complained of pains in his back and head and a stinging pain in the back of his neck, and he had dysentery bad, — but that doesn't matter; it's lucky I ain't supposed to tell a woman all the symptoms. The Boss stuck to the job as long as he could, but we managed the cattle and made it as easy as we could for him. He'd just take it easy, and ride on from camp to camp, and rest. One night I rode to a town off the route (or you did, if you like) and got some medicine for him; that made him better for a while, but at last, a day or two this side of Mulgatown, he had to give up. A squatter there drove him into town in his buggy and put him up at the best hotel. The publican knew the Boss and did all he could for him — put him in the best room and wired for another doctor. We wired for Ned as soon as we saw how bad the Boss was, and Ned rode night and day and got there three days before the Boss died. The Boss was a bit off his head some of the time with the fever, but was calm and quiet towards the end and died easy. He talked a lot about his wife and children, and told us to tell the wife not to fret but to cheer up for the children's sake. How does that sound?"

I'd been thinking while I listened, and an idea struck me.

"Why not let her know the truth?" I asked. "She's sure to hear of it sooner or later; and if she knew he was only a selfish, drunken blackguard she might get over it all the sooner."

"You don't know women, Jack." said Andy quietly. "And, anyway, even if she is a sensible woman, we've got a dead mate to consider as well as a living woman."

"But she's sure to hear the truth sooner or later," I said, "the Boss was so well known."

"And that's just the reason why the truth might be kept from her," said Andy. "If he wasn't well known — and nobody could help liking him, after all, when he was straight — if he wasn't so well known the truth might leak out unawares. She won't know if I can help it, or at least not yet a while. If I see any chaps that come from the North I'll put them up to it. I'll tell M'Grath, the publican at Solong, too: he's a straight man — he'll keep his ears open and warn chaps. One of Mrs. Baker's sisters is staying with her, and I'll

give her a hint so that she can warn off any women that
might get hold of a yarn. Besides, Mrs. Baker is sure to go
and live in Sydney, where all her people are — she was a
Sydney girl; and she's not likely to meet any one there that
will tell her the truth. I can tell her that it was the last wish
of the Boss that she should shift to Sydney."

We smoked and thought a while, and by-and-by Andy
had what he called a "happy thought". He went to his
saddle-bags and got out the small canvas packet that Ned
had given him: it was sewn up with packing-thread, and
Andy ripped it open with his pocket-knife.

"What are you doing, Andy?" I asked.

"Ned's an innocent old fool, as far as sin is concerned,"
said Andy. "I guess he hasn't looked through the Boss's
letters, and I'm just going to see that there's nothing here
that will make liars of us."

He looked through the letters and papers by the light of
the fire. There were some letters from Mrs. Baker to her
husband, also a portrait of her and the children; these Andy
put aside. But there were other letters from barmaids and
women who were not fit to be seen in the same street with the
Boss's wife; and there were portraits — one or two flash
ones. There were two letters from other men's wives too.

"And one of these men, at least, was an old mate of his!"
said Andy, in a tone of disgust.

He threw the lot into the fire; then he went through the
Boss's pocket-book and tore out some leaves that had notes
and addresses on them, and burnt them too. Then he sewed
up the packet again and put it away in his saddle-bag.

"Such is life!" said Andy, with a yawn that might have
been half a sigh.

We rode into Solong early in the day, turned our horses
out in a paddock, and put up at M'Grath's pub until such
time as we made up our minds as to what we'd do or where
we'd go. We had an idea of waiting until the shearing
season started and then making Out-Back to the big sheds.

Neither of us was in a hurry to go and face Mrs. Baker.
"We'll go after dinner," said Andy at first; then after dinner
we had a drink, and felt sleepy — we weren't used to big
dinners of roast-beef and vegetables and pudding, and,
besides, it was drowsy weather — so we decided to have a
snooze and then go. When we woke up it was late in the
afternoon, so we thought we'd put it off till after tea. "It
wouldn't be manners to walk in while they're at tea," said
Andy — "it would look as if we only came for some grub."

But while we were at tea a little girl came with a message
that Mrs. Baker wanted to see us, and would be very much
obliged if we'd call up as soon as possible. You see, in those
small towns you can't move without the thing getting round
inside of half an hour.

"We'll have to face the music now!" said Andy, "and no
get out of it." He seemed to hang back more than I did.
There was another pub opposite where Mrs. Baker lived,
and when we got up the street a bit I said to Andy —

"Suppose we go and have another drink first, Andy? We
might be kept in there an hour or two."

"You don't want another drink," said Andy, rather short.
"Why, you seem to be going the same way as the Boss!" But
it was Andy that edged off towards the pub when we got
near Mrs. Baker's place. "All right!" he said. "Come on!
We'll have this other drink, since you want it so bad."

We had the drink, then we buttoned up our coats and
started across the road — we'd bought new shirts and
collars, and spruced up a bit. Half-way across Andy grabbed
my arm and asked —

"How do you feel now, Jack?"

"Oh, *I'm* all right," I said.

"For God's sake!" said Andy, "don't put your foot in it and
make a mess of it."

"I won't, if you don't."

Mrs. Baker's cottage was a little weather-board box affair
back in a garden. When we went in through the gate Andy
gripped my arm again and whispered —

"For God's sake stick to me now, Jack!"

"I'll stick all right," I said — "you've been having too
much beer, Andy."

I had seen Mrs. Baker before, and remembered her as a
cheerful, contented sort of woman, bustling about the house
and getting the Boss's shirts and things ready when we
started North. Just the sort of woman that is contented with
housework and the children, and with nothing particular
about her in the way of brains. But now she sat by the fire
looking like the ghost of herself. I wouldn't have recognized
her at first. I never saw such a change in a woman, and it
came like a shock to me.

Her sister let us in, and after a first glance at Mrs. Baker I
had eyes for the sister and no one else. She was a Sydney girl,
about twenty-four or twenty-five, and fresh and fair — not
like the sun-browned women we were used to see. She was a
pretty, bright-eyed girl, and seemed quick to understand,

and very sympathetic. She had been educated, Andy had told me, and wrote stories for the Sydney *Bulletin* and other Sydney papers. She had her hair done and was dressed in the city style, and that took us back a bit at first.

"It's very good of you to come," said Mrs., Baker in a weak, weary voice, when we first went in. "I heard you were in town."

"We were just coming when we got your message," said Andy. "We'd have come before, only we had to see to the horses."

"It's very kind of you, I'm sure," said Mrs. Baker.

They wanted us to have tea, but we said we'd just had it. Then Miss Standish (the sister) wanted us to have tea and cake; but we didn't feel as if we could handle cups and saucers and pieces of cake successfully just then.

There was something the matter with one of the children in a back-room, and the sister went to see to it. Mrs. Baker cried a little quietly.

"You mustn't mind me," she said. "I'll be all right presently, and then I want you to tell me all about poor Bob. It's seeing you, that saw the last of him, that set me off."

Andy and I sat stiff and straight, on two chairs against the wall, and held our hats tight, and stared at a picture of Wellington meeting Blucher on the opposite wall. I thought it was lucky that that picture was there.

The child was calling "mumma", and Mrs. Baker went in to it, and her sister came out. "Best tell her all about it and get it over," she whispered to Andy. "She'll never be content until she hears all about poor Bob from some one who was with him when he died. Let me take your hats. Make yourselves comfortable."

She took the hats and put them on the sewing-machine. I wished she'd let us keep them, for now we had nothing to hold on to, and nothing to do with our hands; and as for being comfortable, we were just about as comfortable as two cats on wet bricks.

When Mrs. Baker came into the room she brought little Bobby Baker, about four years old; he wanted to see Andy. He ran to Andy at once, and Andy took him up on his knee. He was a pretty child, but he reminded me too much of his father.

"I'm so glad you've come, Andy!" said Bobby.

"Are you, Bobby?"

"Yes. I wants to ask you about daddy. You saw him go away, didn't you?" and he fixed his great wondering eyes on Andy's face.

"Yes," said Andy.

"He went up among the stars, didn't he?"

"Yes," said Andy.

"And he isn't coming back to Bobby any more?"

"No," said Andy. "But Bobby's going to him by-and-by."

Mrs. Baker had been leaning back in her chair, resting her head on her hand, tears glistening in her eyes; now she began to sob, and her sister took her out of the room.

Andy looked miserable. "I wish to God I was off this job!" he whispered to me.

"Is that the girl that writes the stories?" I asked.

"Yes," he said, staring at me in a hopeless sort of way, "and poems too."

"Is Bobby going up among the stars?" asked Bobby.

"Yes," said Andy — "if Bobby's good."

"And auntie?"

"Yes."

"And mumma?"

"Yes."

"Are you going, Andy?"

"Yes," said Andy hopelessly.

"Did you see daddy go up amongst the stars, Andy?"

"Yes," said Andy, "I saw him go up."

"And he isn't coming down again any more?"

"No," said Andy.

"Why isn't he?"

"Because he's going to wait up there for you and mumma, Bobby."

There was a long pause, and then Bobby asked —

"Are you going to give me a shilling, Andy?" with the same expression of innocent wonder in his eyes.

Andy slipped half-a-crown into his hand. "Auntie" came in and told him he'd see Andy in the morning and took him away to bed, after he'd kissed us both solemnly; and presently she and Mrs. Baker settled down to hear Andy's story.

"Brace up now, Jack, and keep your wits about you," whispered Andy to me just before they came in.

"Poor Bob's brother Ned wrote to me," said Mrs. Baker, "but he scarcely told me anything. Ned's a good fellow, but he's very simple, and never thinks of anything."

Andy told her about the Boss not being well after he crossed the border.

"I knew he was not well,' said Mrs. Baker, "before he left. I didn't want him to go. I tried hard to persuade him not to go this trip. I had a feeling that I oughtn't to let him go. But he'd never think of anything but me and the children. He promised he'd give up droving after this trip, and get something to do near home. The life was too much for him — riding in all weathers and camping out in the rain, and living like a dog. But he was never content at home. It was all for the sake of me and the children. He wanted to make money and start on a station again. I shouldn't have let him go. He only thought of me and the children! Oh! my poor, dear, kind, dead husband!' She broke down again and sobbed, and her sister comforted her, while Andy and I stared at Wellington meeting Blucher on the field of Waterloo. I thought the artist had heaped up the dead a bit extra, and I thought that I wouldn't like to be trod on by horses, even if I was dead.

"Don't you mind," said Miss Standish, "she'll be all right presently," and she handed us the *Illustrated Sydney Journal.* This was a great relief, — we bumped our heads over the pictures.

Mrs. Baker made Andy go on again, and he told her how the Boss broke down near Mulgatown. Mrs. Baker was opposite him and Miss Standish opposite me. Both of them kept their eyes on Andy's face: he sat, with his hair straight up like a brush as usual, and kept his big innocent grey eyes fixed on Mrs. Baker's face all the time he was speaking. I watched Miss Standish. I thought she was the prettiest girl I'd ever seen; it was bad case of love at first sight, but she was far and away above me, and the case was hopeless. I began to feel pretty miserable, and to think back into the past: I just heard Andy droning away by my side.

"So we fixed him up comfortable in the waggonette with the blankets and coats and things," Andy was saying, "and the squatter started into Mulgatown . . . . It was about thirty miles, Jack, wasn't it?" he asked, turning suddenly to me. He always looked so innocent that there were times when I itched to knock him down.

"More like thirty-five," I said, waking up.

Miss Standish fixed her eyes on me, and I had another look at Wellington and Blucher.

"They were all very good and kind to the Boss," said Andy. "They thought a lot of him up there. Everybody was fond of him."

"I know it," said Mrs. Baker. "Nobody could help liking him. He was one of the kindest men that ever lived."

"Tanner, the publican, couldn't have been kinder to his

own brother," said Andy. "The local doctor was a decent chap, but he was only a young fellow, and Tanner hadn't much faith in him, so he wired for an older doctor at Mackintyre, and he even sent out fresh horses to meet the doctor's buggy. Everything was done that could be done, I assure you, Mrs. Baker."

"I believe it," said Mrs. Baker. "And you don't know how it relieves me to hear it. And did the publican do all this at his own expense?"

"He wouldn't take a penny, Mrs. Baker."

"He must have been a good true man. I wish I could thank him."

"Oh, Ned thanked him for you," said Andy, though without meaning more than he said.

"I wouldn't have fancied that Ned would have thought of that," said Mrs. Baker. "When I first heard of my poor husband's death, I thought perhaps he'd been drinking again — that worried me a bit."

"He never touched a drop after he left Solong, I can assure you, Mrs. Baker," said Andy quickly.

Now I noticed that Miss Standish seemed surprised or puzzled, once or twice, while Andy was speaking, and leaned back in her chair and clasped her hands behind her head and looked at him, with half-shut eyes, in a way I didn't like. Once or twice she looked at me as if she was going to ask me a question, but I always looked away quick and stared at Blucher and Wellington, or into the empty fireplace, till I felt that her eyes were off me. Then she asked Andy a question or two, in all innocence I believe now, but it scared him, and at last he watched his chance and winked at her sharp. Then she gave a little gasp and shut up like a steel trap.

The sick child in the bedroom coughed and cried again. Mrs. Baker went to it. We there sat little a deaf-and-dumb institution, Andy and I staring all over the place: presently Miss Standish excused herself, and went out of the room after her sister. She looked hard at Andy as she left the room, but he kept his eyes away.

"Brace up now, Jack," whispered Andy to me, "the worst is coming."

When they came in again Mrs. Baker made Andy go on with his story.

"He — he died very quietly," said Andy, hitching round, and resting his elbows on his knees, and looking into the fireplace so as to have his face away from the light. Miss

Standish put her arm round her sister. "He died very easy," said Andy. "He was a bit off his head at times, but that was while the fever was on him. He didn't suffer much towards the end — I don't think he suffered at all. . . . He talked a lot about you and the children." (Andy was speaking very softly now.) "He said that you were not to fret, but to cheer up for the children's sake. . . . It was the biggest funeral ever seen round there."

Mrs. Baker was crying softly. Andy got the packet half out of his pocket, but shoved it back again.

"The only thing that hurts me now," says Mrs. Baker presently, "is to think of my poor husband buried out there is the lonely Bush, so far from home. It's — cruel!" and she was sobbing again.

"Oh, that's all right, Mrs. baker," said Andy, losing his head a little. "Ned will see to that. Ned is going to arrange to have him brought down and buried in Sydney." Which was about the first thing Andy had told her that evening that wasn't a lie. Ned had said he would do it as soon as he sold his wool.

"It's very kind indeed of Ned," sobbed Mrs. Baker. "I'd never have dreamed he was so kind-hearted and thoughtful. I misjudged him along. And that is all you have to tell me about poor Robert?"

"Yes," said Andy — then one of his "happy thoughts" struck him. "Except that he hoped you'd shift to Sydney, Mrs. Baker, where you've got friends and relations. He thought it would be better for you and the children. He told me to tell you that."

"He was thoughtful up to the end," said Mrs. Baker. "It was just like poor Robert — always thinking of me and the children. We are going to Sydney next week."

Andy looked relieved. We talked a little more, and Miss Standish wanted to make coffee for us, but we had to go and see to our horses. We got up and bumped against each other, and got each other's hats, and promised Mrs. Baker we'd come again.

"Thank you very much for coming," she said, shaking hands with us. "I feel much better now. You don't know how much you have relieved me. Now, mind, you have promised to come and see me again for the last time."

Andy caught her sister's eye and jerked his head towards the door to let her know he wanted to speak to her outside.

"Good-bye, Mrs. Baker," he said, holding on to her hand. "And don't you fret. You've — you've got the children yet.

It's — it's all for the best; and, besides, the Boss said you wasn't to fret." And he blundered out after me and Miss Standish.

She came out to the gate with us, and Andy gave her the packet.

"I want you to give that to her," he said; "it's his letters and papers. I hadn't the heart to give it to her, somehow."

"Tell me, Mr. M'Culloch," she said. "You've kept something back — you haven't told her the truth. It would be better and safer for me to know. Was it an accident — or the drink?"

"It was the drink," said Andy. "I was going to tell you — I thought it would be best to tell you. I had made up my mind to do it, but, somehow, I couldn't have done it if you hadn't asked me."

"Tell me all," she said. "It would be better for me to know."

"Come a little farther away from the house," said Andy. She came along the fence a piece with us, and Andy told her as much of the truth as he could.

"I'll hurry her off to Sydney," she said. "We can get away this week as well as next." Then she stood for a minute before us, breathing quickly, her hands behind her back and her eyes shining in the moonlight. She looked splendid.

"I want to thank you for her sake," she said quickly. "You are good men! I like the Bushmen! They are grand men — they are noble! I'll probably never see either of you again, so it doesn't matter," and she put her white hand on Andy's shoulder and kissed him fair and square on the mouth. "And you, too!" she said to me. I was taller than Andy, and had to stoop. "Good-bye!" she said, and ran to the gate and in, waving her hand to us. We lifted our hats again and turned down the road.

I don't think it did either of us any harm.

Joe Wilson's Courtship

There are many times in this world when a healthy boy is happy. When he is put into knickerbockers, for instance, and "comes a man today", as my little Jim used to say. When they're cooking something at home that he likes. When the "sandy-blight" or measles breaks out amongst the children, or the teacher or his wife falls dangerously ill — or dies, it doesn't matter which — "and there ain't no school". When a boy is naked and in his natural state for a warm climate like Australia, with three or four of his schoolmates, under the shade of the creek-oaks in the bend where there's a good clear pool with a sandy bottom. When his father buys him a gun, and he starts out after kangaroos or 'possums. When he gets a horse, saddle, and bridle, of his own. When he has his arm in splints or a stitch in his head — he's proud then, the proudest boy in the district.

I wasn't a healthy-minded, average boy: I reckon I was born for a poet by mistake, and grew up to be a Bushman, and didn't know what was the matter with me — or the world — but that's got nothing to do with it.

There are times when a man is happy. When he finds out that the girl loves him. When he's just married. When he's a lawful father for the first time, and everything is going on all right: some men make fools of themselves then — I know I did. I'm happy tonight because I'm out of debt and can see clear ahead, and because I haven't been easy for a long time.

But I think that the happiest time in a man's life is when he's courting a girl and finds out for sure that she loves him and hasn't a thought for any one else. Make the most of your courting days, you young chaps, and keep them clean, for they're about the only days when there's a chance of poetry and beauty coming into this life. Make the best of them and you'll never regret it the longest day you live. They're the days that the wife will look back to, anyway, in the brightest

of times as well as in the blackest, and there shouldn't be
anything in those days that might hurt her when she looks
back. Make the most of your courting days, you young
chaps, for they will never come again.

A married man knows all about it — after a while: he sees
the woman world through the eyes of his wife; he knows
what an extra moment's pressure of the hand means, and, if
he has had a hard life, and is inclined to be cynical, the
knowledge does him no good. It leads him into awful messes
sometimes, for a married man, if he's inclined that way, has
three times the chance with a woman that a single man has
— because the married man knows. He is privileged; he can
guess pretty closely what a woman means when she says
something else; he knows just how far he can go; he can go
farther in five minutes towards coming to the point with a
woman than an innocent young man dares go in three
weeks. Above all, the married man is more decided with
women; he takes them and things for granted. In short he is
— well, he is a married man. And, when he knows all this,
how much better or happier is he for it? Mark Twain says
that he lost all the beauty of the river when he saw it with a
pilot's eye — and there you have it.

But it's all new to a young chap, provided he hasn't been a
young blackguard. It's all wonderful, new, and strange to
him. He's a different man. He finds that he never knew
anything about women. He sees none of woman's little ways
and tricks in his girl. He is in heaven one day and down near
the other place the next; and that's the sort of thing that
makes life interesting. He takes his new world for granted.
And, when she says she'll be his wife ——!

Make the most of your courting days, you young chaps, for
they've got a lot of influence on your married life afterwards
— a lot more than you'd think. Make the best of them, for
they'll never come any more, unless we do our courting over
again in another world. If we do, I'll make the most of mine.

But, looking back, I didn't do so badly after all. I never
told you about the days I courted Mary. The more I look
back the more I come to think that I made the most of them,
and if I had no more to regret in married life than I have in
my courting days, I wouldn't walk to and fro in the room, or
up and down the yard in the dark sometimes, or lie awake
some nights thinking . . . . Ah well!

I was between twenty-one and thirty then: birthdays had
never been any use to me, and I'd left off counting them.
You don't take much stock in birthdays in the Bush. I'd

knocked about the country for a few years, shearing and fencing and droving a little, and wasting my life without getting anything for it. I drank now and then, and made a fool of myself. I was reckoned "wild"; but I only drank because I felt less sensitive, and the world seemed a lot saner and better and kinder when I had a few drinks: I loved my fellow-man then and felt nearer to him. It's better to be thought "wild" than to be considered eccentric or ratty. Now, my old mate, Jack Barnes, drank — as far as I could see — first because he'd inherited the gambling habit from his father along with his father's luck: he'd the habit of being cheated and losing very bad, and when he lost he drank. Till drink got a hold on him. Jack was sentimental too, but in a different way. I was sentimental about other people — more fool I! — whereas Jack was sentimental about himself. Before from a spree, he'd write rhymes about "Only a boy, drunk by the roadside", and that sort of thing; and he'd call 'em poetry, and talk about signing them and sending them to the *Town and Country Journal*. But he generally tore them up when he got better. The Bush is breeding a race of poets, and I don't know what the country will come to in the end.

Well. It was after Jack and I had been out shearing at Beenaway shed in the Big Scrubs. Jack was living in the little farming town of Solong, and I was hanging round. Black, the squatter, wanted some fencing done and a new stable built, or buggy and harness-house, at his place at Haviland, a few miles out of Solong. Jack and I were good Bush carpenters, so we took the job to keep us going till something else turned up. "Better than doing nothing," said Jack.

"There's a nice little girl in service at Black's," he said. "She's more like an adopted daughter, in fact, than a servant. She's a real good little girl, and good-looking into the bargain. I hear that young Black is sweet on her, but they say she won't have anything to do with him. I know a lot of chaps that have tried for her, but they've never had any luck. She's a regular little dumpling, and I like dumplings. They call her 'Possum. You ought to try a bear up in that direction, Joe."

I was always shy with women — except perhaps some that I should have fought shy of; but Jack wasn't — he was afraid of no woman, good, bad, or indifferent. I haven't time to explain why, but somehow, whenever a girl took any notice of me I took it for granted that she was only playing with me, and felt nasty about it. I made one or two mistakes, but — ah well!

"My wife knows little 'Possum," said Jack. "I'll get her to ask her out to our place and let you know.

I reckoned that he wouldn't get me there then, and made a note to be on the watch for tricks. I had a hopeless little love-story behind me, of course. I suppose most married men can look back to their lost love; few marry the first flame. Many a married man looks back and thinks it was damned lucky that he didn't get the girl he couldn't have. Jack had been my successful rival, only he didn't know it — I don't think his wife knew it either. I used to think her the prettiest and sweetest little girl in the district.

But Jack was mighty keen on fixing me up with the little girl at Haviland. He seemed to take it for granted that I was going to fall in love with her at first sight. He took too many things for granted as far as I was concerned, and got me into awful tangles sometimes.

"You let me alone, and I'll fix you up, Joe," he said, as we rode up to the station. "I'll make it all right with the girl. You're rather a good-looking chap. You've got the sort of eyes that take with girls, only you don't know it; you haven't got the go. If I had your eyes along with my other attractions, I'd be in trouble on account of a woman about once a-week."

"For God's sake shut up, Jack," I said.

Do you remember the first glimpse you got of your wife? Perhaps not in England, where so many couples grow up together from childhood; but it's different in Australia, where you may hail from two thousand miles away from where your wife was born, and yet she may be a country-woman of yours, and a countrywoman in ideas and politics too. I remember the first glimpse I got of Mary.

It was a two-storey brick house with wide balconies and verandahs all round, and a double row of pines down to the front gate. Parallel at the back was an old slab-and-shingle place, one room deep and about eight rooms long, with a row of skillions at the back: the place was used for kitchen, laundry, servants' rooms, etc. This was the old homestead before the new house was built. There was a wide, old-fashioned, brick-floored verandah in front, with an open end; there was ivy climbing up the verandah post on one side and a baby-rose on the other, and a grape-vine near the chimney. We rode up to the end of the verandah, and Jack called to see if there was any one at home, and Mary came trotting out; so it was in the frame of vines that I first saw her.

More than once since then I've had a fancy to wonder whether the rose-bush killed the grape-vine or the ivy smothered 'em both in the end. I used to have a vague idea of riding that way some day to see. You do get strange fancies at odd times.

Jack asked her if the boss was in. He did all the talking. I saw a little girl, rather plump, with a complexion like a New England or Blue Mountain girl, or a girl from Tasmania or from Gippsland in Victoria. Red and white girls were very scarce in the Solong district. She had the biggest and brightest eyes I'd seen round there, dark hazel eyes, as I found out afterwards, and bright as a 'possum's. No wonder they called her "'Possum". I forgot at once that Mrs. Jack Barnes was the prettiest girl in the district. I felt a sort of comfortable satisfaction in the fact that I was on horseback: most Bushmen look better on horseback. It was a black filly, a fresh young thing, and she seemed as shy of girls as I was myself. I noticed Mary glanced in my direction once or twice to see if she knew me; but, when she looked, the filly took all my attention. Mary trotted in to tell old Black he was wanted, and after Jack had seen him, and arranged to start work next day, we started back to Solong.

I expected Jack to ask me what I thought of Mary — but he didn't. He squinted at me sideways once or twice and didn't say anything for a long time, and then he started talking of other things. I began to feel wild at him. He seemed so damnably satisfied with the way things were going. He seemed to reckon that I was a gone case now; but, as he didn't say so, I had no way of getting at him. I felt sure he'd go home and tell his wife that Joe Wilson was properly gone on little 'Possum at Haviland. That was all Jack's way.

Next morning we started to work. We were to build the buggy-house at the back near the end of the old house, but first we had to take down a rotten old place that might have been the original hut in the Bush before the old house was built. There was a window in it, opposite the laundry window in the old place, and the first thing I did was to take out the sash. I'd noticed Jack yarning with 'Possum before he started work. While I was at work at the window he called me round to the other end of the hut to help him lift a grindstone out of the way; and when we'd done it, he took the tips of my ear between his fingers and thumb and stretched it and whispered into it —

"Don't hurry with that window, Joe; the strips are hard-wood and hard to get off — you'll have to take the sash out

very carefully so as not to break the glass." then he stretched
my ear a little more and put his mouth closer —

"Make a looking-glass of that window, Joe," he said.

I was used to Jack, and when I went back to the window I
started to puzzle out what he meant, and presently I saw it
by chance.

That window reflected the laundry window: the room was
dark inside and there was a good clear reflection; and
presently I saw Mary come to the laundry window and stand
with her hands behind her back, thoughtfully watching me.
The laundry window had an old-fashioned hinged sash, and
I like that sort of window — there's more romance about it, I
think. There was thick dark-green ivy all round the window,
and Mary looked prettier than a picture. I squared up my
shoulders and put my heels together and put as much style as
I could into the work. I couldn't have turned round to save
my life.

Presently Jack came round, and Mary disappeared.

"Well?" he whispered.

"You're a fool, Jack," I said. "She's only interested in the
old house being pulled down."

"That's all right," he said. "I've been keeping an eye on
the business round the corner, and she ain't interested when
I'm round this end."

"You seem mighty interested in the business," I said.

"Yes," said Jack. "This sort of thing just suits a man of my
rank in times of peace."

"What made you think of the window?" I asked.

"Oh, that's as simple as striking matches. I'm up to all
those dodges. Why, where there wasn't a window, I've fixed
up a piece of looking-glass to see if a girl was taking any
notice of me when she thought I wasn't looking."

He went away, and presently Mary was at the window
again, and this time she had a tray with cups of tea and a
plate of cake and bread-and-butter. I was prizing off the
strips that held the sash, very carefully, and my heart
suddenly commenced to gallop, without any reference to
me. I'd never felt like that before, except once or twice. It
was just as if I'd swallowed some clockwork arrangement,
unconsciously, and it had started to go, without warning. I
reckon it was all on account of that blarsted Jack working me
up. He had a quiet way of working you up to a thing, that
made you want to hit him sometimes — after you'd made an
ass of yourself.

I didn't hear Mary at first. I hoped Jack would come

round and help me out of the fix, but he didn't.

"Mr. — Mr. Wilson!" said Mary. She had a sweet voice. I turned round.

"I thought you and Mr. Barnes might like a cup of tea."

"Oh, thank you!" I said, and I made a dive for the window, as if hurry would help it. I trod on an old cask-hoop; it sprang up and dinted my shin and I stumbled — and that didn't help matters much.

"Oh! did you hurt yourself, Mr. Wilson?" cried Mary.

"Hurt myself! Oh no, not at all, thank you," I blurted out. "It takes more than that to hurt me."

I was about the reddest shy lanky fool of a Bushman that was ever taken at a disadvantage on foot, and when I took the tray my hands shook so that a lot of the tea was spilt into the saucers. I embarrassed her too, like the damned fool I was, till she must have been as red as I was, and it's a wonder we didn't spill the whole lot between us. I got away from the window in as much of a hurry as if Jack had cut his leg with a chisel and fainted, and I was running with whisky for him. I blundered round to where he was, feeling like a man feels when he's just made an ass of himself in public. The memory of that sort of thing hurts you worse and makes you jerk your head more impatiently than the thought of a past crime would, I think.

I pulled myself together when I got to where Jack was.

"Here, Jack!" I said. "I've struck something all right; here's some tea and brownie — we'll hang out here all right."

Jack took a cup of tea and a piece of cake and sat down to enjoy it, just as if he'd paid for it and ordered it to be sent out about that time.

He was silent for a while, with the sort of silence that always made me wild at him. Presently he said, as if he'd just thought of it —

"That's a very pretty little girl, 'Possum, isn't she, Joe? Do you notice how she dresses? — always fresh and trim. But she's got on her best bib-and-tucker today, and a pinafore with frills to it. And it's ironing-day, too. It can't be on your account. If it was Saturday or Sunday afternoon, or some holiday, I could understand it. But perhaps one of her admirers is going to take her to the church bazaar in Solong tonight. That's what it is."

He gave me time to think over that.

"But yet she seems interested in you, Joe," he said. "Why didn't you offer to take her to the bazaar instead of letting another chap get in ahead of you? You miss all your chances, Joe."

Then a thought struck me. I ought to have known Jack well enough to have thought of it before.

"Look here, Jack," I said. "What have you been saying to that girl about me?"

"Oh, not much," said Jack. "There isn't much to say about you."

"What did you tell her?"

"Oh, nothing in particular. She'd heard all about you before."

"She hadn't heard much good, I suppose," I said.

"Well, that's true, as far as I could make out. But you've only got yourself to blame. I didn't have the breeding and rearing of you. I smoothed over matters with her as much as I could."

"What did you tell her?" I said. "That's what I want to know."

"Well, to tell the truth, I didn't tell her anything much. I only answered questions."

"And what questions did she ask?"

"Well, in the first place, she asked if your name wasn't Joe Wilson; and I said it was, as far as I knew. Then she said she heard that you wrote poetry, and I had to admit that that was true."

"Look here, Jack," I said, "I've two minds to punch your head."

"And she asked me if it was true that you were wild," said Jack, "and I said you was, a bit. She said it seemed a pity. She asked me if it was true that you drank, and I drew a long face and said that I was sorry to say it was true. She asked me if you had any friends, and I said none that I knew of, except me. I said that you'd lost all your friends; they stuck to you as long as they could, but they had to give you best, one after the other."

"What next?"

"She asked me if you were delicate, and I said no, you were as tough as fencing-wire. She said you looking rather pale and thin, and asked me if you'd had an illness lately. And I said no — it was all on account of the wild, dissipated life you'd led. She said it was a pity you hadn't a mother or a sister to look after you — it was a pity that something couldn't be done for you, and I said it was, but I was afraid that nothing could be done. I told her that I was doing all I could to keep you straight."

I knew enough of Jack to know that most of this was true.
And so she only pitied me after all. I felt as if I'd been
courting her for six months and she'd thrown me over — but
I didn't know anything about women yet.

"Did you tell her I was in jail?" I growled.

"No, by Gum! I forgot that. But never mind. I'll fix that
up all right. I'll tell her that you got two years' hard for
horse-stealing. That ought to make her interested in you, if
she isn't already."

We smoked a while.

"And was that all she said?" I asked.

"Who? — Oh! 'Possum," said Jack rousing himself. "Well
— no; let me think — We got chatting of other things —
you know a married man's privileged, and can say a lot more
to a girl than a single man can. I got talking nonsense about
sweethearts, and one thing led to another till at last she said,
'I suppose Mr. Wilson's got a sweetheart, Mr. Barnes?'"

"And what did you say?" I growled.

"Oh, I told her that you were a holy terror amongst the
girls," said Jack. "You'd better take back that tray, Joe, and
let us get to work."

I wouldn't take back the tray — but that didn't mend
matters, for Jack took it back himself.

I didn't see Mary's reflection in the window again, so I
took the window out. I reckoned that she was just a
big-hearted, impulsive little thing, as many Australian girls
are, and I reckoned that I was a fool for thinking for a
moment that she might give me a second thought, except by
way of kindness. Why! young Black and half a dozen better
men than me were sweet on her, and young Black was to get
his father's station and the money — or rather his mother's
money, for she held the stuff (she kept it close too, by all
accounts). Young Black was away at the time, and his
mother was dead against him about Mary, but that didn't
make any difference, as far as I could see. I reckoned that it
was only just going to be a hopeless, heart-breaking, stand-
far-off-and-worship affair, as far as I was concerned — like
my first love affair, that I haven't told you about yet. I didn't
know women then. If I had known, I think I might have
made more than one mess of my life.

Jack rode home to Solong every night. I was staying at a
pub some distance out of town, between Solong and Haviland. There were three or four wet days, and we didn't get
on with the work. I fought shy of Mary till one day she was
hanging out clothes and the line broke. It was the old-style

sixpenny clothes-line. The clothes were all down, but it was clean grass, so it didn't matter much. I looked at Jack.

"Go and help her, you capital Idiot!" he said, and I made the plunge.

"Oh, thank you, Mr. Wilson!" said Mary, when I came to help. She had the broken end of the line and was trying to hold some of the clothes off the ground, as if she could pull it an inch with the heavy wet sheets and table-cloths and things on it, or as if it would do any good if she did. But that's the way with women — especially little women — some of 'em would try to pull a store bullock if they got the end of the rope on the right side of the fence. I took the line from Mary, and accidentally touched her soft, plump little hand as I did so: it sent a thrill right through me. She seemed a lot cooler than I was.

Now, in cases like this, especially if you lose your head a bit, you get hold of the loose end of the rope that's hanging from the post with one hand, and the end of the line with the clothes on with the other, and try to pull 'em far enough together to make a knot. And that's about all you do for the present, except look like a fool. Then I took off the post end, spliced the line, took it over the fork, and pulled, while Mary helped me with the prop. I thought Jack might have come and taken the prop from her, but he didn't; he just went on with his work as if nothing was happening inside the horizon.

She'd got the line about two-thirds full of clothes, it was a bit short now, so she had to jump and catch it with one hand and hold it down while she pegged a sheet she'd thrown over. I'd made the plunge now, so I volunteered to help her. I held down the line while she threw the things over and pegged out. As we got near the post and higher I straightened out some ends and pegged myself. Bushmen are handy at most things. We laughed, and now and again Mary would say, "No, that's not the way, Mr. Wilson; that's not right; the sheet isn't far enough over; wait till I fix it," etc. I'd a reckless idea once of holding her up while she pegged, and I was glad afterwards that I hadn't made such a fool of myself.

"There's only a few more things in the basket, Miss Brand," I said. "You can't reach — I'll fix 'em up."

She seemed to give a little gasp.

"Oh, those things are not ready yet," she said, "they're not rinsed," and she grabbed the basket and held it away from me. The things looked the same to me as the rest on the line; they looked rinsed enough and blued too. I reckoned that she didn't want me to take the trouble, or thought that I mightn't like to be seen hanging out clothes, and was only doing it out of kindness.

"Oh, it's no trouble," I said, "let me hang 'em out. I like it. I've hung out clothes at home on a windy day," and I made a reach into the basket. But she flushed red, with temper I thought, and snatched the basket away.

"Excuse me, Mr. Wilson," she said, "but those things are not ready yet!" and she marched into the wash-house.

"Ah well! you've got a little temper of your own," I thought to myself.

When I told Jack, he said that I'd made another fool of myself. He said I'd both disappointed and offended her. He said that my line was to stand off a bit and be serious and melancholy in the background.

That evening when we'd started home, we stopped some time yarning with a chap we met at the gate; and I happened to look back, and saw Mary hanging out the rest of the things — she thought that we were out of sight. Then I understood why those things weren't ready while we were round.

For the next day or two Mary didn't take the slightest notice of me, and I kept out of her way. Jack said I'd disillusioned her — and hurt her dignity — which was a thousand times worse. He said I'd spoilt the thing altogether. He said that she'd got an idea that I was shy and poetic, and I'd only shown myself the usual sort of Bush-whacker.

I noticed her talking and chatting with other fellows once or twice, and it made me miserable. I got drunk two evenings running, and then, as it appeared afterwards, Mary consulted Jack, and at last she said to him, when we were together —

"Do you play draughts, Mr. Barnes?"

"No," said Jack.

"Do you, Mr. Wilson?" she asked, suddenly turning her big, bright eyes on me, and speaking to me for the first time since last washing-day.

"Yes," I said, "I do a little." Then there was a silence, and I had to say something else.

"Do you play draughts, Miss Brand?" I asked.

"Yes," she said, "but I can't get any one to play with me here of an evening, the men are generally playing cards or reading." Then she said, "It's very dull these long winter evenings when you've got nothing to do. Young Mr. Black used to play draughts, but he's away."

I saw Jack winking at me urgently.

"I'll play a game with you, if you like," I said, "but I ain't much of a player."

"Oh, thank you, Mr. Wilson! When shall you have an evening to spare?"

We fixed it for that same evening. We got chummy over the draughts. I had a suspicion even then that it was a put-up job to keep me away from the pub.

Perhaps she found a way of giving a hint to old Black without committing herself. Women have ways — or perhaps Jack did it. Anyway, next day the Boss came round and said to me —

"Look here, Joe, you've got no occasion to stay at the pub. Bring along your blankets and camp in one of the spare rooms of the old house. You can have your tucker here."

He was a good sort, was Black the squatter: a squatter of the old school, who'd shared the early hardships with his men, and couldn't see why he should not shake hands and have a smoke and a yarn over old times with any of his old station hands that happened to come along. But he'd married an Englishwoman after the hardships were over, and she'd never got any Australian notions.

Next day I found one of the skillion rooms scrubbed out and a bed fixed up for me. I'm not sure to this day who did it, but I supposed that good-natured old Black had given one of the women a hint. After tea I had a yarn with Mary, sitting on a log of the wood-heap. I don't remember exactly how we both came to be there, or who sat down first. There was about two feet between us. We got very chummy and confidential. She told me about her childhood and her father.

He'd been an old mate of Black's, a younger son of a well-to-do English family (with blue blood in it, I believe), and sent out to Australia with a thousand pounds to make his way, as many younger sons are, with more or less. They think they're hard done by; they blue their thousand pounds in Melbourne or Sydney, and they don't make any more nowadays, for the Roarin' Days have been dead these thirty years. I wish I'd had a thousand pounds to start on!

Mary's mother was the daughter of a German immigrant, who selected up there in the old days. She had a will of her own as far I could understand, and bossed the home till the day of her death. Mary's father made money, and lost it, and drank — and died. Mary remembered him sitting on the verandah one evening with his hand on her head, and singing a German song (the "Lorelei", I think it was) softly, as if to himself. Next day he stayed in bed, and the children were kept out of the room; and, when he died, the children were adopted round (there was a little money coming from England).

Mary told me all about her girlhood. She went first to live with a sort of cousin in town, in a house where they took in cards on a tray, and then she came to live with Mrs. Black, who took a fancy to her at first. I'd had no boyhood to speak of, so I gave her some of my ideas of what the world ought to be, and she seemed interested.

Next day there were sheets on my bed, and I felt pretty cocky until I remembered that I'd told her I had no one to care for me; then I suspected pity again.

But next evening we remembered that both our fathers and mothers were dead, and discovered that we had no friends except Jack and old Black, and things went on very satisfactorily.

And next day there was a little table in my room with a crocheted cover and a looking-glass.

I noticed the other girls began to act mysterious and giggle when I was round, but Mary didn't seem aware of it.

We got very chummy. Mary wasn't comfortable at Haviland. Old Black was very fond of her and always took her part, but she wanted to be independent. She had a great idea of going to Sydney and getting into the hospital as a nurse. She had friends in Sydney, but she had no money. There was a little money coming to her when she was twenty-one — a few pounds — and she was going to try and get it before that time.

"Look here, Miss Brand," I said, after we'd watched the moon rise. "I'll lend you the money. I've got plenty — more than I know what to do with."

But I saw I'd hurt her. She sat up very straight for a while, looking before her; then she said it was time to go in, and said "Good-night, Mr. Wilson."

I reckoned I'd done it that time; but Mary told me afterwards that she was only hurt because it struck her that what she said about money might have been taken for a hint. She didn't understand me yet, and I didn't know human nature. I didn't say anything to Jack — in fact about this time I left off telling him about things. He didn't seem hurt; he worked hard and seemed happy.

I really meant what I said to Mary about the money. It was pure good nature. I'd be a happier man now, I think, and richer man perhaps, if I'd never grown any more selfish than I was that night on the wood-heap with Mary. I felt a great sympathy for her — but I got to love her. I went through all the ups and downs of it. One day I was having tea in the kitchen, and Mary and another girl, named Sarah, reached me a clean plate at the same time: I took Sarah's plate because she was first, and Mary seemed very nasty about it, and that gave me great hopes. But all next evening she played draughts with a drover that she'd chummed up with. I pretended to be interested in Sarah's talk, but it didn't seem to work.

A few days later a Sydney Jackaroo visited the station. He had a good pea-rifle, and one afternoon he started to teach Mary to shoot at a target. They seemed to get very chummy. I had a nice time for three or four days, I can tell you. I was worse than a wall-eyed bullock with the pleuro. The other chaps had a shot out of the rifle. Mary called "Mr. Wilson" to have a shot, and I made a worse fool of myself by sulking. If it hadn't been a blooming Jackaroo I wouldn't have minded so much.

Next evening the Jackaroo and one or two other chaps and the girls went out 'possum-shooting. Mary went. I could have gone, but I didn't. I mooched round all the evening like an orphan bandicoot on a burnt ridge, and then I went up to the pub and filled myself with beer, and damned the world, and came home and went to bed. I think that evening was the only time I ever wrote poetry down on a piece of paper. I got so miserable that I enjoyed it.

I felt better next morning, and reckoned I was cured. I ran against Mary accidentally and had to say something.

"How did you enjoy yourself yesterday evening, Miss Brand?" I asked.

"Oh, very well, thank you, Mr. Wilson," she said. Then she asked, "How did you enjoy yourself, Mr. Wilson?"

I puzzled over that afterwards, but couldn't make anything out of it. Perhaps she only said it for the sake of saying something. But about this time my handkerchiefs and collars disappeared from the room and turned up washed and ironed and laid tidily on my table. I used to keep an eye out, but could never catch anybody near my room. I straightened up, and kept my room a bit tidy, and when my handkerchief got too dirty, and I was ashamed of letting it go to the wash, I'd slip down to the river after dark and wash it out, and dry it next day, and rub it up to look as if it hadn't been washed, and leave it on my table. I felt so full of hope and joy that I worked twice as hard as Jack, till one morning he remarked casually —

"I see you've made a new mash, Joe. I saw the half-caste cook tidying up your room this morning and taking your collars and things to the wash-house."

I felt very much off colour all the rest of the day, and I had such a bad night of it that I made up my mind next morning to look the hopelessness square in the face and live the thing down.

It was the evening before Anniversary Day. Jack and I had put in a good day's work to get the job finished, and Jack was having a smoke and a yarn with the chaps before he started home. We sat on an old log along by the fence at the back of the house. There was Jimmy Nowlett the bullock-driver, and long Dave Regan the drover, and big Jim Bullock the fencer, and one or two others. Mary and the station girls and one or two visitors were sitting under the old verandah. The Jackaroo was there too, so I felt happy. It was the girls who used to bring the chaps hanging round. They were getting up a dance party for Anniversary night. Along in the evening another chap came riding up to the station: he was a big shearer, a dark, handsome fellow, who looked like a gipsy: it was reckoned that there was foreign blood in him. He went by the name of Romany. He was supposed to be shook after Mary too. He had the nastiest temper and the best violin in the district, and the chaps put up with him a lot because they wanted him to play at Bush dances. The moon had risen over Pine Ridge, but it was dusky where we were. We saw Romany loom up, riding in from the gate; he rode round the end of the coach-house and across towards where we were — I suppose he was going to tie up his horse at the fence; but about half-way across the grass he disappeared. It struck me that there was something peculiar about the way he got down, and I heard a sound like a horse stumbling.

"What the hell's Romany trying to do?" said Jimmy Nowlett. "He couldn't have fell off his horse — or else he's drunk."

A couple of chaps got up and went to see. Then there was that waiting, mysterious silence that comes when something happens in the dark and nobody knows what it is. I went over, and the thing dawned on me. I'd stretched a wire clothes-line across there during the day, and had forgotten all about it for the moment. Romany had no idea of the line, and, as he rode up, it caught him on a level with his elbows and scraped him off his horse. He was sitting on the grass, swearing in a surprised voice, and the horse looked surprised too. Romany wasn't hurt, but the sudden shock had spoilt his temper. He wanted to know who'd put up that bloody line. He came over and sat on the log. The chaps smoked a while.

"What did you git down so sudden for, Romany?" asked Jim Bullock presently. "Did you hurt yerself on the pommel?"

"Why didn't you ask the horse to go round?" asked Dave Regan.

"I'd only like to know who put up that bleeding wire!" growled Romany.

"Well," said Jimmy Nowlett, "if we'd put up a sign to beware of the line you couldn't have seen it in the dark."

"Unless it was a transparency with a candle behind it," said Dave Regan. "But why didn't you get down on one end, Romany, instead of all along? It wouldn't have jolted yer so much."

All this with the Bush drawl, and between the puffs of their pipes. But I didn't take any interest in it. I was brooding over Mary and the Jackaroo.

"I've heard of men getting down over their horse's head," said Dave presently, in a reflective sort of way — "in fact I've done it myself — but I never saw a man get off backwards over his horse's rump."

But they saw that Romany was getting nasty, and they wanted him to play the fiddle next night, so they dropped it.

Mary was singing an old song. I always thought she had a sweet voice, and I'd have enjoyed it if that damned Jackaroo hadn't been listening too. We listened in silence until she'd finished.

"That gal's got a nice voice," said Jimmy Nowlett.

"Nice voice!" snarled Romany, who'd been waiting for a chance to be nasty. "Why, I've heard a tom-cat sing better."

I moved, and Jack, he was sitting next me, nudged me to keep quiet. The chaps didn't like Romany's talk about 'Possum at all. They were all fond of her: she wasn't a pet or a tomboy, for she wasn't built that way, but they were fond of her in such a way that they didn't like to hear anything said about her. They said nothing for a while, but it meant a lot. Perhaps the single men didn't care to speak for fear that it would be said that they were gone on Mary. But presently Jimmy Nowlett gave a big puff at his pipe and spoke —

"I suppose you got bit too in that quarter, Romany?"

"Oh, she tried it on, but it didn't go," said Romany. "I've met her sort before. She's setting her cap at that Jackaroo now. Some girls will run after anything with trousers on," and he stood up.

Jack Barnes must have felt what was coming, for he grabbed my arm, and whispered, "Sit still, Joe, damn you! He's too good for you!" but I was on my feet and facing Romany as if a giant hand had reached down and wrenched me off the log and set me there.

"You're a damned crawler, Romany!" I said.

Little Jimmy Nowlett was between us and the other fellows round us before a blow got home. "Hold on, you damned fools!" they said. "Keep quiet till we get away from the house!" There was a little clear flat down by the river and plenty of light there, so we decided to go down there and have it out.

Now I never was a fighting man; I'd never learnt to use my hands. I scarcely knew how to put them up. Jack often wanted to teach me, but I wouldn't bother about it. He'd say, "You'll get into a fight some day, Joe, or out of one, and shame me;" but I hadn't the patience to learn. He'd wanted me to take lessons at the station after work, but he used to get excited, and I didn't want Mary to see him knocking me about. Before he was married Jack was always getting into fights — he generally tackled a better man and got a hiding; but he didn't seem to care so long as he made a good show — though he used to explain the thing away from a scientific point of view for weeks after. To tell the truth, I had a horror of fighting; I had a horror of being marked about the face; I think I'd sooner stand off and fight a man with revolvers than fight him with fists; and then I think I would say, last thing, "Don't shoot me in the face!" Then again I hated the idea of hitting a man. It seemed brutal to me. I was too sensitive and sentimental, and that was what the matter was. Jack seemed very serious on it as we walked down to the river, and he couldn't help hanging out blue lights.

"Why didn't you let me teach you to use your hands?" he said. "The only chance now is that Romany can't fight after all. If you'd waited a minute I'd have been at him." We were a bit behind the rest, and Jack started giving me points about lefts and rights, and "half-arms", and that sort of thing. "He's left-handed, and that's the worst of it," said Jack. "You must only make as good a show as you can, and one of us will take him on afterwards."

But I just heard him and that was all. It was to be my first fight since I was a boy, but, somehow, I felt cool about it — sort of dulled. If the chaps had known all they would have set me down as a cur. I thought of that, but it didn't make any difference with me then; I knew it was a thing they couldn't understand. I knew I was reckoned pretty soft. But I knew one thing that they didn't know. I knew that it was going to be a fight to a finish, one way or the other. I had more brains and imagination than the rest put together, and I suppose that that was the real cause of most of my trouble. I kept saying to myself, "You'll have to go through with it now, Joe, old man! It's the turning-point of your life." If I won the fight, I'd set to work and win Mary; if I lost, I'd leave the district for ever. A man thinks a lot in a flash sometimes; I used to get excited over little things, because of the very paltriness of them, but I was mostly cool in a crisis — Jack was the reverse. I looked ahead: I wouldn't be able to marry a girl who could look back and remember when her husband was beaten by another man — no matter what sort of brute the other man was.

I never in my life felt so cool about a thing. Jack kept whispering instructions, and showing with his hands, up to the last moment, but it was all lost on me.

Looking back, I think there was a bit of romance about it: Mary singing under the vines to amuse a Jackaroo dude, and a coward going down to the river in the moonlight to fight for her.

It was very quiet in the little moonlit flat by the river. We took off our coats and were ready. There was no swearing or barracking. It seemed an understood thing with the men that if I went out first round Jack would fight Romany; and if Jack knocked him out somebody else would fight Jack to square matters. Jim Bullock wouldn't mind obliging for one; he was a mate of Jack's but he didn't mind who he fought so long as it was for the sake of fair play — or "peace and quietness", as he said. Jim was very good-natured. He backed Romany, and of course Jack backed me.

As far as I could see, all Romany knew about fighting was to jerk one arm up in front of his face and duck his head by way of a feint, and then rush and lunge out. But he had the weight and strength and length of reach, and my first lesson was a very short one. I went down early in the round. But it did me good; the blow and the look I'd seen in Romany's eyes knocked all the sentiment out of me. Jack said nothing, — he seemed to regard it as a hopeless job from the first.

Next round I tried to remember some things Jack had told me, and made a better show, but I went down in the end.

I felt Jack breathing quick and trembling as he lifted me up.

"How are you, Joe?" he whispered.

"I'm all right," I said.

"It's all right," whispered Jack in a voice as if I was going to be hanged, but it would soon be all over. "He can't use his hands much more than you can — take your time, Joe — try to remember something I told you, for God's sake!"

When two men fight who don't know how to use their hands, they stand a show of knocking each other about a lot. I got some awful thumps, but mostly on the body. Jimmy Nowlett began to get excited and jump round — he was an excitable little fellow.

"Fight! you — !" he yelled. "Why don't you fight? That ain't fightin'. Fight, and don't try to murder each other. Use your crimson hands or, by God, I'll chip you! Fight, or I'll blanky well bullock-whip the pair of you;" then his language got awful. They said we went like windmills, and that nearly every one of the blows we made was enough to kill a bullock if it had got home. Jimmy stopped us once, but they held him back.

Presently I went down pretty flat, but the blow was well up on the head and didn't matter much — I had a good thick skull. And I had one good eye yet.

"For God's sake, hit him!" whispered Jack — he was trembling like a leaf. "Don't mind what I told you. I wish I was fighting him myself! Get a blow home, for God's sake! Make a good show this round and I'll stop the fight."

That showed how little even Jack, my old mate, understood me.

I had the Bushman up in me now, and wasn't going to be beaten while I could think. I was wonderfully cool, and learning to fight. There's nothing like a fight to teach a man. I was thinking fast, and learning more in three seconds than Jack's sparring could have taught me in three weeks. People think that blows hurt in a fight, but they don't — not till afterwards. I fancy that a fighting man, if he isn't altogether an animal, suffers more mentally than he does physically.

While I was getting my wind I could hear through the moonlight and still air the sound of Mary's voice singing up at the house. I thought hard into the future, even as I fought. The fight only seemed something that was passing.

I was on my feet again and at it, and presently I lunged out and felt such a jar in my arm that I thought it was telescoped. I thought I'd put out my wrist and elbow. And Romany was lying on the broad of his back.

I heard Jack draw three breaths of relief in one. He said nothing as he straightened me up, but I could feel his heart beating. He said afterwards that he didn't speak because he thought a word might spoil it.

I went down again, but Jack told me afterwards that he *felt* I was all right when he lifted me.

Then Romany went down, then we fell together, and the chaps separated us. I got another knockdown blow in, and was beginning to enjoy the novelty of it, when Romany staggered and limped.

"I've done," he said. "I've twisted my ankle." He'd caught his heel against a tuft of grass.

"Shake hands," yelled Jimmy Nowlett.

I stepped forward, but Romany took his coat and limped to his horse.

"If yer don't shake hands with Wilson, I'll lamb yer!" howled Jimmy; but Jack told him to let the man alone, and Romany got on his horse somehow and rode off.

I saw Jim Bullock stoop and pick up something from the grass, and heard him swear in surprise. There was some whispering, and presently Jim said —

"If I thought that, I'd kill him."

"What is it?" asked Jack.

Jim held up a butcher's knife. It was common for a man to carry a butcher's knife in a sheath fastened to his belt.

"Why did you let your man fight with a butcher's knife in his belt?" asked Jimmy Nowlett.

But the knife could easily have fallen out when Romany fell, and we decided it that way.

"Any way," said Jimmy Nowlett, "if he'd stuck Joe in hot blood before us all it wouldn't be so bad as if he sneaked up and stuck him in the back in the dark. But you'd best keep an eye over yer shoulder for a year or two, Joe. That chap's got Eye-talian blood in him somewhere. And now the best thing you chaps can do is to keep your mouth shut and keep all this dark from the gals."

Jack hurried me on ahead. He seemed to act queer, and when I glanced at him I could have sworn that there was water in his eyes. I said that Jack had no sentiment except for himself, but I forgot, and I'm sorry I said it.

"What's up, Jack?" I asked.

"Nothing," said Jack.

"What's up, you old fool?" I said.

"Nothing," said Jack, "except that I'm damned proud of you, Joe, you old ass!" and he put his arm round my shoulders and gave me a shake. "I didn't know it was in you, Joe — I wouldn't have said it before, or listened to any other man say it, but I didn't think you had the pluck — God's truth, I didn't. Come along and get your face fixed up."

We got into my room quietly, and Jack got a dish of water, and told one of the chaps to sneak a piece of fresh beef from somewhere.

Jack was as proud as a dog with a tin tail as he fussed round me. He fixed up my face in the best style he knew, and he knew a good many — he'd been mended himself so often.

While he was at work we heard a sudden hush and a scraping of feet amongst the chaps that Jack had kicked out of the room, and a girl's voice whispered, "Is he hurt? Tell me. I want to know, — I might be able to help."

It made my heart jump, I can tell you. Jack went out at once, and there was some whispering. When he came back he seemed wild.

"What is it, Jack?" I asked.

"Oh, nothing," he said, "only that damned slut of a half-caste cook overhead some of those blanky fools arguing as to how Romany's knife got out of the sheath, and she's put a nice yarn round amongst the girls. There's a regular bobbery, but it's all right now. Jimmy Nowlett's telling 'em lies at a great rate."

Presently there was another hush outside, and a sauce with vinegar and brown paper was handed in.

One of the chaps brought some beer and whisky from the pub, and we had a quiet little time in my room. Jack wanted to stay all night, but I reminded him that his little wife was waiting for him in Solong, so he said he'd be round early in the morning, and went home.

I felt the reaction pretty bad. I didn't feel proud of the affair at all. I thought it was a low, brutal business all round. Romany was a quiet chap after all, and the chaps had no right to chyack him. Perhaps he'd had a hard life, and carried a big swag of trouble that we didn't know anything about. He seemed a lonely man. I'd gone through enough myself to teach me not to judge men. I made up my mind to tell him how I felt about the matter next time we met. Perhaps I made my usual mistake of bothering about

"feelings" in another party that hadn't any feelings at all —
perhaps I didn't; but it's generally best to chance it on the
kind side in a case like this. Altogether I felt as if I'd made
another fool of myself and been a weak coward. I drank the
rest of the beer and went to sleep.

About daylight I woke and heard Jack's horse on the
gravel. He came round the back of the buggy-shed and up to
my door, and then, suddenly, a girl screamed out. I pulled
on my trousers and 'lasticside boots and hurried out. It was
Mary herself, dressed, and sitting on an old stone step at the
back of the kitchen with her face in her hands, and Jack was
off his horse and stooping by her side with his hand on her
shoulder. She kept saying, "I thought you were ——! I
thought you were ——!" I didn't catch the name. An old
single-barrel, muzzle-loader shot-gun was lying in the grass
at her feet. It was the gun they used to keep loaded and
hanging in straps in a room of the kitchen ready for a shot at
a cunning old hawk that they called ""Tarnal Death", and
that used to be always after the chickens.

When Mary lifted her face it was as white as note-paper,
and her eyes seemed to grow wilder when she caught sight of
me.

"Oh, you did frighten me, Mr. Barnes," she gasped. Then
she gave a little ghost of a laugh and stood up, and some
colour came back.

"Oh, I'm a little fool!" she said quickly. "I thought I heard
old 'Tarnal Death at the chickens, and I thought it would be
a great thing if I got the gun and brought him down; so I got
up and dressed quietly so as not to wake Sarah. And then
you came round the corner and frightened me. I don't know
what you must think of me, Mr. Barnes."

"Never mind," said Jack. "You go and have a sleep, or you
won't be able to dance tonight. Never mind the gun — I'll
put that away." And he steered her round to the door of her
room off the brick verandah where she slept with one of the
other girls.

"Well, that's a rum start!" I said.

"Yes, it is," said Jack; "it's very funny. Well, how's your
face this morning, Joe?"

He seemed a lot more serious than usual.

We were hard at work all the morning cleaning out the
big wool-shed and getting it ready for the dance, hanging
hoops for the candles, making seats, etc. I kept out of sight
of the girls as much as I could. One side of my face was a
sight and the other wasn't too classical. I felt as if I had been
stung by a swarm of bees.

"You're a fresh, sweet-scented beauty now, and no mistake, Joe," said Jimmy Nowlett — he was going to play the accordion that night. "You ought to fetch the girls now, Joe. But never mind, your face'll go down in about three weeks. My lower jaw is crooked yet; but that fight straightened my nose, that had been knocked crooked when I was a boy — so I didn't lose much beauty by it."

When we'd done in the shed, Jack took me aside and said —

"Look here, Joe! if you won't come to the dance tonight — and I can't say you'd ornament it — I tell you what you'll do. You get little Mary away on the quiet and take her out for a stroll — and act like a man. The job's finished now, and you won't get another chance like this."

"But how am I to get her out?" I said.

"Never you mind. You be mooching round down by the big peppermint-tree near the river-gate say about half-past ten."

"What good'll that do?"

"Never you mind. You just do as you're told, that's all you've got to do," said Jack, and he went home to get dressed and bring his wife.

After the dancing started that night I had a peep in once or twice. The first time I saw Mary dancing with Jack, and looking serious; and the second time she was dancing with the blarsted Jackaroo dude, and looking excited and happy. I noticed that some of the girls that I could see sitting on a stool along the opposite wall, whispered, and gave Mary black looks as the Jackaroo swung her past. It struck me pretty forcibly that I should have taken fighting lessons from him instead of from poor Romany. I went away and walked about four miles down the river road, getting out of the way into the Bush whenever I saw any chap riding along. I thought of poor Romany and wondered where he was, and thought that there wasn't much to choose between us as far as happiness was concerned. Perhaps he was walking by himself in the Bush, and feeling like I did. I wished I could shake hands with him.

But somehow, about half-past ten, I drifted back to the river slip-rails and leant over them, in the shadow of the peppermint-tree, looking at the rows of river-willows in the moonlight. I didn't expect anything, in spite of what Jack said.

I didn't like the idea of hanging myself: I'd been with a party who found a man hanging in the Bush, and it was no place for a woman round where he was. And I'd helped drag two bodies out of the Cudgeegong river in a flood, and they weren't sleeping beauties. I thought it was a pity that a chap couldn't lie down on a grassy bank in a graceful position in the moonlight and die just by thinking of it — and die with his eyes and mouth shut. But then I remembered that I wouldn't make a beautiful corpse, anyway it went, with the face I had on me.

I was just getting comfortably miserable when I heard a step behind me, and my heart gave a jump. And I gave a start too.

"Oh, is that you, Mr. Wilson?" said a timid little voice.

"Yes," I said. "Is that you, Mary?"

And she said yes. It was the first time I called her Mary, but she did not seem to notice it.

"Did I frighten you?" I asked.

"No — yes — just a little," she said. "I didn't know there was any one ——" then she stopped.

"Why aren't you dancing?" I asked her.

"Oh, I'm tired," she said. "It was too hot in the wool-shed. I thought I'd like to come out and get my head cool and be quiet a little while."

"Yes," I said, "it must be hot in the wool-shed."

She stood looking out over the willows. Presently she said, "It must be very dull for you, Mr. Wilson — you must feel lonely. Mr. Barnes said ——" Then she gave a little gasp and stopped — as if she was just going to put her foot in it.

"How beautiful the moonlight looks on the willows!" she said.

"Yes," I said, "doesn't it? Supposing we have a stroll by the river."

"Oh , thank you, Mr. Wilson. I'd like it very much."

I didn't notice it then, but, now I come to think of it, it was a beautiful scene: there was a horse-shoe of high blue hills round behind the house, with the river running round under the slopes, and in front was a rounded hill covered with pines, and pine ridges, and a soft blue peak away over the ridges ever so far in the distance.

I had a handkerchief over the worst of my face, and kept the best side turned to her. We walked down by the river, and didn't say anything for a good while. I was thinking hard. We came to a white smooth log in a quiet place out of sight of the house.

"Suppose we sit down for a while, Mary," I said.

"If you like, Mr. Wilson," she said.

There was about a foot of log between us.

"What a beautiful night!" she said.

"Yes," I said, "isn't it?"

Presently she said, "I suppose you know I'm going away next month, Mr. Wilson?"

I felt suddenly empty. "No," I said, "I didn't know that."

"Yes," she said, "I thought you knew. I'm going to try and get into the hospital to be trained for a nurse, and if that doesn't come off I'll get a place as assistant public-school teacher."

We didn't say anything for a good while.

"I suppose you won't be sorry to go, Miss Brand?" I said.

"I — I don't know," she said. "Everybody's been so kind to me here."

She sat looking straight before her, and I fancied her eyes glistened. I put my arm round her shoulders, but she didn't seem to notice it. In fact, I scarcely noticed it myself at the time.

"So you think you'll be sorry to go away?" I said.

"Yes, Mr. Wilson. I suppose I'll fret for a while. It's been my home, you know."

I pressed my hand on her shoulder, just a little, so as she couldn't pretend not to know it was there. But she didn't seem to notice.

"Ah, well," I said, "I suppose I'll be on the wallaby again next week."

"Will you, Mr. Wilson?" she said. Her voice seemed very soft.

I slipped my arm round her waist, under her arm. My heart was going like clockwork now.

Presently she said —

"Don't you think it's time to go back now, Mr. Wilson?"

"Oh, there's plenty of time!" I said. I shifted up, and put my arm farther round, and held her closer. She sat straight up, looking right in front of her, but she began to breathe hard.

"Mary," I said.

"Yes," she said.   "Call me Joe," I said.

"I — I don't like to," she said. "I don't think it would be right."

So I just turned her face round and kissed her. She clung to me and cried.

"What is it, Mary?" I asked.

She only held me tighter and cried.

"What is it, Mary?" I said. "Ain't you well? Ain't you happy?"

"Yes, Joe," she said, "I'm very happy." Then she said, "Oh, your poor face! Can't I do anything for it?"

"No," I said. "That's all right. My face doesn't hurt me a bit now."

But she didn't seem right.

"What is it, Mary?" I said. "Are you tired? You didn't sleep last night ——" Then I got an inspiration.

"Mary," I said, "what were you doing out with the gun this morning?"

And after some coaxing it all came out, a bit hysterical.

"I couldn't sleep — I was frightened. Oh! I had such a terrible dream about you, Joe! I thought Romany came back and got into your room and stabbed you with his knife. I got up and dressed, and about daybreak I heard a horse at the gate; then I got the gun down from the wall — and — and Mr. Barnes came round the corner and frightened me. He's something like Romany, you know."

Then I got as much of her as I could into my arms.

And, oh, but wasn't I happy walking home with Mary that night! She was too little for me to put my arm round her waist, so I put it round her shoulder, and that felt just as good. I remember I asked her who'd cleaned up my room and washed my things, but she wouldn't tell.

She wouldn't go back to the dance yet; she said she'd go into her room and rest a while. There was no one near the old verandah; and when she stood on the end of the floor she was just on a level with my shoulder.

"Mary," I whispered, "put your arms round my neck and kiss me."

She put her arms round my neck, but she didn't kiss me; she only hid her face.

"Kiss me, Mary!" I said.

"I — I don't like to," she whispered.

"Why not, Mary?"

Then I felt her crying or laughing, or half crying and half laughing. I'm not sure to this day which it was.

"Why won't you kiss me, Mary? Don't you love me?"

"Because," she said, "because — because I — I don't — I don't think it's right for — for a girl to — to kiss a man unless she's going to be his wife."

Then it dawned on me! I'd forgot all about proposing.

"Mary," I said, "would you marry a chap like me?"

And that was all right.

Next morning Mary cleared out my room and sorted out my things, and didn't take the slightest notice of the other girls' astonishment.

But she made me promise to speak to old Black, and I did the same evening. I found him sitting on the log by the fence, having a yarn on the quiet with an old Bushman; and when the old Bushman got up and went away, I sat down.

"Well, Joe," said Black, "I see somebody's been spoiling your face for the dance." and after a bit he said, "Well, Joe, what is it? Do you want another job? If you do, you'll have to ask Mrs. Black, or Bob" (Bob was his eldest son); "they're managing the station for me now, you know." He could be bitter sometimes in his quiet way.

"No," I said; "it's not that, Boss."

"Well, what is it, Joe?"

"I — well the fact is, I want little Mary."

He puffed at his pipe for a long time, then I thought he spoke.

"What did you say, Boss?" I said.

"Nothing, Joe," he said. "I was going to say a lot, but it wouldn't be any use. My father used to say a lot to me before I was married."

I waited a good while for him to speak.

"Well, Boss," I said, "what about Mary?"

"Oh! I suppose that's all right, Joe," he said. "I — I beg your pardon. I got thinking of the days when I was courting Mrs. Black."

Brighten's Sister-in-law

Jim was born on Gulgong, New South Wales. We used to say "on" Gulgong — and old diggers still talked of being "on th' Gulgong" — though the goldfield there had been worked out for years, and the place was only a dusty little pastoral town in the scrubs. Gulgong was about the last of the great alluvial "rushes" of the "roaring days" — and dreary and dismal enough it looked when I was there. The expression "on" came from being on the "diggings" or goldfield — the workings or the goldfield was all underneath, of course, so we lived (or starved) *on* them — not in nor at 'em.

Mary and I had been married about two years when Jim came —— His name wasn't "Jim", by the way, it was "John Henry", after an uncle godfather; but we called him Jim from the first — (and before it) — because Jim was a popular Bush name, and most of my old mates were Jims. The Bush is full of good-hearted scamps called Jim.

We lived in an old weather-board shanty that had been a sly-grog-shop, and the Lord knows what else! in the palmy days of Gulgong; and I did a bit of digging ("fossicking", rather), a bit of shearing, a bit of fencing, a bit of Bush-carpentering, tank-sinking, — anything, just to keep the billy boiling.

We had a lot of trouble with Jim with his teeth. He was bad with every one of them, and we had most of them lanced — couldn't pull him through without. I remember we got one lanced and the gum healed over before the tooth came through, and we had to get it cut again. He was a plucky little chap, and after the first time he never whimpered when the doctor was lancing his gum: he used to say "tar" afterwards, and want to bring the lance home with him.

The first turn we got with Jim was the worst. I had had the wife and Jim out camping with me in a tent at a dam I was making at Cattle Creek; I had two men working for me, and a boy to drive one of the tip-drays, and I took Mary out to cook for us. And it was lucky for us that the contract was finished and we got back to Gulgong, and within reach of a doctor, the day we did. We were just camping in the house, with our goods and chattels anyhow, for the night; and we were hardly back home an hour when Jim took convulsions for the first time.

Did you ever see a child in convulsions? You wouldn't want to see it again: it plays the devil with a man's nerves. I'd got the beds fixed up on the floor, and the billies on the fire — I was going to make some tea, and put a piece of corned beef on to boil over night — when Jim (he'd been queer all day, and his mother was trying to hush him to sleep) — Jim, he screamed out twice. He'd been crying a good deal, and I was dog-tired and worried (over some money a man owed me) or I'd have noticed at once that there was something unusual in the way the child cried out: as it was I didn't turn round till Mary screamed "Joe! Joe!" You know how a woman cries out when her child is in danger or dying — short, and sharp, and terrible. "Joe! Look! look! Oh, my God! our child! Get the bath, quick! quick! it's convulsions!"

Jim was bent back like a bow, stiff as a bullock-yoke, in his mother's arms, and his eyeballs were turned up and fixed — a thing I saw twice afterwards, and don't want ever to see again.

I was falling over things getting the tub and the hot water, when the woman who lived next door rushed in. She called to her husband to run for the doctor, and before the doctor came she and Mary had got Jim into a hot bath and pulled him through.

The neighbour woman made me up a shake-down in another room, and stayed with Mary that night; but it was a long while before I got Jim and Mary's screams out of my head and fell asleep.

You may depend I kept the fire in, and a bucket of water hot over it, for a good many nights after that: but (it always happens like this) there came a night, when the fright had worn off, when I was too tired to bother about the fire, and that night Jim took us by surprise. Our wood-heap was done, and I broke up a new chair to get a fire, and had to run a quarter of a mile for water; but this turn wasn't so bad as the first, and we pulled him through.

You never saw a child in convulsions? Well, you don't want to. It must be only a matter of seconds, but it seems long minutes; and half an hour afterwards the child might be laughing and playing with you, or stretched out dead. It shook me up a lot. I was always pretty high-strung and sensitive. After Jim took the first fit, every time he cried, or turned over, or stretched out in the night, I'd jump: I was always feeling his forehead in the dark to see if he was feverish, or feeling his limbs to see if he was "limp" yet. Mary and I often laughed about it — afterwards. I tried sleeping in another room, but for nights after Jim's first attack I'd be just dozing off into a sound sleep, when I'd hear him scream, as plain as could be, and I'd hear Mary cry, "Joe! — Joe!" — short, sharp, and terrible — and I'd be up and into their room like a shot, only to find them sleeping peacefully. Then I'd feel Jim's head and his breathing for signs of convulsions, see to the fire and water, and go back to bed and try to sleep. For the first few nights I was like that all night, and I'd feel relieved when daylight came. I'd be in first thing to see if they were all right; then I'd sleep till dinner-time if it was Sunday or I had no work. But then I was run down about that time: I was worried about some money for a wool-shed I put up and never got paid for; and, besides, I'd been pretty wild before I met Mary.

I was fighting hard then — struggling for something better. Both Mary and I were born to better things, and that's what made the life so hard for us.

Jim got on all right for a while: we used to watch him well, and have his teeth lanced in time.

It used to hurt and worry me to see how — just as he was getting fat and rosy and like a natural happy child, and I'd feel proud to take him out — a tooth would come along, and he'd get thin and white and pale and bigger-eyed and old-fashioned. We'd say, "He'll be safe when he gets his eye-teeth": but he didn't get them till he was two; then, "He'll be safe when he gets his two-year-old teeth": they didn't come till he was going on for three.

He was a wonderful little chap — Yes, I know all about parents thinking that their child is the best in the world. If your boy is small for his age, friends will say that small children make big men; that he's a very bright, intelligent child, and that it's better to have a bright, intelligent child than a big, sleepy lump of fat. And if your boy is dull and sleepy, they say that the dullest boys make the cleverest men — and all the rest of it. I never took any notice of that sort of clatter — took it for what it was worth; but, all the same, I don't think I ever saw such a child as Jim was when he turned two. He was everybody's favourite. They spoilt him rather. I

had my own ideas about bringing up a child. I reckoned
Mary was too soft with Jim. She'd say, "Put that" (whatever
it was) "out of Jim's reach, will you, Joe?" and I'd say, "No!
leave it there, and make him understand he's not to have it.
Make him have his meals without any nonsense, and go to
bed at a regular hour," I'd say. Mary and I had many a
breeze over Jim. She'd say that I forgot he was only a baby:
but I held that a baby could be trained from the first week;
and I believed I was right.

But, after all, what are you to do? You'll see a boy that
was brought up strict turn out a scamp; and another that
was dragged up anyhow (by the hair of the head, as the
saying is) turn out well. Then, again, when a child is delicate
— and you might lose him any day — you don't like to spank
him, though he might be turning out a little fiend, as
delicate children often do. Suppose you gave a child a
hammering, and the same night he took convulsions, or
something, and died — how'd you feel about it? You never
know what a child is going to take, any more than you can
tell what some women are going to say or do.

I was very fond of Jim, and we were great chums.
Sometimes I'd sit and wonder what the deuce he was
thinking about, and often, the way he talked, he'd make me
uneasy. When he was two he wanted a pipe above all
things, and I'd get him a clean new clay and he'd sit by my
side, on the edge of the verandah, or on a log of the
wood-heap, in the cool of the evening, and suck away at his
pipe, and try to spit when he saw me do it. He seemed to
understand that a cold empty pipe wasn't quite the thing,
yet to have the sense to know that he couldn't smoke tobacco
yet: he made the best he could of things. And if he broke a
clay pipe he wouldn't have a new one, and there'd be a row;
the old one had to be mended up, somehow, with string or
wire. If I got my hair cut, he'd want his cut too; and it
always troubled him to see me shave — as if he thought there
must be something wrong somewhere, else he ought to have
to be shaved too. I lathered him one day, and pretended to
shave him: he sat through it as solemn as an owl, but didn't
seem to appreciate it — perhaps he had sense enough to
know that it couldn't possible be the real thing. He felt his
face, looked very hard at the lather I scraped off, and
whimpered, "No blood, daddy!"

I used to cut myself a good deal: I was always impatient
over shaving.

Then he went in to interview his mother about it. She
understood his lingo better than I did.

But I wasn't always at ease with him. Sometimes he'd sit looking into the fire, with his head on one side, and I'd watch him and wonder what he was thinking about (I might as well have wondered what a Chinaman was thinking about) till he seemed at least twenty years older than me: sometimes, when I moved or spoke, he'd glance round just as if to see what that old fool of a dadda of his was doing now.

I used to have a fancy that there was something Eastern, or Asiatic — something older than our civilization or religion — about old-fashioned children. Once I started to explain my idea to a woman I thought would understand — and as it happened she had an old-fasioned child, with very slant eyes — a little tartar he was too. I suppose it was the sight of him that unconsciously reminded me of my infernal theory, and set me off on it, without warning me. Anyhow, it got me mixed up in an awful row with the woman and her husband — and all their tribe. It wasn't an easy thing to explain myself out of it, and the row hasn't been fixed up yet. There were some Chinamen in the district.

I took a good-size fencing contract, the frontage of a ten-mile paddock, near Gulgong, and did well out of it. The railway had got as far as the Cudgeegong river — some twenty miles form Gulgong and two hundred from the coast — and "carrying" was good then. I had a couple of draught-horses, that I worked in the tip-drays when I was tank-sinking, and one or two others running in the Bush. I bought a broken-down waggon cheap, tinkered it up myself — christened it "The Same Old Thing" — and started carrying from the railway terminus through Gulgong and along the bush roads and tracks that branch out fanlike through the scrubs to the one-pub towns and sheep and cattle station out there in the howling wilderness. It wasn't much of a team. There were the two heavy horses for "shafters"; a stunted colt, that I'd bought out of the pound for thirty shillings; a light, spring-cart horse; an old grey mare, with points like a big red-and-white Australian store bullock, and with the grit of an old washerwoman to work; and a horse that had spanked along in Cobb & Co.'s mail-coach in his time. I had a couple there that didn't belong to me: I worked them for the feeding of them in the dry weather. And I had all sorts of harness, and I mended and fixed up myself. It was a mixed team, but I took light stuff, got through pretty quick, and freight rates were high. So I got along.

Before this, whenever I made a few pounds I'd sink a shaft

somewhere, prospecting for gold; but Mary never let me rest till she talked me out of that.

I made up my mind to take on a small selection farm — that an old mate of mine had fenced in and cleared, and afterwards chucked up — about thirty miles out west of Gulgong, at a place called Lahey's Creek. (The places were all called Lahey's Creek, or Spicer's Flat, or Murphy's Flat, or Ryan's Crossing, or some such name — round there.) I reckoned I'd have a run for the horses and be able to grow a bit of feed. I always had a dread of taking Mary and the children too far away from a doctor — or a good woman neighbour; but there were some people came to live on Lahey's Creek, and besides, there was a young brother of Mary's — a young scamp (his name was Jim, too, and we called him "Jimmy" at first to make room for our Jim — he hated the name "Jimmy" or James). He came to live with us — without asking — and I thought he'd find enough work at Lahey's Creek to keep him out of mischief. He wasn't to be depended on much — he thought nothing of riding off, five hundred miles or so, "to have a look at the country" — but he was fond of Mary, and he'd stay by her till I got some one else to keep her company while I was on the road. He would be a protection against "sundowners" or any shearers who happened to wander that way in the "D.T.'s" after a spree. Mary had a married sister come to live at Gulgong just before we left, and nothing would suit her and her husband but we must leave little Jim with them for a month or so — till we got settled down at Lahey's Creek. They were newly married.

Mary was to have driven into Gulgong, in the spring-cart, at the end of the month, and taken Jim home; but when the time came she wasn't too well — and, besides, the tyres of the cart were loose, and I hadn't time to get them cut, so we let Jim's time run on a week or so longer, till I happened to come out through Gulgong from the river with a small load of flour for Lahey's Creek way. The roads were good, the weather grand — no chance of it raining, and I had a spare tarpaulin if it did — I would only camp out one night; so I decided to take Jim home with me.

Jim was turning three then, and he was a cure. He was so old-fashioned that he used to frighten me sometimes — I'd almost think that there was something supernatural about him; though, of course, I never took any notice of that rot about some children being too old-fashioned to live. There's always the ghoulish old hag (and some not so old nor haggish either) who'll come round and shake up young parents with such croaks as, "You'll never rear that child — he's too bright for his age." To the devil with them! I say.

But I really thought that Jim was too intelligent for his age, and I often told Mary that he ought to be kept back, and not let talk too much to old diggers and long lanky jokers of Bushmen who rode in and hung their horses outside my place on Sunday afternoons.

I don't believe in parents talking about their own children everlastingly — you get sick of hearing them; and their kids are generally little devils, and turn out larrikins as likely as not.

But, for all that, I really think that Jim, when he was three years old, was the most wonderful little chap in every way, that I ever saw.

For the first hour or so, along the road, he was telling me all about his adventures at his auntie's.

"But they spoilt me too much, dad," he said as solemn as a native bear. "An' besides, a boy ought to stick to his parrans!"

I was taking out a cattle-pup for a drover I knew, and the pup took up a good deal of Jim's time.

Sometimes he'd jolt me, the way he talked; and other times I'd have to turn away my head and cough, or shout at the horses, to keep from laughing outright. And once, when I was taken that way, he outright said —

"What are you jerking your shoulders and coughing, and grunting, and going on that way for, dad? Why don't you tell me something?"

"Tell you what, Jim?"

"Tell me some talk."

So I told him all the talk I could think of. And I had to brighten up, I can tell you, and not draw too much on my imagination — for Jim was a terror at cross-examination when the fit took him; and he didn't think twice about telling you when he thought you were talking nonsense. Once he said —

"I'm glad you took me home with you, dad. You'll get to know Jim."

"What!" I said.

"You'll get to know Jim."

"But don't I know you already?"

"No, you don't. You never has time to know Jim at home."

And, looking back, I saw that it was cruel true. I had known in my heart all along that this was the truth; but it

came to me like a blow from Jim. You see, it had been a
hard struggle for the last year or so; and when I was home
for a day or two I was generally too busy, or too tired and
worried, or full of schemes for the future, to take much
notice of Jim. Mary used to speak to me about it sometimes.
"You never take notice of the child," she'd say. "You could
surely find a few minutes of an evening. What's the use of
always worrying and brooding? Your brain will go with a
snap some day, and, if you get over it, it will teach you a
lesson. You'll be an old man, and Jim a young one, before
you realize that you had a child once. Then it will be too
late."

This sort of talk from Mary always bored me and made
me impatient with her, because I knew it all too well. I never
worried for myself — only for Mary and the children. And
often, as the days went by, I said to myself, "I'll take more
notice of Jim and give Mary more of my time, just as soon as
I can see things clear ahead a bit." And the hard days went
on, and the weeks, and the months, and the years —— Ah,
well!

Mary used to say, when things would get worse, "Why
don't you talk to me, Joe? Why don't you tell me your
thoughts, instead of shutting yourself up in yourself and
brooding — eating your heart out? It's hard for me: I get to
think you're tired of me, and selfish. I might be cross and
speak sharp to you when you are in trouble. How am I to
know, if you don't tell me?"

But I didn't think she'd understand.

And so, getting acquainted, and chumming and dozing,
with the gums closing over our heads here and there, and the
ragged patches of sunlight and shade passing up, over the
horses, over us, on the front of the load, over the load, and
down on to the white, dusty road again — Jim and I got
along the lonely Bush road and over the ridges, some fifteen
miles before sunset, and camped at Ryan's Crossing on
Sandy Creek for the night. I got the horses out and took the
harness off. Jim wanted badly to help me, but I made him
stay on the load; for one of the horses — a vicious, red-eyed
chestnut — was a kicker: he'd broken a man's leg. I got the
feed-bags stretched across the shafts, and the chaff-and-corn
into them; and there stood the horses all round with their
rumps north, south, and west, and their heads between the
shafts, munching and switching their tails. We use double
shafts, you know, for horse-teams — two pairs side by side,
— and prop them up, and stretch bags between them,

letting the bags sag to serve as feed-boxes. I threw the spare tarpaulin over the wheels on one side, letting about half of it lie on the ground in case of damp, and so making a floor and a break-wind. I threw down bags and the blankets and 'possum rug against the wheel to make a camp for Jim and the cattle-pup, and got a gin-case we used for a tucker-box, the frying-pan and billy down, and made a good fire at a log close handy, and soon everything was comfortable. Ryan's Crossing was a grand camp. I stood with my pipe in my mouth, my hands behind my back, and my back to the fire, and took the country in.

Reedy Creek came down along a western spur of the range: the banks here were deep and green, and the water ran clear over the granite bars, boulders, and gravel. Behind us was a dreary flat covered with those gnarled, grey-barked, dry-rotted "native apple-trees" (about as much like apple-trees as the native bear is like any other), and a nasty bit of sand-dusty road that I was always glad to get over in wet weather. To the left on our side of the creek were reedy marshes, with frogs croaking, and across the creek the dark box-scrub-covered ridges ended in steep "sidings" coming down to the creek-bank, and to the main road that skirted them, running on west up over a "saddle" in the ridges and on towards Dubbo. The road by Lahey's Creek to a place called Cobborah branched off, though dreary apple-tree and stringy bark flats, to the left, just beyond the crossing: all these fanlike branch tracks from the Cudgeegong were inside a big horse-shoe in the Great Western Line, and so they gave small carriers a chance, now that Cobb & Co.'s coaches and the big teams and vans had shifted out of the main western terminus. There were tall she-oaks all along the creek, and a clump of big ones over a deep water-hole just above the crossing. The creek oaks have rough barked trunks, like English elms, but are much taller, and higher to the branches — and the leaves are reedy; Kendall, the Australian poet, calls them the "she-oak harps Aeolian". Those trees are always sigh-sigh-sighing — more of a sigh than a sough or the "whoosh" of gum-trees in the wind. You always hear them sighing, even when you can't feel any wind. It's the same with telegraph wires: put your head against a telegraph-post on a dead, still day, and you'll hear and feel the far-away roar of the wires. But then the oaks are not connected with the distance, where there might be wind; and they don't *roar* in a gale, only sigh louder and softer according to the wind, and never seem to go above or below a certain pitch — like a big harp with all the strings the same. I used to have a theory that those creek oaks got the wind's voice telephoned to them, so to speak, through the ground.

I happened to look down, and there was Jim (I thought he was on the tarpaulin, playing with the pup): he was standing close beside me with his legs wide apart, his hands behind his back, and his back to the fire.

He held his head a little on one side, and there was such an old, old, wise expression in his big brown eyes — just as if he'd been a child for a hundred years or so, or as though he were listening to those oaks and understanding them in a fatherly sort of way.

"Dad!" he said presently — "Dad! do you think I'll ever grow up to be a man?"

"Wh — why, Jim?" I gasped.

"Because I don't want to."

I couldn't think of anything against this. It made me uneasy. But I remember *I* used to have a childish dread of growing up to be a man.

"Jim." I said, to break the silence, "do you hear what the she-oaks say?"

"No, I don't. Is they talking?"

"Yes," I said, without thinking.

"What is they saying?" he asked.

I took the bucket and went down to the creek for some water for tea. I thought Jim would follow with a little tin billy he had, but he didn't: when I got back to the fire he was again on the 'possum rug, comforting the pup. I fried some bacon and eggs that I'd brought out with me. Jim sang out from the waggon —

"Don't cook too much, dad — I mightn't be hungry."

I got the tin plates and pint-pots and things out on a clean new flour-bag, in honour of Jim, and dished up. He was leaning back on the rug looking at the pup in a listless sort of way. I reckoned he was tired out, and pulled the gin-case up close to him for a table and put his plate on it. But he only tried a mouthful or two, and then he said —

"I ain't hungry, dad! You'll have to eat it all."

It made me uneasy — I never liked to see a child of mine turn from his food. They had given him some tinned salmon in Gulgong, and I was afraid that that was upsetting him. I was always against tinned muck.

"Sick, Jim?" I asked.

"No, dad, I ain't sick; I don't know what's the matter with me."

"Have some tea, sonny?"

"Yes, dad."

I gave him some tea, with some milk in it that I'd brought in a bottle from his aunt's from him. He took a sip or two and then put the pint-pot on the gin-case.

"Jim's tired, dad," he said.

I made him lie down while I fixed up a camp for the night. It had turned a bit chilly, so I let the big tarpaulin down all round — it was made to cover a high load, the flour in the waggon didn't come above the rail, so the tarpaulin came down well on to the ground. I fixed Jim up a comfortable bed under the tail-end of the waggon: when I went to lift him in he was lying back, looking up at the stars in a half-dreamy, half-fascinated way that I didn't like. Whenever Jim was extra old-fashioned, or affectionate, there was danger.

"How do you feel now, sonny?"

It seemed a minute before he heard me and turned from the stars.

"Jim's better, dad." Then he said something like, "The stars are looking at me." I thought he was half asleep. I took off his jacket and boots, and carried him in under the waggon and made him comfortable for the night.

"Kiss me 'night-night, daddy," he said.

I'd rather he hadn't asked me — it was a bad sign. As I was going to the fire he called me back.

"What is it, Jim?"

"Get me my things and the cattle-pup, please, daddy."

I was scared now. His things were some toys and rubbish he'd brought from Gulgong, and I remembered, the last time he had convulsions, he took all his toys and a kitten to bed with him. And "night-night" and "daddy" were two-year-old language to Jim. I'd thought he'd forgotten those words — he seemed to be going back.

"Are you quite warm enough, Jim?"

"Yes, dad."

I started to walk up and down — I always did this when I was extra worried.

I was frightened now about Jim, though I tried to hide the fact from myself. Presently he called me again.

"What is it, Jim?"

"Take the blankets off me, fahver — Jim's sick!" (They'd been teaching him to say father.)

I was scared now. I remembered a neighbour of ours had a little girl die (she swallowed a pin), and when she was going she said —

"Take the blankets off me, muvver — I'm dying."

And I couldn't get that out of my head.

I threw back a fold of the 'possum rug, and felt Jim's head — he seemed cool enough.

"Where do you feel bad, sonny?"

No answer for a while; then he said suddenly, but in a voice as if he were talking in his sleep —

"Put my boots on, please, daddy. I want to go home to muvver!"

I held his hand, and comforted him for a while; then he slept — in a restless, feverish sort of way.

I got the bucket I used for water for the horses and stood it over the fire; I ran to the creek with the big kerosene-tin bucket and got it full of cold water and stood it handy. I got the spade (we always carried one to dig wheels out of bogs in wet weather) and turned a corner of the tarpaulin back, dug a hole, and trod the tarpaulin down into the hole, to serve for a bath, in case of the worst. I had a tin of mustard, and meant to fight a good round for Jim, if death came along.

I stooped in under the tail-board of the waggon and felt Jim. His head was burning hot, and his skin parched and dry as a bone.

Then I lost nerve and started blundering backward and forward between the waggon and the fire, and repeating what I'd heard Mary say the last time we fought for Jim: "God! don't take my child! God! don't take my boy!" I'd never had much faith in doctors, but, my God! I wanted one then. The nearest was fifteen miles away.

I threw back my head and stared up at the branches, in desperation; and — Well, I don't ask you to take much stock in this, though most old Bushmen will believe anything of the Bush by night; and — Now, it might have been that I was all unstrung, or it might have been a patch of sky outlined in the gently moving branches, or the blue smoke rising up. But I saw the figure of a woman, all white, come down, down, nearly to the limbs of the trees, point on up the main road, and then float up and up and vanish, still pointing. I thought Mary was dead! Then it flashed on me —

Four or five miles up the road, over the "saddle", was an old shanty that had been a half-way inn before the Great Western Line got round as far as Dubbo and took the coach traffic off those old Bush roads. A man named Brighten lived there. He was a selector; did a little farming, and as much sly-grog selling as he could. He was married — but it wasn't that: I'd thought of them, but she was a childish, worn-out, spiritless woman, and both were pretty "ratty" from hardship and loneliness — they weren't likely to be of any use to me. But it was this: I'd heard talk, among some women in Gulgong, of a sister of Brighten's wife who'd gone out to live with them lately: she'd been a hospital matron in the city, they said; and there were yarns about her. Some said she got the sack for exposing the doctors — or carrying on with them — I didn't remember which. The fact of a city woman going out to live in such a place, with such people, was enough to make talk among women in a town twenty miles away, but then there must have been something extra about her, else Bushmen wouldn't have talked and carried her name so far; and I wanted a woman out of the ordinary now. I even reasoned this way, thinking like lightning, as I knelt over Jim between the big back wheels of the waggon.

I had an old racing mare that I used as a riding hack, following the team. In a minute I had her saddled and bridled; I tied the end of a half-full chaff-bag, shook the chaff into each end and dumped it on to the pommel as a cushion or buffer for Jim; I wrapped him in a blanket, and scrambled into the saddle with him.

The next minute we were stumbling down the steep bank, clattering and splashing over the crossing, and struggling up the opposite bank to the level. The mare, as I told you, was an old racer, but broken-winded — she must have run without wind after the first half mile. She had the old racing instinct in her strong, and whenever I rode in company I'd have to pull her hard else she'd race the other horse or burst. She ran low fore and aft, and was the easiest horse I ever rode. She ran like wheels on rails, with a bit of a tremble now and then — like a railway carriage — when she settled down to it.

The chaff-bag had slipped off, in the creek I suppose, and I let the bridle-rein go and held Jim up to me like a baby the whole way. Let the strongest man, who isn't used to it, hold a baby in one position for five minutes — and Jim was fairly heavy. But I never felt the ache in my arms that night — it must have gone before I was in a fit state of mind to feel it. And at home I'd often growled about being asked to hold the baby for a few minutes. I could never brood comfortably and nurse a baby at the same time. It was a ghostly moonlight night. There's no timber in the world so ghostly as the Australian Bush moonlight — or just about daybreak. The all-shaped patches of moonlight falling between ragged, twisted boughs; the ghostly blue-white bark of the "white-box" trees; a dead naked white ring-barked tree, or dead white stump starting out here and there, and the ragged patches of shade and light on the road that made anything, from the shape of a spotted bullock to a naked corpse laid out stark. Roads and tracks through the Bush made by moonlight — every one seeming straighter and clearer than the real one: you have to trust to your horse then. Sometimes the naked white trunk of a red stringy bark-tree, where a sheet of bark had been taken off, would start out like a ghost from the dark Bush. And dew or frost glistening on these things, according to the season. Now and again a great grey kangaroo, that had been feeding on a green patch down by the road, would start with a "thump-thump", and away up the siding.

The Bush seemed full of ghosts that night — all going my way — and being left behind by the mare. Once I stopped to look at Jim: I just sat back and the mare "propped" — she'd been a stock-horse, and was used to "cutting-out". I felt Jim's hands and forehead; he was in a burning fever. I bent forward, and the old mare settled down to it again. I kept saying out loud — and Mary and me often laughed about it (afterwards): "He's limp yet! — Jim's limp yet!" (the words seemed jerked out of me by sheer fright) — "He's limp yet!" till the mare's feet took it up. Then, just when I thought she was doing her best and racing her hardest, she suddenly started forward, like a cable tram gliding along on its own and the grip put on suddenly. It was just what she'd do when I'd be riding alone and a strange horse drew up from behind — the old racing instinct. I *felt* the thing too! I felt as if a strange horse *was* there! And then — the words just jerked out of me by sheer funk — I started saying, "Death is riding tonight! . . . Death is racing tonight! . . . Death is riding tonight!" till the hoofs took that up. And I believe the old mare felt the black horse at her side and was going to beat him or break her heart.

I was mad with anxiety and fright: I remember I kept saying, "I'll be kinder to Mary after this! I'll take more notice of Jim!" and the rest of it.

I don't know how the old mare got up the last "pinch". She must have slackened pace, but I never noticed it: I just held Jim up to me and gripped the saddle with my knees — I remember the saddle jerked from the desperate jumps of her till I thought the girth would go. We topped the gap and were going down into a gully they called Dead Man's

Hollow, and there, at the back of a ghostly clearing that opened from the road where there were some black-soil springs, was a long, low, oblong weatherboard-and-shingle building, with blind, broken windows in the gable-ends, and a wide steep verandah roof slanting down almost to the level of the window-sills — there was something sinister about it, I thought — like the hat of a jailbird slouched over his eyes. The place looked both deserted and haunted. I saw no light, but that was because of the moonlight outside. The mare turned in at the corner of the clearing to take a short cut to the shanty, and, as she struggled across some marshy ground, my heart kept jerking out the words, "It's deserted! They've gone away! It's deserted!" The mare went round to the back and pulled up between the back door and a big bark-and-slab kitchen. Some one shouted from inside —

"Who's there?"

"It's me. Joe Wilson. I want your sister-in-law — I've got the boy — he's sick and dying!"

Brighten came out, pulling up his moleskins. "What boy?" he asked.

"Here, take him," I shouted, "and let me get down."

"What's the matter with him?" asked Brighten, and he seemed to hang back. And just as I made to get my leg over the saddle, Jim's head went back over my arm, he stiffened, and I saw his eyeballs turned up and glistening in the moonlight.

I felt cold all over then and sick in the stomach — but *clear-headed* in a way: strange, wasn't it? I don't know why I didn't get down and rush into the kitchen to get a bath ready. I only felt as if the worst had come, and I wished it were over and gone. I even thought of Mary and the funeral.

Then a woman ran out of the house — a big, hard-looking woman. She had on a wrapper of some sort, and her feet were bare. She laid her hand on Jim, looked at his face, and then snatched him from me and ran into the kitchen — and me down and after her. As great good luck would have it, they had some dirty clothes on to boil in a kerosene tin — dish-cloths or something.

Brighten's sister-in-law dragged a tub out from under the table, wrenched the bucket off the hook, and dumped in the water, dish-clothes and all, snatched a can of cold water from a corner, dashed that in, and felt the water with her hand — holding Jim up to her hip all the time — and I won't say how he looked. She stood him in the tub and started dashing water over him, tearing off his clothes between the splashes.

"Here, that tin of mustard — there on the shelf!" she shouted to me.

She knocked the lid off the tin on the edge of the tub, and went on splashing and spanking Jim.

It seemed an eternity. And I? Why, I never thought clearer in my life. I felt cold-blooded — I felt as if I'd like an excuse to go outside till it was all over. I thought of Mary and the funeral — and wished that that was past. All this in a flash, as it were. I felt that it would be a great relief, and only wished the funeral was months past. I felt — well, altogether selfish. I only thought for myself.

Brighten's sister-in-law splashed and spanked him hard — hard enough to break his back I thought, and — after about half an hour it seemed — the end came: Jim's limbs relaxed, he slipped down into the tub, and the pupils of his eyes came down. They seemed dull and expressionless, like the eyes of a new baby, but he was back for the world again.

I dropped on the stool by the table.

"It's all right," she said. "It's all over now. I wasn't going to let him die." I was only thinking, "Well it's over now, but it will come on again. I wish it was over for good. I'm tired of it."

She called to her sister, Mrs. Brighten, a washed-out, helpless little fool of a woman, who'd been running in and out and whimpering all the time —

"Here, Jessie! bring the new white blanket off my bed. And you, Brighten, take some of that wood off the fire, and stuff something in that hole there to stop the draught."

Brighten — he was a nuggety little hairy man with no expression to be seen for whiskers — had been running in with sticks and back logs from the wood-heap. He took the wood out, stuffed up the crack, and went inside and brought out a black bottle — got a cup from the shelf, and put both down near my elbow.

Mrs. Brighten started to get some supper or breakfast, or whatever it was, ready. She had a clean cloth, and set the table tidily. I noticed that all the tins were polished bright (old coffee- and mustard-tins and the like, that they used instead of sugar-basins and tea-caddies and salt-cellars), and the kitchen was kept as clean as possible. She was all right at little things. I knew a haggard, worked-out Bushwoman who put her whole soul — or all she'd got left — into polishing old tins till they dazzled your eyes.

I didn't feel inclined for corned beef and damper, and post-and-rail tea. So I sat and squinted, when I thought she

wasn't looking, at Brighten's sister-in-law. She was a big
woman, her hands and feet were big, but well-shaped and
all in proportion — they fitted her. She was a handsome
woman — about forty I should think. She had a square
chin, and a straight thin-lipped mouth — straight save for a
hint of a turn down at the corners, which I fancied (and I
have strange fancies) had been a sign of weakness in the days
before she grew hard. There was no sign of weakness now.
She had hard grey eyes and blue-black hair. She hadn't
spoken yet. She didn't ask me how the boy took ill or I got
there, or who or what I was — at least not until the next
evening at tea-time.

She sat upright with Jim wrapped in the blanket and laid
across her knees, with one hand under his neck and the other
laid lightly on him, and she just rocked him gently.

She sat looking hard and straight before her, just as I've
seen a tired needlewoman sit with her work in her lap, and
look away back into the past. And Jim might have been the
work in her lap, for all she seemed to think of him. Now and
then she knitted her forehead and blinked.

Suddenly she glanced round and said — in a tone as if I
was her husband and she didn't think much of me —

"Why don't you eat something?"

"Beg pardon?"

"Eat something!"

I drank some tea, and sneaked another look at her. I was
beginning to feel more natural, and wanted Jim again, now
that the colour was coming back into his face, and he didn't
look like an unnaturally stiff and staring corpse. I felt a
lump rising, and wanted to thank her. I sneaked another
look at her.

She was staring straight before her — I never saw a
woman's face change so suddenly — I never saw a woman's
eyes so haggard and hopeless. Then her great chest heaved
twice, I heard her draw a long shuddering breath, like a
knocked-out horse, and two great tears dropped from her
wide open eyes down her cheeks like rain-drops on a face of
stone. And in the firelight they seemed tinged with blood.

I looked away quick, feeling full up myself. And presently
(I hadn't seen her look round) she said —

"Go to bed."

"Beg pardon?" (Her face was the same as before the
tears.)

"Go to bed. There's a bed made for you inside on the
sofa."

"But — the team — I must ——"

"What?"

"The team. I left it at the camp. I must look to it."

"Oh! Well, Brighten will ride down and bring it up in the morning — or send the half-caste. Now you go to bed, and get a good rest. The boy will be all right. I'll see to that."

I went out — it was a relief to get out — and looked to the mare. Brighten had got her some corn[1] and chaff in a candle-box, but she couldn't eat yet. She just stood or hung resting one hind-leg and then the other, with her nose over the box — and she sobbed. I put my arms round her neck and my face down on her ragged mane, and cried for the second time since I was a boy.

As I started to go in I heard Brighten's sister-in-law say, suddenly and sharply —

"Take *that* away, Jessie."

And presently I saw Mrs. Brighten go into the house with the black bottle.

The moon had gone behind the range. I stood for a minute between the house and the kitchen and peeped in through the kitchen window.

She had moved away from the fire and sat near the table. She bent over Jim and held him up close to her and rocked herself to and fro.

I went to bed and slept till the next afternoon. I woke just in time to hear the tail-end of a conversation between Jim and Brighten's sister-in-law. He was asking her out to our place and she promising to come.

"And now," says Jim, "I want to go home to 'muffer' in 'The Same Ol' Fling.'"

"What?"

Jim repeated.

"Oh! 'The Same Old Thing,' — the waggon."

The rest of the afternoon I poked round the gullies with old Brighten, looking at some "indications" (of the existence of gold) he had found. It was no use trying to "pump" him concerning his sister-in-law; Brighten was an "old hand", and had learned in the old Bush-ranging and cattle-stealing days to know nothing about other people's business. And, by the way, I noticed then that the more you talk and listen to a bad character, the more you lose your dislike for him.

I never saw such a change in a woman as in Brighten's sister-in-law that evening. She was bright and jolly, and

1. Maize or Indian corn — wheat is never called corn in Australia.

seemed at least ten years younger. She bustled round and helped her sister to get tea ready. She rooted out some old china that Mrs. Brighten had stowed away somewhere, and set the table as I seldom saw it set out there. She propped Jim up with pillows, and laughed and played with him like a great girl. She described Sydney and Sydney life as I'd never heard it described before; and she knew as much about the Bush and old diggings day as I did. She kept old Brighten and me listening and laughing till nearly midnight. And she seemed quick to understand everything when I talked. If she wanted to explain anything that we hadn't seen, she wouldn't say that it was "like a — like a" — and hesitate (you know what I mean); she'd hit the right thing on the head at once. A squatter with a very round, flaming red face and a white cork hat had gone by in the afternoon: she said it was "like a mushroom on the rising moon". She gave me a lot of good hints about children.

But she was quiet again next morning. I harnessed up, and she dressed Jim and gave him his breakfast, and made a comfortable place for him on the load with the 'possum rug and a spare pillow. She got up on the wheel to do it herself. Then was the awkward time. I'd half start to speak to her, and then turn away and go fixing up round the horses, and then make another false start to say good-bye. At last she took Jim up in her arms and kissed him, and lifted him on the wheel; but he put his arms tight round her neck, and kissed her — a thing Jim seldom did with anybody, except his mother, for he wasn't what you'd call an affectionate child, — he'd never more than offer his cheek to me, in his old-fashioned way. I'd got up the other side of the load to take him from her

"Here, take him," she said.

I saw his mouth twitching as I lifted him. Jim seldom cried nowadays — no matter how much he was hurt. I gained some time fixing Jim comfortable.

"You'd better make a start," she said. "You want to get home early with that boy."

I got down and went round to where she stood. I held out my hand and tried to speak, but my voice went like an ungreased waggon wheel, and I gave it up, and only squeezed her hand.

"That's all right," she said; then tears came into her eyes, and she suddenly put her hand on my shoulder and kissed me on the cheek. "You be off — you're only a boy yourself. Take care of that boy; be kind to your wife, and take care of yourself."

"Will you come to see us?"

I started the horses, and looked round once more. She was looking up at Jim, who was waving his hand to her from the top of the load. And I saw that haggard, hungry, hopeless look come into her eyes in spite of the tears.

I smoothed over that story and shortened it a lot, when I told it to Mary — I didn't want to upset her. But, some time after I brought Jim home from Gulgong, and while I was at home with the team for a few days, nothing would suit Mary but she must go over to Brighten's shanty and see Brighten's sister-in-law. So James drove her over one morning in the spring-cart: it was a long way, and they stayed at Brighten's overnight and didn't get back till late the next afternoon. I'd got the place in a pig-muck, as Mary said, "doing for" myself, and I was having a snooze on the sofa when they got back. The first thing I remember was some one stroking my head and kissing me, and I heard Mary saying, "My poor boy! My poor old boy!"

I sat up with a jerk. I thought that Jim had gone off again. But it seems that Mary was only referring to me. Then she started to pull grey hairs out of my head and put 'em in an empty match-box — to see how many she'd get. She used to do this when she felt a bit soft. I don't know what she said to Brighten's sister-in-law or what Brighten's sister-in-law said to her, but Mary was extra gentle for the next few days.

"Water Them Geraniums"

I. A Lonely Track

The time Mary and I shifted out into the Bush from Gulgong to "settle on the land" at Lahey's Creek.

I'd sold the two tip-drays that I used for tank-sinking and dam-making, and I took the traps out in the waggon on top of a small load of rations and horse-feed that I was taking to a sheep-station out that way. Mary drove out in the spring-cart. You remember we left little Jim with his aunt in Gulgong till we got settled down. I'd sent James (Mary's brother) out the day before, on horseback, with two or three cows and some heifers and steers and calves we had, and I'd told him to clean up a bit, and make the hut as bright and cheerful as possible before Mary came.

We hadn't much in the way of furniture. There was the four-poster cedar bedstead that I bought before we were married, and Mary was rather proud of it: it had "turned" posts and joints that bolted together. There was a plain hardwood table, that Mary called her "ironing-table", up-side down on top of the load, with the bedding and blankets between the legs; there were four of those common black kitchen-chairs — with apples painted on the hard board backs — that we used for the parlour; there was a cheap batten sofa with arms at the ends and turned rails between the uprights of the arms (we were a little proud of the turned rails); and there was the camp-oven, and the three-legged pot, and pans and buckets, stuck about the load and hanging under the tail-board of the waggon.

There was the little Wilcox & Gibb's sewing-maching — my present to Mary when we were married (and what a present, looking back to it!). There was a cheap little rocking-chair, and a looking-glass and some pictures that were presents from Mary's friends and sister. She had her mantel-shelf ornaments and crockery and nick-nacks packed away, in the linen and old clothes, in a big tub made of half a cask, and a box that had been Jim's cradle. The live stock was a cat in one box, and in another an old rooster, and three hens that formed cliques, two against one, turn about, as three of the same sex will do all over the world. I had my old cattle-dog, and of course a pup on the load — I always had a pup that I gave away, or sold and didn't get paid for, or had "touched" (stolen) as soon as it was old enough. James had his three spidery, sneaking, thieving, cold-blooded kangaroo-dogs with him. I was taking out three months' provisions in the way of ration-sugar, tea, flour, and potatoes, etc.

I started early, and Mary caught up to me at Ryan's Crossing on Sandy Creek, where we boiled the billy and had some dinner.

Mary bustled about the camp and admired the scenery and talked too much, for her, and was extra cheerful, and kept her face turned from me as much as possible. I soon saw what was the matter. She'd been crying to herself coming along the road. I thought it was all on account of leaving little Jim behind for the first time. She told me that she couldn't make up her mind till the last moment to leave him and that, a mile or two along the road, she'd have turned back for him, only that she knew her sister would laugh at her. She was always terribly anxious about the children.

We cheered each other up, and Mary drove with me the rest of the way to the creek, along the lonely branch track, across native-apple-tree flats. It was a dreary, hopeless track. There was no horizon, nothing but the rough ashen trunks of the gnarled and stunted trees in all directions, little or no undergrowth, and the ground, save for the coarse, brownish tufts of dead grass, as bare as the road, for it was a dry season: there had been no rain for months, and I wondered what I should do with the cattle if there wasn't more grass on the creek.

In this sort of country a stranger might travel for miles without seeming to have moved, for all the difference there is in the scenery. The new tracks were "blazed" — that is, slices of bark cut off from both sides of trees, within sight of each other, in a line, to mark the track until the horses and wheelmarks made it plain. A smart Bushman, with a sharp tomahawk, can blaze a track as he rides. But a Bushman a little used to the country soon picks out differences amongst the trees, half unconsciously as it were, and so finds his way about.

Mary and I didn't talk much along this track — we couldn't have heard each other very well, anyway, for the "clock-clock" of the waggon and the rattle of the cart over the hard lumpy ground. And I suppose we both began to feel pretty dismal as the shadows lengthened. I'd noticed lately that Mary and I had got out of the habit of talking to each other — noticed it in a vague sort of way that irritated me (as vague things will irritate one) when I thought of it. But then I thought, "It won't last long — I'll make life brighter for her by-and-by."

As we went along — and the track seemed endless — I got brooding, of course, back into the past. And I feel now, when it's too late, that Mary must have been thinking that way too. I thought of my early boyhood, of the hard life of "grubbin" and "milkin" and "fencin" and "ploughin" and "ring-barkin", etc., and all for nothing. The few months at the little bark-school, with a teacher who couldn't spell. The cursed ambition or craving that tortured my soul as a boy — ambition or craving for — I didn't know what for! For something better and brighter, anyhow. And I made the life harder by reading at night.

It all passed before me as I followed on in the waggon, behind Mary in the spring-cart. I thought of these old things more than I thought of her. She had tried to help me to better things. And I tried too — I had the energy of half-a-dozen men when I saw a road clear before me, but shied at the first check. Then I brooded, or dreamed of making a home — that one might call a home — for Mary — some day. Ah, well!——

And what was Mary thinking about, along the lonely, changeless miles? I never thought of that. Of her kind, careless, gentleman father, perhaps. Of her girlhood. Of her homes — not the huts and camps she lived in with me. Of our future? — she used to plan a lot, and talk a good deal of our future — but not lately. These things didn't strike me at the time — I was so deep in my own brooding. Did she think now — did she begin to feel now that she had made a great mistake and thrown away her life, but must make the best of it? This might have roused me, had I thought of it. But whenever I thought Mary was getting indifferent towards me, I'd think, "I'll soon win her back. We'll be sweethearts again — when things brighten up a bit."

It's an awful thing to me, now I look back to it, to think how far apart we had grown, what strangers we were to each other. It seems, now, as though we had been sweethearts long years before, and had parted, and had never really met since.

The sun was going down when Mary called out —

"There's our place, Joe!"

She hadn't seen it before, and somehow it came new and with a shock to me, who had been out here several times. Ahead, through the trees to the right, was a dark green clump of the oaks standing out of the creek, darker for the dead grey grass and blue-grey bush on the barren ridge in the background. Across the creek (it was only a deep, narrow gutter — a water-course with a chain of water-holes after rain), across on the other bank, stood the hut, on a narrow flat between the spur and the creek, and a little higher than this side. The land was much better than on our old selection, and there was good soil along the creek on both sides: I expected a rush of selectors out here soon. A few acres round the hut was cleared and fenced in by a light two-rail fence of timber split from logs and saplings. The man who took up this selection left it because his wife died here.

It was a small oblong hut built of split slabs, and he had roofed it with shingles which he split in spare times. There was no verandah, but I built one later on. At the end of the house was a big slab-and-bark shed, bigger than the hut itself, with a kitchen, a skillion for tools, harness, and horse-feed, and a spare bedroom partitioned off with sheets of bark and old chaff-bags. The house itself was floored roughly, with cracks between the boards; there were cracks between the slabs all round — though he'd nailed strips of tin, from old kerosene-tins, over some of them; the partitioned-off bedroom was lined with old chaff-bags with newspapers pasted over them for wall-paper. There was no ceiling, calico or otherwise, and we could see the round pine rafters and battens, and the under ends of the shingles. But ceilings make a hut hot and harbour insects and reptiles — snakes sometimes. There was one small glass window in the "dining-room" with three panes and a sheet of greased paper, and the rest were rough wooden shutters. There was a pretty good cow-yard and calf-pen, and — that was about all. There was no dam or tank (I made one later on); there was a water-cask, with the hoops falling off and the staves gaping, at the corner of the house, and spouting, made of lengths of bent tin, ran round under the eaves. Water from a new shingle roof is wine-red for a year or two, and water from a stringy bark roof is like tan-water for years. In dry weather the selector had got his house water from a cask sunk in the gravel at the bottom of the deepest water-hole in the creek. And the longer the drought lasted, the farther he had to go down the creek for his water, with a cask on a cart, and take his cows to drink, if he had any. Four, five, six, or seven miles — even ten miles to water is nothing in some places.

James hadn't found himself called upon to do more than milk old "Spot" (the grandmother cow of our mob), pen the calf at night, make a fire in the kitchen, and sweep out the house with a bough. He helped me unharness and water and feed the horses, and then started to get the furniture off the waggon and into the house. James wasn't lazy — so long as one thing didn't last too long; but he was too uncomfortably practical and matter-of-fact for me. Mary and I had some tea in the kitchen. The kitchen was permanently furnished with a table of split slabs, adzed smooth on top, and supported by four stakes driven into the ground, a three-legged stool and a block of wood, and two long stools made of half-round slabs (sapling trunks split in halves) with auger-holes bored in the round side and sticks stuck into them for legs. The floor was of clay; the chimney of slabs and tin; the fireplace was about eight feet wide, lined with clay, and with a blackened pole across, with sooty chains and wire hooks on it for the pots.

Mary didn't seem able to eat. She sat on the three-legged stool near the fire, though it was warm weather, and kept her face turned from me. Mary was still pretty, but not the little dumpling she had been: she was thinner now. She had big dark hazel eyes that shone a little too much when she was pleased or excited. I thought at times that there was something very German about her expression; also something aristocratic about the turn of her nose, which nipped in at the nostrils when she spoke. There was nothing aristocratic about me. Mary was German in figure and walk. I used sometimes to call her "Little Duchy" and "Pigeon Toes". She had a will of her own, as shown sometimes by the obstinate knit in her forehead between the eyes.

Mary sat still by the fire, and presently I saw her chin tremble.

"What is it, Mary?"

She turned her face farther from me. I felt tired, disappointed, and irritated — suffering from a reaction.

"Now, what is it, Mary?" I asked; "I'm sick of this sort of

thing. Haven't you got everything you wanted? You've had your own way. What's the matter with you now?"

"You know very well, Joe."

"But I *don't* know," I said. I knew too well.

She said nothing.

"Look here, Mary," I said, putting my hand on her shoulder, "don't go on like that; tell me what's the matter?"

"It's only this," she said suddenly, "I can't stand this life here; it will kill me!"

I had a pannikin of tea in my hand, and I banged it down on the table.

"This is more than a man can stand!" I shouted. "You know very well that it was you that dragged me out here. You run me on to this! Why weren't you content to stay in Gulgong?"

"And what sort of a place was Gulgong, Joe?" asked Mary quietly.

(I thought even then in a flash what sort of a place Gulgong was. A wretched remnant of a town on an abandoned goldfield. One street, each side of the dusty main road; three or four one-storey square brick cottages with hip roofs of galvanized iron that glared in the heat — four rooms and a passage — the police-station, bank-manager and schoolmaster's cottages, etc. Half-a-dozen tumble-down weather-board shanties — the three pubs., the two stores, and the post-office. The town tailing off into weather-board boxes with tin tops, and old bark huts — relics of the digging days — propped up by many rotting poles. The men, when at home, mostly asleep or droning over their pipes or hanging about the verandah posts of the pubs., saying, "'Ullo, Bill!" or "'Ullo, Jim!" — or sometimes drunk. The women, mostly hags, who blackened each other's and girls' characters with their tongues, and criticized the aristocracy's washing hung out on the line: "And the colour of the clothes! Does that woman wash her clothes at all? or only soak 'em and hang 'em out?" — that was Gulgong.)

"Well, why didn't you come to Sydney, as I wanted you to?" I asked Mary.

"You know very well, Joe," said Mary quietly.

(I knew very well, but the knowledge only maddened me. I had had an idea of getting a billet in one of the big wool-stores — I was a fair wool expert — but Mary was afraid of the drink. I could keep well away from it so long as I worked hard in the Bush. I had gone to Sydney twice since I met Mary, once before we were married, and she forgave

me when I came back; and once afterwards. I got a billet
there then, and was going to send for her in a month. After
eight weeks she raised the money somehow and came to
Sydney and brought me home. I got pretty low down that
time.)

"But, Mary," I said, "it would have been different this
time. You would have been with me. I can take a glass now
or leave it alone."

"As long as you take a glass there is danger," she said.

"Well, what did you want to advise me to come out here
for, if you can't stand it? Why didn't you stay where you
were?" I asked.

"Well," she said, "why weren't you more decided?"

I'd sat down, but I jumped to my feet then.

"Good God!" I shouted, "this is more than any man
can stand. I'll chuck it all up! I'm damned well sick and tired
of the whole thing."

"So am I, Joe," said Mary wearily.

We quarrelled badly then — that first hour in our new
home. I know now whose fault it was.

I got my hat and went out and started to walk down the
creek. I didn't feel bitter against Mary — I had spoken too
cruelly to her to feel that way. Looking back, I could see
plainly that if I had taken her advice all through, instead of
now and again, things would have been all right with me. I
had come away and left her crying in the hut, and James
telling her, in a brotherly way, that it was all her fault. The
trouble was that I never liked to "give in" or go half-way to
make it up — not half-way — it was all the way or nothing
with our natures.

"If I don't make a stand now," I'd say, "I'll never be
master. I gave up the reins when I got married, and I'll have
to get them back again."

What women some men are! But the time came, and not
many years after, when I stood by the bed where Mary lay,
white and still; and, amongst other things, I kept saying,
"I'll give in, Mary — I'll give in," and then I'd laugh. They
thought that I was raving mad, and took me from the room.
But that time was to come.

As I walked down the creek track in the moonlight the
question rang in my ears again, as it had done when I first
caught sight of the house that evening —

"Why did I bring her here?"

I was not fit to "go on the land". The place was only fit for
some stolid German, or Scotsman, or even Englishman and

his wife, who had no ambition but to bullock and make a farm of the place. I had only drifted here through careless-ness, brooding, and discontent.

I walked on and on till I was more than half-way to the only neighbours — a wretched selector's family, about four miles down the creek — and I thought I'd go on to the house and see if they had any fresh meat.

A mile or two farther I saw the loom of the bark hut they lived in, on a patchy clearing in the scrub, and heard the voice of the selector's wife — I had seen her several times: she was a gaunt, haggard Bushwoman, and, I supposed, the reason why she hadn't gone mad through hardship and loneliness was that she hadn't either the brains or the memory to go farther than she could see through the trunks of the "apple-trees".

"You, An-nay!" (Annie.)

"Ye-es" (from somewhere in the gloom).

"Didn't I tell yer to water them geraniums!"

"Well, didn't I?"

"Don't tell lies or I'll break yer young back!"

"I did, I tell yer — the water won't soak inter the ashes."

Geraniums were the only flowers I saw grow in the drought out there. I remembered this woman had a few dirty grey-green leaves behind some sticks against the bark wall near the door; and in spite of the sticks the fowls used to get in and scratch beds under the geraniums, and scratch dust over them, and ashes were thrown there — with an idea of helping the flower, I suppose; and greasy dish-water, when fresh water was scarce — till you might as well try to water a dish of fat.

Then the woman's voice again —

"You, Tom-may!" (Tommy.)

Silence, save for an echo on the ridge.

"Y-o-u, T-o-m-*may*!"

"Y-e-e-s!" shrill shriek from across the creek.

"Didn't I tell you to ride up to them new people and see if they want any meat or any think?" in one long screech.

"Well — I karnt find the horse."

"Well-find-it-first-think-in-the-morning and. And-don't-forget-to-tell-Mrs.-Wi'son-that-mother'll-be-up-as-soon-as-she-can."

I didn't feel like going to the woman's house that night. I felt — and the thought came like a whip-stroke on my heart — that this was what Mary would come to if I left her here.

I turned and started to walk home, fast. I'd made up my mind. I'd take Mary straight back to Gulgong in the morning — forgot about the load I had to take to the sheep station. I'd say, "Look here, Girlie" (that's what I used to call her), "we'll leave this wretched life; we'll leave the Bush for ever! We'll go to Sydney, and I'll be a man! and work my way up." And I'd sell waggon, horses, and all, and go.

When I got to the hut it was lighted up. Mary had the only kerosene lamp, a slush lamp, and two tallow candles going. She had got both rooms washed out — to James's disgust, for he had to move the furniture and boxes about. She had a lot of things unpacked on the table; she had laid clean news-papers on the mantel-shelf — a slab on two pegs over the fireplace — and put the little wooden clock in the centre and some of the ornaments on each side, and was tacking a trip of vandyked American oil-cloth round the rough edge of the slab.

"How does that look, Joe? We'll soon get things ship-shape."

I kissed her, but she had her mouth full of tacks. I went out in the kitchen, drank a pint of cold tea, and sat down.

Somehow I didn't feel satisfied with the way things had gone.

II   *"Past Carin'"*

Next morning things looked a lot brighter. Things always look brighter in the morning — more so in the Australian Bush, I should think, than in most other places. It is when the sun goes down on the dark bed of the lonely Bush, and the sunset flashes like a sea of fire and then fades, and then glows out again, like a bank of coals, and then burns away to ashes — it is then that old things come home to one. And strange, new-old things too, that haunt and depress you terribly, and that you can't understand. I often think how, at sunset, the past must come home to new-chum black-sheep, sent out to Australia and drifted into the Bush. I used to think that they couldn't have much brains, or the loneliness would drive them mad.

I'd decided to let James take the team for a trip or two. He could drive alright; he was a better business man, and no doubt would manage better than me — as long as the novelty lasted; and I'd stay at home for a week or so, till Mary got used to the place, or I could get a girl from somewhere to come and stay with her. The first weeks or few months of loneliness are the worst, as a rule, I believed, as they say the first weeks in jail are — I was never there. I know it's so with tramping or hard graft[1]: the first day or two are twice as hard as any of the rest. But, for my part, I could never get used to loneliness and dulness; the last days used to be the worst with me: then I'd have to make a move, or drink. When you've been too much and too long alone in a lonely place, you begin to do queer things and think queer thoughts — provided you have any imagination at all. You'll sometimes sit of an evening and watch the lonely track, by the hour, for a horseman or a cart or some one that's never likely to come that way — some one, or a stranger, that you can't and don't really expect to see. I think that most men who have been alone in the Bush for any length of time — and married couples too — are more or less mad. With married couples it is generally the husband who is painfully shy and awkward when strangers come. The woman seems to stand the loneliness better, and can hold her own with strangers, as a rule. It's only afterwards, and looking back, that you see how queer you got. Shepherds and boundary-riders, who are alone for months, *must* have their periodical spree, at the nearest shanty, else they'd go raving mad. Drink is the only break in the awful monotony, and the yearly or half-yearly spree is the only thing they've got to look forward to: it keeps their minds fixed on something definite ahead.

But Mary kept her head pretty well through the first months of loneliness. *Weeks*, rather, I should say, for it wasn't as bad as it might have been farther up-country: there was generally some one came of a Sunday afternoon — a spring-cart with a couple of women, or maybe a family — or a lanky shy Bush native or two on lanky shy horses. On a quiet Sunday, after I'd brought Jim home, Mary would dress him an herself — just the same as if we were in town — and make me get up on one end and put on a collar and take her and Jim for a walk along the creek. She said she wanted to keep me civilized. She tried to make a gentleman of me for years, but gave it up gradually.

Well. It was the first morning on the creek: I was greasing the waggon-wheels, and James out after the horse, and Mary hanging out clothes, in an old print dress and a big ugly white hood, when I heard her being hailed as "Hi, missus!" from the front slip-rails.

---

1. "Graft", work. The term is now applied, in Australia, to all sorts of work, from bullock-driving to writing poetry.

It was a boy on horseback. He was a light-haired, very much freckled boy of fourteen or fifteen, with a small head, but with limbs, especially his bare sun-blotched shanks, that might have belonged to a grown man. He had a good face and frank grey eyes. An old, nearly black cabbage-tree hat rested on the butts of his ears, turning them out at right angles from his head, and rather dirty sprouts they were. He wore a dirty torn Crimean shirt; and a pair of man's moleskin trousers rolled up above the knees, with the wide waistband gathered under a greenhide belt. I noticed, later on, that, even when he wore trousers short enough for him, he always rolled 'em up above the knees when on horseback, for some reason of his own: to suggest leggings, perhaps, for he had them rolled up in all weathers, and he wouldn't have bothered to save them from the sweat of the horse, even if that horse ever sweated.

He was seated astride a three-bushel bag thrown across the ridge-pole of a big grey horse, with a coffin-shaped head, and built astern something after the style of a roughly put up hip-roofed box-bark humpy.[2] His colour was like old box-bark, too, a dirty bluish-grey; and, one time, when I saw his rump looming out of the scrub, I really thought it was some old shepherd's hut that I hadn't noticed there before. When he cantered it was like the humpy starting off on its corner-posts.

"Are you Mrs. Wilson?" asked the boy.

"Yes," said Mary.

"Well, mother told me to ride acrost and see if you wanted anythink. We killed lars' night, and I've fetched a piece er cow."

"Piece of *what?*" asked Mary.

He grinned, and handed a sugar-bag across the rail with something heavy in the bottom of it, that nearly jerked Mary's arm out when she took it. It was a piece of beef, that looked as if it had been cut off with a wood-axe, but it was fresh and clean.

"Oh, I'm so glad!" cried Mary. She was always impulsive, save to me sometimes. "I was just wondering where we were going to get any fresh meat. How kind of your mother! Tell her I'm very much obliged to her indeed." And she felt behind her for a poor little purse she had. "And now — how much did your mother say it would be?"

The boy blinked at her, and scratched his head.

2. "Humpy", a rough hut.

"How much will it be," he repeated, puzzled. "Oh — how much does it weigh I-s'pose-yer-mean. Well, it ain't been weighed at all — we ain't got no scales. A butcher does all that sort of think. We just kills it, and cooks it, and eats it — and goes by guess. What won't keep we salts down in the cask. I reckon it weighs about a ton by the weight of it if yer wanter know. Mother thought that if she sent any more it would go bad before you could scoff it. I can't see ——"

"Yes, yes," said Mary, getting confused. "But what I want to know is, how do you manage when you sell it?"

He glared at her, and scratched his head. "Sell it? Why, we only goes halves in a steer with some one, or sells steers to the butcher — or maybe some meat to a party of fencers or surveyors, or tank-sinkers, or them sorter people ——"

"Yes, yes; but what I want to know is, how much am I to send your mother for this?"

"How much what?"

"Money, of course, you stupid boy," said Mary. "You seem a very stupid boy."

Then he saw what she was driving at. He began to fling his heels convulsively against the sides of his horse, jerking his body backward and forward at the same time, as if to wind up and start some clockwork machinery inside the horse, that made it go, and seemed to need repairing or oiling.

"We ain't that sorter people, missus," he said. "We don't sell meat to new people that come to settle here." Then, jerking his thumb contemptuously towards the ridges, "Go over ter Wall's if yer wanter buy meat; they sell meat ter strangers." (Wall was the big squatter over the ridges.)

"Oh!" said Mary, "I'm *so* sorry. Thank your mother for me. She *is* kind."

"Oh, that's nothink. She said to tell yer she'll be up as soon as she can. She'd have come up yisterday evening — she thought yer'd feel lonely comin' new to a place like this — but she couldn't git up."

The machinery inside the old horse showed signs of starting. You almost heard the wooden joints *creak* as he lurched forward, like an old propped-up humpy when the rotting props give way; but at the sound of Mary's voice he settled back on his foundations again. It must have been a very poor selection that couldn't afford a better spare horse than that.

"Reach me that lump er wood, will yer, missus?" said the boy, and he pointed to one of my "spreads" (for the team-chains) that lay inside the fence. "I'll fling it back agin over the fence when I git this ole cow started."

"But wait a minute — I've forgotten your mother's name," said Mary.

He grabbed at his thatch impatiently. "Me mother — oh! — the old woman's name's Mrs. Spicer. (Git up, karnt yer!)" He twisted himself round, and brought the stretcher down on one of the horse's "points" (and he had many) with a crack that must have jarred his wrist.

"Do you go to school?" asked Mary. There was a three-days-a-week school over the ridges at Wall's station.

"No!" he jerked out, keeping his legs going. "Me — why I'm going on fur fifteen. The last teacher at Wall's finished me. I'm going to Queensland next month drovin'." (Queensland border was over three hundred miles away.)

"Finished you? How?" asked Mary.

"Me edgercation, of course! How do yer expect me to start this horse when yer keep talkin'?"

He split the "spread" over the horse's point, threw the pieces over the fence, and was off, his elbows and legs flinging wildly, and the old saw-stool lumbering along the road like an old working bullock trying a canter. That horse wasn't a trotter.

And next month he *did* start for Queensland. He was a young son and a surplus boy on a wretched, poverty-stricken selection; and as there was "northin' doin'" in the district, his father (in a burst of fatherly kindness, I suppose) made him a present of the old horse and a new pair of Blucher boots, and I gave him an old saddle and a coat, and he started for the Never-Never Country.

And I'll bet he got there. But I'm doubtful if the old horse did.

Mary gave the boy five shillings, and I don't think he had anything more except a clean shirt and an extra pair of white cotton socks.

"Spicer's farm" was a big bark humpy on a patchy clearing in the native apple-tree scrub. The clearing was fenced in by a light "dog-legged" fence (a fence of sapling poles resting on forks and X-shaped uprights) and the dusty ground round the house was almost entirely covered with cattle-dung. There was no attempt at cultivation when I came to live on the creek; but there were old furrow-marks amongst the stumps of another shapeless patch in the scrub near the hut. There was a wretched sapling cow-yard and calf-pen, and a cow-bail with one sheet of bark over it for shelter. There was no dairy to be seen, and I suppose the milk was set in one of the two skillion rooms, or lean-to's behind the hut, — the other was "the boys' bedroom". The Spicers kept a few cows and steers, and had thirty or forty sheep. Mrs. Spicer used to drive down the creek once a week, in her rickety old spring-cart, to Cobborah, with butter and eggs. The hut was nearly as bare inside as it was out — just a frame of "round-timber" (sapling poles) covered with bark. The furniture was permanent (unless you rooted it up), like in our kitchen: a rough slab table on stakes driven into the ground, and seats made the same way. Mary told me afterwards that the beds in the bag-and-bark partitioned-off room ("mother's bedroom") were simply poles laid side by side on cross-pieces supported by stakes driven into the ground, with straw mattresses and some worn-out bed-clothes. Mrs. Spicer had an old patchwork quilt, in rags, and the remains of a white one, and Mary said it was pitiful to see how these things would be spread over the beds — to hide them as much as possible — when she went down there. A packing-case, with something like an old print skirt draped round it, and a cracked looking-glass (without a frame) on top, was the dressing-table. There were a couple of gin-cases for a wardrobe. The boys' beds were three-bushel bags stretched between poles fastened to uprights. The floor was the original surface, tramped hard, worn uneven with much sweeping, and with puddles in rainy weather where the roof leaked. Mrs. Spicer used to stand old tins, dishes, and buckets under as many of the leaks as she could. The saucepans, kettles, and boilers were old kerosene-tins and billies. They used kerosene-tins, too, cut longways in halves, for setting the milk in. The plates and cups were of tin; there were two or three cups without saucers, and a crockery plate or two — also two mugs, cracked and without handles, one with "For a Good Boy" and the other with "For a Good Girl" on it; but all these were kept on the mantel-shelf for ornament and for company. They were the only ornaments in the house, save a little wooden clock that hadn't gone for years. Mrs. Spicer had a superstition that she had "some things packed away from the children".

The pictures were cut from old copies of the *Illustrated Sydney News* and pasted on to the bark. I remember this, because I remember, long ago, the Spencers, who were our neighbours when I was a boy, had the walls of their bedroom covered with illustrations of the American Civil War, cut from illustrated London papers, and I used to "sneak" into "mother's bedroom" with Fred Spencer whenever we got the chance, and gloat over the prints. I gave him a blade of a pocket-knife once, for taking me in there.

I saw very little of Spicer. He was a big, dark, dark-haired and whiskered man. I had an idea that he wasn't a selector at all, only a "dummy" for the squatter of the Cobborah run. You see, selectors were allowed to take up land on runs, or pastoral leases. The squatters kept them off as much as possible, by all manner of dodges and paltry persecution. The squatter would get as much freehold as he could afford, "select" as much land as the law allowed one man to take up, and then employ dummies (dummy selectors) to take up bits of land that he fancied about his run, and hold them for him.

Spicer seemed gloomy and unsociable. He was seldom at home. He was generally supposed to be away shearin', or fencin', or workin' on somebody's station. It turned out that the last six months he was away it was on the evidence of a cask of beef and a hide with the brand cut out, found in his camp on a fencing contract up-country, and which he and his mates couldn't account for satisfactorily, while the squatter could. Then the family lived mostly on bread and honey, or bread and treacle, or bread and dripping, and tea. Every ounce of butter and every egg was needed for the market, to keep them in flour, tea, and sugar. Mary found that out, but couldn't help them much — except by "stuffing" the children with bread and meat or bread and jam whenever they came up to our place — for Mrs. Spicer was proud with the pride that lies down in the end and turns its face to the wall and dies.

Once, when Mary asked Annie, the eldest girl at home, if she was hungry, she denied it — but she looked it. A ragged mite she had with her explained things. The little fellow said —

"Mother told Annie not to say we was hungry if yer asked; but if yer give us anythink to eat, we was to take it an' say thenk yer, Mrs. Wilson."

"I wouldn't 'a' told yer a lie; but I thought Jimmy would split on me, Mrs. Wilson," said Annie. "Thenk yer, Mrs. Wilson."

She was not a big woman. She was gaunt and flat-chested, and her face was "burnt to a brick", as they say out there. She had brown eyes, nearly red, and a little wild-looking at times, and a sharp face — ground sharp by hardship — the cheeks drawn in. She had an expression like — well, like a woman who had been very curious and suspicious at one time, and wanted to know everybody's business and hear everything, and had lost all her curiosity, without losing the expression or the quick suspicious movements of the head. I don't suppose you understand. I can't explain it any other way. She was not more than forty.

I remember the first morning I saw her. I was going up the creek to look at the selection for the first time, and called at the hut to see if she had a bit of fresh mutton, as I had none and was sick of "corned beef".

"Yes — of — course," she said, in a sharp nasty tone, as if to say "Is there anything more you want while the shop's open?" I'd met just the same sort of woman years before while I was carrying swag between the shearing-sheds in the awful scrubs out west of the Darling river, so I didn't turn on my heels and walk away. I waited for her to speak again.

"Come — inside," she said, "and sit down. I see you've got the waggon outside. I s'pose your name's Wilson, ain't it? You're thinkin' about takin' on Harry Marshfield's selection up the creek, so I heard. Wait till I fry you a chop and boil the billy."

Her voice sounded, more than anything else, like a voice coming out of a phonograph — I heard one in Sydney the other day — and not like a voice coming out of her. But sometimes when she got outside her everyday life on this selection she spoke in a sort of — in a sort of lost groping-in-the-dark kind of voice.

She didn't talk much this time — just spoke in a mechanical way of the drought, and the hard times, "an' butter 'n' eggs bein' down, an' her husban' an' eldest son bein' away, an' that makin' it so hard for her."

I don't know how many children she had. I never got a chance to count them, for they were nearly all small, and shy as piccaninnies, and used to run and hide when anybody came. They were mostly nearly as black as piccaninnies too. She must have averaged a baby a year for years — and God only knows how she got over her confinements! Once, they said, she only had a black gin with her. She had an elder boy and girl, but she seldom spoke of them. The girl, "Liza", was "in service in Sydney". I'm afraid I knew what that meant. The elder son was "away". He had been a bit of a favourite round there, it seemed.

Some one might ask her, "How's your son Jack, Mrs. Spicer?" or, "Heard of Jack lately? and where is he now?"

"Oh, he's somewheres up country," she'd say in the "groping" voice, or "He's drovin' in Queenslan'," or "Shearin' on the Darlin' the last time I heerd from him." "We ain't had a line from him since — les' see — since Chris'mas 'fore last."

And she'd turn her haggard eyes in a helpless, hopeless sort of way towards the west — towards "up-country" and "Out-Back".[3]

The eldest girl at home was nine or ten, with a little old face and lines across her forehead: she had an older expression than her mother. Tommy went to Queensland, as I told you. The eldest son at home, Bill (older than Tommy), was "a bit wild".

I've passed the place in smothering hot mornings in December, when the droppings about the cow-yard had crumpled to dust that rose in the warm, sickly, sunrise wind, and seen that woman at work in the cow-yard, "bailing up" and leg-roping cows, milking, or hauling at a rope round the neck of a half-grown calf that was too strong for her (and she was tough as fencing-wire), or humping great buckets of sour milk to the pigs or the "poddies" (hand-fed calves) in the pen. I'd get off the horse and give her a hand sometimes with a young steer, or a cranky old cow that wouldn't "bail-up" and threatened her with her horns. She'd say —

"Thenk yer, Mr. Wilson. Do yer think we're ever goin' to have any rain?"

I've ridden past the place on bitter black rainy mornings in June or July, and seen her trudging about the yard — that was ankle-deep in black liquid filth — with an old pair of Blucher boots on, and an old coat of her husband's, or maybe a three-bushel bag over her shoulders. I've seen her climbing on the roof by means of the water-cask at the corner, and trying to stop a leak by shoving a piece of tin in under the bark. And when I'd fixed the leak —

"Thenk yer, Mr. Wilson. This drop of rain's a blessin'! Come in and have a dry at the fire and I'll make yer a cup of tea." And, if I was in a hurry, "Come in, man alive! Come in! and dry yerself a bit till the rain holds up. Yer can't go home like this! Yer'll git yer death o' cold."

I've even seen her, in the terrible drought, climbing she-oaks and apple-trees by a makeshift ladder, and awkwardly lopping off boughs to feed the starving cattle.

"Jist tryin' ter keep the milkers alive till the rain comes."

They said that when the pleuro-pneumonia was in the district and amongst her cattle she bled and physicked them herself, and fed those that were down with slices of half-ripe pumpkins (from a crop that had failed).

"An', one day," she told Mary, "there was a big barren

3.   "Out-Back" is always west of the Bushman, no matter how far out he be.

heifer (that we called Queen Elizabeth) that was down with the ploorer. She'd been down for four days and hadn't moved, when one mornin' I dumped some wheaten chaff — we had a few bags that Spicer brought home — I dumped it in front of her nose, an' — would yer b'lieve me, Mrs. Wilson? — she stumbled onter her feet an' chased me all the way to the house! I had to pick up me skirts an' run! Wasn't it redic'lus?"

They had a sense of the ridiculous, most of those poor sun-dried Bushwomen. I fancy that that helped save them from madness.

"We lost nearly all our milkers," she told Mary. "I remember one day Tommy came running to the house and screamed: 'Marther! [mother] there's another milker down with the ploorer!' Jist as if it was great news. Well, Mrs. Wilson, I was dead-beat, an' I giv' in. I jist sat down to have a good cry, and felt for my han'kerchief — it *was* a rag of a han'kerchief, full of holes (all me others was in the wash). Without seein' what I was doin' I put me finger through one hole in the han'kerchief an' me thumb through the other, and poked me fingers into me eyes, instead of wipin' them. Then I had to laugh."

There's a story that once, when the Bush, or rather grass, fires were out all along the creek on Spicer's side, Wall's station hands were up above our place, trying to keep the fire back from the boundary, and towards evening one of the men happened to think of the Spicers: they saw smoke down that way. Spicer was away from home, and they had a small crop of wheat, nearly ripe, on the selection.

"My God! that poor devil of a woman will be burnt out, if she ain't already!" shouted young Billy Wall. "Come along, three or four of you chaps" — (it was shearing-time, and there were plenty of men on the station).

They raced down the creek to Spicer's, and were just in time to save the wheat. She had her sleeves tucked up, and was beating out the burning grass with a bough. She'd been at it for an hour, and was as black as a gin, they said. She only said when they'd turned the fire: "Thenk yer! Wait an' I'll make some tea."

After tea the first Sunday she came to see us, Mary asked —

"Don't you feel lonely, Mrs. Spicer, when your husband goes away?"

"Well — no, Mrs. Wilson," she said in the groping sort of

voice. "I uster, once. I remember, when we lived on the Cudgeegong river — we lived in a brick house then — the first time Spicer had to go away from home I nearly fretted my eyes out. And he was only goin' shearin' for a month. I muster bin a fool; but then we were only jist married a little while. He's been away drovin' in Queenslan' as long as eighteen months at a time since then. But" (her voice seemed to grope in the dark more than ever) "I don't mind, — I somehow seem to have got past carin'. Besides — besides, Spicer was a very different man then to what he is now. He's got so moody and gloomy at home, he hardly ever speaks."

Mary sat silent for a minute thinking. Then Mrs. Spicer roused herself —

"Oh, I don't know what I'm talkin' about! You mustn't take any notice of me, Mrs. Wilson, — I don't often go on like this. I do believe I'm gittin' a bit ratty at times. It must be the heat and the dulness."

But once or twice afterwards she referred to a time "when Spicer was a different man to want he was now".

I walked home with her a piece along the creek. She said nothing for a long time, and seemed to be thinking in a puzzled way. Then she said suddenly —

"What-did-you-bring-her-here-for? She's only a girl."

"I beg pardon, Mrs. Spicer."

"Oh, I don't know what I'm talkin' about! I b'lieve I'm gittin' ratty. You mustn't take any notice of me, Mr. Wilson."

She wasn't much company for Mary; and often, when she had a child with her, she'd start taking notice of the baby while Mary was talking, which used to exasperate Mary. But poor Mrs. Spicer couldn't help it, and she seemed to hear all the same.

Her great grouble was that she "couldn't git no reg'lar schoolin' for the children".

"I learns 'em at home as much as I can. But I don't git a minute to call me own; an' I'm ginerally that dead-beat at night that I'm fit for nothink."

Mary had some of the children up now and then later on, and taught them a little. When she first offered to do so, Mrs. Spicer laid hold of the handiest youngster and said —

"There — do you hear that? Mrs. Wilson is goin' to teach yer, an' it's more than yer deserve!" (the youngster had been "cryin'" over something). "Now, go up an' say 'Thenk yer, Mrs. Wilson.' And if yer ain't good, and don't do as she tells yer, I'll break every bone in yer young body!"

The poor little devil stammered something, and escaped.

The children were sent by turns over to Wall's to Sunday-school. When Tommy was at home he had a new pair of elastic-side boots, and there was no end of rows about them in the family — for the mother made him lend them to his sister Annie, to go to Sunday-school in, in her turn. There were only about three pairs of anyway decent boots in the family, and these were saved for great occasions. The children were always as clean and tidy as possible when they came to our place.

And I think the saddest and most pathetic sight on the face of God's earth is the children of very poor people made to appear well: the broken wornout boots polished or greased, the blackened (inked) pieces of string for laces; the clean patched pinafores over the wretched threadbare frocks. Behind the little row of children hand-in-hand — and no matter where they are — I always see the worn face of the mother.

Towards the end of the first year on the selection our little girl came. I'd sent Mary to Gulgong for four months that time, and when she came back with the baby Mrs. Spicer used to come up pretty often. She came up several times when Mary was ill, to lend a hand. She wouldn't sit down and condole with Mary, or waste her time asking questions, or talking about the time when she was ill herself. She'd take off her hat — a shapeless little lump of black straw she wore for visiting — give her hair a quick brush back with the palms of her hands, roll up her sleeves, and set to work to "tidy up". She seemed to take most pleasure in sorting out our children's clothes, and dressing them. Perhaps she used to dress her own like that in the days when Spicer was a different man from what he was now. She seemed interested in the fashion-plates of some women's journals we had, and used to study them with an interest that puzzled me, for she was not likely to go in for fashion. She never talked of her early girlhood; but Mary, from some things she noticed, was inclined to think that Mrs. Spicer had been fairly well brought up. For instance, Dr. Balanfantie, from Cudgee-gong, came out to see Wall's wife, and drove up the creek to our place on his way back to see how Mary and the baby were getting on. Mary got out some crockery and some table-napkins that she had packed away for occasions like this; and she said that the way Mrs. Spicer handled the things, and helped set the table (though she did it in a mechanical sort of way), convinced her that she had been used to table-napkins at one time in her life.

Sometimes, after a long pause in the conversation, Mrs.
Spicer would say suddenly —

"Oh, I don't think I'll come up next week, Mrs. Wilson."

"Why, Mrs. Spicer?"

"Because the visits doesn't do me any good. I git the
dismals afterwards."

"Why, Mrs. Spicer? What on earth do you mean?"

"Oh, I-don t-know-what-I'm-talkin'-about. You mustn't
take any notice of me." And she'd put on her hat, kiss the
children — and Mary too, sometimes, as if she mistook her
for a child — and go.

Mary thought her a little mad at times. But I seemed to
understand.

Once, when Mrs. Spicer was sick, Mary went down to her,
and down again next day. As she was coming away the
second time, Mrs. Spicer said —

"I wish you wouldn't come down any more till I'm on me
feet, Mrs. Wilson. The children can do for me."

"Why, Mrs. Spicer?"

"Well, the place is in such a muck, and it hurts me."

We were the aristocrats of Lahey's Creek. Whenever we
drove down on Sunday afternoon to see Mrs. Spicer, and as
soon as we got near enough for them to hear the rattle of the
cart, we'd see the children running to the house as fast as
they could split, and hear them screaming —

"Oh, marther! Here comes Mr. and Mrs. Wilson in their
spring-cart."

And we'd see her bustle round, and two or three fowls fly
out the front door, and she'd lay hold of a broom (made of a
bound bunch of "broom-stuff" — coarse reedy grass or bush
from the ridges — with a stick stuck in it) and flick out the
floor, with a flick or two round in front of the door perhaps.
The floor nearly always needed at least one flick of the
broom on account of the fowls. Or she'd catch a youngster
and scrub his face with a wet end of a cloudy towel, or twist
the towel round her finger and dig out his ears — as if she
was anxious to have him hear every word that was going to
be said.

No matter what state the house would be in she'd always
say, "I was jist expectin' yer, Mrs. Wilson." And she was
original in that, anyway.

She had an old patched and darned white table-cloth that
she used to spread on the table when we were there, as a
matter of course ("The others is in the wash, so you must
excuse this, Mrs. Wilson"), but I saw by the eyes of the

children that the cloth was rather a wonderful thing to them. "I must really git some more knives an' forks next time I'm in Cobborah," she'd say. "The children break an' lose 'em till I'm ashamed to ask Christians ter sit down ter the table."

She had many Bush yarns, some of them very funny, some of them rather ghastly, but all interesting, and with a grim sort of humour about them. But the effect was often spoilt by her screaming at the children to "Drive out them fowls, karnt yer," or "Take yer maulies [hands] outer the sugar," or "Don't touch Mrs. Wilson's baby with them dirty maulies," or "Don't stand starin' at Mrs. Wilson with yer mouth an' ears in that vulgar way."

Poor woman! she seemed everlastingly nagging at the children. It was a habit, but they didn't seem to mind. Most Bushwomen get the nagging habit. I remember one, who had the prettiest, dearest, sweetest, most willing, and affectionate little girl I think I ever saw, and she nagged that child from daylight till dark — and after it. Taking it all round, I think that the nagging habit in a mother is often worse on ordinary children, and more deadly on sensitive youngsters, than the drinking habit in a father.

One of the yarns Mrs. Spicer told us was about a squatter she knew who used to go wrong in his head every now and again, and try to commit suicide. Once, when the station-hand, who was watching him, had his eye off him for a minute, he hanged himself to a beam in the stable. The men ran in and found him hanging and kicking. "They let him hang for a while," said Mrs. Spicer, "till he went black in the face and stopped kicking. Then they cut him down and threw a bucket of water over him."

"Why! what on earth did they let the man hang for?" asked Mary.

"To give him a good bellyful of it: they thought it would cure him of tryin' to hang himself again."

"Well, that's the coolest thing I ever heard of," said Mary.

"That's jist what the magistrate said, Mrs. Wilson," said Mrs. Spicer.

"One morning," said Mrs. Spicer, "Spicer had gone off on his horse somewhere, and I was alone with the children, when a man came to the door and said —

"'For God's sake, woman, give me a drink!'

"Lord only knows where he came from! He was dressed like a new chum — his clothes was good, but he looked as if he'd been sleepin' in them in the Bush for a month. He was very shaky. I had some coffee that mornin', so I gave him some in a pint pot; he drank it, and then he stood on his head till he tumbled over, and then he stood up on his feet and said, 'Thenk yer, mum.'

"I was so surprised that I didn't know what to say, so I jist said, 'Would you like some more coffee?'

"'Yes, thenk yer,' he said — 'about two quarts.'

"I nearly filled the pint pot, and he drank it and stood on his head as long as he could, and when he got right end up he said, 'Thenk yer, mum — it's a fine day,' and then he walked off. He had two saddle-straps in his hands."

"Why, what did he stand on his head for?" asked Mary.

"To wash it up and down, I suppose, to get twice as much taste of the coffee. He had no hat. I sent Tommy across to Wall's to tell them that there was a man wanderin' about the Bush in the horrors of drink, and to get some one to ride for the police. But they was too late, for he hanged himself that night."

"O Lord!" cried Mary.

"Yes, right close to here, jist down the creek where the track to Wall's branches off. Tommy found him while he was out after the cows. Hangin' to the branch of a tree with the two saddle-straps."

Mary stared at her, speechless.

"Tommy came home yellin' with fright. I sent him over to Wall's at once. After breakfast, the minute my eyes was off them, the children slipped away and went down there. They came back screamin' at the tops of their voices. I did give it to them. I reckon they won't want ter see a dead body again in a hurry. Every time I'd mention it they'd huddle together, or ketch hold of me skirts and howl.

"'Yer'll go agen when I tell yer not to,' I'd say.

"'Oh no, mother,' they'd howl.

"'Yer wanted ter see a man hangin',' I said.

"'Oh, don't, mother! Don't talk about it.'

"'Yer wouldn't be satisfied till yer see it,' I'd say; 'yer had to see it or burst. Yer satisfied now, ain't yer?'

"'Oh, don't, mother!'

"'Yer run all the way there, I s'pose?'

"'Don't, mother!'

"'But yer run faster back, didn't yer?'

"'Oh, don't, mother.'

"But," said Mrs. Spicer, in conclusion, "I'd been down to see it myself before they was up."

"And ain't you afraid to live alone here, after all these horrible things?" asked Mary.

"Well, no; I don't mind. I seem to have got past carin' for anythink now. I felt it a little when Tommy went away — the first time I felt anythink for years. But I'm over that now."

"Haven't you got any friends in the district, Mrs. Spicer?"

"Oh yes. There's me married sister near Cobborah, and a married brother near Dubbo; he's got a station. They wanted to take me an' the children between them, or take some of the younger children. But I couldn't bring my mind to break up the home. I want to keep the children together as much as possible. There's enough of them gone, God knows. But it's a comfort to know that there's some one to see to them if anythink happens to me."

One day — I was on my way home with the team that day — Annie Spicer came running up the creek in terrible trouble.

"Oh, Mrs. Wilson! something terribl's happened at home! A trooper" (mounted policeman — they called them "mounted troopers" out there), "a trooper's come and took Billy!" Billy was the eldest son at home.

"What?"

"It's true, Mrs. Wilson."

"What for? What did the policeman say?"

"He — he — he said, 'I — I'm very sorry, Mrs. Spicer; but — I — I want William.'"

It turned out that William was wanted on account of a horse missed from Wall's station and sold down-country.

"An' mother took on awful," sobbed Annie; "an' now she'll only sit stock-still an' stare in front of her, and won't take no notice of any of us. Oh! it's awful, Mrs. Wilson. The policeman said he'd tell Aunt Emma" (Mrs Spicer's sister at Cobborah), "and send her out. But I had to come to you, an' I've run all the way."

James put the horse to the cart and drove Mary down.

Mary told me all about it when I came home.

"I found her just as Annie said; but she broke down and cried in my arms. Oh, Joe! it was awful! She didn't cry like a woman. I heard a man at Haviland cry at his brother's funeral, and it was just like that. She came round a bit after a while. Her sister's with her now. . . . Oh, Joe! you must take me away from the Bush."

Later on Mary said —

"How the oaks are sighing tonight, Joe!"

Next morning I rode across to Wall's station and tackled the old man; but he was a hard man, and wouldn't listen to me — in fact, he ordered me off the station. I was a selector, and that was enough for him. But young Billy Wall rode after me.

"Look here, Joe!" he said, "it's a blanky shame. All for the sake of a horse! And as if that poor devil of a woman hasn't got enough to put up with already! I wouldn't do it for twenty horses. *I'll* tackle the boss, and if he won't listen to me, I'll walk off the run for the last time, if I have to carry my swag."

Billy Wall managed it. The charge was withdrawn, and we got young Billy Spicer off up-country.

But poor Mrs. Spicer was never the same after that. She seldom came up to our place unless Mary dragged her, so to speak; and then she would talk of nothing but her last trouble, till her visits were painful to look forward to.

"If it only could have been kep' quiet — for the sake of the other children; they are all I think of now. I tried to bring 'em all up decent, but I s'pose it was my fault, somehow. It's the disgrace that's killin' me — I can't bear it."

I was at home one Sunday with Mary and a jolly Bush-girl named Maggie Charlsworth, who rode over sometimes from Wall's station (I must tell you about her some other time; James was "shook after her"), and we got talkin' about Mrs. Spicer. Maggie was very warm about old Wall.

"I expected Mrs. Spicer up today," said Mary. "She seems better lately."

"Why!" cried Maggie Charlsworth, "if that ain't Annie coming running up along the creek. Something's the matter!"

We all jumped up and ran out.

"What is it, Annie?" cried Mary.

"Oh, Mrs. Wilson! Mother's asleep, and we can't wake her!"

"What?"

"It's — it's the truth, Mrs. Wilson."

"How long has she been asleep?"

"Since lars' night."

"My God!" cried Mary, *"since last night?"*

"No, Mrs. Wilson, not all the time; she woke wonst, about daylight this mornin'. She called me and said she didn't feel well, and I'd have to manage the milkin'."

"Was that all she said?"

"No. She said not to go for you; and she said to feed the

pigs and calves; and she said to be sure and water them geraniums."

Mary wanted to go, but I wouldn't let her. James and I saddled our horses and rode down the creek.

Mrs. Spicer looked very little different from what she did when I last saw her alive. It was some time before we could believe that she was dead. But she was "past carin'" right enough.

A Double Buggy at
Lahey's Creek

I. Spuds, and a Woman's Obstinacy

Ever since we were married it had been Mary's great ambition to have a buggy. The house or furniture didn't matter so much — out there in the Bush where we were — but, where there were no railways or coaches, and the roads were long, and mostly hot and dusty, a buggy was the great thing. I had a few pounds when we were married, and was going to get one then; but new buggies went high, and another party got hold of a second-hand one that I'd had my eye on, so Mary thought it over and at last she said, "Never mind the buggy, Joe; get a sewing-machine and I'll be satisfied. I'll want the machine more than the buggy, for a while. Wait till we're better off."

After that, whenever I took a contract — to put up a fence or wool-shed, or sink a dam or something — Mary would say, "You ought to knock a buggy out of this job, Joe"; but something always turned up — bad weather or sickness. Once I cut my foot with the adze and was laid up; and, another time, a dam I was making was washed away by a flood before I finished it. Then Mary would say, "Ah, well — never mind, Joe. Wait till we are better off." But she felt it hard the time I built a wool-shed and didn't get paid for it, for we'd as good as settled about another second-hand buggy then.

I always had a fancy for carpentering, and was handy with tools. I made a spring-cart — body and wheels — in spare time, out of colonial hardwood, and got Little the blacksmith to do the ironwork; I painted the cart myself. It wasn't much lighter than one of the tip-drays I had, but it *was* a spring-cart, and Mary pretended to be satisfied with it: anyway, I didn't hear any more of the buggy for a while.

I sold that cart, for fourteen pounds, to a Chinese gardener who wanted a strong cart to carry his vegetables round through the Bush. It was just before our first youngster came: I told Mary that I wanted the money in case of extra expense — and she didn't fret much at losing that cart. But the fact was, that I was going to make another try for a buggy, as a present for Mary when the child was born. I thought of getting the turn-out while she was laid up, keeping it dark from her till she was on her feet again, and then showing her the buggy standing in the shed. But she had a bad time, and I had to have the doctor regularly, and get a proper nurse, and a lot of things extra; so the buggy idea was knocked on the head. I was set on it, too: I'd thought of how, when Mary was up and getting strong, I'd say one morning, "Go round and have a look in the shed, Mary; I've got a few fowls for you," or something like that — and follow her round to watch her eyes when she saw the buggy. I never told Mary about that — it wouldn't have done any good.

Later on I got some good timber — mostly scraps that were given to me — and made a light body for a spring-cart. Galletly, the coach-builder at Cudgeegong, had got a dozen pairs of American hickory wheels up from Sydney, for light spring-carts, and he let me have a pair for cost price and carriage. I got him to iron the cart, and he put it through the paint-shop for nothing. He sent it out, too, at the tail of Tom Tarrant's big van — to increase the surprise. We were swells then for a while; I heard no more of a buggy until after we'd been settled at Lahey's Creek for a couple of years.

I told you how I went into the carrying line, and took up a selection at Lahey's Creek — for a run for the horses and to grow a bit of feed — and shifted Mary and little Jim out there from Gulgong, with Mary's young scamp of a brother James to keep them company while I was on the road. The first year I did well enough carrying, but I never cared for it — it was too slow; and, besides, I was always anxious when I was away from home. The game was right enough for a single man — or a married one whose wife had got the nagging habit (as many Bushwomen have — God help 'em!), and who wanted peace and quietness sometimes. Besides, other small carriers started (seeing me getting on); and Tom Tarrant, the coach-driver at Cudgeegong, had another heavy spring-van built, and put it on the roads, and he took a lot of the light stuff.

The second year I made a rise — out of "spuds", of all the things in the world. It was Mary's idea. Down at the lower end of our selection — Mary called it "the run" — was a shallow watercourse called Snake's Creek, dry most of the

year, except for a muddy water-hole or two; and, just above
the junction, where it ran into Lahey's Creek, was a low
piece of good black-soil flat, on our side — about three
acres. The flat was fairly clear when I came to the selection
— save for a few logs that had been washed up there in some
big "old man" flood, way back in black-fellows' times; and
one day, when I had a spell at home, I got the horses and
trace-chains and dragged the logs together —·those that
wouldn't split for fencing timber — and burnt them off. I
had a notion to get the flat ploughed and make a lucern-
paddock of it. There was a good water-hole, under a
clump of she-oak in the bend, and Mary used to take her
stools and tubs and boiler down there in the spring-cart in
hot weather, and wash the clothes under the shade of the
trees — it was cooler, and saved carrying water to the house.
And one evening after she'd done the washing she said to
me —

"Look here, Joe; the farmers out here never seem to get a
new idea: they don't seem to me ever to try and find out
beforehand what the market is going to be like — they just
go on farming the same old way and putting in the same old
crops year after year. They sow wheat, and, if it comes on
anything like the thing, they reap and thresh it; if it doesn't,
they mow it for hay — and some of 'em don't have the brains
to do that in time. Now, I was looking at that bit of flat you
cleared, and it struck me that it wouldn't be a half bad idea
to get a bag of seed-potatoes, and have the land ploughed —
old Corny George would do it cheap — and get them put in
at once. Potatoes have been dear all round for the last
couple of years."

I told her she was talking nonsense, that the ground was
no good for potatoes, and the whole district was too dry.
"Everybody I know has tried it, one time or another, and
made nothing of it," I said.

"All the more reason why you should try it, Joe," said
Mary. "Just try one crop. It might rain for weeks, and then
you'll be sorry you didn't take my advice."

"But I tell you the ground is not potato-ground," I said.

"How do you know? You haven't sown any there yet."

"But I've turned up the surface and looked at it. It's not
rich enough, and too dry, I tell you. You need swampy,
boggy ground for potatoes. Do you think I don't know land
when I see it?"

"But you haven't *tried* to grow potatoes there yet, Joe.
How do you know ——"

I didn't listen to any more. Mary was obstinate when she got an idea into her head. It was no use arguing with her. All the time I'd be talking she'd just knit her forehead and go on thinking straight ahead, on the track she'd started — just as if I wasn't there — and it used to make me mad. She'd keep driving at me till I took her advice or lost my temper — I did both at the same time, mostly.

I took my pipe and went out to smoke and cool down.

A couple of days after the potato breeze, I started with the team down to Cudgeegong for a load of fencing-wire I had to bring out; and after I'd kissed Mary good-bye, she said —

"Look here, Joe, if you bring out a bag of seed-potatoes, James and I will slice them, and old Corny George down the creek would bring his plough up in the dray and plough the ground for very little. We could put the potatoes in ourselves if the ground were only ploughed."

I thought she'd forgotten all about it. There was no time to argue — I'd be sure to lose my temper, and then I'd either have to waste an hour comforting Mary or go off in a "huff", as the women call it, and be miserable for the trip. So I said I'd see about it. She gave me another hug and a kiss. "Don't forget, Joe," she said as I started. "Think it over on the road." I reckon she had the best of it that time.

About five miles along, just as I turned into the main road, I heard some one galloping after me, and I saw young James on his hack. I got a start, for I thought that something had gone wrong at home. I remember, the first day I left Mary on the creek, for the first five or six miles I was half-a-dozen times on the point of turning back — only I thought she'd laugh at me.

"What is it, James?" I shouted, before he came up — but I saw he was grinning.

"Mary says to tell you not to forget to bring a hoe out with you."

"You clear off home!" I said, "or I'll lay the whip about your young hide; and don't come riding after me again as if the run was on fire."

"Well, you needn't get shirty with me!" he said. "*I* don't want to have anything to do with a hoe." And he rode off.

I *did* get thinking about those potatoes, though I hadn't meant to. I knew of an independent man in that district who'd made his money out of a crop of potatoes; but that was away back in the roaring 'Fifties — '54 — when spuds went up to twenty-eight shillings a hundredweight (in Sydney), on account of the gold rush. We might get good rain now, and, anyway, it wouldn't cost much to put the potatoes in. If they came on well, it would be a few pounds in my pocket; if the crop was a failure, I'd have a better show with Mary next time she was struck by an idea outside housekeeping, and have something to grumble about when I felt grumpy.

I got a couple of bags of potatoes — we could use those that were left over; and I got a small iron plough and a harrow that Little the blacksmith had lying in his yard and let me have cheap — only about a pound more than I told Mary I gave for them. When I took advice, I generally made the mistake of taking more than was offered, or adding notions of my own. It was vanity, I suppose. If the crop came on well I could claim the plough-and-harrow part of the idea, anyway. (It didn't strike me that if the crop failed Mary would have the plough and harrow against me, for old Corny would plough the ground for ten or fifteen shillings.) Anyway, I'd want a plough and harrow later on, and I might as well get it now; it would give James something to do.

I came out by the western road, by Guntawang, and up the creek home; and the first thing I saw was old Corny George ploughing the flat. And Mary was down on the bank superintending. She'd got James with the trace-chains and the spare horses, and had made him clear off every stick and bush where another furrow might be squeezed in. Old Corney looked pretty grumpy on it — he'd broken all his ploughshares but one, in the roots; and James didn't look much brighter. Mary had an old felt hat and a new pair of 'lastic-side boots of mine on, and the boots were covered with clay, for she'd been down hustling James to get a rotten old stump out of the way by the time Corny came round with his next furrow.

"I thought I'd make the boots easy for you, Joe," said Mary.

"It's all right, Mary," I said. "I'm not going to growl." Those boots were a bone of contention between us; but she generally got them off before I got home.

Her face fell a little when she saw the plough and harrow in the waggon, but I said that would be all right — we'd want a plough anyway.

"I thought you wanted old Corny to plough the ground," she said.

"I never said so."

"But when I sent Jim after you about the hoe to put the spuds in, you didn't say you wouldn't bring it," she said.

I had a few days at home, and entered into the spirit of the thing. When Corny was done, James and I cross-ploughed the land, and got a stump or two, a big log, and some scrub out of the way at the upper end and added nearly an acre, and ploughed that. James was all right at most Bushwork: he'd bullock so long as the novelty lasted; he liked ploughing or fencing, or any graft he could make a show at. He didn't care for grubbing out stumps, or splitting posts and rails. We sliced the potatoes of an evening — and there was trouble between Mary and James over cutting through the "eyes". There was no time for the hoe — and besides it wasn't a novelty to James — so I just ran furrows and they dropped the spuds in behind me, and I turned another furrow over them, and ran the harrow over the ground. I think I hilled those spuds, too, with furrows — or a crop of Indian corn I put in later on.

It rained heavens-hard for over a week: we had regular showers all through, and it was the finest crop of potatoes ever seen in the district. I believe at first Mary used to slip down at daybreak to see if the potatoes were up; and she'd write to me about them, on the road. I forget how many bags I got; but the few who had grown potatoes in the district sent theirs to Sydney, and spuds went up to twelve and fifteen shillings a hundredweight in that district. I made a few quid out of mine — and saved carriage too, for I could take them out on the waggon. Then Mary began to hear (through James) of a buggy that some one had for sale cheap, or a dogcart that somebody else wanted to get rid of — and let me know about it, in an offhand way.

II. *Joe Wilson's Luck*

There was good grass on the selection all the year. I'd picked up a small lot — about twenty head — of half-starved steers for next to nothing, and turned them on the run; they came on wonderfully, and my brother-in-law (Mary's sister's husband), who was running a butchery at Gulgong, gave me a good price for them. His carts ran out twenty or thirty miles, to little bits of gold-rushes that were going on at th' Home Rule, Happy Valley, Guntawang, Tallawang, and Cooyal, and those places round there, and he was doing well.

Mary had heard of a light American waggonette, when the steers went — a tray-body arrangement, and she thought she'd do with that. "It would be better than the buggy, Joe," she said — "there'd be more room for the children, and, besides, I could take butter and eggs to Gulgong, or Cobborah, when we get a few more cows." Then James heard of a small flock of sheep that a selector — who was about starved off his selection out Talbragar way — wanted to get rid of. James reckoned he could get them for less than half-a-crown a-head. We'd had a heavy shower of rain, that came over the ranges and didn't seem to go beyond our boundaries. Mary said, "It's a pity to see all that grass going to waste, Joe. Better get those sheep and try your luck with them. Leave some money with me, and I'll send James over for them. Never mind about the buggy — we'll get that when we're on our feet."

So James rode across to Talbragar and drove a hard bargain with that unfortunate selector, and brought the sheep home. There were about two hundred, wethers and ewes, and they were young and looked a good breed too, but so poor they could scarcely travel: they soon picked up, though. The drought was blazing all round and Out-Back, and I think that my corner of the ridges was the only place where there was any grass to speak of. We had another shower or two, and the grass held out. Chaps began to talk of "Joe Wilson's luck".

I would have liked to shear those sheep; but I hadn't time to get a shed or anything ready — along towards Christmas there was a bit of a boom in the carrying line. Wethers in wool were going as high as thirteen to fifteen shillings at the Homebush yards at Sydney, so I arranged to truck the sheep down from the river by rail, with another small lot that was going, and I started James off with them. He took the west road, and down Guntawang way a big farmer who saw James with the sheep (and who was speculating, or adding to his stock, or took a fancy to the wool) offered James as much for them as he reckoned I'd get in Sydney, after paying the carriage and the agents and the auctioneer. James put the sheep in a paddock and rode back to me. He was all there where riding was concerned. I told him to let the sheep go. James made a Greener shot-gun, and got his saddle done up, out of that job.

I took up a couple more forty-acre blocks — one in James's name, to encourage him with the fencing. There was a good slice of land in an angle between the range and the creek, farther down, which everybody thought belonged to Wall, the squatter, but Mary got an idea, and went to the local land office and found out that it was "unoccupied Crown land", and so I took it up on pastoral lease, and got a few more sheep — I'd saved some of the best-looking ewes from the last lot.

One evening — I was going down next day for a load of fencing-wire for myself — Mary said —

"Joe! do you know that the Matthews have got a new double buggy?"

The Matthews were a big family of cockatoos, along up the main road, and I didn't think much of them. The sons were all "bad-eggs", though the old woman and girls were right enough.

"Well, what of that?" I said. "They're up to their neck in debt, and camping like black-fellows in a big bark humpy. They do well to go flashing round in a double buggy."

"But that isn't what I was going to say," said Mary. "They want to sell their old single buggy, James says. I'm sure you could get it for six or seven pounds; and you could have it done up."

"I wish James to the devil!" I said. "Can't he find anything better to do than ride round after cock-and-bull yarns about buggies?"

"Well," said Mary, "it was James who got the steers and the sheep."

Well, one word led to another, and we said things we didn't mean — but couldn't forget in a hurry. I remember I said something about Mary always dragging me back just when I was getting my head above water and struggling to make a home for her and the children; and that hurt her, and she spoke of the "homes" she'd had since she was married. And that cut me deep.

It was about the worst quarrel we had. When she began to cry I got my hat and went out and walked up and down by the creek. I hated anything that looked like injustice — I was so sensitive about it that it made me unjust sometimes. I tried to think I was right, but I couldn't — it wouldn't have made me feel any better if I could have thought so. I got thinking of Mary's first year on the selection and the life she'd had since we were married.

When I went in she'd cried herself to sleep. I bent over and, "Mary," I whispered.

She seemed to wake up.

"Joe — Joe!" she said.

"What is it Mary?" I said.

"I'm pretty well sure that old Spot's calf isn't in the pen.

Make James go at once!"

Old Spot's last calf was two years old now; so Mary was talking in her sleep, and dreaming she was back in her first year.

We both laughed when I told her about it afterwards; but I didn't feel like laughing just then.

Later on in the night she called out in her sleep —

"Joe — Joe! Put that buggy in the shed, or the sun will blister the varnish!"

I wish I could say that that was the last time I ever spoke unkindly to Mary.

Next morning I got up early and fried the bacon and made the tea, and took Mary's breakfast in to her — like I used to do, sometimes, when we were first married. She didn't say anything — just pulled my head down and kissed me.

When I was ready to start Mary said —

"You'd better take the spring-cart in behind the dray and get the tyres cut and set. They're ready to drop off, and James has been wedging them up till he's tired of it. The last time I was out with the children I had to knock one of them back with a stone: there'll be an accident yet."

So I lashed the shafts of the cart under the tail of the waggon, and mean and ridiculous enough the cart looked, going along that way. It suggested a man stooping along handcuffed, with his arms held out and down in front of him.

It was dull weather, and the scrubs looked extra dreary and endless — and I got thinking of old things. Everything was going all right with me, but that didn't keep me from brooding sometimes — trying to hatch out stones, like an old hen we had at home. I think, taking it all round, I used to be happier when I was mostly hard-up — and more generous. When I had ten pounds I was more likely to listen to a chap who said, "Lend me a pound-note, Joe," than when I had fifty; *then* I fought shy of careless chaps — and lost mates that I wanted afterwards — and got the name of being mean. When I got a good cheque I'd be as miserable as a miser over the first ten pounds I spent; but when I got down to the last I'd buy things for the house. And now that I was getting on, I hated to spend a pound on anything. But then, the farther I got away from poverty the greater the fear I had of it — and, besides, there was always before us all the thought of the terrible drought, with blazing runs as bare and dusty as the road, and dead stock rotting every yard, all along the barren creeks.

I had a long yarn with Mary's sister and her husband that night in Gulgong, and it brightened me up. I had a fancy that that sort of a brother-in-law made a better mate than a nearer one; Tom Tarrant had one, and he said it was sympathy. But while we were yarning I couldn't help thinking of Mary, out there is the hut on the Creek, with no one to talk to but the children, or James, who was sulky at home, or Black Mary or Black Jimmy (our black boy's father and mother), who weren't over-sentimental. Or maybe a selector's wife (the nearest was five miles away), who could talk only of two or three things — "lambin" and "shearin" and "cookin" for the men, and what she said to her old man, and what he said to her — and her own ailments — over and over again.

It's a wonder it didn't drive Mary mad! — I know I could never listen to that woman more than an hour. Mary's sister said, —

"Now if Mary had a comfortable buggy, she could drive in with the children oftener. Then she wouldn't feel the loneliness so much."

I said "Good night" then and turned in. There was no getting away from that buggy. Whenever Mary's sister started hinting about a buggy, I reckoned it was a put-up job between them.

III. The Ghost of Mary's Sacrifice

When I got to Cudgeegong I stopped at Galletly's coach-shop to leave the cart. The Galletlys were good fellows: there were two brothers — one was a saddler and harness-maker. Big brown-bearded men — the biggest men in the district, 'twas said.

Their old man had died lately and left them some money; they had men, and only worked in their shops when they felt inclined, or there was a special work to do; they were both first-class tradesmen. I went into the painter's shop to have a look at a double buggy that Galletly had built for a man who couldn't pay cash for it when it was finished — and Galletly wouldn't trust him.

There it stood, behind a calico screen that the coach-painters used to keep out the dust when they were varnishing. It was a first-class piece of work — pole, shafts, cushions, whip, lamps, and all complete. If you only wanted to drive one horse you could take out the pole and put in the shafts, and there you were. There was a tilt over the front seat; if you only wanted the buggy to carry two, you could fold down the back seat, and there you had a handsome, roomy, single buggy. It would go near fifty pounds.

While I was looking at it, Bill Galletly came in, and slapped me on the back.

"Now, there's a chance for you, Joe!" he said. "I saw you rubbing your head round that buggy the last time you were in. You wouldn't get a better one in the colonies, and you won't see another like it in the district again in a hurry — for it doesn't pay to build 'em. Now you're a full-blown squatter, and it's time you took little Mary for a fly round in her own buggy now and then, instead of having her stuck out there in the scrub, or jolting through the dust in a cart like some old Mother Flourbag."

He called her "little Mary" because the Galletly family had known her when she was a girl.

I rubbed my head and looked at the buggy again. It was a great temptation.

"Look here, Joe," said Bill Galletly in a quieter tone. "I'll tell you what I'll do. I'll let *you* have the buggy. You can take it out and send along a bit of a cheque when you feel you can manage it, and the rest later on — a year will do, or even two years. You've had a hard pull, and I'm not likely to be hard up for money in a hurry."

They were good fellows the Galletlys, but they knew their men. I happened to know that Bill Galletly wouldn't let the man he built the buggy for take it out of the shop without cash down, though he was a big-bug round there. But that didn't make it easier for me.

Just then Robert Galletly came into the shop. He was rather quieter than his brother, but the two were very much alike.

"Look here, Bob," said Bill; "here's a chance for you to get rid of your harness. Joe Wilson's going to take that buggy off my hands."

Bob Galletly put his foot up on a saw-stool, took one hand out of his pockets, rested his elbow on his knee and his chin on the palm of his hand, and bunched up his big beard with his fingers, as he always did when he was thinking. Presently he took his foot down, put his hand back in his pocket, and said to me, "Well, Joe, I've got a double set of harness made for the man who ordered that damned buggy, and if you like I'll let you have it. I suppose when Bill there has squeezed all he can out of you I'll stand a show of getting something. He's a regular Shylock, he is."

I pushed my hat forward and rubbed the back of my head and stared at the buggy.

"Come across to the Royal, Joe," said Bob.

But I knew that a beer would settle the business, so I said I'd get the wool up to the station first and think it over, and have a drink when I came back.

I thought it over on the way to the station, but it didn't seem good enough. I wanted to get some more sheep, and there was the new run to be fenced in, and the instalments on the selections. I wanted lots of things that I couldn't well do without. Then, again, the farther I got away from debt and hard-upedness the greater the horror I had of it. I had two horses that would do; but I'd have to get another later on, and altogether the buggy would run me nearer a hundred than fifty pounds. Supposing a dry season threw me back with that buggy on my hands. Besides, I wanted a spell. If I got the buggy it would only mean an extra turn of hard graft for me. No, I'd take Mary for a trip to Sydney, and she'd have to be satisfied with that.

I'd got it settled, and was just turning in through the big white gates to the goods-shed when young Black, the squatter, dashed past to the station in his big new waggonette, with his wife and a driver and a lot of portmanteaus and rugs and things. They were going to do the grand in Sydney over Christmas. Now it was young Black who was so shook after Mary when she was in service with the Blacks before the old man died, and if I hadn't come along — and if girls never cared for vagabonds — Mary would have been mistress of Haviland homestead, with servants to wait on her; and she was far better fitted for it than the one that was there. She would have been going to Sydney every holiday and putting up at the old Royal, with every comfort that a woman could ask for, and seeing a play every night. And I'd have been knocking around amongst the big stations Out-Back, or maybe drinking myself to death at the shanties.

The Blacks didn't see me as I went by, ragged and dusty, and with an old, nearly black, cabbage-tree hat drawn over my eyes. I didn't care a damn for them, or any one else, at most times, but I had moods when I felt things.

One of Black's big wool teams was just coming away from the shed, and the driver, a big, dark, rough fellow, with some foreign blood in him, didn't seem inclined to wheel his team an inch out of the middle of the road. I stopped my

horses and waited. He looked at me and I looked at him —
hard. Then he wheeled off, scowling, and swearing at his
horses. I'd given him a hiding, six or seven years before, and
he hadn't forgotten it. And I felt then as if I wouldn't mind
trying to give some one a hiding.

The goods clerk must have thought that Joe Wilson was
pretty grumpy that day. I was thinking of Mary, out there in
the lonely hut on a barren creek in the Bush — for it was
little better — with no one to speak to except a haggard,
worn-out Bushwoman or two, that came to see her on
Sunday. I thought of the hardships she went through in the
first year — that I haven't told you about yet; of the time she
was ill, and I away, and no one to understand; of the time
she was alone with James and Jim sick; and of the loneliness
she fought through out there. I thought of Mary, outside in
the blazing heat, with an old print dress and a felt hat, and
pair of 'lastic-siders of mine on, doing the work of a station
manager as well as that of a housewife and mother. And her
cheeks were getting thin, and her colour was going: I
thought of the gaunt, brick-brown, saw-file voiced, hopeless
and spiritless Bushwomen I knew — and some of them not
much older than Mary.

When I went back down into the town, I had a drink with
Bill Galletly at the Royal, and that settled the buggy; then
Bob shouted, and I took the harness. Then I shouted, to wet
the bargain. When I was going, Bob said, "Send in that
young scamp of a brother of Mary's with the horses: if the
collars don't fit I'll fix up a pair of makeshifts, and alter the
others." I thought they both gripped my hand harder than
usual, but that might have been the beer.

IV.   The Buggy Comes Home

I "whipped the cat" a bit, the first twenty miles or so, but
then, I thought, what did it matter? What was the use of
grinding to save money until we were too old to enjoy it. If
we had to go down in the world again, we might as well fall
out of a buggy as out of a dray — there'd be some talk about
it, anyway, and perhaps a little sympathy. When Mary had
the buggy she wouldn't be tied down so much to that
wretched hole in the Bush; and the Sydney trips needn't be of
off either. I could drive down to Wallerawang on the main
line, where Mary had some people, and leave the buggy and
horses there, and take the train to Sydney; or go right on, by

the old coach-road, over the Blue Mountains: it would be a grand drive. I thought best to tell Mary's sister at Gulgong about the buggy; I told her I'd keep it dark from Mary till the buggy came home. She entered into the spirit of the thing, and said she'd give the world to be able to go out with the buggy, if only to see Mary open her eyes when she saw it; but she couldn't go, on account of a new baby she had. I was rather glad she couldn't, for it would spoil the surprise a little, I thought. I wanted that all to myself.

I got home about sunset next day, and, after tea, when I'd finished telling Mary all the news, and a few lies as to why I didn't bring the cart back, and one or two other things, I sat with James, out on a log of the wood-heap, where we generally had our smokes and interviews, and told him all about the buggy. He whistled, then he said —

"But what do you want to make it such a Bushranging business for? Why can't you tell Mary now? It will cheer her up. She's been pretty miserable since you've been away this trip."

"I want it to be a surprise," I said.

"Well, I've got nothing to say against a surprise, out in a hole like this; but it 'ud take a lot to surprise me. What am I to say to Mary about taking the two horses in? I'll only want one to bring the cart out, and she's sure to ask."

"Tell her you're going to get yours shod."

"But he had a set of slippers only the other day. She knows as much about horses as we do. I don't mind telling a lie so long as a chap has only got to tell a straight lie and be done with it. But Mary asks so many questions."

"Well, drive the other horse up the creek early, and pick him up as you go."

"Yes. And she'll want to know what I want with two bridles. But I'll fix her — *you* needn't worry."

"And, James," I said, "get a chamois leather and sponge — we'll want 'em anyway — and you might give the buggy a wash down in the creek, coming home. It's sure to be covered with dust."

"Oh! — orlright."

"And if you can, time yourself to get here in the cool of the evening, or just about sunset."

"What for?"

I'd thought it would be better to have the buggy there in the cool of the evening, when Mary would have time to get excited and get over it — better than in the blazing hot morning, when the sun rose as hot as at noon, and we'd have the long broiling day before us.

"What do you want me to come at sunset for?" asked James. "Do you want me to camp out in the scrub and turn up like a blooming sundowner?"

"Oh well," I said, "get here at midnight if you like."

We didn't say anything for a while — just sat and puffed at our pipes. Then I said, —

"Well, what are you thinking about?"

"I'm thinking it's time you got a new hat, the sun seems to get in through your old one too much," and he got out of my reach and went to see about penning the calves. Before we turned in he said —

"Well, what am I to get out of the job, Joe?"

He had his eye on a double-barrel gun that Franca the gunsmith in Cudgeegong had — one barrel shot, and the other rifle; so I said —

"How much does Franca want for that gun?"

"Five-ten; but I think he'd take my single barrel off it. Anyway, I can squeeze a couple of quid out of Phil Lambert for the single barrel." (Phil was his bosom chum.)

"All right," I said. "Make the best bargain you can."

He got his own breakfast and made an early start next morning, to get clear of any instructions or messages that Mary might have forgotten to give him overnight. He took his gun with him.

I'd always thought that a man was a fool who couldn't keep a secret from his wife — that there was something womanish about him. I found out. Those three days waiting for the bugggy were about the longest I ever spent in my life. It made me scotty with every one and everything; and poor Mary had to suffer for it. I put in the time patching up the harness and mending the stockyard and the roof, and, the third morning, I rode up the ridges to look for trees for fencing-timber. I remember I hurried home that afternoon because I thought the buggy might get there before me.

At tea-time I got Mary on to the buggy business.

"What's the good of a single buggy to you, Mary?" I asked. "There's only room for two, and what are you going to do with the children when we go out together?"

"We can put them on the floor at our feet, like other people do. I can always fold up a blanket or 'possum rug for them to sit on."

But she didn't take half so much interest in buggy talk as she would have taken at any other time, when I didn't want her to. Women are aggravating that way. But the poor girl was tired and not very well, and both the children were cross. She did look knocked up.

"We'll give the buggy a rest, Joe," she said. (I thought I heard it coming then.) "It seems as far off as ever. I don't know why you want to harp on it today. Now, don't look so cross, Joe — I didn't mean to hurt you. We'll wait until we can get a double buggy, since you're so set on it. There'll be plenty of time when we're better off."

After tea, when the youngsters were in bed, and she'd washed up, we sat outside on the edge of the verandah floor, Mary sewing, and I smoking and watching the track up the creek.

"Why don't you talk, Joe?" asked Mary. "You scarcely ever speak to me now: it's like drawing blood out of a stone to get a word from you. What makes you so cross, Joe?"

"Well, I've got nothing to say."

"But you should find something. Think of me — it's very miserable for me. Have you anything on your mind? Is there any new trouble? Better tell me, no matter what it is, and not go worrying and brooding and making both our lives miserable. If you never tell one anything, how can you expect me to understand?"

I said there was nothing the matter.

"But there must be, to make you so unbearable. Have you been drinking, Joe — or gambling?"

I asked her what she'd accuse me of next.

"And another thing I want to speak to you about," she went on. "Now, don't knit up your forehead like that, Joe, and get impatient —— "

"Well, what is it?"

"I wish you wouldn't swear in the hearing of the children. Now, little Jim today, he was trying to fix his little go-cart and it wouldn't run right, and — and —— "

"Well, what did he say?"

"He — he" (she seemed a little hysterical, trying not to laugh) — "he said 'damn it!'"

I had to laugh. Mary tried to keep serious, but it was no use.

"Never mind, old woman," I said, putting an arm round her, for her mouth was trembling, and she was crying more than laughing. "It won't be always like this. Just wait till we're a bit better off."

Just then a black boy we had (I must tell you about him some other time) came sidling along by the wall, as if he were afraid somebody was going to hit him — poor little devil! I never did.

"What is it, Harry?" said Mary.

"Buggy comin', I bin thinkit."

"Where?"

He pointed up the creek.

"Sure it's a buggy?"

"Yes, missus."

"How many horses?"

"One — two."

We knew that he could hear and see things long before we could. Mary went and perched on the wood-heap, and shaded her eyes — though the sun had gone — and peered through between the eternal grey trunks of the stunted trees on the flat across the creek. Presently she jumped down and came running in.

"There's some one coming in a buggy, Joe!" she cried, excitedly. "And both my white table-cloths are rough dry. Harry! put two flat-irons down to the fire, quick, and put on some more wood. It's lucky I kept those new sheets packed away. Get up out of that Joe! What are you sitting grinning like that for? Go and get on another shirt. Hurry — Why! It's only James — by himself."

She stared at me, and I sat there, grinning like a fool.

"Joe!" she said, "whose buggy is that?"

"Well, I suppose it's yours," I said.

She caught her breath, and stared at the buggy and then at me again. James drove down out of sight into the crossing, and came up close to the house.

"Oh, Joe! what have you done?" cried Mary. "Why, it's a new double buggy!" Then she rushed at me and hugged my head. "Why didn't you tell me, Joe? You poor old boy! — and I've been nagging at you all day!" and she hugged me again.

James got down and started taking the horses out — as if it was an everyday occurrence. I saw the double-barrel gun sticking out from under the seat. He'd stopped to wash the buggy, and I suppose that's what made him grumpy. Mary stood on the verandah, with her eyes twice as big as usual, and breathing hard — taking the buggy in.

James skimmed the harness off, and the horses shook themselves and went down to the dam for a drink. "You'd better look under the seats," growled James, as he took his gun out with great care.

Mary dived for the buggy. There was a dozen of lemonade and ginger-beer in a candle-box from Galletly — James said that Galletly's men had a gallon of beer, and they cheered him, James (I suppose he meant they cheered the buggy), as he drove off; there was a "little bit of a ham" from Pat Murphy, the storekeeper at Home Rule, that he'd "cured himself" — it was the biggest I ever saw; there were three loaves of baker's bread, a cake, and a dozen yards of something "to make up for the children", from Aunt Gertrude at Gulgong; there was a fresh-water cod, that long Dave Regan had caught the night before in the Macquarie river, and sent out packed in salt in a box; there was a holland suit for the black boy, with red braid to trim it; and there was a jar of preserved ginger, and some lollies (sweets) ("for the lil' boy"), and a rum-looking Chinese doll and a rattle ("for lil' girl") from Sun Tong Lee, our storekeeper at Gulgong — James was chummy with Sun Tong Lee, and got his powder and shot and caps there on tick when he was short of money. And James said that the people would have loaded the buggy with "rubbish" if he'd waited. They all seemed glad to see Joe Wilson getting on — and these things did me good.

We got the things inside, and I don't think either of us knew what we were saying or doing for the next half-hour. Then James put his head in and said, in a very injured tone, —

"What about my tea? I ain't had anything to speak of since I left Cudgeegong. I want some grub."

Then Mary pulled herself together.

"You'll have your tea directly," she said. "Pick up that harness at once, and hang it on the pegs in the skillion; and you, Joe, back that buggy under the end of the verandah, the dew will be on it presently — and we'll put wet bags up in front of it tomorrow, to keep the sun off. And James will have to go back to Cudgeegong for the cart — we can't have that buggy to knock about in."

"All right," said James — "anything! Only get me some grub."

Mary fried the fish, in case it wouldn't keep till the morning, and rubbed over the tablecloths, now the irons were hot — James growling all the time — and got out some crockery she had packed away that had belonged to her mother, and set the table in a style that made James uncomfortable.

"I want some grub — not a blooming banquet!" he said. And he growled a lot because Mary wanted him to eat his fish without a knife, "and that sort of Tommy-rot." When he'd finished he took his gun, and the black boy, and the dogs, and went out 'possum-shooting.

When we were alone Mary climbed into the buggy to try the seat, and made me get up alongside her. We hadn't had such a comfortable seat for years; but we soon got down, in case any one came by, for we began to feel like a pair of fools up there.

Then we sat, side by side, on the edge of the verandah, and talked more than we'd done for years — and there was a good deal of "Do you remember?" in it — and I think we got to understand each other better that night.

And at last Mary said, "Do you know, Joe, why, I feel tonight just — just like I did the day we were married."

And somehow I had that strange, shy sort of feeling too.

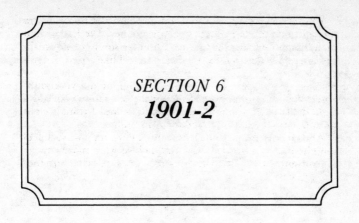

SECTION 6
1901-2

Editor's Note

The article on the *Bulletin* was written with an English audience in mind, and while in England Lawson had hoped to include it in a collection of literary essays. It remained unpublished in his lifetime. "The Shearers" provided the epigraph to *Children of the Bush*, in which "Send Round the Hat" and "A Sketch of Mateship" appeared. "Drifting Apart" was written before Lawson returned to Australia, "A Child in the Dark" soon after (and published in the *Bulletin*). Neither was published in book form until *Triangles of Life* in 1913 (which provides the text here).

The text of the extract from the article on the *Bulletin* is transcribed from the undated typescript in the Mitchell Library. The texts of "Send Round the Hat" and "A Sketch of Mateship" are taken from *Children of the Bush*, and of "The Shearers" from *When I Was King*.

The Sydney *Bulletin*
(extract)

II.   A Sketch of Archibald

On the second floor, in the right hand room of three narrow little partitioned off rooms (boxes rather) that box in the front windows — an editorial den — certainly smaller and scarcely less bare than the one hinted at twenty years ago, in the beginning of this article — sits an elderly man, tallish and of spare proportions — a man who is little known personally — working hard at a formidable pile of manuscripts (much of it beautifully written on foolscap) on a small, plain desk where there is barely room for a stack of MSS. on each hand and writing space between. Most men could draw his hat over their ears, though his head does not appear nearly so large as it is. It is somewhat greyer and balder than it was twenty years ago. When he turns from his work to you — which he does with some effort — you see that his eyes are kind and his manner very gentle. He is a man whose kindly tone (as if he had known you well as a boy) and altogether unworldly and unaffected manner, you remember long after you have forgotten his features.

He is going through the copy for next issue, from left to right and down into the waste-paper basket (the *Bulletin* "W.P.B.") sheet by sheet, and, in the case of accepted work, line for line and word for word: reconsidering, revising, recondensing matter which has been through the hands of at least one sub-editor (whose sole work consists of condensing) and, in doubtful cases, copy that has been under the spectacles, blue pencils, and red-inked pens of the three who comprise the working staff. He uses the scissors only to reduce the bulk of the copy by clipping off — over the Waste Paper Basket — half sheets, three quarter sheets — whole sheets save for a line or two — of marked off foolscap. Practically every line of the literary matter which appears in the Sydney *Bulletin* runs under the point of the Editor's fountain pen — which explains the marvellously uniform variety of the *Bulletin's* paragraph columns. The Editor works — or "grinds" — six and seven hours a day, and when the paper is printed, he goes through the damp sheets, hungry pen or pencil in hand and wishes that he had cut out about half of it.

On his right sits his typewriter clerk, secretary, and book-keeper, a young man with a quiet, resigned voice and prematurely grey, who, when he has occasion to leave the room on a busy day, locks the Editor in behind him. Behind the editorial chair, and leaving just room to turn round, stand tall, wide cases of pigeon-holes, covering that wall, and containing (some of us believe) thousands of pounds worth of old contributions — stories, sketches, and articles — in original and in duplicate; and the cases are always kept locked. I know that some of those contributions were sold to the *Bulletin* ten years ago. They say that the Editor has copies of most of them at home. It is supposed that the value of the whole of the pigeon-holed contributions, including others and artists' sketches in a big chest and elsewhere, would run well into four figures. The Editor, if still in doubt between the W.P.B. and the compositors' room *re* the copy of an Australian sketch or article held by him, would, if put to the point, rather pay for it and pigeon-hole it than rerturn it to the author.

Some say that this collecting and hoarding of copy is a mania born of an old fear of an opposition backed by both brains and capital. The Editor once condescended to explain: "I buy while the market's open; by and by it may be closed." I have always regarded him as being one of the most far-seeing men in Australasia. Some of that copy, bought long ago for £1.10 per column is now, because of the deaths or successes of the writers, worth two to three guineas a column. We (the old *Bulletin* contributors) have a dreary joke to the effect that the Editor is only waiting for our deaths, so that the copy in his hands might gain weight and literary value, and be of more interest to Australian readers, when published as "found amongst the papers of the late So-and-So". And, to carry the alleged joke further, it is often considered a case of waiting for the Editor's death, for, when he goes on his short annual holiday, he leaves his hoards of copy locked up and takes the keys with him. But there is copy there which could not be boiled down to *Bulletin* length, even though the three witches and their master assisted; and much that is and will always be out of the

Bulletin line; for the *Bulletin* could not change either its policy or literary style and maintain its position. This is the literary advertisement:

> *The Editor will carefully read and acknowledge in the "Correspondence" column all contributions submitted — whether in the form of Political, Social, or other Articles, Verse, Short Tales or Sketches (those dealing with Australian subjects, and not exceeding two columns in length, or, say, 3000 words, are specially acceptable), Paragraphs, Letters, or Newspaper-Clippings. All communications will be regarded as strictly confidential.*
>
> *The Bulletin will return all unsuitable MS. when the address is specified and stamps are enclosed. But we desire those sending MS. to distinctly understand that we are not responsible for its preservation or transmission.*

The Editor very rarely reprints at length (more than half a column) and, when he does, you may be sure the matter is especially good in his opinion. Years ago I published some rhymes anonymously, in another paper; they were reprinted in the *Bulletin*, and I felt rather proud of the fact. But the Editor would not print the best copy (from a literary point of view) in the world, if he thought it out of the *Bulletin's* line. He recently published a rhyme of mine with which, to use his words, he was "not particularly in love". It was quoted in a leading review which I, rather triumphantly, showed him. "Now, look here," he said. "The very fact that So-and-So (the editor of the review) reprinted that, proves that it should never have gone in the *Bulletin*."

"Well, *what* shall I write?" I asked rather impatiently. "Can you suggest anything?"

"Write according to your liver, old man. That's what I do."

I went home and wrote four columns in strict accordance with my liver, but he wouldn't look at it. It was printed by another editor, however, and extensively quoted in England and America, and I'm not likely to hear the last of it the longest day I live.

But "write in your own style" is the key-note of the Editor's advice. He'd often say to a young writer whose "style" was changing — or who was trying new lines: "Yes, the sketch (or whatever it is) is very good, but it isn't *you* somehow. Why don't you lay to your book? This is out of your line."

"But it's in the *Bulletin* line."

"It may be, but I don't care to use it with your name to it; it's out of *your* line."

Years ago, when Phil May went to Rome with some idea of painting, the Editor would say:

"You're not laying to your book, you're like Phil May — the best black and white artist I know. He wants to paint; it's like a man with a fat wife who wants a thin one. You've got a fat wife in your line, and now you'll never be satisfied till you get a thin one."

The Editor says that if the angel Gabriel came down with copy he wouldn't print it if he did not think it good, and suitable for the *Bulletin*. The reply in the answers to correspondents' column would probably run like this:

> . . . Gabriel: Your formidable looking screed received. May possibly boil down to a par. Please write with black ink and on less transparent paper. We are all nearly blind in this office and wear fearsome goggles. . . .

Which last is true — bad light and the infernal vibration of the machinery.

Or the reply may be like this:

> You seem to have struck something new, but nearly missed us by writing in faint blue pencil on both sides of the paper. Will be glad to hear from you again.

Or this:

> Will gladly print your pretty and musical verses. You must drop in when you are down in Sydney.

Gabriel goes irresolutely up stairs, knocks timidly at the Editor's door, and gives his card:

The Editor: "Oh, come in! How do you do?" Shakes hands without rising and lifts a pile of MS. off the only other seat, (an old piano stool I think) by his side. "Sit down!" He proceeds in a kindly, fatherly manner and tone to give the angel some advice: ". . . Every man has at least one story in him. Some more. . . . Write as simply as you can. . . . Don't strain after effect. . . . Write carefully and write only when you have something to tell the people. . . . Go over your copy and blot out every word you can possibly do without. How are you off? What are you doing for a living? Are you hard up? — Have you got your fare back? — Well, if you like, you can go downstairs to Mr —— (the manager or cashier) and I daresay they'll fix you up. Good-bye, old man."

Gabriel would be a new writer, a fresh discovery (and the Australian field of writers has been petering of late years). Now, I have been a regular contributor for fourteen years — and a most consistent persecutor of the Editor on busy days, *re* the delay in publishing stories and sketches which I wanted for a forthcoming book. Now, if I flew to Sydney tonight, and dropped into the *Bulletin* office tomorrow morning (Tuesday and the busy day) the Editor, after I had rapped hard and coughed, would probably say, without taking his eyes clear of the copy:

"For the Lord's sake , don't bother me today, old man!" Then appealingly, "Look at that pile I've got to go through!"

And, if I waited round till lunch hour, he'd probably cross the street to me, shake hands and say:

"Hello Lawson! How are you? By the way, you've been to London, haven't you? How did you get on there?"

And, probably, before I could reply, a wreck — periodically "sacked" reporter from one of the dailies, and old contributor to the *Bulletin* — would touch the Editor's elbow, start to speak, and, the voice breaking into a sound between a cry of agony and a whine, would stand and let crumpled, soiled linen, white face and jerking limbs explain.

The Editor: "Dear, Dear! Good Lord! how did you get like this? Eh?" (finger and thumb dredging waistcoat pocket) "You've got some copy in the office? Well, for God's sake don't go down there — they've had So-and-So worrying the lives out of them all the morning. Send your wife down. I'll leave word not to give you the money. Here, take this, and get a drink and get squared up for God's sake. Better leave an order in the office to pay your wife in future — that's the most sensible plan. . . . And — hold on! Look here!" (palm and forefinger to work) "when you've squared up, start with a clean sheet — you needn't knock it off altogether; take wine, red wine, take a glass in the morning and afternoon and before going to bed, don't go beyond that. — Make up your mind to — etc. —"

To me: "Well, so-long, Lawson. I haven't had a bite of lunch yet. See you tomorrow morning." (Wednesay, his off day) "So-long."

If you follow him a few steps from the office on Wednesday or Saturday, noon, you'll see him standing outside a fishmonger's round the corner, finger and thumb dredging waistcoat pocket — as if he is vaguely doubtful whether he has any silver on him or not — and his eye on fresh bait prawns in the window; for he is going fishing off the rocks this afternoon — by himself preferred. He grinds for six or seven hours a day in the office. He goes for a short holiday once a year but doesn't enjoy himself for more than three days — then, the story is, he gets a daily paper — he depends mostly on the Sydney *Daily Telegraph* for reliable news — and goes through it with a blue pencil. He comes back looking ten years older, but completely recovers his old form after a week's work that would blind and turn the brain of another man. His portrait, if it is in existence, would be hard to get. He is a man whose kindly voice and manner you remember better than his features. His name rarely appears in print — never if he could help it. Certainly never in the literary columns of his paper.

"Literary Contributions to be addressed to J.F. Archibald."

He has had his hard-up days. He has been in the Bush and on the goldfields, and sometimes, when a new young writer with, say a goldfield story or sketch, starts to explain some detail which he fears the Editor will not understand, he says kindly, "Oh, that's all right, old man. *I've* been there."

III. *A Clear Field*

Mr. Archibald says "Hard graft and brains" did it; but there must have been other reasons contributing to the success of an outspoken and decidedly republican journal, starting without capital twenty years ago, in Australia, and always paying its contributors. In the first place there was no Australian humorous and satirical paper. There was the Sydney *Punch* — the name should be sufficient — a very weak and sad imitation of the original, with alleged humorous dialogues between ridiculously dressed Bushmen, standing in attitudes which would have been impossible unless they were shockingly deformed; and, now and then, with a vague idea that something "Bushy" would be looked for, an alleged picture of, say, "Going to Mudgee-Budgee Races", which might have been drawn in England, from letters from Uncle William in Australia by the good young lady who died. The *Illustrated Sydney News*, *Town and Country Journal*, and other Australian weeklies have "comic" sheets (sometimes coloured) at Christmas, depicting the improbable "adventures of a New-chum in the Bush" — the cockney sportsman style of humour, done by new-chum artists (at least they said they were artists), who knew nothing of the Bush, and as regards humour and artistic merit, barely on a level with *Komick Kutts* and other penny prints that are offered outside theatres as "all the comic papers, sir"! But the new-chum joke was dropped eventually, because the editors were mostly new-chums, and the established Australian press — save always the *Bulletin* and sometimes a few other papers — was, is, and has always been toady to England and all that is English. Even some London Conservative dailies come wonderfully refreshing to me after the *Sydney Morning Herald* ("Grannie"), which paper hasn't been known to "say anything" within the memory of the present generation. "It is not so much that we do not wish to become more Australian, as that we do not wish to become less English," was, I think, Grannie's most brilliant remark, concerning Australian Federation.

Then we had, for an "Australian Christmas Supplement" say a lonely new-chum in a hut in the Bush — the interior seemingly as spacious as the inside of St Paul's; hero dressed in cords, red shirt, and Wellington boots, and reclining, in the most approved Young Ladies Journal fashion on an alleged 'possum rug. In the picture I'm thinking of, a savage who might have represented the King of the Cannibal Islands (he certainly wasn't an Australian aborigine) was shown reaching round the door post for a gun that stood handy, and his mates, with sheaves of spears, were visible through the open window. Up in the corner of the picture was a smoke-framed "vision of the future", an ideal English scene (the "run" as it was going to be) with the squatter (in fancy rig) riding with his bride down by the riverside — both on race horses. This abortion of mediocrity was called the "Squatter's Dream". It did duty for several alternate Christmas numbers, and, the last time it came out, there were some rhymes underneath explaining how the squatter leaps (as he can't leap the picture) to his feet, seizes the gun, shoots two of the stealthy savages and brains the rest.

Then there was "Christmas in the Bush", "Christmas on the Mountains", "A Christmas Picnic", "Christmas Down the Harbour", "Jim's Ride — A Christmas Story", and all the sickening slush about a time on which nothing out of the ordinary (except booze) happens in any country, and which is perhaps the least popular holiday of any in Australia. The

Bulletin cleverly cartooned, in colours, the Australian
Christmas Supplement and killed it for some years, but the
last Christmas I was in Australia, the most popular
supplement in Sydney (where they know as much about the
Bush as you do here in England) was a picture called "The
Miner's Daughter", a soft, fresh-faced English village girl,
standing behind the windlass and winding up a large-size
digger (in top boots!) *with her left hand*.

I remember, the only commission I could get from one of
the oldest and wealthiest of Australian weeklies was to write
rhymes, or a Christmas story to fit an old block to be used in
the Christmas issue. I once wrote some rhymes for an old
picture called "The Teamster" and supposed to represent a
bullock-driver on the roads up-country. I got the block man
to scrape an English village out of the background, and the
grass from under the bullock's feet — then the illustration
passed. Another was a picture of an old-fashioned English
home in winter; and I couldn't manage it at all, though at
first I had an idea of having the stone lions removed from
the gate-posts, calling the snow dust, and writing a drought
story round the picture. And this was a wealthy journal with
the latest machinery. Do you wonder that most of the best
Austraian artists have cleared out of the country, and the
rest only want a chance to get away?

The *Bulletin* cartoons are never crude or vulgar, and they
are always portraits in the sense that a cartoon can be a
portrait. The *Bulletin* artists' sketches are true to the Bush
and Bush humour — and drawn by young Australians —
men who know the Bush, or go out and study it. The work is
most original, and the *Bulletin* pays its men. The illustrations of the stories in the *Bulletin* Christmas number are
works of art and true pictures of real Bush life.

When the *Bulletin* started there was a strong Democratic
or national feeling struggling for an outlet in Australia (it
broke loose in the extraordinary republican demonstrations
in connection with the proposed Jubilee celebrations in '87,
when a serious riot was only averted by Lady Carrington —
who was very popular — coming on the platform at a critical
moment in the last big meeting). Australian Democracy was
only represented by un-organized unionism and a few
free-thought and socialistic rags, edited, and in some cases
written, set-up, printed, folded, wrapped and posted by
enthusiasts who were too deadly in earnest to be read by
more than a few. The *Bulletin* filled the vacancy. The
Bulletin caught on almost from the jump, and other news-

paper men (and some of the daily proprietors) seeing what they had missed, started rival journals. There have been many since then, some going so far as to imitate the *Bulletin's* red cover and title as closely as they dared, but they are all dead now. Now and again a "smart" paper starts on "*Bulletin* lines", hates and slangs the *Bulletin* for half-a-dozen issues, and then dies viciously with a final spiteful issue. — The *Bulletin* buries it with a cheerful paragraph.

The literary standard of the principal Australian weeklies, when the *Bulletin* started, was practically the same as it is now; the only difference, if any, being that the other great weeklies have been forced, because of the *Bulletin*, and for very shame's sake, to pay for decent original Australian sketches and stories for their Christmas numbers. The weeklies are run in connection with and in the same office as the "Great Australian Dailies" (*vide Review of Reviews*) and filled with matter which has done duty in the dailies during the week. The hopeless monotony of the weekly pages is not relieved by sketches and portraits of race winners, imported cows, bulls and sheep (also hogs); the "landing of the Governor" and his inevitable visit to Mudgee-Budgee or some such place, and portraits of prominent Australian political humbugs. These papers are owned by old and wealthy first families who have nothing in common with the future of Australia as a nation; and the present proprietors have retained or inherited the old camp-idea (the old spirit which was ever the curse of new, and specially of gold-bearing countries) the old idea of making as much out of the country as they could and then going "Home". The editors and sub-editors are mostly new-chums who feel as much of the spirit of Australia and know as much about the Bush as Downing Street knows about the Colonies in general. Until recently the usual answer to an Australian writer or artist was "We are very sorry, but we have already exceeded our allowance for outside contributions. We may be able to give a small sum — it would only be an honorarium — for a suitable short Christmas story for our next Christmas number."

The *Bulletin* paragraphic style is bright and unique, and the stories and sketches are Australian, written by men who know Australia. *Bulletin* contributors range from lords to swagmen, tramps and felons. If a good story is heard in the Bush — "You must send that to the *Bulletin*" or "Someone ought to send that to the *Bulletin*". If an act of tyranny or injustice comes to light — "Write to the *Bulletin* about it."

Every line that goes into the *Bulletin* is original, as far as mortal editors can be sure. And every line is paid for. Even suggestions for the artists, no matter how crude in the original, are paid for liberally if used.

It was through the existence of the *Bulletin* alone that a purely Australian school of Art and Literature became possible. When I say art, I mean also painting, for the successful young Australian artists of recent years made bread and butter by sketching for the *Bulletin* while painting their pictures.

Before the advent of the *Bulletin,* no Australian writer could hope for more than the barest notice of the existence of his work in book form unless the book bore the name of a London publishing firm. Australian literature had to fight its way home to its own country by way of England. Australian editors seemed not to have the courage to judge an Australian's work on its merits, nor to notice it until it had been reviewed by an English magazine, and then only, or barely so far as it had been noticed. The Australian writer until he got a "London hearing" was sometimes grudgingly accepted as "the Australian Burns", "the Australian Bret Harte", etc. etc. and, later on, as "the Australian Kipling".

There was no criticism worthy of the name. An Australian writer published a volume of short stories which happened to include a goldfield story, and the best that could be said of him was that his work was "an excellent specimen of that style of writing which Bret Harte set the world imitating in vain, and, being full of local colour, was no unworthy copy of the Great Master". The critic evidently had not either read the book or studied the great master; and he knew nothing of Australian goldfields' life. The Australian wrote a short story, and a story of the diggings; Bret Harte wrote short stories and stories of mining; Bret Harte was a big name — that was enough for the critic.

Then there was all the paltry journalistic caddishness, jealousy and toadyism of a small city where journals were edited by surplus little men of London journalism who could not make bread and butter in their own country and had an ignorant contempt for Australia and all that was Australian.

Neither the Press nor the Government seemed to recognize the possibility of Australian Letters. They made no distinction between an Australian writer in their offices and the veriest dead-beat political billet hunter; but, were it the case of a well-connected chump from home, everything was possible, even to the running of a special train. It was easy for a Britisher "dood" — especially one with an eye-glass to his eye and a letter of introduction to "His Nibs" of the time, and who claimed to represent some Mud-hole, or Eat-and-Swill Gazette "at home" — to obtain and hold for years a free pass over our railways and have his slush printed in the journals.

But mark! so soon as a southern writer went "Home" and got some recognition there, he became "So-and-So", the well-known Australian author whose work had attracted attention in London lately, and we first heard of him, by cable perhaps, even though he might have been writing at his best for years in Australia.

It was not the fault of the Australian people, either, for, when the journal, which holds, in its time and country, and with regard to the position of its contemporaries (and perhaps in the history of the world's journalism), an unique position — when the *Bulletin* proved to the people of Australia that they had artists and writers and the material for a distinct literature, they took the first opportunity of showing their appreciation of the fact, and that the shameful neglect of the past could not be charged to them. The first of the purely Australian series of books published by Angus & Robertson of Sydney — and a book of verse by the way, published at 5/- — is now going into its thirtieth thousand. For their courage and enterprise with regard to Australian literature, Angus & Robertson take second place to the *Bulletin*, and richly deserve their success. Even the *Bulletin,* until recently, held that the Australian writer who attempted to publish his work in Australia "did himself a cruel and irreparable injury".

The *Bulletin* has always sought out and encouraged Australian writers, and taken their work in preference to any other. I remember, if you took work to Archibald which was not distinctly Australian, he'd say: "Yes, that's a very good little thing, old man, but it might have been written in Greenland. We want Australian stuff — we want the Australian atmosphere."

And he has it. The Australian atmosphere is in the *Bulletin*, and the *Bulletin* is the spirit of Australia.

And all this without prejudice, by the way, for my work has never been so severly criticized, and I have never been so severely kicked for my shortcomings, as in the pages of the *Bulletin*.

The *Bulletin* recently remarked humorously that when it started it couldn't afford to pay its contributors to say nothing, consequently they were constantly breaking out and saying things — and they've got the habit to this day.

The following, from a Sydney daily, is a fair example of the art of saying nothing.

> As foreshadowed in a recent issue, everything seems to point to one of two things: either a speedy termination of the war on account of the apparently complete demoralisation of the Boer forces opposed to General Roberts, or a struggle to the bitter end, prolonged into many months of irritating guerilla warfare. How far we are in the right time alone can show. We leave it to our readers to . . . etc., etc.

Or this, from another daily:

> We believe that we may safely affirm that all right thinking Australians realize that the willingness evinced by the various peoples of the Australian Colonies to federate and become a single Commonwealth does not rise from a wish to become less English, but from a healthy desire to become, if possible, more Australian in fact . . . etc., etc.

And recently the Cockney editor of a leading Australian daily spoke of Australian horses as being able to travel day and night for an indefinite period, and, in time of drought, being perfectly satisfied with a bunch of mulga at the end of the day (*mulga* is a coarse scrub only eaten by sheep or cattle in the last stage of starvation). The blunders made by the Australian City Press with regard to the Bush are scarcely less ridiculous than the blunders made by the Home papers in matters concerning Australia in general. (I recently saw, in a leading London illustrated, a picture of "Hobart, the capital of Victoria, Australia"!)

So you see there was room in Australia for a much less outspoken and brilliant paper than the Sydney *Bulletin*. . . . [Lawson then includes an article on "The Push" from the *Bulletin*, 21 January 1899, before concluding.]

Send Round the Hat

> Now this is the creed from the Book of the Bush —
> Should be simple and plain to a dunce:
> "If a man's in a hole you must pass round the hat —
> Were he jail-bird or gentleman once."

"Is it any harm to wake yer?"

It was about nine o'clock in the morning, and, though it was Sunday morning, it was no harm to wake me; but the shearer had mistaken me for a deaf Jackeroo, who was staying at the shanty and was something like me, and had good-naturedly shouted almost at the top of his voice, and he woke the whole shanty. Anyway he woke three or four others who were sleeping on beds and stretchers, and one on a shake-down on the floor, in the same room. It had been a wet night, and the shanty was full of shearers from Big Billabong Shed which had cut-off the day before. My room mates had been drinking and gambling over night, and they swore luridly at the intruder for disturbing them.

He was six-foot-three or thereabout. He was loosely built, bony, sandy-complexioned and grey eyed. He wore a good-humoured grin at most times, as I noticed later on; he was of a type of Bushman that I always liked — the sort that seem to get more good-natured the longer they grow, yet are hard-knuckled and would accommodate a man who wanted to fight, or thrash a bully in a good-natured way. The sort that like to carry somebody's baby round, and cut wood, carry water and do little things for overworked married Bush-women. He wore a saddle-tweed sac suit two sizes too small for him, and his face, neck, great hands and bony wrists were covered with sun blotches and freckles.

"I hope I ain't disturbing yer," he shouted, as he bent over my bunk, "but there's a cove —"

"You needn't shout!" I interrupted, "I'm not deaf."

"Oh — I beg your pardon!" he shouted. "I didn't know I was yellin'. I thought you was the deaf feller."

"Oh, that's all right," I said. "What's the trouble?"

"Wait till them other chaps is done swearin' and I'll tell yer," he said. He spoke with a quiet, good-natured drawl, with something of the nasal twang, but tone and drawl distinctly Australian — altogether apart from that of the Americans.

"Oh, spit it out for Christ's sake, Long-un!" yelled One-eyed Bogan, who had been the worst swearer in a rough shed, and he fell back on his bunk as if his previous remarks had exhausted him.

"It's that there sick Jackeroo that was pickin'-up at Big Billabong," said the Giraffe. "He had to knock off the first week, an' he's been here ever since. They're sendin' him away to the hospital in Sydney by the speeshall train. They're just goin' to take him up in the waggonette to the railway station, an' I thought I might as well go round with the hat an' get him a few bob. He's got a missus and kids in Sydney."

"Yer always goin' round with yer gory hat!" growled Bogan. "Yer'd blanky well take it round in hell!"

"That's what he's doing, Bogan," muttered "Gentleman Once", on the shake down, with his face to the wall.

The hat was a genuine "cabbage tree", one of the sort that "last a lifetime", it was well coloured, almost black in fact with weather and age, and it had a new strap round the base of the crown. I looked into it and saw a dirty pound note and some silver. I dropped in half a crown, which was more than I could spare, for I had only been a green hand at Big Billabong.

"Thank yer!" he said. "Now then, you fellers!"

"I wish you'd keep your hat on your head, and your money in your pockets and your sympathy somewhere else," growled Jack Moonlight as he raised himself painfully on his elbow and felt under his pillow for two half-crowns. "Here," he said, "here's two half-casers. Chuck 'em in and let me sleep for God's sake!"

"Gentleman Once", the gambler, rolled round on his shake-down, bringing his good-looking, dissipated face from the wall. He had turned in in his clothes and with consider-able exertion he shoved his hand down into the pocket of his trousers, which were a tight fit. He brought up a roll of pound notes and could find no silver.

"Here," he said to the Giraffe, "I might as well lay a quid. I'll chance it anyhow. Chuck it in."

"You've got rats this mornin', Gentleman Once," growled

the Bogan. "It ain't a blanky horse race."

"P'r'aps I have," said Gentleman Once, and he turned to
the wall again with his head on his arm.

"Now, Bogan, yer might as well chuck in somethin'," said
the giraffe.

"What's the matter with the —— Jackeroo?" asked the
Bogan, tugging his trousers from under the mattress.

Moonlight said somethiing in a low tone.

"The —— he has!" said Bogan. "Well, I pity the ——!
Here, I'll chuck in half a —— quid!" and he dropped half a
sovereign into the hat.

The fourth man, who was known to his face as "Barcoo-
Rot", and behind his back as "the Mean Man", had been
drinking all night, and not even Bogan's stump-splitting
adjectives could rouse him. So Bogan got out of bed, and
calling on us (as blanky female cattle) to witness what he was
about to do, he rolled the drunkard over, prospected his
pockets till he made up five shillings (or a "caser" in Bush
language), and "chucked" them into the hat.

And Barcoo-Rot is probably unconscious to this day that
he was ever connected with an act of charity.

The Giraffe struck the deaf jackeroo in the next room. I
heard the chaps cursing "Long-'un" for waking them, and
"Deaf-'un" for being, as they thought at first, the indirect
cause of the disturbance. I heard the Giraffe and his hat
being condemned in other rooms and cursed along the
verandah where more shearers were sleeping; and after a
while I turned out.

The Giraffe was carefully fixing a mattress and pillows on
the floor of a waggonette, and presently a man, who looked
like a corpse, was carried out and lifted into the trap.

As the waggonette started, the shanty keeper — a fat,
soulless-looking man — put his hand in his pocket and
dropped a quid into the hat which was still going round, in
the hands of the Giraffe's mate, little Teddy Thompson, who
was as far below medium height as the Giraffe was above it.

The Giraffe took the horse's head and led him along on the
most level parts of the road towards the railway station, and
two or three chaps went along to help get the sick man into
the train.

The shearing season was over in that district, but I got a
job of house painting, which was my trade, at the Great
Western Hotel (a two-storey brick place), and I stayed in
Bourke for a couple of months.

The Giraffe was a Victorian native from Bendigo. He was well known in Bourke and to many shearers who came through the great dry scrubs from hundreds of miles round. He was stakeholder, drunkard's banker, peacemaker where possible, referee or second to oblige the chaps when a fight was on, big brother or uncle to most of the children in town, final court of appeal when the youngsters had a dispute over a footrace at the school picnic, referee at their fights, and he was the stranger's friend.

"The feller as knows can battle around for himself," he'd say. "But I always like to do what I can for a hard-up stranger cove. I was a green hand Jackeroo once meself, and I know what it is."

"You're always bothering about other people, Giraffe," said Tom Hall, the Shearers' Union Secretary, who was only a couple of inches shorter than the Giraffe. "There's nothing in it, you can take it from me — I ought to know."

"Well, what's a feller to do?" said the Giraffe. "I'm only hangin' round here till shearin' starts agen, an' a cove might as well be doin' something. Besides, it ain't as if I was like a cove that had old people or a wife an' kids to look after. I ain't got no responsibilities. A feller can't be doin' nothing'. Besides, I like to lend a helpin' hand when I can."

"Well, all I've got to say," said Tom, most of whose screw went in borrowed quids, etc. "All I've got to say is that you'll get no thanks, and you might blanky well starve in the end."

"There ain't no fear of me starvin' so long as I've got me hands about me; an' I ain't a cove as wants thanks," said the Giraffe.

He was always helping someone or something. Now it was a bit of a "darnce" that we was gettin' up for the girls; again it was Mrs. Smith, the woman whose husban' was drowned in the flood in the Bogan river lars' Crismas, or that there poor woman down by the Billabong — her husban' cleared out and left her with a lot o'kids. Or Bill Something, the bullocky, who was run over by his own waggon, while he was drunk, and got his leg broke.

Toward the end of his spree One-eyed Bogan broke loose and smashed nearly all the windows of the Carriers' Arms, and next morning he was fined heavily at the police court. About dinner time I encountered the Giraffe and his hat, with two half-crowns in it for a start.

"I'm sorry to trouble yer," he said, "but One-eyed Bogan carn't pay his fine, an' I thought we might fix it up for him. He ain't half a bad sort of feller when he ain't drinkin'. It's only when he gets too much booze in him."

After shearing, the hat usually started round with the Giraffe's own dirty crumpled pound note in the bottom of it as a send-off, later on it was half a sovereign, and so on down to half a crown and a shilling, as he got short of stuff; till in the end he would borrow a "few bob" — which he always repaid after next shearing — "just to start the thing goin'."

There were several yarns about him and his hat. 'Twas said that the hat had belonged to his father, whom he resembled in every respect, and it had been going round for so many years that the crown was worn as thin as paper by the quids, half-quids, casers, half-casers, bobs and tanners or sprats — to say nothing of the scrums — that had been chucked into it in its time and shaken up.

They say that when a new governor visited Bourke the Giraffe happened to be standing on the platform close to the exit, grinning good-humouredly, and the local toady nudged him urgently and said in an awful whisper, "Take off your hat! Why don't you take off your hat?"

"Why?" drawled the Giraffe, "he ain't hard up, is he?"

And they fondly cherish an anecdote to the effect that, when the One-Man-One-Vote Bill was passed (or Payment of Members, or when the first Labour Party went in — I forget on which occasion they said it was) the Giraffe was carried away by the general enthusiasm, got a few beers in him, "chucked" a quid into his hat, and sent it round. The boys contributed by force of habit, and contributed largely, because of the victory and the beer. And when the hat came back to the Giraffe, he stood holding it in front of him with both hands and stared blankly into it for a while. Then it dawned on him.

"Blowed if I haven't bin an' gone an' took up a bloomin' collection for meself!" he said.

He was almost a teetotaller, but he stood his shout in reason. He mostly drank ginger beer.

"I ain't a feller that boozes, but I ain't got nothin' agen chaps enjoyin' themselves, so long as they don't go too far."

It was common for a man on the spree to say to him —

"Here! here's five quid. Look after it for me, Giraffe, will yer, till I git off the booze."

His real name was Bob Brothers, and his Bush names, "Long-'un", "The Giraffe", "Send-round-the-hat", "Chuck-in-a-bob", and "Ginger-ale".

Some years before, camels and Afghan drivers had been imported to the Bourke district; the camels did very well in the dry country, they went right across country and carried everything from sardines to flooring boards. And the teamsters loved the Afghans nearly as much as Sydney furniture makers love the cheap Chinese in the same line. They loved 'em even as union shearers on strike love blacklegs brought up-country to take their places.

Now the Giraffe was a good, straight unionist, but in cases of sickness or trouble he was as apt to forget his unionism, as all Bushmen are, at all times (and for all time), to forget their creed. So, one evening, the Giraffe blundered into the "Carriers' Arms" — of all places in the world — when it was full of teamsters; he had his hat in his hand and some small silver and coppers in it.

"I say, you fellers, there's a poor, sick Afghan in the camp down there along the —"

A big, brawny bullock driver took him firmly by the shoulders, or, rather by the elbows, and ran him out before any damage was done. The Giraffe took it as he took most things, good-humouredly; but, about dusk, he was seen slipping down towards the Afghan camp with a billy of soup.

"I believe," remarked Tom Hall, "that when the Giraffe goes to heaven — and he's the only one of us, as far as I can see, that has a ghost of a show — I believe that when he goes to heaven, the first thing he'll do will be to take his infernal hat round amongst the angels — getting up a collection for this damned world that he left behind."

"Well, I don't think there's so much to his credit, after all," said Jack Mitchell, shearer. "You see, the Giraffe is ambitious; he likes public life, and that accounts for him shoving himself forward with his collections. As for bothering about people in trouble, that's only common curiosity; he's one of those chaps that are always shoving their noses into other people's troubles. And, as for looking after sick men — why! there's nothing the Giraffe likes better than pottering round a sick man, and watching him and studying him. He's awfully interested in sick men, and they're pretty scarce out here. I tell you there's nothing he likes better — except, maybe, it's pottering round a corpse. I believe he'd ride forty miles to help and sympathize and potter round a funeral. The fact of the matter is that the Giraffe is only enjoying himself with other people's troubles — that's all it is. Its only vulgar curiosity and selfishness. I set it down to his ignorance; the way he was brought up."

A few days after the Afghan incident the Giraffe and his hat had a run of luck. A German, one of a party who were building a new wooden bridge over the Big Billabong, was helping unload some girders from a truck at the railway station, when a big log slipped on the skids and his leg was smashed badly. They carried him to the Carrier's Arms, which was the nearest hotel, and into a bedroom behind the bar, and sent for the doctor. The Giraffe was in evidence as usual.

"It vas not that at all," said German Charlie, when they asked him if he was in much pain. "It vas not that at all. I don't cares a damn for der bain; but dis is der tird year — und I vas going home dis year — after der gontract — und der contract yoost commence!"

That was the burden of his song all through, between his groans.

There were a good few chaps sitting quietly about the bar and verandah when the doctor arrived. The Giraffe was sitting at the end of the counter, on which he had laid his hat while he wiped his face, neck and forehead with a big speckled "sweat-rag". It was a very hot day.

The doctor, a good-hearted young Australian, was heard saying something. Then German Charlie, in a voice that rung with pain —

"Make that leg right, doctor — quick! Dis is der tird pluddy year — und I must go home!"

The doctor asked him if he was in great pain.

"Neffer mind der pluddy bain, doctor! Neffer mind der pluddy bain! Dot vas nossing. Make dat leg well quick, doctor. Dis vas der last gontract, and I was going home dis year." Then the words jerked out of him by physical agony: "Der girl vas vaiting dree year, und — by Got! I must go home."

The publican — Watty Braithwaite, known as "Watty Broadweight", or, more familiarly, "Watty Bothways" — turned over the Giraffe's hat in a tired, bored sort of way, dropped a quid into it, and nodded resignedly at the Giraffe.

The Giraffe caught up the hint and the hat with alacrity. The hat went all round town, so to speak; and, as soon as his leg was firm enough not to come loose on the road German Charlie went home.

It was well known that I contributed to the *Sydney Bulletin* and several other papers. The Giraffe's bump of revence was very large, and swelled especially for sick men and poets. He treated me with much more respect than is due from a Bushman to a man, and with an odd sort of extra gentleness I sometimes fancied. But one day he rather surprised me.

"I'm sorry to trouble yer," he said in a shamefaced way. "I don't know as you go in for sportin', but One-eyed Bogan an' Barcoo-Rot is goin' to have a bit of a scrap down the Billybong this evenin', an' —"

"A bit of a what?" I asked.

"A bit of fight to a finish," he said apologetically. "An' the chaps is tryin' to fix up a fiver to put some life into the thing. There's bad blood between One-eyed Bogan and Barcoo-Rot, an' it won't do them any harm to have it out."

It was a great fight, I remember. There must have been a couple of score blood-soaked handkerchiefs (or "sweat-rags") buried in a hole on the field of battle, and the Giraffe was busy the rest of the evening helping to patch up the principals. Later on he took up a small collection for the loser, who happened to be Barcoo-Rot in spite of the advantage of an eye.

The Salvation Army lassie, who went round with the *War Cry*, nearly always sold the Giraffe three copies.

A new-chum parson, who wanted a subscription to build or enlarge a chapel, or something, sought the assistance of the Giraffe's influence with his mates.

"Well," said the Giraffe, "I ain't a churchgoer meself. I ain't what you might call a religious cove, but I'll be glad to do what I can to help yer. I don't suppose I can do much. I ain't been to church since I was a kiddy."

The parson was shocked, but later on he learned to appreciate the Giraffe and his mates, and to love Australia for the Bushman's sake, and it was he who told me the above anecodote.

The Giraffe helped fix some stalls for a Catholic church bazaar, and some of the chaps chaffed him about it in the union office.

"You'll be taking up a collection for a Joss-House down in the Chinamen's camp next," said Tom Hall in conclusion.

"Well, I ain't got nothin' agen the Roming Carflics," said the Giraffe. "An' Father O'Donovan's a very decent sort of cove. He stuck up for the unions all right in the strike anyway." ("He wouldn't be Irish if he wasn't," someone commented.) "I carried swags once for six months with a feller that was a Carflick, an' he was a very straight feller. And a girl I knowed turned Carflick to marry a chap that had got her into trouble, an' she was always jes' the same to me after as she was before. Besides, I like to help everything that's goin' on."

Tom Hall and one or two others went out hurriedly to

have a drink. But we all loved the Giraffe.

He was very innocent and very humorous, especially when he meant to be most serious and philosophical.

"Some of them Bush girls is regular tomboys," he said to me solemnly one day. "Some of them is too cheeky altogether. I remember once I was stoppin' at a place — they was sort of relations o' mine — an' they put me to sleep in a room off the verander, where there was a glass door an' no blinds. An' the first mornin' the girls — they was sort o' cousins o' mine — they come gigglin' and foolin' round outside the door on the verander, an' kep' me in bed till nearly ten o'clock. I had to put me trowsis on under the bedclothes in the end. But I got back on 'em the next night," he reflected.

"How did you do that, Bob?" I asked.

"Why, I went to bed in me trowsis!"

One day I was on a plank, painting the ceiling of the bar of the Great Western Hotel. I was anxious to get the job finished. The work had been kept back most of the day by chaps handing up long beers to me, and drawing my attention to the alleged fact that I was putting on the paint wrong side out. I was slapping it on over the last few boards when —

"I'm very sorry to trouble yer; I always seem to be troublin' yer; but there's that there woman and them girls—"

I looked down — about the first time I had looked down on him — and there was the Giraffe, with his hat brim up on the plank and two half-crowns in it.

"Oh, that's all right, Bob," I said, and I dropped in half a crown.

There were shearers in the bar, and presently there was some barracking. It appeared that that there woman and them girls were strange women, in the local as well as the Biblical sense of the word, who had come from Sydney at the end of the shearing season, and had taken a cottage on the edge of the scrub on the outskirts of the town. There had been trouble this week in connection with a row at their establishment, and they had been fined, warned off by the police, and turned out by their landlord.

"This is a bit too red hot, Giraffe," said one of the shearers. "Them ——s has made enough out of us coves. They've got plenty of stuff, don't you fret. Let 'em go to ——! I'm blanked if I give a sprat."

"They ain't got their fares to Sydney," said the Giraffe. "An', what's more, the little 'un is sick, an' two of them has kids in Sydney."

"How the —— do you know?"

"Why, one of 'em come to me an' told me all about it."

There was an involuntary guffaw.

"Look here, Bob," said Billy Woods, the Rouseabout's Secretary, kindly. "Don't you make a fool of yourself. You'll have all the chaps laughing at you. Those girls are only working you for all you're worth. I suppose one of 'em came crying and whining to you. Don't you bother about them. *You* don't know them; they can pump water a moment's notice. You haven't had any experience with women yet, Bob."

"She didn't come whinin' and cryin' to me," said the Giraffe, dropping his twanging drawl a little. "She looked me straight in the face an' told me all about it."

"I say, Giraffe," said Box-o'-Tricks, "what have you been don'? You've bin down there on the nod. I'm surprised at yer, Giraffe."

"An' he pretends to be so gory soft an' innocent too," growled the Bogan. "We know all about you, Giraffe."

"Look here, Giraffe," said Mitchell the shearer. "I'd never have thought it of you. We all thought you were the only virgin youth west the river; I always thought you were a moral young man. You mustn't think that because your conscience is pricking you everyone else's is."

"I ain't had anythin' to do with them," said the Giraffe, drawling again. "I ain't a cove that goes in for that sort of thing. But other chaps has, and I think they might as well help 'em out of their fix."

"They're a rotten crowd," said Billy Woods. "You don't know them, Bob. Don't bother about them — they're not worth it. Put your money in your pocket. You'll find a better use for it before next shearing."

"Better shout, Giraffe," said Box-o'-Tricks.

Now in spite of the Giraffe's softness he was the hardest man in Bourke to move when he'd decided on what he thought was "the fair thing to do". Another peculiarity of his was that on occasion, such for instance as "sayin' a few words" at a strike meeting, he would straighten himself, drop the twang, and rope in his drawl, so to speak.

"Well, look here, you chaps," he said now. "I don't know anything about them women. I s'pose they're bad, but I don't suppose they're worse than men has made them. All I know is that there's four women turned out, without any stuff, and every woman in Bourke, an' the police, an' the law agen 'em. An' the fact that they is women is agenst 'em most of all. You don't expect 'em to hump their swags to Sydney! Why, only I ain't got the stuff I wouldn't trouble yer. I'd pay their fares meself. Look," he said, lowering his voice, "there they are now, an' one of the girls is cryin'. Don't let 'em see yer lookin'."

I dropped softly from the plank and peeped out with the rest.

They stood by the fence on the opposite side of the street, a bit up towards the railway station, with their portmanteaux and bundles at their feet. One girl leant with her arms on the fence rail and her face buried in them, another was trying to comfort her. The third girl and the woman stood facing our way. The woman was good-looking; she had a hard face, but it might have been made hard. The third girl seemed half defiant, half inclined to cry. Presently she went to the other side of the girl who was crying on the fence and put her arm round her shoulder. The woman suddenly turned her back on us and stood looking away over the paddocks.

The hat went round. Billy Woods was first, then Box-o'-Tricks, and then Mitchell.

Billy contributed with eloquent silence. "I was only jokin', Giraffe," said Box-o'-Tricks, dredging his pockets for a couple of shillings. It was some time after the shearing, and most of the chaps were hard up.

"Ah, well," sighed Mitchell. "There's no help for it. If the Giraffe would take up a collection to import some decent girls to this God-forgotten hole there might be some sense in it. . . . It's bad enough for the Giraffe to undermine our religious prejudices, and tempt us to take a morbid interest in sick chows and Afghans, and blacklegs and widows; but when he starts mixing us up with strange women it's time to buck." And he prospected his pockets and contributed two shillings, some old pennies, and a pinch of tobacco dust.

"I don't mind helping the girls, but I'm damned if I'll give a penny to help the old ——" said Tom Hall.

"Well, she was a girl once herself," drawled the Giraffe.

The Giraffe went round to the other pubs and to the union offices, and when he returned he seemed satisfied with the plate, but troubled about something else.

"I don't know what to do for them for tonight," he said. "None of the pubs or boardin'-houses will hear of them, an' there ain't no empty houses, an' the women is all agen 'em."

"Not all," said Alice, the big, handsome barmaid from Sydney. "Come here, Bob." She gave the Giraffe half a sovereign and a look for which some of us would have paid him ten pounds — had we had the money, and had the look been transferable.

"Wait a minute, Bob," she said, and she went in to speak to the landlord.

"There's an empty bedroom at the end of the store in the yard," she said when she came back. "They can camp there for tonight if they behave themselves. You'd better tell 'em, Bob."

"Thank yer, Alice," said the Giraffe.

Next day, after work, the Giraffe and I drifted together and down by the river in the cool of the evening, and sat on the edge of the steep, drought-parched bank.

"I heard you saw your lady friends off this morning, Bob," I said, and was sorry I said it, even before he answered.

"Oh, they ain't no friends of mine," he said. "Only four poor devils of women. I thought they mightn't like to stand waitin' with the crowd on the platform, so I jest offered to get their tickets an' told 'em to wait round at the back of the station till the bell rung. . . . An' what do yer think they did, Harry?" he went on, with an exasperatingly unintelligent grin. "Why, they wanted to kiss me."

"Did they?"

"Yes. An' they would have done it, too, if I hadn't been so long. . . . Why, I'm blessed if they didn't kiss me hands."

"You don't say so."

"God's truth. Somehow I didn't like to go on the platform with them after that; besides they was cryin', and I can't stand women cryin'. But some of the chaps put them into an empty carriage." He thought a moment. Then —

"There's some terrible good-hearted fellers in the world," he reflected.

I thought so too.

"Bob," I said, "you're a single man. Why don't you get married and settle down?"

"Well," he said, "I ain't got no wife an' kids, that's a fact. But it ain't my fault."

He may have been right about the wife. But I thought of the look that Alice had given him, and —

"Girls seem to like me right enough," he said, "but it don't go no further than that. The trouble is that I'm so long, and I always seem to get shook after little girls. At least, there one little girl in Bendigo that I was properly gone on."

"And wouldn't she have you?"

"Well, it seems not."

"Did you ask her?"

"Oh, yes, I asked her right enough."

"Well, and what did she say?"

"She said it would be rediculus for her to be seen trottin' alongside of a chimbly like me."

"Perhaps she didn't mean that. There are any amount of little women who like tall men."

"I thought of that too — afterwards. P'r'aps she didn't mean it that way. I s'pose the fact of the matter was that she didn't cotton on to me, and wanted to let me down easy. She didn't want to hurt me feelin's, if yer understand — she was a very good-hearted little girl. There's some terrible tall fellers where I come from, and I know two as married little girls."

He seemed a hopeless case.

"Sometimes," he said, "sometimes I wish that I wasn't so blessed long."

"There's that there deaf Jackeroo," he reflected presently. "He's something in the same fix about girls as I am. He's too deaf and I'm too long."

"How do you make that out?" I asked. "He's got three girls, to my knowledge, and, as for being deaf, why, he gasses more than any man in the town, and knows more of what's going on than old Mother Brindle the washer-woman."

"Well, look at that now!" said the Giraffe, slowly, "Who'd have thought it? He never told me he had three girls, an' as for hearin' news, I always tell him anything that's goin' on that I think he doesn't catch. He told me his trouble was that whenever he went out with a girl people could hear what they was sayin' — at least they could hear what she was sayin' to him, an' draw their own conclusions, he said. He said he went out one night with a girl, and some of the chaps foxed 'em an' heard her sayin' 'don't' to him, an' put it all round town."

"What did she say 'don't' for?" I asked.

"He didn't tell me that, but I s'pose he was kissin' her or huggin' her or something."

"Bob," I said presently, "didn't you try the little girl in Bendigo a second time?"

"No," he said. "What was the use. She was a good little girl, and I wasn't goin' to go botherin' her. I ain't the sort of cove that goes hangin' round where he isn't wanted. But somehow I couldn't stay about Bendigo after she gave me the hint, so I thought I'd come over an' have a knock round on this side for a year or two."

"And you never wrote to her?"

"No. What was the use of goin' pesterin' her with letters? I know what trouble letters give me when I have to answer one. She'd have only had to tell me the straight truth in a letter an' it wouldn't have done me any good. But I've pretty well got over it by this time."

A few days later I went to Sydney. The Giraffe was the last I shook hands with from the carriage window, and he slipped something in a piece of newspaper into my hand.

"I hope yer won't be offended," he drawled, "but some of the chaps thought you mightn't be too flush of stuff — you've been shoutin' a good deal; so they put a quid or two together. They thought it might help yer to have a bit of a fly round in Sydney.

I was back in Bourke before next shearing. On the evening of my arrival I ran against the Giraffe; he seemed strangely shaken over something, but he kept his hat on his head.

"Would yer mind takin' a stroll as fur as the Billerbong?" he said. "I got something I'd like to tell yer."

His big, brown, sun-burnt hands trembled and shook as he took a letter from his pocket and opened it.

"I've just got a letter," he said. "A letter from that little girl at Bendigo. It seemed it was all a mistake. I'd like you to read it. Somehow I feel as if I want to talk to a feller, and I'd rather talk to you than any of them other chaps."

It was a good letter, from a big-hearted little girl. She had been breaking her heart for the great ass all these months. It seemed that he had left Bendigo without saying good-bye to her. "Somehow I couldn't bring meself to it," he said, when I taxed him with it. She had never been able to get his address until last week; then she got it from a Bourke man who had gone South. She called him "an' awful long fool", which he was, without the slightest doubt, and she implored him to write, and come back to her.

"And will you go back, Bob?" I asked.

"My oath! I'd take the train tomorrer only I ain't got the stuff. But I've got a stand in Big Billerbong shed an' I'll soon knock a few quid together. I'll go back as soon as ever shearin's over. I'm goin' to write away to her tonight."

The Giraffe was the "ringer" of Big Billabong Shed that season. His tallies averaged 120 a day. He only sent his hat round once during shearing, and it was noticed that he hesitated at first and only contributed half a crown. But then it was a case of a man being taken from the shed by the police for wife desertion.

"It's always that way," commented Mitchell. "Those soft, good-hearted fellows always end by getting hard and selfish. The world makes 'em so. It's the thought of the soft fools they've been that finds out sooner or later and makes 'em repent. Like as not the Giraffe will be the meanest man out-back before he's done."

When Big Billabong cut out, and we got back to Bourke with our dusty swags and dirty cheques, I spoke to Tom Hall —

"Look here, Tom," I said. "That long fool, the Giraffe, has been breaking his heart for a little girl in Bendigo ever since he's been out-back, and she's been breaking her heart for him, and the ass didn't know it till he got a letter from her just before Big Billabong started. He's going tomorrow morning."

That evening Tom stole the Giraffe's hat. "I s'pose it'll turn up in the mornin'", said the Giraffe. "I don't mind a lark," he added, "but it does seem a bit red hot for the chaps to collar a cove's hat and a feller goin's away for good, p'r'aps, in the mornin'."

Mitchell started the thing going with a quid.

"It's worth it," he said, "to get rid of him. We'll have some peace now. There won't be so many accidents or women in trouble when the Giraffe and his blessed hat are gone. Anyway, he's an eyesore in the town, and he's getting on my nerves for one. . . . Come on, you sinners! Chuck 'em in; we're only taking quids and half-quids."

About daylight next morning Tom Hall slipped into the Giraffe's room at the Carriers' Arms. The Giraffe was sleeping peacefully. Tom put the hat on a chair by his side. The collection had been a record one, and, besides the packet of money in the crown of the hat, there was a silver-mounted pipe with case — the best that could be bought in Bourke, a gold brooch, and several trifles — besides an ugly valentine of a long man in his shirt walking the room with a twin on each arm.

Tom was about to shake the Giraffe by the shoulder, when he noticed a great foot, with about half a yard of big-boned ankle and shank, sticking out at the bottom of the bed. The temptation was too great. Tom took up the hair-brush, and, with the back of it, he gave a smart rap on the point of an in-growing toe-nail, and slithered.

We heard the Giraffe swearing good-naturedly for a while,

and then there was a pregnant silence. He was staring at the hat we supposed.

We were all up at the station to see him off. It was rather a long wait. The Giraffe edged me up to the other end of the platform.

He seemed overcome.

"There's — there's some terrible good-hearted fellers in this world," he said. "You mustn't forget 'em, Harry, when you make a big name writin'. I'm — well, I'm blessed if I don't feel as if I was jist goin' to blubber!"

I was glad he didn't. The Giraffe blubberin' would have been a spectacle. I steered him back to his friends.

"Ain't you going to kiss me, Bob?" said the Great Western's big, handsome barmaid, as the bell rang.

"Well, I don't mind kissin' you, Alice," he said, wiping his mouth. "But I'm goin' to be married, yer know." And he kissed her fair on the mouth.

"There's nothin' like gettin' into practice," he said, grinning round.

We thought he was improving wonderfully; but at the last moment something troubled him.

"Look here, you chaps," he said hesitatingly, with his hand in his pocket, "I don't know what I'm going to do with all this stuff. There's that there poor washerwoman that scalded her legs liftin' the boiler of clothes off the fire —"

We shoved him into the carriage. He hung — about half of him — out the window, wildly waving his hat, till the train disappeared in the scrub.

And, as I sit here writing by lamplight at mid-day, in the midst of a great city of shallow social sham, of hopeless, squalid poverty, of ignorant selfishness, cultured or brutish, and of noble and heroic endeavour frowned down or callously neglected, I am almost aware of a burst of sunshine in the room, and a long form leaning over my chair, and —

"Excuse me for troublin' yer; I'm always troublin' yer; but there's that there poor woman. . . ."

And I wish I could immortalize him!

THE SHEARERS

No church-bell rings them from the Track,
    No pulpit lights their blindness—
'Tis hardship, drought and homelessness
    That teach those Bushmen kindness:
The mateship born of barren lands,
    Of toil and thirst and danger—
The camp-fare for the stranger set,
    The first place to the stranger.

They do the best they can today—
    Take no thought of the morrow;
Their way is not the old-world way—
    They live to lend and borrow.
When shearing's done and cheques gone wrong,
    They call it "time to slither"—
They saddle up and say "So-long!"
    And ride — the Lord knows whither.

And though he may be brown or black,
    Or wrong man there or right man,
The mate that's honest to his mates
    They call that man a "white man"!
They tramp in mateship side by side—
    The Protestant and "Roman"—
They call no biped lord or "sir",
    And touch their hats to no man!

They carry in their swags, perhaps,
    A portrait and a letter—
And, maybe, deep down in their hearts,
    The hope of "something better".
Where lonely miles are long to ride,
    And all days seem recurrent,
There's lots of time to think of men
    They might have been — but weren't.

They turn their faces to the west
    And leave the world behind them—
(Their drought-dried graves are seldom green
    Where even mates can find them).
They know too little of the world
    To rise to wealth or greatness:
But in this book of mine I pay
    My tribute to their straightness.

A Sketch of Mateship

Bill and Jim, professional shearers, were coming into Bourke from the Queensland side. They were horsemen and had two pack-horses. At the last camp before Bourke Jim's pack-horse got disgusted and homesick during the night and started back for the place where he was foaled. Jim was little more than a newchum-Jackeroo; he was no Bushman and generally got lost when he went down the next gully. Bill was a Bushman, so it was decided that he should go back to look for the horse.

Now Bill was going to sell his pack-horse, a well-bred mare, in Bourke, and he was anxious to get her into the yards before the horse sales were over; this was to be the last day of the sales. Jim was the best "barracker" of the two; he had great imagination; he was a very entertaining story-teller and conversationalist in social life, and a glib and a most impressive liar in business, so it was decided that he should hurry on into Bourke with the mare and sell her for Bill. Seven pounds, reserve.

Next day Bill turned up with the missing horse and saw Jim standing against a verandah post of the "Carriers' Arms", with his hat down over his eyes, and thoughtfully spitting in the dust. Bill rode over to him.

"Ullo, Jim."

"'Ullo, Bill. I see you got him."

"Yes, I got him."

Pause.

"Where'd yer find him?"

"'Bout ten mile back. Near Ford's Bridge. He was just feedin' along."

Pause. Jim shifted his feet and spat in the dust.

"Well," said Bill at last. "How did you get on, Jim?"

"Oh, all right," said Jim. "I sold the mare."

"That's right," said Bill. "How much did she fetch?"

"Eight quid;" then, rousing himself a little and showing some emotion, "An' I could 'a' got ten quid for her if I hadn't been a dam' fool."

"Oh, that's good enough," said Bill.

"I could 'a' got ten quid if I'd 'a' waited."

"Well, it's no use cryin'. Eight quid is good enough. Did you get the stuff?"

"Oh, yes. They parted all right. If I hadn't been such a dam' fool an' rushed it, there was a feller that would 'a' given ten quid for that mare."

"Well, don't break yer back about it," said Bill. "Eight is good enough."

"Yes. But I could 'a' got ten," said Bill, languidly, putting his hand in his pocket.

Pause. Bill sat waiting for him to hand over the money; but Jim withdrew his hand empty, stretched, and said —

"Ah, well, Bill, I done it in. Lend us a couple o' notes."

Jim had been drinking and gambling all night and he'd lost the eight pounds as well as his own money.

Bill didn't explode. What was the use? He should have known that Jim wasn't to be trusted with money in town. It was he who had been the fool. He sighed and lent Jim a pound, and they went in to have a drink.

Now it strikes me that if this had happened in a civilized country (like England) Bill would have had Jim arrested and jailed for larceny as a bailee, or embezzlement, or whatever it was. And would Bill or Jim or the world have been any better for it?

Drifting Apart

I told you how we took up a selection at Lahey's Creek, and how little Jim had convulsions on the road out, and Brighten's sister-in-law saved him; and about the hard struggle we had for years, and poor Mrs. Spicer, who was "past carin'", and died like a broken-down horse; and how I was lucky, got to be a squatter, and bought a brand-new, first-class double buggy for Mary — and how her brother James brought it as a surprise to Lahey's Creek. And before that I told you all about how I first met Mary at Haviland Station, and how we fell in love, courted, and got married. Ah, well! How the times goes by!

I had luck, and did well for three or four seasons running. I was always going to build a new brick-and-shingle house for Mary — bricks and shingles are cooler than slabs and iron — but that was one of the houses I never built — except in the air. I've lived on the bank of the creek, and the place looked about the same as ever — and about as dreary and lonely and God-forsaken. I didn't even get any more furniture, in a good many of 'em.

So we still lived in the old slab-and-bark house and Mary got tired of bothering me about it. I'd always say, "Wait till the new house is built." It was no home for a woman. I can see that now.

You remember how I was always talking about making a nice home for Mary, and giving her more of my time, and trying to make her life a little brighter when things brightened up. I tried to do it by taking her trips to Sydney whenever I could get her to go, leaving her brother James to look after the station. At first I'd send the black boy ahead with fresh horses, and we'd flash down in the buggy the hundred miles or so of glorious mountain and valley road to Wallerawang, leave the buggy and two horses there, and take the train over the Blue Mountains to the Big Smoke.

Then again, when wool was up, I'd take berths in a sleeping carriage from Dubbo, and put up at the *Royal* in Sydney, and do the thing in great style. But Mary thought the sleeping carriage was unnecessary expense, and she didn't like stopping at an hotel. She was always anxious about me and the drink. She preferred some "cheap, quiet place". "A run of bad seasons might come along at any time, Joe," she said, "and then you'll be sorry for the money you throw away now."

I thought it was very unjust of her to talk of throwing away money when I was only trying to give her pleasure — but then women were always unjust and unreasonable.

"If we don't enjoy ourselves when we've got the chance, we never will," I said.

"We could do that just as well at home, Joe," said Mary, "if you only knew — if you'd listen to me, and go the right way to work about it. Why can't you settle down in your own home, and make it bright, and be contented?"

"Well, what's the use of furniture, or a new house for that matter, when there's no one but Bushies to look at it?" I said. "We might just as well live in a tent. What's the use of burying ourselves in the blasted Bush altogether? We've got two pretty children, and you're good-looking yet, Mary, and it isn't as if we were an old man and woman."

"I'm nearly twenty-seven," said Mary. "I only thought of it today, and it came like a shock to me. I feel like an old woman."

I'd learned enough of women not to argue with Mary while she was in that mood. The fact of the matter was that after the first trip or two she didn't seem to enjoy herself in the city. You see, she always insisted on taking the children with her. She couldn't bring herself to trust them at home with the girl, and I knew that if she did, she'd be worrying all the time, and spoil her pleasure and mine, and so we always took them with us. But they were an awful drag in the city. Mary wouldn't trust 'em with a strange woman or girl, except perhaps for a few hours when they were in bed, and we went to one of the theatres. So we always carted them round the town with us. I soon got tired of humping one or the other of 'em. But crossing the streets was the worst. It was bad enough with Mary when we were out alone. She would hang back when the crossing was clear, and suddenly make a start when there was a rush of traffic, and baulk as often as not, and sometimes turn and run back to the kerb from the middle of the street — me trying to hang on to her all the time — till I'd get rippin' wild, and go for her.

"Damn it all!" I said, "why can't you trust to me and come when I tell you? One would think I came out with the fixed intention of getting you run over, and getting rid of you." And Mary would lose her temper, and say, "Ah, well, Joe, I sometimes think you do want to get rid of me, the way you go on," or something like that, and our pleasure would be spoilt for the day. But with the children! What with one or the other of them always whimpering or crying, and Jim always yelling when we got into a tram, or 'bus, or boat, or into some place that he didn't trust, or when we reckoned we were lost, which was about every twenty minutes — and, what with Mary losing her temper every time I lost mine, there were times when I really wished in my heart I was on my own. . . . Ah, well, there came a day when I had my wish.

I forgot about the hard life in huts and camps in the Bush, and the bitter, heart-breaking struggle she'd shared with me since we were married, and how she'd slaved and fought through the blazing drought on that wretched, lonely selection, in the first year, while I was away with the team most of the time — how she'd stuck to me through thick and thin. I only thought she was very irritable and selfish and unreasonable, and that she ought to be able to keep the children in better order. I believed that she had spoilt them. And I was wild to think how our holiday was being wasted.

After the first time or two, Mary didn't seem to enjoy the theatre. She told me one night, when we got a bit confidential, that the play had depressed her, and made her sad.

"How's that?" I asked.

"Well, Joe," she said, "I don't want to hurt you, Joe, but, if you must know, I was thinking all the time of the past — of our own lives."

That hurt me and made me wild. I'd been thinking, too, all the time I was watching the play, of life as it was, and my own dull, sordid, hopeless, monotonous life in particular. But I hadn't been thinking of hers. The truth seemed that we were getting on each other's nerves — we'd been too long together alone in the Bush; and it isn't good for a man and his wife to be too much alone. I at least had come to think that when Mary said unpleasant things she only did it to irritate me.

"What are you always raking up the past for?" I said. "Can't you have done with it? Ain't I doing my best to make you happy? What more do you want?"

"I want a good many little things, Joe," said Mary.

We quarrelled then, but in the hard, cold, quiet, sarcastic way we'd got into lately — not the old short, fierce quarrel of other days, when we'd make it up, and love each other all the more afterwards. I don't know how much I hurt her, but I know she cut me to the heart sometimes, as a woman can cut a man.

Next evening I went out alone, and didn't get back to the hotel till after twelve. Mary was up, waiting; but she didn't say much, only that she had been afraid to go to bed. Next morning she asked me to stay in and watch the children while she went shopping, and bought the things she wanted to take home, and I did, and we made it up, and got along smoothly until after tea; then I wanted to go out, and Mary didn't want me to — she wanted me to sit on the balcony with her.

I remember she was very earnest about me staying in with her that evening, and if I hadn't been drinking the night before I would have stayed. I waited awhile, and then I got restless, and found I was out of tobacco.

"I will send out for it, Joe," said Mary.

"What nonsense," I said. "I'll run out and get it myself. I'm all right. I'll only be a few minutes."

"Well, if you must go, you must," she said, in the hard tone again.

"I'll only be a few minutes, I tell you," I said. "Don't start the thing again, for God's sake."

"Well, promise me you won't be more than a quarter of an hour," said Mary, "and I'll wait here for you. I don't like being left alone in a place full of strange men."

"That's all right, Mary," I said, and I stepped out for half an hour. I was restless as a hen that didn't know where to lay. I wanted to walk, and was fond of the noise and bustle of the streets. They fascinated me, and dragged me out.

I didn't get back to the hotel till daylight.

I hoped to find Mary asleep, and I went into the bedroom very softly. She was in bed, but she was awake. She took the thing so quietly that it made me uneasy. When an impulsive, determined little woman begins to take things very quietly, it's time for the man to straighten up and look out. She didn't even ask me where I'd been, and that made me more uneasy (I had a good yarn readied up), and when she spoke of a murder case in the *Herald* and asked me if I'd read the divorce case, where a wife sued her husband for drunkenness and adultery, I began to get scared. I wished she'd go for me, and have done with it, but she didn't. At last, at breakfast, she said —

"I think we'll go home today, Joe; we'll take the evening train from Redfern. You can get any business done that you want to do by that time."

And I thought so, too.

It was a miserable journey — one of the most dreary and miserable I ever made in my life. Both the children were peevish all the way. While there were other passengers in the carriage I couldn't talk to Mary, and when we were alone she wouldn't talk to me — except to answer yes and no.

The worst of it was that I didn't know what she thought, or how much she suspected. I wondered whether she believed that I had deceived her, and that worried me a lot. I hadn't been drinking much, and I came home sober that morning, so drink was no excuse for me being out all night. I thought once or twice that it would have been much better if I'd come home drunk, with a muddled yarn about meeting an old chum and having a glorious "auld-lang-syne" night at some club.

I was very attentive all the way. I got tea and cake and sandwiches at every refreshment room, and whatever fruit I could lay hands on, and nursed the children to sleep by turns; but it didn't soften Mary. She wasn't a child any longer. She only said, "Thank you, Joe," and as I watched her face it seemed to grow harder and more set and obstinate.

"Mary," I said at last, when we were going down the Great Zig-zag, "suppose we get out at Wallerawang, and go up through Cudgegong? We can rest there for a day, and then go on to Gulgong, and see your sister and Dick, and stay there for a night perhaps."

"If you like, Joe," said Mary.

"You'll like to see Hilda, Mary, wouldn't you?"

"Yes, Joe," she said, in the same cold, disinterested tone, "I would like to see her."

The case seemed hopeless. I had first-class tickets through to Dubbo, and would have to get others for the Cudgegong (Mudgee) line; besides, the coach fares would be extra, and I thought Mary would rouse herself, and buck at the waste of money, but she didn't seem to mind that a bit. But Haviland cattle station was on the Cudgegong line, and it was at Haviland where I first met Mary. She was brought up there from a child, and I thought that the sight of the place would break her down, if anything would.

We changed trains at Wallerawang Junction at midnight,
and passed the great Capertee Valley and Macdonald's Hole
in the moonlight — a great basin in the mountains, where
"Starlight" and the Marsdens used to ride, and hide sometimes for months together, in *Robbery Under Arms*, and
where thousands of tourists will go some day. All along the
Western line I saw old roads and tracks where I came
droving as a boy, and old camps where I camped; and the
ruins of one old Halfway House, dismal and haunted, in the
heavy scrub, where my old chum Jack Barnes and I had a
glorious spree one time; and Gerty — but never mind that;
and lonely, deserted old roads, where I carried when I grew
up, and often tramped beside the bullocks or horses, and
spouted Gordon's poetry till it lifted me, and wished to God
that I could write like that, or do something, or break away
from the life that was driving me mad. And it all made me
feel very dismal now and hopeless, and I hated the Bush
worse than ever, and made up my mind to take Mary and
the children out of it, just as soon as I could get rid of the
station. I'd take the first reasonable offer that came.

Mary slept, or pretended to sleep, most of the time. and I
kept the children quiet. I watched her face a good deal, and
tried to persuade myself that she hadn't changed much since
the days when I had courted her at Haviland; but somehow,
Mary and the girl I got to love me years ago seemed very
different. It seemed to me as if — well, as if I'd courted a girl
and married a woman. But perhaps it was time and distance
— or I might have changed most. I began to feel myself
getting old (forty was very near), but it had never struck me
that Mary would feel that way too.

We had breakfast at Rylstone. After that Mary talked a
little, but still in a hard, cold way. She wondered how things
were at home, and hoped it would rain soon. She said the
weather looked and smelt like the beginning of a drought.
Hanging out blue lights, I thought. Then she'd be silent for
miles, except to speak to the children; and then I got a
suspicion that she was talking at me through them, and it
made me wild, and I had a job to keep from breaking out. It
was during that journey that I first began to wonder what
my wife was thinking about, and to worry over it — to
distrust her silence. I wished she'd cry, and then it struck me
that I hadn't seen tears in Mary's eyes for God knows how
long — and the thought of it hurt me a lot.

We had the carriage to ourselves after Dungaree, and
Haviland was the next station. I wished we could have
passed Haviland by moonlight, or in the evening, instead of

the garish morning. I thought it would have been more likely to soften Mary. I'd rehearsed the business, half unconsciously, humbugging myself, as men will. I was going to be very silent, and look extra sad, and keep gazing out of the window, and never look at Mary, and try, if possible, to squeeze some suspicious moisture into my eyes, as we passed the place. But I felt by instinct that my barneying and pleading and bluffing and acting and humbugging days were past — also my bullying days. I couldn't work on Mary's feelings now like I used to. I knew, or thought I knew, that she saw through me, and felt that she knew I knew it. Most men's wives see through their husbands sooner or later, and when a wife does, it's time for a husband to drop his nonsense, and go straight. She'll know when he's sincere and when he's not — he needn't be afraid of that.

And so, the nearer we got to Haviland, the more helpless and unprepared I felt. But when the train swung round the horn of the crescent of hills in which Haviland lay there wasn't any need for acting. There was the old homestead, little changed, and as fair as it seemed in those far-away days, nearly eight years ago, when that lanky scamp, Joe Wilson, came hanging round after "Little 'Possum", who was far too good for the likes of him. There was the stable and buggy house that Jack Barnes and I built between shearings. There was the wide, brick-floored, vine-covered verandah where I first saw Mary; and there was the little green flat by the river where I stood up, that moonlight night, like a man, and thrashed big "Romany", the station hand, because he'd said something nasty about little Mary Brand — all the time she was sitting singing with the other girls under the verandah to amuse a new chum Jackeroo. And there, near the willows by the river, was the same old white, hardwood log where Mary and I sat in the moonlight next night, while all the rest were dancing in the big woolshed — when I made her understand how awfully fond of her I was. And there ——

There was no need for humbugging now. The trouble was to swallow the lumps in my throat, and keep back the warm gush of suspicious moisture that came to my eyes. Mary sat opposite, and I stole a glance at her. She was staring out with wide-opened eyes, and there were tears in them — and a scared look, I fancied for the moment. Then suddenly she turned from the window and looked at me, her eyes wide and brimming, and — well, it was the same little Mary, my sweetheart, after our first quarrel years ago.

I jumped up and sat down by her side, and put my arm round her; and she just put her arms round my neck and her head down on my chest, and cried till the children cried too, and little Jim interfered — he thought I was hurting his mother. Then Mary looked up and smiled. She comforted the children, and told them to kiss their father, and for the rest of the journey we talked of those old days, and at last Mary put her arms round my neck, and said —

"You never did deceive me, Joe, did you? I want you to swear that to me."

"No, Mary," I said, "I never did. I swear to God I never did!"

And God knew whether I had done so or not.

"You've got the scar on the bridge of your nose still," said Mary, kissing it, "and" — as if she'd just noticed it for the first time —" why! your hair is greyer than ever," and she pulled down my head, and her fingers began to go through my hair as in the days of old. And when we got to the hotels at Cudgegong, she made me have a bath and lie down on the bed and go to sleep. And when I awoke, late in the afternoon, she was sitting by my side, smoothing my hair.

A Child in the Dark, and a Foreign Father

New Year's Eve! A hot night in midsummer in the drought. It was so dark — with a smothering darkness — that even the low loom of the scrub-covered ridges, close at hand across the creek, was not to be seen. The sky was not clouded for rain, but with drought haze and the smoke of distant bush fires.

Down the hard road to the crossing at Pipeclay Creek sounded the footsteps of a man. Not the crunching steps of an English labourer, clod-hopping contentedly home; these sounded more like the foot-steps of one pacing steadily to and fro, and thinking steadily and hopelessly — sorting out the past. Only the steps went on. A glimmer of white moleskin trousers and a suggestion of light-coloured tweed jacket, now and again, as if in the glimmer of a faint ghost light in the darkness.

The road ran along by the foot of a line of low ridges, or spurs, and, as he passed the gullies or gaps, he felt a breath of hotter air, like blasts from a furnace in the suffocating atmosphere. He followed a two-railed fence for a short distance, and turned in at a white batten gate. It seemed lighter now. There was a house, or, rather, a hut suggested, with white-washed slab walls and a bark roof. He walked quietly round to the door of a detached kitchen, opened it softly, went in and struck a match. A candle stood, stuck in a blot of its own grease, on one end of the dresser. He lit the candle and looked round.

The walls of the kitchen were of split slabs, the roof box-bark, the floor clay, and there was a large clay-lined fireplace, the sides a dirty brown, and the back black. It had evidently never been whitewashed. There was a bed of about a week's ashes, and above it, suspended by a blackened hook and chain from a grimy cross-bar, hung a black bucket full of warm water. The man got a fork, explored the bucket, and found what he expected — a piece of raw corned-beef in water, which had gone off the boil before the meat had been heated through.

The kitchen was furnished with a pine table, a well-made flour bin, and a neat safe and side-board, or dresser — evidently the work of a carpenter. The top of the safe was dirty — covered with crumbs and grease and tea stains. On one corner lay a school exercise book, with a stone ink-bottle and a pen beside it. The book was open at a page written in the form of verse, in a woman's hand, and headed —

"Misunderstood."

He took the edges of the book between his fingers and thumbs, and made to tear it, but, the cover being tough, and resisting the first savage tug, he altered his mind, and put the book down. Then he turned to the table. There was a jumble of dirty crockery on one end, and on the other, set on a sheet of stained newspaper, the remains of a meal — a junk of badly-hacked bread, a basin of dripping (with the fat over the edges), and a tin of treacle. The treacle had run down the sides of the tin on to the paper. Knives, heavy with treacle, lay glued to the paper. There was a dish with some water, a rag, and a cup or two in it — evidently an attempt to wash-up.

The man took up a cup and pressed it hard between his palms, until it broke. Then he felt relieved. He gathered the fragments in one hand, took the candle, and stumbled out to where there was a dust-heap. Kicking a hole in the ashes, he dropped in the bits of broken crockery, and covered them. Then his anger blazed again. He walked quickly to the back door of the house, thrust the door open, and flung in, but a child's voice said from the dark —

"Is that you, father? Don't tread on me, father."

The room was nearly as bare as the kitchen. There was a table, covered with cheap American oilcloth, and, on the other side, a sofa on which a straw mattress, a cloudy blanket, and a pillow without a slip had been thrown in a heap. On the floor, between the sofa and the table, lay a boy — child almost — on a similar mattress, with a cover of coarse sacking, and a bundle of dirty clothes for a pillow. A pale, thinfaced, dark-eyed boy.

"What are you doing here, sonny?" asked the father.

"Mother's bad again with her head. She says to tell you to come in quiet, and sleep on the sofa tonight. I started to wash up and clean up the kitchen, father, but I got sick."

"Why, what is the matter with you, sonny?" His voice quickened, and he held the candle down to the child's face.

"Oh, nothing much, father. I felt sick, but I feel better now."

"What have you been eating?"

"Nothing that I know of; I think it was the hot weather, father."

The father spread the mattress, blew out the candle, and lay down in his clothes. After a while the boy began to toss restlessly.

"Oh, it's too hot, father," he said. "I'm smothering."

The father got up, lit the candle, took a corner of the newspaper-covered "scrim" lining that screened the cracks of the slab wall, and tore it away; then he propped open the door with a chair.

"Oh, that's better already, father," said the boy.

The hut was three rooms long and one deep, with a verandah in front and a skillion, harness and tool room, about half the length, behind. The father opened the door of the next room softly, and propped that open, too. There was another boy on the sofa, younger than the first, but healthy and sturdy-looking. He had nothing on him but a very dirty shirt, a patch-work quilt was slipping from under him, and most of it was on the floor; the boy and the pillow were nearly off, too.

The father fixed him as comfortably as possible, and put some chairs by the sofa to keep him from rolling off. He noticed that somebody had started to scrub this room, and left it. He listened at the door of the third room for a few moments to the breathing within; then he opened it and gently walked in. There was an old-fashioned four-poster cedar bedstead, a chest of drawers, and a baby's cradle made out of a gin-case. The woman was fast asleep. She was a big, strong, and healthy-looking woman, with dark hair and strong, square features. There was a plate, a knife and fork, and egg-shells, and a cup and saucer on the top of the chest of drawers; also two candles, one stuck in a mustard tin, and one in a pickle bottle, and a copy of *Ardath*.

He stepped out into the skillion, and lifted some harness on to its pegs from chaff-bags in the corner. Coming in again, he nearly stumbled over a bucket half-full of dirty water on the floor, with a scrubbing brush, some wet rags, and half a bar of yellow soap beside it. He put these things in the bucket, and carried it out. As he passed through the first room the sick boy said —

"I couldn't lift the saddle of the harness on to the peg, father. I had to leave the scrubbing to make some tea and cook some eggs for mother, and put baby to bed, and then I felt too bad to go on with the scrubbing — and I forgot about the bucket."

"Did the baby have any tea, sonny?"

"Yes. I made her bread and milk, and she ate a big plateful. The calves are in the pen alright, and I fixed the gate. And I brought a load of wood this morning, father, before mother took bad."

"You should not have done that. I told you not to. I could have done that on Sunday. Now, are you sure you didn't lift a log into the cart that was too heavy for you?"

"Quite sure, father. Oh, I'm plenty strong enough to put a load of wood on the cart."

The father lay on his back on the sofa, with his hands behind his head, for a few minutes.

"Aren't you tired, father?" asked the boy.

"No, sonny, not very tired; you must try and go to sleep now," and he reached across the table for the candle, and blew it out.

Presently the baby cried, and in a moment the mother's voice was heard.

"Nils! Nils! Are you there, Nils?"

"Yes, Emma."

"Then for God's sake come and take this child away before she drives me mad! My head's splitting."

The father went in to the child and presently returned for a cup of water.

"She only wanted a drink," the boy heard him say to the mother.

"Well, didn't I tell you she wanted a drink? I've been calling for the last half-hour, with that child screaming, and not a soul to come near me, and me lying here helpless all day, and not a wink of sleep for two nights."

"But, Emma, you were asleep when I came in."

"How can you tell such infernal lies? I ——. To think I'm chained to a man who can't say word of truth! God help me! To have to lie night after night in the same bed with a liar!"

The child in the first room lay quaking with terror, dreading one of those cruel and shameful scenes which had made a hell of his childhood.

"Hush, Emma!" the man kept saying. "Do be reasonable. Think of the children. They'll hear us."

"I don't care if they do. They'll know soon enough, God

knows! I wish I was under the turf!"

"Emma, do be reasonable."

"Reasonable! I ——"

The child was crying again. The father came back to the first room, got something from his coat pocket, and took it in.

"Nils, are you quite mad, or do you want to drive me mad? Don't give the child that rattle! You must be either mad or a brute, and my nerves in this state. Haven't you got the slightest consideration for ——"

"It's not a rattle, Emma; it's a doll."

"There you go again! Flinging your money away on rubbish that'll be on the dust-heap tomorrow, and your poor wife slaving her finger-nails off for you in this wretched hole, and not a decent rag to her back. Me, your clever wife that ought to be ——. Light those candles and bring me a wet towel for my head. I must read now, and try and compose my nerves, if I can."

When the father returned to the first room, the boy was sitting up in bed, looking deathly white.

"Why, what's the matter, sonny?" said the father, bending over him, and putting a hand to his back.

"Nothing, father. I'll be all right directly. Don't you worry, father."

"Where do you feel bad, sonny?"

"In my head and stomach, father; but I'll be all right d'rectly. I've often been that way."

In a minute or two he was worse.

"For God's sake, Nils, take that boy into the kitchen, or somewhere," cried the woman, "or I'll go mad. It's enough to kill a horse. Do you want to drive me into a lunatic asylum?"

"Do you feel better now, sonny?" asked the father.

"Yes, ever so much better, father," said the boy, white and weak. "I'll be all right in a minute, father."

"You had best sleep on the sofa tonight, sonny. It's cooler there."

"No, father, I'd rather stay here; it's much cooler now."

The father fixed the bed as comfortably as he could, and, despite the boy's protest, put his own pillow under his head. Then he made a fire in the kitchen, and hung the kettle and a big billy of water over it. He was haunted by recollections of convulsions amongst the children while they were teething. He took off his boots, and was about to lie down again when the mother called—

"Nils, Nils, have you made a fire?"

"Yes, Emma."

"Then for God's sake make me a cup of tea. I must have it after all this."

He hurried up the kettle — she calling every few minutes to know if "that kettle was boiling yet". He took her a cup of tea, and then a second. She said the tea was slush, and as sweet as syrup, and called for more, and hot water.

"How do you feel now, sonny?" he asked as he lay down on the sofa once more.

"Much better, father. You can put out the light now if you like."

The father blew out the candle, and settled back again, still dressed, save for his coat, and presently the small, weak hand sought the hard, strong, horny, knotted one; and so they lay, as was customary with them. After a while the father leaned over a little and whispered —

"Asleep, sonny?"

"No, father."

"Feel bad again?"

"No, father."

Pause.

"What are you thinking about, sonny?"

"Nothing, father."

"But what is it? What are you worrying about? Tell me."

"Nothing, father, only — It'll be a good while yet before I grow up to be a man, won't it, father?"

The father lay silent and troubled for a few moments.

"Why do you ask me that question tonight, sonny? I thought you'd done with all that. You were always asking me that question when you were a child. You're getting too old for those foolish fancies now. Why have you always had such a horror of growing up to be a man?"

"I don't know, father. I always had funny thoughts — you know, father. I used to think that I'd been a child once before, and grew up to be a man, and grew old and died."

"You're not well tonight, sonny — that's what's the matter. You're queer, sonny; it's a touch of sun — that's all. Now, try to go to sleep. You'll grow up to be a man, in spite of laying awake worrying about it. If you do, you'll be a man all the sooner."

Suddenly the mother called out —

"Can't you be quiet? What do you mean by talking at this hour of the night? Am I never to get another wink of sleep? Shut those doors, Nils, for God's sake, if you don't want to drive me mad — and make that boy hold his tongue!"

The father closed the doors.

"Better try to go to sleep now, sonny," he whispered, as he lay down again.

The father waited for some time, then, moving very softly, he lit the candle at the kitchen fire, put it where it shouldn't light the boy's face, and watched him. And the child knew he was watching him, and pretended to sleep, and, so pretending, he slept. And the old year died as many old years had died.

The father was up about four o'clock — he worked at his trade in a farming town about five miles away, and was struggling to make a farm and a home between jobs. He cooked bacon for breakfast, washed up the dishes and tidied the kitchen, gave the boys some bread and bacon fat, of which they were very fond, and told the eldest to take a cup of tea and some bread and milk to his mother and the baby when they woke.

The boy milked the three cows, set the milk, and heard his mother calling —

"Nils! Nils!"

"Yes, mother."

"Why didn't you answer when I called you? I've been calling here for the last three hours. Is your father gone out?"

"Yes, mother."

"Thank God! It's a relief to be rid of his everlasting growling. Bring me a cup of tea and the *Australian Journal*, and take this child out and dress her; she should have been up hours ago."

And so the New Year began.

Select Bibliography

Lawson's Major Collections of Verse And Prose

Short Stories in Prose and Verse. Sydney: Louisa Lawson, 1894.

In the Days When the World Was Wide and Other Verses. Sydney: Angus and Robertson, 1896.

While the Billy Boils. Angus and Robertson, 1896.

On the Track and *Over the Sliprails*. Sydney: Angus and Robertson, 1900. (These were also combined in the one volume, with composite title, in the same year)

Verses, Popular and Humorous. Sydney: Angus and Robertson, 1900. (These were also issued as separate volumes, *Popular Verses* and *Humorous Verses*, in the same year.)

The Country I Come From. Edinburgh and London: William Blackwood and Sons, 1901.

Joe Wilson and His Mates. Edinburgh and London: William Blackwood and Sons, 1901.

Children of the Bush. London: Methuen, 1902. (First published in Australia in two volumes, *Send Around the Hat* and *The Romance of the Swag*. Sydney: Angus and Robertson, 1907.)

When I was King and Other Verses. Sydney: Angus and Robertson, 1905.

The Rising of the Court and Other Sketches in Prose and Verse. Sydney: Angus and Robertson, 1910.

The Skyline Riders and Other Verses. Sydney and Dunedin: Fergusson Ltd., N.D. (1910).

For Australia and Other Poems. Melbourne: Standard Publishing Co., 1913.

Triangles of Life and Other Stories. Melbourne: Standard Publishing Co., 1913.

My Army, O, My Army! and Other Songs. Sydney: Tyrrell's Ltd, 1915.

Modern Editions

Cronin, Leonard, ed.   *Henry Lawson: Collected Works.* 2 vols. Sydney: Lansdowne, 1984.

Roderick, Colin, ed.   *Henry Lawson: Collected Verse.* 3 vols. Sydney: Angus and Robertson, 1967-69.

————   *Henry Lawson: Letters.* Sydney: Angus and Robertson, 1970.

————   *Henry Lawson: Short Stories and Sketches.* Sydney: Angus and Robertson, 1972.

————   *Henry Lawson: Autobiographical and Other Writings.* Sydney: Angus and Robertson, 1972.

————   *Henry Lawson: The Master Story-Teller* (a selection from the two 1972 collections of the prose). Sydney: Angus and Robertson, 1984.

Selected Biographical And Critical Studies

Clark, Manning.   *In Search of Henry Lawson.* South Melbourne: Macmillan, 1978.

Kiernan, Brian.   "A Critical Biography of Henry Lawson", introduction to *The Essential Henry Lawson.* South Yarra: Currey O'Neil, 1982.

Matthews, Brian.   *The Receding Wave: Henry Lawson's Prose.* Melbourne: Melbourne University Press, 1972.

Murray-Smith, Stephen. *Henry Lawson.* (Australian Writers and Their Work). Melbourne: Oxford University Press, rev. ed. 1975.

Phillips, A.A.   *Henry Lawson* (Twayne World Author Series). New York: Twayne, 1970.

Pons, Xavier.   *Out of Eden: Henry Lawson's Life and Works — A Psychoanalytic View.* Sydney: Angus and Robertson, Sirius Books, 1984.

Prout, Denton.   *Henry Lawson: The Grey Dreamer.* Adelaide: Rigby, 1963; republished Seal Books, 1973.

Roderick, Colin.   *Henry Lawson Criticism: 1894-1971.* Sydney: Angus and Robertson, 1972.

————   *The Real Henry Lawson.* Adelaide: Rigby, 1982.

————   *Henry Lawson: Commentaries on His Prose Writings.* Sydney: Angus and Robertson, 1985.

UQP AUSTRALIAN AUTHORS

The Australian Short Story
edited by Laurie Hergenhan
Outstanding contemporary short stories alongside some of the best from the past. This volume encompasses the short story in Australia from its *Bulletin* beginnings in the 1890s to its vigorous revival in the 1970s and 1980s.

Catherine Helen Spence
edited by Helen Thomson
An important early feminist writer, Catherine Helen Spence was one of the first women in Australia to break through the constraints of gender and class and enter public life. This selection contains her most highly regarded novel, *Clara Morison*, her triumphant autobiography, and much of her political and social reformist writing.

Christopher Brennan
edited by Terry Sturm
Christopher Brennan was a legend in his own time, and his art was an unusual amalgam of Victorian, symbolist and modernist tendencies. This selection draws on the whole range of Brennan's work: poetry, literary criticism and theory, autobiographical writing, and letters.

Robert D. FitzGerald
edited by Julian Croft
FitzGerald's long and distinguished literary career is reflected in this selection of his poetry and prose. There is poetry from the 1920s to the 1980s, samples from his lectures on poetics and essays on family origins and philosophical preoccupations, a short story, and his views on Australian poetry.

Australian Science Fiction
edited by Van Ikin
An exotic blend of exciting recent works with a selection from Australia's long science fiction tradition. Classics by Erle Cox, M. Barnard Eldershaw and others are followed by stories from major contemporary writers Damien Broderick, Frank Bryning, Peter Carey, A. Bertram Chandler, Lee Harding, David J. Lake, Philippa C. Maddern, Dal Stivens, George Turner, Wynne N. Whiteford, Michael Wilding and Jack Wodhams.

Barbara Baynton
edited by Sally Krimmer and Alan Lawson

Bush writing of the 1890s, but very different from Henry Lawson. Baynton's stories are often macabre and horrific, and her bush women express a sense of outrage. The revised text of the brilliant *Bush Studies*, the novel *Human Toll*, poems, articles and an interview, all reveal Baynton's disconcertingly independent viewpoint.

Joseph Furphy
edited by John Barnes

Such is Life is an Australian classic. Written by an ex-bullock driver, half-bushman and half-bookworm, it is an extraordinary achievement. The accompanying selection of novel extracts, stories, verse, *Bulletin* articles and letters illustrates the astounding range of Furphy's talent, and John Barnes's notes reveal the intellectual and linguistic richness of his prose.

James McAuley
edited by Leonie Kramer

James McAuley was a poet, intellectual, and leading critic of his time. This volume represents the whole range of his poetry and prose, including the Ern Malley hoax that caused such a sensation in the 1940s, and some new prose pieces published for the first time. Leonie Kramer's introduction offers new critical perspectives on his work.

Rolf Boldrewood
edited by Alan Brissenden

Australia's most famous bushranging novel, *Robbery Under Arms*, together with extracts from the original serial version. The best of Boldrewood's essays and short stories are also included; some are autobiographical, most deal with life in the bush.

Marcus Clarke
edited by Michael Wilding

The convict classic *For the Term of His Natural Life*, and a varied selection of short stories, critical essays and journalism. Autobiographical stories provide vivid insights into the life of this prolific and provocative man of letters.

Nettie Palmer
edited by Vivian Smith

Nettie Palmer was a distinguished poet, biographer, literary critic, diarist, letter-writer, editor and translator, who played a vital role in the development and appreciation of Australian literature. Her warm and informative diary, *Fourteen Years*, is reproduced as a facsimile of the original illustrated edition, along with a rich selection of her poems, reviews and literary journalism.

Writing of the Eighteen Nineties
edited by Leon Cantrell

A retrospective collection, bringing together the work of 32 Australian poets, storytellers and essayists. The anthology challenges previous assumptions about this romantic period of galloping ballads and bush yarns, bohemianism and creative giants.

Colonial Voices
edited by Elizabeth Webby

The first anthology to draw on the fascinating variety of letters, diaries, journalism and other prose accounts of nineteenth-century Australia. These colonial voices belong to adults and children, some famous or infamous, others unknown, whose accounts reveal unusual aspects of Australia's colourful past.

Eight Voices of the Eighties
edited by Gillian Whitlock

These eight voices represent the crest of the wave of women's writing that has characterised the 1980s. Short fiction by Kate Grenville, Barbara Hanrahan, Beverley Farmer, Thea Astley, Elizabeth Jolley, Jessica Anderson, Olga Masters, and Helen Garner is supported by a selection of their criticism, reviews, interviews and commentary, to give an unusual perspective on the phenomenon of women's writing in Australia today.

Randolph Stow
edited by Anthony J. Hassall

Stow's most powerful novel, *Visitants*, is reproduced in full, together with episodes from *To the Islands*, *Tourmaline*, the semi-autobiographical *The Merry-go-Round in the Sea*, the satiric comedy *Midnite* and *The Girl Green as Elderflower*, as well as a generous selection of his poems, many not previously collected.

David Malouf
edited by James Tulip

A well-balanced, compact selection of David Malouf's intricately connected work. Short stories, poems, essays, interviews and the classic novel *Johnno*, reproduced in full, show the range of his remarkable achievement.

John Shaw Neilson
edited by Cliff Hanna

John Shaw Neilson was the most original poet of his time, able to imbue the Australian landscape with a universal significance. This volume gathers together Neilson's poetry, arranged chronologically from his earliest work to the confidence and maturity of his last poems, his autobiography, and correspondence. It also includes an interview with members of his family.

Kenneth Slessor
edited by Dennis Haskell
This collection of Kenneth Slessor's writing — poetry, essays, journalism, war despatches and diaries, personal notes and letters — allows a fuller, more rounded view of his work than has previously been possible. Slessor emerges as a sensitive, complex and sophisticated person and writer — in any medium.